BETWEEN
FANG & CLAW

The Butcher of the Bronx

D.R. SIMPSON

LADERO
FICTION

LADERO FICTION published by
Ladero Press
915 Doyle Road, Suite 303, Box #101
Deltona, Florida 32725

First Ladero Press Printing, February 2024
Official Release Publication, June 2024

ISBNs
978-1-946981-92-9 Paperback
978-1-946981-93-6 EPUB
978-1-946981-94-3 Kindle

Cover Designed by Donald Simpson, Alex Segura, and SheerGenius

Edited by Zaundra George, Ladero Press

Dedication

To my 96-year-old mother, Julia M. Simpson, along with my father, Walter S. Simpson Sr. (now deceased).

Not only did they love, raise and spiritually guide me along with my siblings throughout our lives, but she continues to support me as I move forward.

This is a true testimony of her love of family, and above all, her love for Christ.

Table of Contents

Acknowledgements

First, I want to give thanks to my Lord and Savior Jesus Christ for this opportunity in publishing.

I would like to also acknowledge my initial editor Aisha Brantley, whose insight helped me with my growth as a writer.

My beta reader, Hap Schneider, who helped with the flow.

Zaundra George, my final editor, who along with L.D. Robinson, my publisher, took my understanding of my craft to another level; their input proved to be invaluable.

Also, I would like to give special thanks to L.D. Robinson, owner of Ladero Press, for providing the opportunity to publish my work through her company.

BETWEEN
FANG & CLAW

The Butcher of the Bronx

Prologue

After the fall of the Roman Empire, the age of enlightenment had dimmed. Throughout Europe, invading forces that had pressed her borders were now able to enter without resistance. Through the void left by her fall, many looted, raped, and pillaged towns left along the way. Not even the mighty city of Rome was exempt from their plunder.

In the centuries that followed, new kingdoms slowly began to rise along her outermost borders; to the north the Goths and the Ottomans, to the south the Vandals, and to the east the Huns, along with others of lesser-known origins that had begun to stake their own claims along frontiers to the east.

One such conqueror was a young warlord named Nicholai Bultizar. Cruel and ruthless, he was driven from his people because of the heinous acts committed against the females of his clan. This caused his expulsion and the loss of inheritance. Stripped not only of his title and the family name of Wolvenhunt by his father, but now he no longer held claim to lands or allegiance to his people. Although void of a title, he still wore the family emblem around his neck—a round wooden medallion trimmed in gold with the head of a wolf at its center. This was a symbol of his savagery, as he was feared wherever he went.

As a castaway, he ventured far from his former lands and people in order to begin his own rise to power. Slowly, he built an army of his own, filled with thieves and ruthless mercenaries that too were feared by all, taking whatever they wanted and destroying anyone and anything that stood in the way. As his forces grew in power, they raided and looted other lands until he found a place that was ripe for the taking. A region to the east, a land called

Sargonia. It was the year 743 A.D. when he and his forces seized the land. To the east of the region lay the Caucasus Mountains, and to the north the Black Sea. Surrounded by rolling hills, thick forests, and fertile plains, it was the secret jewel of what was once part of the mighty Roman Empire.

With an army of mercenaries loyal to him, they provided the mechanism, allowing the takeover of the fallen empire's most diverse and peaceful region. Like a wolf amongst sheep, his conquest was one that was swift, cruel, and complete. He ravaged the land and its people, doing so without prejudice. He proclaimed himself King while no one dared to oppose him.

For years he drained its people, stripping the land of its wealth, seizing lands, imposing heavy taxation, and murdering and torturing many of its people. With an increasing appetite for blood, he took great pleasure in the torture that he inflicted upon his subjects. Any who resisted him were thrown into the dungeon while he contemplated the method of their death.

Even with all he had inflicted, there was an even darker side to the king's persona—one that was beyond the knowledge of the people. Only those closest to him knew the truth. It was his lust for young women of a tender age that met his preference. They were what truly brought the beast out of the man.

Whispers of his sadistic and brutal acts toward these women that were forced into his bed chambers quickly spread throughout the land. No one dared to speak openly however the word had spread across the countryside like a rushing winter wind. By his authority, his most loyal subjects within his inner circle would go out in the late hours of the night to abduct those he desired the most. They were the ones who rejected the king's advances and had no desire to be one of his concubines.

Late at night, screams could be heard from the king's chambers by the young women he had abducted against their will. He experienced great pleasure and sexual gratification in inflicting pain upon these women. Once he was finished, many were thrown onto the street, some barely able to stand, and were covered in blood from his violent acts. If any spoke of what happened, the consequences of their actions would be most severe for both them and their families. They were the lucky ones; others were not so fortunate.

There were a chosen few that he found to fulfill his twisted fantasies with absolute compliance. They were the ones that never returned home. Many were brutally murdered as if savaged by some kind of wild animal. Each woman's heart was removed from her body while she was still alive. He held the belief that by possessing their hearts he would also possess their souls, thereby making them a part of him.

Despite the whispers, many clamored at the palace gates seeking justice for these crimes. Knowing that he himself was responsible, Bultizar pledged he would do everything in his power to bring the culprit to justice. For months, he brought many that were innocent to trial for these acts, falsely accusing them while planting lies and false evidence as facts.

Bultizar devised a host of cruel, unimaginable punishments for crimes he knew they had not committed. Many were burned alive while others were drawn, quartered, and fed to starving wolves that he captured. The abductions and murders continued until, finally, the truth found its way to the ears of the people through one woman who miraculously escaped with the aid of a guard. At the cost of his own life, he had grown tired of the secret acts of a madman.

Chapter 1:
The Fall of a Tyrant

After years of oppression and murder, the people had finally reached their limit. They began to place their hopes on the shoulders of a young warrior named Jahir Amid. After seeking adventures far to the east, he and his Greek companion—a young warrior named Adonis Argyros—had finally returned home to the land of their birth after a ten-year quest.

Jahir was a tall, broad, and muscular warrior of African descent. His complexion was a smooth, dark shade of brown. His hair was long and coarse, formed into locks that streamed just below his shoulders. His beard outlined the contour of a low and defined masculine chin.

Atop his stallion, black as midnight, he sat, adorned in armor etched with the scars of battle. The armor glistened under the sun and served as a testament to any that dared to doubt his word. His breastplate was crafted to his form; its color was the shade of finely polished brass protecting him from the neck to his knees. He wielded a scimitar with edges that could split a single hair in two.

Jahir was raised by an old and noble warrior named Omon Escar. He had journeyed to these lands from beyond the frontiers of the fallen empire from far to the east. At the request of Jahir's dying father stricken with the plague, Omon agreed to take him and raise him as his own. He taught him honor, respect, compassion, and the ways of a true warrior. He excelled in them all.

After Omon's death, Jahir and Adonis left these lands seeking a more adventurous life. He followed the footsteps of the man who raised him not long before Bultizar's arrival. After years of wandering, seeking a life of adventure and grandeur, the only things they found were death and despair.

Returning home with hopes of finding the peace he had left behind, only misery and more despair greeted Jahir instead. Not long after his return, he met and fell in love with a farmer's daughter named Kolliana who tamed the warrior inside of him. After years of war and finally finding peace, one day he found her murdered at the hands of the brutal king who had carried out his dark desires. It was said he had sent his henchman to abduct her as he had done to many others during the night since his reign.

Stricken with grief and hatred, Jahir formed a rebel army with the aid of his friend, Adonis. Together, they trained an army of farmers, turning them into skilled fighters. Facing Bultizar's forces, they fought with vigor and unmeasurable ferocity to match Bultizar's forces blade for blade until they defeated Bultizar's army.

Fearing the repercussions of his actions, Bultizar and those left of his most loyal soldiers, fled into the wilderness. Determined to make Bultizar pay for his crimes, Jahir pursued him throughout the eastern frontier. For nearly two years, Bultizar continued to elude the grasp of the young warrior.

While fleeing Jahir's pursuit, Bultizar came upon a domed shaped hut made of wood and bark in the forest. An old man who heard the gallop of Bultizar's horses approaching emerged from the hut. The man stepped forward in his woven cloak toward the army as they surrounded him.

Bultizar peered down from his horse at the old man. His thoughts were to kill him. Due to his nature and the darkness of his heart, nothing short of a miracle would save him, placing his hand on his sword. Fearing his intentions the old man cried out. "My name is Methuel! I am of the order of Sayers, the teller of foreseen truths."

Unimpressed, Bultizar dismounted his horse, drawing his sword as he walked toward him. Methuel knew his fate by the look in Bultizar's eyes. Fearing for his life, he pleaded for him to stop, but his words fell upon deaf ears.

"I know who you are," Methuel said, just as Bultizar drew near. With his sword unsheathed, he was nearly upon him while Methuel hastened his words.

"I foresaw your coming! Your name is Nicholai Bultizar, the King of Sargonia—before your fall!"

With his sword drawn, Bultizar reared back to strike, but Methuel's words caused Bultizar to hesitate for an instant, but they did little to change his thoughts. Methuel continued to speak hastily. "You're being pursued by a young warrior with the intent of ending your life," he said.

"Knowing my identity is all the more reason for you to die," Bultizar replied, as he stood over him. "It is not good to have so great a knowledge, old man."

With a sword raised above him, Methuel shouted, "I can help restore you to that power which you lost! More power than you could possibly imagine!"

Bultizar stopped just short of killing him as curiosity took hold. Slowly lowering his sword, he commanded him to continue.

"There is a book and a key that opens it," Methuel revealed, "one of great power. It is called the Apoxius."

"Old man!" Bultizar shouted, once again raising his sword. "I don't believe in fantasies. I don't have the time to hear them, nor do you to tell them!"

"He that possesses and opens the book shall become invincible," Methuel replied, "commanding an army of a supernatural origin, one that is not of this world, but one no army of man nor any other can defeat."

"What do you take me for, old man," Bultizar snapped, "a fool? You would say anything that would spare your worthless life."

"No, it is the truth!" Methuel urged. "There is an old castle fortress that was once ruled by a powerful sorceress. They called her the mother of darkness. No one knows who she truly is or where she came from. All that is known is the woman possesses the power to summon demons, and everyone that had ever faced her was never seen again." Bultizar glared at him as he explained.

"The book is held within her fortress walls," Methuel continued. "Its age dates back before written history. Its name comes from an ancient tongue that has long been lost. No one knows the true meaning of the word. It is believed that this book holds unspeakable power and whoever opens it shall possess the power to wield it.

"It is said that she and twelve of her followers were its guardian. No one had ever dared to enter those castle walls to take possession in fear that a curse would fall upon them, save but Ramnard the Great of the North. He, along with his finest warriors, entered to possess it after hearing of its power. Legend says that he and his men entered the castle and were never seen again."

Bultizar looked at him and laughed. "I have heard enough! If you speak the truth, and it is guarded by such power, then I, too, shall meet the same fate. I have grown weary of this. It's time I put an end to this."

"No! There's more!" Methuel shouted.

"The castle has been abandoned for over a hundred years. No one has seen the sorceress or her followers since they vanished. Thorns and thickets now cover and protect the land and its walls. Believing that the fortress is cursed, no one has dared to enter since the time of Ramnard."

"If no one has ever returned to tell of it, then how is it that you know?" With his sword raised once again to strike him, Methuel quickly replied.

"I was blessed with the sight of things not seen, as well as, events that may soon come to pass. It is through a dream that I knew you would come. How else would I know your name and what had taken place?"

"That information could have come from anyone that has crossed your path," Bultizar replied.

"That is true, but look around you," Methuel replied. "Who would follow such a path in this harsh wilderness from a distance so far away? I speak the truth, great master. I can take you there and show you."

"Tell me where I can find this castle," Bultizar commanded.

"The path is a difficult one to follow with spoken words, but I can take you there," the old sayer responded.

While accepting his offer, Bultizar never took his eyes off him. He looked over to his enforcer Boris the Beheader, then commanded one of his men to get the old man a horse. Looking back toward Methuel, he gave a warning.

"Old man! If you are lying, then I will make you regret the day your worthless mother gave birth to you. I will strip the flesh off your bones while you still have breath."

"I speak the truth!" Methuel asserted. "It is a three-day journey from this place at the steps of the great mountains."

Immediately, Bultizar gave the command as they galloped away.

***

Still on Bultizar's trail, Jahir and his forces had been slowly gaining ground. Although Bultizar had been difficult to track as he was a master at evading his enemies, Jahir himself was also skilled. Determination and strength of will had taught him the ways of the evasive warlord. No matter how elusive Bultizar proved to be, Jahir would always pick up his trail, making up for lost ground. He never repeated the same mistakes nor fell for the same tricks that Bultizar had lain before them. Despite this fact, Bultizar's trail had gone cold once again.

Adonis looked to Jahir and asked, "What is our next recourse? He has lost us once again."

Jahir sat quietly for a moment atop his horse while slowly scanning the trees and terrain around him. After gathering his thoughts, he looked back to Adonis.

"We have not lost him," he replied. "There is a pattern in which he follows. In the past, we always followed the most obvious and roundabout trails before he chose a different one. Usually, his was the most direct, regardless of how unlikely the route allowed him to fall behind us while we remained on the terrain that was most difficult and unlikely to follow. Once he fell behind us, our mistake was moving in the opposite direction from him, thereby spreading the distance between us farther apart. Once he accomplishes this, he then gains the advantage once again."

Jahir galloped north to find a vantage point high upon a hill nearby. He looked around to see the thickness of the forest while judging the difficulty of the terrain. Jahir discerned Bultizar's pattern in eluding his pursuit. Instead of following his trail, he decided to move directly through terrain that was both treacherous and uncertain.

After nearly a day of pursuit, his gamble paid off. Instead of the path taking a couple of days, he had cut his time to a day. This brought him onto a path in which he could rapidly pursue him.

***

Bultizar was confident that he had lost Jahir. Bultizar looked to Methuel who was leading them on the horse.

"Which direction do we go from here, and how far away are we from the castle?" Bultizar asked.

"Beyond that ridge lies the fortress," Methuel responded. "We are but a day away. There you shall find . . . "

Before he could finish, Bultizar rode up close to the old man before running his sword through Methuel's back, dropping him off his horse to the ground and onto his side. Methuel looked up at the one who had just betrayed him.

While Methuel gasped for air, Bultizar said to him, "Your task is complete, and you are no longer needed."

Methuel lay silent before closing his eyes. With no further thought, Bultizar was confident that he had acquired all the knowledge he needed to press forth, leaving Methuel for dead.

***

Hours later of following Bultizar's trail, one of Jahir's men heard movement in the thicket. Riding over to investigate, he shouted, "Jahir!" The warrior turned towards Jahir and waved for him to come.

When Jahir arrived, he looked down and saw the old man lying on the ground dying. With the little energy that remained, the man was attempting to crawl.

Seeing that he was still alive, Jahir dismounted his horse and turned him on his back so that he could face him while Adonis stood behind him.

"Who are you?" Jahir asked. "Why did someone do this to you?"

The old man opened his eyes and replied, "I was betrayed by the one you now pursue. My name is no longer important, but what I have to say to you is—" Hesitating for a moment, he continued. "I foresaw your coming and why you are here."

While he spoke, Jahir listened closely. He shared with him everything that he had revealed to Bultizar. He told Jahir everything he needed to know in finding him, including where he was headed and what he was planning to do once he arrived. He told him of the book, the nature of it, and how he was trying to claim it for himself.

"If you follow the trail that is before you," he told Jahir, "You will be too late to stop him. There is another way, one that will cut your quest in half. Follow the path of the spiraling hills southwest, beyond the trees, and you shall be able to cut him off before he reaches the fortress."

As he uttered his final words, both breath and life left his body. His eyes stared into the abyss. Jahir looked back at Adonis with a fierce urgency as they mounted their horses, wasting no moment in pursuing the path that the old man had revealed.

***

Believing that Jahir was far from him, Bultizar continued to move forward at a steady pace. For more than a day, he and his men stayed on their path with hardly any breaks. Exhausted, his men were ready to take a needed rest, but Bultizar was determined to continue. Bultizar ignored their needs and held a deaf ear to their words to push them even harder, despite their exhaustion. He refused to stop while threatening to kill anyone who did. A day later, they finally crossed over the ridge and down into the valley. He was only a short distance from where the castle was supposed to lie.

Bultizar and his men pressed forward, believing the path was clear and the castle was just beyond the trees. As they galloped across the open field, suddenly Jahir and his men emerged from the forest to intercept them, riding toward them in full stride. Outnumbering Bultizar's men five to one, Jahir's men were well rested and had been awaiting his arrival for hours.

With Jahir on one side and Adonis on the other, they caught Bultizar and his forces in the middle. As they clashed, Bultizar's men were in no condition to fight. Outnumbered, weary, and weakened by all that had transpired, they were unable to match the tenacity and ferocity that Jahir and his warriors had brought to the fight.

As swords and shields met on the field of battle, Bultizar's men began to fall by the wayside. Driven by their determination for vengeance against anyone loyal to their tyrant king, Bultizar's men were all put to justice by the blades of Jahir's army. The battle was over almost as quickly as it had begun.

12

Chapter 2:
The Curse

With his men falling all around him, Bultizar's time was fleeting and had begun to run out. With the battle raging around him swords and shields clashing from all sides and during the clamor, Bultizar saw an opening to escape. This was his chance to seize the prize that lay somewhere behind the walls of the sorceress's castle. With that opportunity, he rode his horse as quickly as it would carry him.

Engaged in battle a short distance away, Jahir watched Bultizar as he began to ride off in the direction of the fortress. Desperately, he attempted to reach him, but swinging swords and axes of the battle before him stood in his way. Determined to end this conflict once and for all, he fought through them. Intercepted by two of Bultizar's men, he watched Bultizar put distance between them. He quickly dispatched one of the fighters as the other was killed by Adonis, who had arrived to aid him.

Jahir looked to Adonis and said, "Finish this, I will pursue Bultizar while he attempts to flee his due justice."

He then rode off in pursuit, leaving the battlefield behind him. He was now on Bultizar's trail alone. In the distance, he saw Bultizar before him, fleeing toward the fortress gates. Bultizar drove his horse as hard as he could, and he was not going to escape Jahir this time. He was prepared to pursue him to the ends of the earth, and in his heart, the end was going to happen there within the castle walls as he followed Bultizar into the fortress.

In thinking he had escaped, Bultizar did not realize that Jahir was still in pursuit. As he remembered everything Methuel had told him in the woods,

Bultizar slowly moved within the narrow corridor that led to a set of stairs at the end of the hallway.

Once he reached the top of the stairs, he saw there was a large oval chamber with twelve open doorways that were on the circumference of the chamber on all sides. At the center of the room was a wooden shrine surrounded by unlit candles and a large book overlaid in thick layers of cobwebs. Upon moving closer, Bultizar saw that the book had a small compartment on its top cover with a keyhole at its center. On the book were the markings of symbols—a language he could not understand. Beside the book was what appeared to be an old rusted key.

Above the chamber were three small bell-shaped windows where the sunlight shined directly upon the book. As he stood in front of it, he marveled at what lay within it. When he reached to take possession of both the book and the key, he heard his name.

"Bultizar!" Jahir shouted, entering the chamber with his sword drawn. "Your time on this earth is about to come to an end."

Bultizar turned and drew his sword in return. He stared into Jahir's eyes and began to laugh.

"You have come a long way to die," he replied. "If you seek vengeance, then it shall not come in this life, nor in the next, and certainly not by you. I have come to claim what is mine and I will not be denied by one such as you!"

"I care nothing for that in which you seek," Jahir responded. "I have but one desire—to end your life for the misery you've caused and for the death of my woman."

Slowly, Jahir approached as Bultizar stepped away from the book with his sword drawn and a smile on his face, anticipating an attack. Wasting little time, Jahir moved in as their swords began to clash. With the intent to end this conflict as quickly as it had begun, Jahir fought with unbridled rage, while Bultizar responded with the force of a deranged madman.

Their swords rang like a symphony as the two matched one another blow for blow. As the battle raged between them, Jahir grew stronger. Bultizar relied on his savviness and experience that had always carried him through such battles. The two fought with neither finding their mark that would end this struggle. Jahir drew first blood, leaving a jagged wound on the side of Bultizar's face.

Finally, seeing an opportunity to end this, Bultizar spun around like a windmill with the intent to separate Jahir's head from his body. In reaction to Bultizar's attempt, Jahir countered the assault, weaving beneath Bultizar's swing to move in close. Jahir delivered an elbow strike to Bultizar's face that momentarily dazed him as he fell onto the floor.

Bultizar shook his head as he attempted to regain his senses and get back on his feet. He only made it to his knees while Jahir moved in to finish him.

Jahir, looking down at Bultizar with fire in his eyes—his sword raised over his head—cried out to him, "Prepare to die!"

Before he could deliver the killing blow, Jahir stood over him like a statue, his body frozen in place along with Bultizar, who was still on his knees awaiting the blow that never came. Both were unable to speak. Emerging from one of the rooms surrounding the chamber was an old white-haired woman. She came forth wearing the lines of time upon her face. She raised her frail hand slightly with her right palm facing down. As she lowered her hand, it caused Jahir to drop to his knees.

Slowly, she approached them both, walking around and between them. Both Bultizar and Jahir were unable to move; they could only follow her movements with their eyes. Finally, she stopped between them both to stare at each of them. She gazed upon the book that rested atop the wooden pedestal.

"You entered within these walls to stage your battle," she said. Her voice was calm but stern. "I sense your purpose was not for simple conflict, but to take that which belongs to me as others before you have never succeeded."

She looked down at Jahir and continued. "I have looked into your heart and it is one driven by vengeance." She turned to Bultizar and said, "But you have come driven by greed and lust, seeking to steal that which belongs to me—a prize that you shall never possess."

With the gesture of a thought on her face, both warriors fell to the floor. She stood over them, first looking at one and then the other. She balled her hand into a fist, which caused them to close their eyes. She stood over them and decreed, "For your acts, I shall lay a curse on you both, causing a sleep to fall upon you. It will last for centuries, and you shall hear my voice. You will remember my words as if I had spoken them yesterday.

"When you awaken," the old woman continued, "all that you have ever known or loved will be lost to you through time. Nothing will remain except the hatred you share for one another on this day. That hatred—buried deep within your hearts—will grow like an insatiable hunger, and will plague you both throughout the ages."

First, she looked to Bultizar, gazing at the medallion he wore around his neck with the head of a golden wolf at its center. Closing her eyes, she sensed Bultizar was like herself. They both shared the same dark, cold, and evil spirit. Seeing that his head was covered with long blond hair, she reached down to take a strand from atop his head.

She then expressed to Bultizar, "For five hundred years shall you sleep, and when you awaken, the curse of a werewolf shall I bestow upon you. Like the hair on your head, so shall your body be covered, and you shall be transformed into a werewolf with golden hair whenever you transform into the beast.

Neither silver nor garlic will be able to bring you harm; only the claws of the one I have yet to curse. If he buries them deep into your chest to take your beating heart from its cradle while still in the form of the beast, only then will your life be forfeited and all will come to an end."

She made a declaration as she looked deeper into his heart. "Because your heart resembles that of my own, I shall grant you a small reprieve. With the setting of the sun you shall change at will, only to grow stronger when the moon is at its fullest and the rage of the beast shall increase.

"Since the power you sought is what brought you to this chamber—to claim my book that you can never possess—I offer you an alternative to satisfy that lust in the distant centuries to come. There will be two moons rising in the future that will give you the power that you seek. Since the hearts of those desired have been your ultimate prize, the time before their rising shall you claim them in your grasp while they still yet beat. The path in which you take them shall form a five-pointed star.

"At the stroke of midnight—in that instant—you must claim the sixth, at the heart of the star. At that moment, your heart's desire will be fulfilled, and you will achieve that ultimate prize. With a single bite, you will be able to raise a matchless army that no one on earth can defeat. You will become invincible, able to change from man to beast at will, with the whole world at your feet. Nothing will be able to harm you, not by man or the claws of the other cursed beast.

"If you fail to take that final victim at the exact moment the moon reaches its highest height--midnight," she warned, "then all will be lost, and the one I aforementioned will be able to take your heart and life."

She then looked over at Jahir. When she stepped forward, half of the symbols that were written on the book suddenly began to glow, catching her eye. As a thought had entered her mind, she stared back at Jahir. She looked deep into his heart and soul.

She made another decree. Looking down at his hair flowing in locks and then at the smooth dark contours of his skin, she began to speak.

"In the form of a cat—the panthiem you shall be called—I shall lay your curse," she decreed. "Like velvet to the touch, you shall be covered in it with smooth black fur, a panther who stands like a man. A beast you shall remain both day and night, one that can never change. For six hundred years shall you sleep, only to open your eyes to renew your search on the trail of the Golden Wolf. It will be his victims that will lead you on your path in finding him.

"Through their eyes, you shall witness their deaths and feel the pain of his claws as surely as if you had met their fate. When the blood of the werewolf begins to boil, you will sense his presence, but only when he transforms into the beast will you be able to find him. In human form, his identity will be as a blur to your memory, and you will not know him if you stood at his side. Like your enemy, nothing in this world can harm you except his fangs sunk deep into your throat.

"Your only reprieve from your curse is to take the heart of the living werewolf while he is in his beastly form. However, your time to do so has its limit. When that century arrives, then you must take his life before he claims the heart of his final victim before midnight on the night of the scarlet moon. If you fail before that time arrives, then the power to slay him will pass, you will be at his mercy from that time forth."

While the two lay helpless and asleep at the feet of the old sorceress, she commanded her servants to come forth. Each began to emerge from the surrounding rooms. Twelve hooded figures dressed in dark gray robes came forth. She commanded them to take each of the men to a place she had designated where they could not be found.

Before they were taken away, one of her servants humbly approached the sorceress and asked in a whisper, "Master, you let them live?"

She looked to the servant, smiled, and said, "Each of them has a quality that I seek. It is that which is in their hearts that holds the key to what I need. Only through time can they fulfil that purpose."

The sorceress turned her back to the warriors. "Now, go!" she commanded, "Then return back to me."

Her loyal servants bowed their heads and did as they were told. Within the hour they returned, each taking their place around the temple shrine, only to find Adonis and his men. After the dispatching of what remained of Bultizar's followers, Adonis along with his men had gone into the castle in search of Jahir.

Remembering the words of the old man who died along the path, Adonis was already prepared for what could follow. With their weapons drawn, they were circumspect in entering the castle and going up the stairs until they moved into the chamber.

The old sorceress felt their presence and turned to face them. As Adonis ordered his archers to release their arrows immediately, they blanketed her servants with them. Before her servants could defend their master, she fell to her knees. The sorceress looked and then smiled as Adonis ran over to her with his sword to finish her. As he looked down at her, his demeanor had turned dark, his voice vexed with anger.

"Witch!" he shouted. "Where is he? Where is he?"

She looked up at him and continued to smile. "You are too late," she uttered and then laughed. When she stared into his eyes, he froze momentarily as though she was connecting with his mind. She then told him what she had done but never revealed the secret of Jahir's resting place or that of the tyrant Bultizar.

As Adonis faced what seemed to be an inevitable death, he prepared to strike. The sorceress showed no fear but only continued to laugh. It was like she was taunting him, knowing she would never reveal her secret to him.

Adonis sensed the danger that she posed to the world. Without another thought, he thrust his sword into her chest. Immediately, her body turned into dark smoke and fiery ash, after which the bodies of her disciples quickly followed. Adonis and his men stood and pondered what their eyes had witnessed. A sudden rush of wind scattered the ashes throughout the corridors of the castle.

"My Lord," Adonis responded. "God help us all." Looking to his men, he said, "Search this place from the dungeon to the loft. Let no brick be unturned until we find him." He looked over at the book. "As for the book, burn it and melt down the key."

As instructed, they set a torch to it, but it would neither burn nor was the key able to melt. There was not even a scorch on either one, no matter how long they attempted to incinerate them.

Finally, Adonis said, "Since fire cannot harm them, we must take them to a place where they will never be found."

One of his men nearby him shouted, "We can take them to Jerusalem, where the holy can stand watch over them!"

"No!" Adonis replied. "They have no place amongst the holy. We will take the book far from here, high atop the mountains, and bury it in secret. The key we shall cast far away, deep into the Black Sea. We shall take an oath before God that we shall never reveal their resting place as long as life and breath remain within our bodies. Bring me my journal. I shall record these events and the words that the old witch shared with me before I took her life. I must write of what has happened here today, warning all the people that is to come."

For days, they searched for Jahir—the man that had led them to freedom—without finding a trace of him. Distraught after searching every corner, corridor, and room of the castle's chamber, they began to finally accept that Jahir was lost to them forever.

Adonis looked to his men. "We have searched everywhere, and I fear we will never find him." he said. Frustrated, Adonis continued. "Set this accursed place aflame."

As they obliged, they watched the old fortress burn from the chamber out, crumbling into rubble and smoldering ashes.

In the months that followed, Adonis took the key, journeyed into the Black Sea, and chartered a small boat, where he placed the key in a small sack and anchored it with stones before casting it into the black waters. He returned to his men who were waiting on the shore for him. They began to search for the most inaccessible and unforgiving place they could find in order to hide the book.

Finally, they found the perfect hiding place. Near the peak on the weather worn side of a mountain, they found a cave with an opening barely wide enough for one person to enter. Adonis took the book alone and hid it deep inside. When he emerged, he looked around and saw a boulder nearby large enough to cover its opening. He gave the order for twenty men to move it since its weight was so great. Once finished, each man swore an oath to never reveal its secret.

Chapter 3:
The Awakenings

Five centuries later, surrounded in darkness and enclosed in a musty tomb, Bultizar opened his eyes. He didn't know where he was and felt trapped, entombed in some sort of cold stone casing. He was unable to move from side to side. He needed to get out, but all he could do was push up. With all his might, he pushed the stone lid to the side with strength he did not know he had.

His last memories were hearing the voice of the witch that had put him there after being locked in battle with his most hated enemy. The words she spoke were cemented in his mind as though she had spoken them yesterday. As he held the medallion he kept around his neck in front of him, he stood and stared at it, remembering what it now meant. The engraved head of a wolf plated in gold. It represented the form the sorceress had cursed him to take, upon the setting of the sun.

His appetite for blood was now stronger than before; his hunger for power even greater. To most, this would be a curse, to him, it was a blessing. The old sorceress gave him a purpose and a goal, which was to achieve the power he desired in his heart. All that was needed was time and patience, something of which he now had plenty. Once he made his way up the cellar steps and arrived at the top, he found the once mighty fortress scorched from a fire and in ruins.

There was neither a trace of his enemy Jahir nor of the white-haired sorceress that had placed him there. His men were all gone. The once mighty castle was a relic of the past scorched from a fire. Bultizar observed how the castle was now covered in foliage and his garments were worn away from time.

Although he had not eaten in centuries, there was a hunger inside him that surpassed a natural one. As he turned his face to the sky—his vision adjusting to the light—he attempted to gain his bearing and decided to choose a course of direction. With his clothes old and tattered, Bultizar did not want to be seen so he decided to follow the direction of the setting sun where darkness would conceal his appearance. Only a few hours remained before nightfall, so he would not have much longer to wait.

Moving through the underbrush that blanketed the forest floor, Bultizar heard the wheels of a cart just beyond the trees. As he looked around, he saw a small tree with broken branches. It resembled a spiked club—a makeshift weapon that was easy to conceal. He carried it by his side as he moved toward the sound of the cart nearby.

Atop the cart was a man guiding it as it was being pulled by an old mare. As he moved toward him, Bultizar stood there while placing his stick behind him. He blocked the old man's path and waved his free arm for the man to stop the cart.

"Hold!" Bultizar proclaimed.

The man looked Bultizar up and down, seeing that his clothing was ragged and torn. "Stranger," he shouted, "who are thee to block this road? Be gone and out of my way so that I can go to my home!"

"I shall let you pass without bother," Bultizar replied, "but I was robbed and beaten. My memory lapsed. I need to know the whereabouts of this place, and the year in which it is."

The man, skeptical of his questions at first, proceeded to answer, "It is the year 1162, the year of our Lord. What is your name? Surely you can remember that."

"I know not," Bultizar expressed. "All memory has left me. I cannot remember my last meal. Do you have any food that you can spare to relieve me from my hunger?"

"If it will cause me no further delay in reaching my family before the sun sets, I have a few pieces of fruit I can give you," the man responded.

He turned around and reached for a woven sac. Before he could obtain it, Bultizar jumped onto the cart and hit the man across his head. The impact was so hard that it sounded like a tree being chopped, echoing throughout the forest. It caused him to fall off the cart and onto the ground.

As the man lay helpless, bludgeoned and dazed, Bultizar continued to beat him beyond recognition until his club was soaked in blood. Quickly he rummaged through his belongings, taking everything of value.

Amongst his belongings were a knife and a few bags of grain he had traded for at the marketplace. He decided to remove the man of his clothing, leaving him naked, before dragging his body off the road into the woods. Finally, he covered it with sticks and leaves. Like a ravenous beast, he ate everything he could, but no matter how much he consumed, his hunger never subsided as the orange glow of the setting sun shined through the trees.

Without delay, he jumped onto the cart and continued to follow the old dirt road. In the distance, he heard a young voice that caught his attention. But there was something else he noticed. Something happening within himself that he could not explain.

His insides felt as though they were bursting in flames. His senses began to heighten, and his hunger drove him in the direction of a young voice. As he drew near, he crouched down to peer through the bushes and trees.

The force inside him began to erupt through his pores as his whole body became engulfed in pain. From his fingertips grew three-inch claws, along with changes to his face. Quickly, he turned his attention back toward the young voice he had heard.

She was a girl of six years, playing in the small wooded area near her cottage. Upon hearing her mother's call, she headed back toward her home. The sun had just breached the trees as it was now dusk. As her mother called out to her a second time, she heard the screams of her child.

In a panic she ran toward her daughter's cry, only to find blood splattered along the ground and upon the leaves of bushes nearby, along with her daughter's shredded garments. What her eyes beheld was more than she could bear. She collapsed to the ground, lying there unconscious. When she had awakened, she found herself in the arms of a young man who was carrying her toward her cottage.

"Madam, are you all right?" he asked.

Still in shock by what she had seen in perceiving the fate of her daughter, she cried, "My daughter, Anne! My precious Anne! Something has taken my baby. Her blood—it was everywhere!"

As they approached the door, the woman shouted, "Let me down! We must find her!" She kept pleading with the stranger.

"What do you think has taken her?" the young man asked.

Hysterically she shouted, "A wolf! It must have been a wolf."

As he opened the door, he placed a finger to his mouth and gestured for her to calm down in a gentle voice.

"No!" she shouted. "I have to find my baby!" She was suddenly perplexed by his calmness, which was unusual for such an extreme moment. She also began to wonder where she was.

"We will find her," he assured. "Where is the child's father?"

"He went to the marketplace. He should have returned by now!"

With a soothing voice, he tried to calm the mother. "Let me fetch you some water," he said as he grabbed a goblet of water set on a table nearby. After giving her a drink, she became upset once more. She repeatedly screamed out her daughter's name as she attempted to rise from her seat and run toward the door.

Immediately, he took hold of her with both hands and grabbed her by both shoulders and gave her a brief shrug. "You must calm down," he said.

"No!" she shouted. "Let me go! I must find my baby."

In response to her cries, he pushed her backward until she was sitting on the bed. "We will go, but let me first get my weapon. I cannot do anything to help or protect you unless I get my sword."

For a moment, she began to calm as he looked into her eyes, ensuring her that he would be able to help her. As she sat, the young man turned and walked toward the door. As he was walking away, she asked, "Stranger, who are you?" She had been so upset she had not thought to ask.

With his back turned toward her, he responded, "It matters not what my name is, only that we find your precious daughter. That is the only thing that matters."

When he reached the door, instead of opening it to leave, he drew the bolt and locked it. With his back still toward her and a smile spread across his face, he said, "I shall take you to join her."

"You know where to find my daughter?" she asked, puzzled by his words. "You know where my baby is? Why have you not taken me to her?"

When he turned, the blue eyes she first looked upon had turned gray and wild. She became frightened, realizing her position on the bed.

"Who are you?" she asked again.

The young man then began to laugh and said, "I am the one who shall take you to join your daughter, as promised."

With those words, he smiled as six-inch fangs emerged through his gums. His face became elongated and his rounded human ears took the shape of a wolf's. As he grew in size while standing on two feet, his head pressed against the ceiling of the small cottage. He became completely covered with blond fur, giving him a golden appearance.

Horrified by what was now standing before her, the mother began to scream. But it served no value as the howl of the beast blanketed her screams until she could no longer be heard. Taking the goblet in her hand, she struck the beast across the face with all her might. He barely noticed as he grabbed her by the throat with a clawed hand. He savagely ravaged her body like a crazed hungry animal, leaving her lying on the floor in a pool of blood with the goblet still in her grasp, her lifeless body ripped apart.

Immediately afterward, he reverted to his human form. With his hunger satisfied and his unwavering thirst for blood intact, he realized that this was something that afforded him tremendous pleasure, and the beast within would always be a part of him. He no longer felt the need to return to the place of his exile, for he had received the answers that he sought. He also realized there was no longer a need for him to confine himself to any lands or walls in order to obtain the power he so desired. The power now flowed through his veins, and his only threat was but a distant memory. With that thought engrained in his mind, he realized the whole world was his playground in which to go wherever he so chose. Until the time that he and Jahir would meet again, there was no one else that could stop him from carrying out his desires. Whatever direction his blackened heart would lead him, that would be the direction he would go. A trail of blood and terror would mark the wake of his wrath.

*****

One hundred years later, Jahir was disoriented as he opened his eyes. He sensed something different about himself. For six hundred years he had slept, never once waking to see the light of day. While he lay there, he found that his movement was also restricted. He felt like a caged animal that yearned for its freedom. Anxiety set his heart racing as the adrenaline flowed through him greater than he ever remembered.

He could feel the strength in his arms increasing. Pressing against a heavy slab that imprisoned him, he moved it with relative ease to send it crashing thunderously to the floor, shaking the dust from the walls around him. As he sat upright in his stone coffin, his senses slowly began to clear. He was surrounded in total darkness but his eyes pierced through it as though it was the height of the noonday sun. His last memory was one that both he and Bultizar shared, being locked in battle before hearing the words of the white-haired witch, decreeing their fates before both fell into centuries of sleep.

As he lifted himself from his stone coffin, there was barely enough room to stand. He needed to free himself from this prison. He pushed with all his might, placing both hands against the walls of his tomb, causing one of its walls to crumble and fall.

He emerged from his hidden chamber into a dark, narrow hallway. Moving silently, he came upon another room akin to the one he had left. When he looked inside, its wall had also been breached some time ago.

As he continued, he heard a faint sound behind him. Quickly, he turned to see what it may have been. He turned to face no one so he surmised the sound was simply an echo of his own steps bouncing off the wall. There was a smell in the air with which he was not familiar. He heard the sound again and paused for a moment. *I must be hearing things*, he thought.

Believing his time asleep there had done something that affected his mind, he quickly dismissed the thought that he had heard something. Jahir moved along until he heard the same sound again. He turned once more; again, he saw nothing.

He stood there a moment before hearing it again. Looking down along the edges of the dirt floor next to the wall, he saw a mouse scampering along the corridor. This was a scent that would have been impossible for him to detect at any time before now.

What's happening to me? he asked himself before continuing until he came across a narrow stairwell that spiraled upward. It was the same path his nemesis had followed a century earlier. As he began to climb them, specs of light began to shred the darkness from above.

The closer to the top of the stairs he climbed, the more intense the light became. It blinded him for a moment until his eyes began to adjust. Once at the top, he found that the castle he had entered was in ruins unlike it was before. It was nothing like he remembered.

As he looked down at the armor he was wearing, he saw how it had aged and rusted, a far contrast to the brassey and untarnished armor he last remembered with the scars of battle etched upon it. He passed another room that was filled with debris and shattered glass that had fallen from a mirror. It was still partially intact. As he went by it, something caught his eye startling him, causing him to jump back.

At first, he thought it was a creature of some sort, ready to attack, until its movements mimicked his own. What frightened him most was that the beast was draped in rusted armor covered in short black fur. What he saw was incomprehensible to him. He realized that he was not staring at a beastly creature in the doorway, but into an old shattered mirror reflecting his own image. He stood, staring. Slowly moving toward, he placed his gloved hands on his face, turning his head slowly from side to side in disbelief. This had become a nightmare—one from which he could not awake.

His face was covered with short black fur that resembled a panther's. His ears were round and oval in shape with long black locks covering his head, streaming down the side of his face. When he opened his mouth, a pair of three-inch fangs projected from his gums. As it was foretold, he had become a catlike creature, a panthiem—part man and part beast.

He looked down at his gloved hands. Until that moment, it never occurred to him to remove them. They had begun to ache slightly before feeling subjected to excruciating pain. When he removed his gloves, he beheld hands like paws with long retractable claws that grew out at least six inches.

Images flashed in his head as he began to remember his battle in the castle chamber when he was locked in a death struggle with the one whose face was clouded from his memory—the one whom he had sworn to bring to justice for all the atrocities he had committed, for murdering young women and removing their hearts after he had ravaged them. Among the victims included Kolliana, the woman that he loved.

He sat contemplating his lot. Seeing that he had been changed into a monster, he wondered what would happen if he were seen in his present condition. He stayed under the protection of the castle ruins, out of the sight of any weary traveler passing by. He waited until nightfall before he decided to leave his temporary sanctuary, exploring a world he was no longer sure of. Under the cover of night, he moved silently throughout the countryside.

After being asleep for six hundred years, Jahir was being driven by immeasurable hunger, along with something else inside him. It went beyond the need for sustenance, which also led him in a specific direction. No longer able to tolerate his desire for flesh, Jahir began to hunt. He had been transformed into a beast, both a hunter and a killer. The flesh he sought was not that of a human, but of a wild beast. As he moved through the wind, thick brush, and trees, he caught the scent of a large deer sorting leaves from a low hanging branch.

Slowly, he moved forward until he got close enough to launch his attack. Overtaking his victim, and with a single blow, he knocked it to the ground, pinning it before delivering a swift bite to its throat.

While he lay there, driven by centuries of hunger, he gorged himself. Covered in blood, he barely noticed. His hunger now satiated, there was something else in the air—another strange scent. Everything was now new to him. Growls in the distance called to him from where they were. A scream followed which was too far away for a normal human to hear, but he was no longer normal.

Quickly springing to his feet before finishing his meal, he moved in the direction of the growls and screams until they ceased. As he drew near, he could see a young girl being ravaged by wolves. Jahir rushed to her aid as she was being torn apart by the pack.

With powerful leg muscles, Jahir leaped into the midst of the animals and began to tear into the pack but he was too late. The wolves, at least a dozen in sequence, began attacking him. Proving too powerful an adversary, he repelled the pack as though they were pups. Swiftly, he downed four, severely wounding them.

Battered and bloody, they retreated from his attack and fled into the forest. Jahir noticed men with arrows and dogs were rapidly approaching, which had caused the wolves to flee. All he could focus upon was the tattered body of the young girl lying bloody and lifeless before him. Memories of his past now haunted him; he had once found the woman he loved shredded in almost the same manner but by the acts of a different kind of killer.

While he stood watching her lifeless body, he was struck with an arrow in his shoulder. It was like a needle pricking his skin; he hardly noticed. Pulling it out he briefly stared at it before casting it aside. The sound of their dogs and horses brought him back to reality. With the body of the girl still at his feet, he was instantly branded the killer, having the appearance of a beast.

Jahir was now faced with a choice—either make a stand or attempt to explain in words that would likely fall upon deaf ears. In this form, in their eyes, he knew he would be viewed as a spawn of Satan. Not wanting to harm them, he fled knowing an attack against him would most certainly end in death of his attackers.

Jahir released a roar that shook the ground while revealing his fangs stopping the men in their tracks while their dogs scattered from their pursuit. While archers took aim once more, Jahir fled deeper into the forest, quickly outdistancing them.

Like the wind, he moved with an effortless stride. Arrows never found their mark as they whisked around him some embedding themselves in the trees and the ground behind him. The sounds of dogs and horses in pursuit had begun to grow faint until they could no longer be heard. Instinctively possessing the characteristics of the creature that resembled his namesake, he took flight leaping high into the trees which had now become his highway. No longer bound to the earth alone, he was free to move above without restriction.

After losing sight and scent of what the archers perceived to be a monster, there was no trail left for the men or their dogs to follow. They all stood silent, looking to one another with fear etched across their faces. No one really knew what it was they had seen just moments earlier.

One of the men came forth and said, "So, the legend is true of the beast. But it has been one hundred years since it was last seen or had taken its last victim, until now."

Another came forth and replied, "No! That is not the beast of legend."

The others looked at him while another spoke out, saying, "How would you know this? For you were not yet born."

"No, that is true. I was not, but the story was passed down to me by my father and his father's father and his father before him who had seen the beast with his own two eyes. What he described was not that of a black furred catlike beast but that of a wolf—a golden werewolf whose body was completely covered in fur as golden as the hair on your head," he said as he turned to yet another that was standing amongst them.

"My great grandfather said it had ravaged the land, killing as it pleased after the sun had set," he continued. "Whether the moon was full or not, it would kill for the love of it, consuming most of his victims. There were a selected few whose hearts he chose to take —mostly that of young females.

"When they finally came upon it with their swords drawn as they surrounded it," he continued, "it stood in defiance hovering over its last victim covered in blood and refusing to flee. As it stood there, it smiled at him and about thirty armed men. He said that its fangs looked like daggers as long as a man's hand, curved and sharp. As they attacked, he said its claws tore through their shields and armor as though they were of cloth. Half of the men fell that day before it chose to end its attack, for reasons that were impossible to know. He could have killed them all but my great grandfather said it was as though it wanted the rest to survive to remember him for all time. While many lay dead or dying, it was at that moment, it chose to flee, and that was the last anyone had seen of the beast until this day."

He looked to the others and said, "What we have seen here today was something else, something new to these lands. May Christ help us all if it strikes again. Let us go and retrieve the child's body and take her home to her mother, that she may grieve for her daughter. Then, we must warn the people of what may soon come."

This would be a tale that over time would plague Jahir's journey—a tale that would become a legend, linking the shadow of the cat to that of the golden wolf. While the men turned and went their way, so had Jahir departed to go his.

He returned to the place he once called home long ago to seek answers. He thought of his friend Adonis and wondered what had become of him. He was not sure whether he had indeed slept for six centuries but he believed the answers he sought would be found in the kingdom he helped to set free from the hands of Bultizar.

The land of Sargonia was a distant journey, but there was something driving him in the opposite direction—one of an unknown force that was near impossible to resist. Cries from the distant past called out to him. Jahir followed that path. It was a trail filled with images of death and terror dancing through his head. A horrid tale that he could not explain.

Careful to remain out of sight during the day only emerging at night when he could move about more freely, his journey took him through places he had never seen and places he had never known to exist. After his fateful encounter with the men in the forest, he knew he had to remain out of sight or risk being hunted like a wild animal.

His instincts were keen, driving him in a direction that he could not refrain. His path led him to an abandoned cottage. It had been abandoned a long time ago. The forest had reclaimed both it and its lands.

Jahir stood quietly and still amongst the thickets as images of a young girl flashed in his head. He heard her screams and felt her pain as she was being ripped apart by images of a golden werewolf.

He moved toward the door of the cottage where he saw images of a young woman also in pain. There he also saw the vision of the woman along with the same images of the golden werewolf.

It had all become overwhelming to him; it was more than he could bear. As he left the old cottage and its lands behind him, it was at that very moment that he realized what he must do. He was determined to do everything in his power to track and kill his sworn enemy, no matter what it took, in order to end the pain of the tortured while freeing himself from his curse along the way.

For months, he moved through the countryside until he found himself in a valley filled with the corpses of Bultizar's victims. The world began to spin around him like a whirlwind as he stood in the midst. With both hands he held his head attempting to sort out all the images and pain. Although he fought his emotions as long as he could, this was all new to him and overwhelming. He blacked out and fell to the ground, lying there unconscious for hours. As he lay there, a parade of images flooded his mind. He beheld visions of his past when he was still a man, as well as the horrors of his future—a trail that would either lead to his salvation or his death.

When he awakened, his timeless search through the ages had just begun. Following a trail of blood, tears, and painful memories of the souls that had succumbed to the werewolf's wrath, he wandered the land for years seeking answers that never came. It was a journey that would eventually return him to his place of birth, only to find that it had been wiped from his memory. Not even where the mighty fortress of Obi once stood could a single stone be found. It was said that the people dismantled it brick by brick, never wanting to be reminded of the horrors that had taken place behind its walls.

From Europe to the Middle East and well into Asia was left a faint and distant trail that Jahir was driven to follow. Throughout the civilized world, Jahir pursued Bultizar as the monster randomly chose his victims, sometimes decades between choosing the next. Over the centuries, Jahir began to close the gaps of his enemy's divergence through time. What began as a century of pursuit gradually narrowed into decades, then months, and now into weeks, until the new millennium had arrived.

Chapter 4:
The Butcher of the Bronx

Present-Day New York City

Shortly after 9 PM, a scream broke the silence of a working-class neighborhood in the Bronx while many were preparing to shut down for the night. Shortly after, another sound followed, just as disturbing, but with a far different tone.

The howl of some kind of animal, perhaps a wolf or a coyote, echoed through the neighborhood like a scene out of the Old West. Those that heard it thought it may have come from the zoo a few blocks away, but no one was certain.

A half hour after everything had quieted, a homeless man decided to take a shortcut through the half-lit alley in the neighborhood. He was heading back to the shelter after his stay in the detox ward of the local hospital. With a bottle in his hand, he was celebrating his completion of the detox program. Less than five minutes into his celebration, he was feeling the buzz that had sent him there in the first place.

While he was walking through the alley, he thought he heard a sound ahead of him of something being dragged along the ground. As he continued on, he saw a trail of blood in front of him leading to a doorway of a vacant building. Fifty feet in front, he was stunned by what he saw.

It was large, standing over what he thought was a pile of rags before realizing it was a female body lying in the doorway. She was mutilated, and covered in blood. Whatever stood over her corpse turned and looked at him. For a second, the man doubted his own eyes along with his own sanity as he stood there shaking. At first, he thought it was a man with long locks but as it stood there staring back at him, he noticed it was something else. In a panic, he turned and ran as fast as he could.

"Help!" he called.

He glanced back as he ran to see if he was being pursued but to his relief, there was no one behind him. Whoever or whatever it was had disappeared into the vacant building. A few residents that passed by ignored him, dismissing him to be a belligerent and ranting alcoholic. Someone had already called the police after hearing the scream and the howl of what sounded like an animal.

Officers Daniels and Pittman pulled up to the scene as the homeless man ran toward them. "There's a body in the alley!" he shouted repeatedly. "I saw it. A woman was ripped apart, and blood was everywhere!"

He was frantic as the two officers subdued him in an attempt to calm him. After several attempts, he began to settle down. They had him sit in the back of the cruiser. Pittman stayed with him while Daniels went to investigate. With one hand on his Glock and the other shining his light in front of him, Daniels moved cautiously down the dark alley where the man claimed he had seen the body.

As he approached, Daniels saw the trail of blood along with what appeared to be a pair of large paw prints leading to an open doorway of the vacant building. The door looked as though it had been forced open. It hung on one hinge, leaning against the wall.

Daniels shined his light inside and saw the gruesome sight of a female that had been shredded. Quickly grabbing his radio, he reported a possible homicide and called for backup, stating the possibility of the unknown assailant still on the scene.

Back in the cruiser, Pittman watched the man from his rearview mirror. Since the man had settled down, the officer began to interview him.

"What's your name, sir?" Pittman calmly asked.

"Harvey Lancaster," he replied, as the officer continued to question him.

"Mr. Lancaster, try to remain calm and explain exactly it was that you saw."

"He—it—had long locks coming from under a hood. But when I saw his face, it had yellow eyes like a cat with black fur. His face was half covered with a scarf or something, though."

What he described was hard for anyone to believe, especially from a man who reeked of alcohol. Pittman believed his judgment had been compromised by his condition causing him to quickly dismiss his account. Then, he heard Daniels's transmission over the radio.

"I've got to run," Pittman said, hopping out the cruiser. "Mr. Lancaster, remain in the back of the cruiser until I return."

He drew his weapon and proceeded down the alley to assist his partner. Once he arrived, he couldn't believe the amount of blood that was everywhere. He looked at his partner.

"Who or what could have done this to a person?" Pittman asked.

"I don't know," Daniels replied, "but whoever it is went into the building. Stay here while I make my way to the front, in case whoever it is attempts to exit."

Shortly afterwards, more police began to arrive along with an EMS unit. When the medics saw the body, they were astounded by the gruesome sight. In all the responses they had encountered over the years, they had never come across anything that even came close to resembling this. Any attempts to resuscitate her were pointless due to the magnitude of her injuries.

A special operations taskforce was sent in to set up a command post. The place became filled with cops and crime scene investigators as they taped off the area while the crowds began to gather. With lights focused on the building, a command was given for the SWAT team to access at every possible point of entry before sending in the search dogs. They searched the building and its perimeter, exhausting all resources. Even the dogs couldn't find a single trail to follow. After a few hours, the area was deemed secure before the search teams were pulled.

The crime scene investigators were called to begin their investigation. First to arrive CSI investigator Gabrielle Acostas, the department's top investigator, led the team. She was thirty-three years old of Puerto Rican descent, looking as though she had just stepped out of a magazine centerfold. As beautiful as she was intelligent, she had a reputation for being efficient and thorough. Once she and her team entered the building, they spread out collecting anything and everything they could find. This was the second such killing in less than a month, almost identical to a previous murder that occurred only a few miles from this Bronx neighborhood.

Shortly after they arrived, the lead homicide detectives assigned to the case pulled up in a black unmarked Crown Victoria. In charge of the investigation was Lieutenant Bobby Grimes and his partner, Sergeant John Poles. Grimes a twenty-year veteran-- tall, dark, and athletically built. Standing about six-two, he wore his head bald with a mid-length beard and mustache.

When Grimes got out of the car, he looked as though he had just stepped out of a fashion magazine. With a tailored Armani suit and a pair of high-end gators, he had the swag to carry that image. A Stanford University graduate with a doctorate of psychology under his belt, he had been a multi-lettered athlete, who also excelled in playing chess. Grimes was one of the sharpest minds in the department, having the unique ability of getting into the heads of the most complicated criminal psyches.

Poles, his partner of Irish Italian descent, was a young and witty law school graduate who had finished Princeton University near the top of his class. Poles had chosen police life over a much more lucrative law career. After his father's death in the line of duty, he made the decision to follow in his footsteps to honor his sacrifice.

Standing six even, Poles was youthful in appearance. He looked more like a freshman in college than a veteran of ten years. He held a third-degree black belt in the art of Hapkido, with two amateur titles under his belt. Poles was the more casually dressed of the officers. He wore tan khakis under a trench with a multicolored tie—a style that matched his personality. Poles, the lighthearted one, constantly broke the ice to keep the day rolling smoothly.

Their styles, one as a hardline cop while the other had a much lighter tone, complimented one another. Both were tested and experienced, with reputations of being tough, persistent, and highly efficient. They had a track record that was unparalleled within the department for solving the toughest of cases, with this one in particular appearing to fill that bill.

With Grimes in mind, the commissioner had personally assigned them to take the lead in this case. The commissioner had taken a personal stake in this case. The victim who had been murdered weeks earlier was Stacy Thomas, the daughter of the commissioner's closest childhood friend. They had been working nonstop on her death, and now this one was added which was nearly identical. Both women were found murdered in the same animalistic way--each with their hearts violently removed. All of this suggested that they were the victims of the same killer. Because of the sheer brutality and savagery involved in the deaths, the commissioner needed the killer found in a hurry. If anyone could find the killer, he believed these two could.

As Grimes and his partner approached, they were greeted by officers Daniels and Pittman who were the first to arrive.

"What do you have for us?" Grimes asked.

"We were approached by a man running out of the alley toward us," Daniels replied. "A guy named Harvey Lancaster, screaming about something he saw in the alley."

He gave the two detectives all the details they had received, telling them what Lancaster had seen was gone. As Daniels relayed what Lancaster had told them, he noticed there was something ambiguous in what the man had seen. *He said it was a very large something, but he couldn't tell whether it was a man or something else when he looked into its face,* Daniels thought to himself.

"That description Lancaster gave sounded sketchy at best," Daniels concluded. "He said it had yellow eyes like a cat, but his face was half covered, and that its long black locks came down from under a hood he was wearing. Lancaster said it was standing next to the body before he turned and ran away from it."

"Where is he now?" Grimes asked.

"In the back of the cruiser," Daniels replied nodding his head in that direction. "Here's our theory: It appears that she was killed in the alley then dragged over to the building before he—it—got away. But here's the thing: There was a strange set of prints in the dirt, like gigantic paws, leading into the building. With the size and shape of them, I'm still trying to figure out what could've made them."

"There was a set of prints found at the site of Stacy Thomas's murder," Poles replied, eyes wide.

"The CSI team has already begun casting the prints. Let's go," Daniels said as the officers headed to the victim's body.

When they got within fifteen feet of the cruiser enroute to where the body lay, they were met by an air of booze coming from the backseat where Lancaster was sitting. The rear window was rolled halfway down as they approached.

After getting a whiff, Poles looked over at Grimes. "With that amount of booze reeking from his pores, I don't know if we'll be able to believe any of his story," Poles said.

They were now outside of the building where the body was. Grimes walked over to where the CSI team had begun setting print casts; he squatted down to get a closer look, careful not to disturb them.

Poles looked down at his partner. "Chief, they look exactly like the ones found at the last murder scene," Poles said.

"Yes," Grimes replied, "they do. When we talk to the forensics team, we'll have a better idea." Grimes turned to Officer Daniels. "Where is the team now?" he asked.

"Inside," Daniels replied.

"Did anything come up on Mr. Lancaster?" Grimes asked.

"Not much," Daniels replied. "Forty-three years of age, homeless, and an Iraqi war vet. He fell on hard times then lost his wife due to the bottle and drug abuse. Been divorced now a few years. His wife took the kids along with everything else, and then moved to the West Coast with her new husband. Since then, he's been married to the bottle fulltime. You know, that down and out story. He's been homeless ever since. He has no real criminal record except a few vagrancy charges. Nothing serious. He also has a history of depression. The guy is really messed up."

"I'm sure he saw something; just nothing we could use in court," Poles said, shaking his head along with Daniels and his partner Pittman.

"What he described didn't make any sense," Pittman said. "He was crazy out his head when he ran up on us. We weren't sure whether to shoot him or arrest him."

"As messy as the scene was, there was no blood found on him, which leads me to believe he wasn't involved," Daniels explained.

After entering the building, Grimes looked over at the covered body, before being approached by Acostas. She had also worked the scene of Stacy Thomas's murder.

Grimes had a particular interest in the prints that were being set in a cast outside. Acostas confirmed their suspicions. "They appeared to be identical to those found at that site," she said. "But what's most baffling is when we examined them, we found that they were comparable to that of a bipedal animal by the weight distribution of the print—a heavy one at that. By the depth of it, it had to weigh at least upwards of four hundred pounds."

Grimes and Poles both found that assessment interesting. "What do we have here, King Kong?" Poles asked, snickering sarcastically with his reply.

"I don't know, but no animal came to mind that could leave *those* type of paw prints, walking on two feet," Acostas replied.

"Have you found anything else that could possibly link the two deaths?" Grimes asked.

"Not yet."

She took the two detectives over to the body. When they got there, she knelt over and drew back the sheets to reveal the mutilated body, which was heavily covered in blood.

Grimes looked over to his partner. Both knew immediately what the other was thinking. "The Butcher of the Bronx kills again," said Poles.

"'The Butcher of the Bronx?'" Grimes asked, repeating his statement.

"Yeah, that's what some are calling him after Stacy's death. Whatever they want to call him, it appears to be the same killer, an apparent serial killer. The body mutilated, and the heart torn from the body just like the last victim."

As they both stood there looking at the gruesome sight, Acostas provided the facts about the victim.

"Kerri Barnes, a twenty-four-year-old female living in the Bronx. An accountant for Horus & Weaver Brokerage. She doesn't have any family here. She had moved here from Belton, Louisiana, after leaving high school to attend a cosmetology academy. After getting her degree, she decided to stay. Her roommate also told the officers that Ms. Barnes said that she was going to Tenley's for happy hour to have a few drinks. She also told her that she had broken it off with her boyfriend and wanted to go there to relax. That was about 6 o'clock this evening, which was the last time she saw her."

"Had anybody spoken to anyone down there at Tenley's?" Grimes asked.

"Yes, a couple of officers were sent down there as well. They filed a report." Going off what information she had on her, she added, "Barnes lived in the Westgate apartment complex. Officers had been sent to her apartment and talked with her roommate, Tonya Springs. We have the phone number," she said, handing it over to Grimes.

"Good. I'll speak with her later to see what we can find out," Grimes replied before she walked away.

"So far, we have one eyewitness to something," Poles forewarned.

"Yes, we do," Grimes replied, "but we also need to go to Tenley's and see if we can find out anything else."

"One thing is for certain—someone saw her," Poles assured.

"Another young female victim the same age and body type," Grimes declared.

"Both twenty-four years old; sounds like a pattern forming to me," Poles insinuated.

Grimes looked over at him and thought about it. He feared that his partner might be right.

"I hope not but it's too early to make that assessment," Grimes declared.

"Our last victim, Stacy Thomas—someone did see her talking with a well-dressed young man wearing a blue tailored suit with long blond hair pinned in a ponytail before she disappeared," Poles responded.

"Yes, but no one got a good look at his face before she disappeared, which means that could be anybody. Besides, that description was sketchy at best. No one actually saw her leave with him, making him a person of interest, not necessarily a suspect," Grimes surmised.

"With no one that fits that description coming forth, we're going to need more than that to push the envelope forward on this," Poles forewarned.

"Well, Tenley's is where we're going first," Grimes replied. Looking over at Daniels and Pittman, Grimes continued, "Take Mr. Lancaster down to the station. Get him a cup of coffee or something. I'll question him there later."

"Okay Lieutenant, you got it," Pittman replied.

Grimes crouched over the body once again to get another look. The victim's chest cavity had been penetrated. As he looked closely, Grimes noticed dried blood on the shredded remains of her clothing. He had surmised that the amount of force from a blow to have done this was remarkable.

"See how the blood splattered?" Grimes asked his partner, looking at him. "You noticed anything else about it?"

Poles looked closely, then took a double take. "Yes," he replied, "the blow was delivered upwardly when she died."

"Exactly," Grimes agreed. "See how the blood traveled down the center of her chest onto her clothes, and onto her abdomen? It flowed much farther down the front of her wounds than on the sides of them."

"Whoever or whatever did this had to be awfully powerful to cave someone's chest in like that and then snatch their heart out in one fluent motion," Poles said, looking at his partner. "Chief, you have a pretty sharp eye for this kind of thing! You ever thought about transferring to forensics and sharing that eye with them?"

"What, and leave the streets?" Grimes queried. "I think I'm just fine here keeping an eye on you."

Grimes continued to look over the body while the CSI team was still searching for evidence. Poles went off on his own to look around, in case the forensics team had missed anything. He encountered in a dark corner some debris that had been dumped. With a small hand light, Poles searched for anything he could find useful to the investigation. A stickler for detail, something caught his eye—something that could have been easily overlooked.

As he leaned over with his flashlight in the only spot everyone had missed among the spotlights that were set up, he squatted down to get a closer look. He called Grimes over who was standing near the doorway.

"Hey, Chief, over here. I think we may have found something!"

Putting on a pair of gloves and using a pair of tweezers that he always kept with him, Poles picked up a long strand of blond hair. It was barely exposed, lying on top of a shattered piece of a window pane among trash and debris. His eye for detail was impeccable. Upon closely examining it, he placed it in a plastic bag as Acostas and Grimes came over.

"I may have found something, or maybe not," Poles said. Walking them over to the light, he showed them what he had found. "The last human seen with Stacy Thomas was a blond male," he continued. "Up to this point, no one remembers the details of his face, so this will have to be the next best thing."

As he handed the bag over to Acostas, she replied, "This is the only real evidence we have—this and the prints. Once we get both the cast and this sample to the lab for DNA analysis, we'll know for sure. My hunch is that they will match. We'll see. Let's give it a few weeks. Finding a match for those animal tracks is going to be interesting."

"Yes," Grimes replied, "and we still have the one witness that we have to interview. Hopefully, he'll be sober enough to make some kind of sense."

"If he can't give us anything that we can use, or if we can't find a link to anything else in the evidence we already have, then we're still at square one," Acostas concluded before she walked off with the sample.

Usually the lighthearted detective, Poles was frustrated. He looked over at his partner and said, "Chief, what's going on here? All of this is beginning to look like a twisted nightmare."

Equally frustrated, Grimes simply shook his head. "We have one woman last seen in the company of a young blond male that no one saw her leave with. Then there's the pattern of their bodies appearing as if they've been attacked by some kind of large animal, and the prints left behind. We have to wait to see if the two sets of prints match. So far, the set we have doesn't match any known species. Living, anyway."

"I think we should go back to where Stacy Thomas was killed and look again," Poles said. "I keep having the feeling that we've missed something.

You may be right, but after a few weeks, I'm sure that scene has already been compromised. It's probably back to being a home for the homeless. We'll just have to wait and see if anything we found tonight will lead us anywhere new or simply nowhere."

"If those prints prove to be something other than a human, what kind of animal do we have running around in the streets of New York, literally?"

"I don't know, but I've never heard of an animal that preferred women of the same age that are built the same,"

"Coincidence, perhaps?"

"Coincidence unlikely. I'm thinking more along the lines of a man in some kind of suit or costume, or a trained animal of some sort."

"It's highly unlikely a large savage creature can roam a city street for weeks at a time that no one has seen," Poles said, "especially a city of this magnitude. I don't know. Hey, remember that fool that had both a tiger and an alligator in that cramped tower apartment complex in Harlem? With all those people around, no one knew they were there until it attacked him."

"Yes, but that was different; that took place inside. Had it gotten out and attacked someone, that would've been a species we could've tracked and seen. Besides, there have been no other attacks in the weeks between these two killings. That, along with the distance between the two locations, just doesn't make sense."

"You're right, Chief, it doesn't. Right now, we have footprints and bite marks, according to the experts, none of which match those of anything they have on file. An autopsy that posed more questions than answers that still hasn't rendered any leads. We also have a cat man seen by an alcoholic; let's not forget that. Until we question him, we haven't an idea. Last, but not least, there still remains the question of the man last seen with Stacy Thomas. There's nothing on him, no reports of a male body found anywhere. Nor are these injuries appearing human related. So far, I don't want to have to play a cat and mouse game with whatever it is we're dealing with because innocent people will die waiting for this thing to play out."

"We have to keep searching," Grimes persisted. "It's still early. We'll start a background search and see if we can find any connections between the two women—who they knew, who they hung out with, or liked being around. We'll see if there are any boyfriends or girlfriends that may have any possible beefs, old or new—places they've been most recently that may tie them together. Once we get her body down to the medical examiner's office, we'll see how all this will match up with our last victim. This time, I want to be there for the autopsy in case there's something we can act on immediately rather than waiting for a report."

Chief, I'm with you. We need to be on top of this before someone else dies. This case has already begun building steam."

Chapter 5:
Hidden Truths

The commissioner and his entourage had just arrived on the scene; Kyle Kuntz, a thirty-five-year veteran of the force, a highly decorated and dedicated commissioner. He had moved up the ranks on his merit and reputation of being one of those incorruptible cops that lived and died by the book. He took a personal interest in the case, with the first victim being the daughter of his closest friend, Guy Thomas. They had grown up playing baseball together back in their neighborhood.

Kuntz became an officer, while Guy chose a career with the fire service. He had Grimes assigned to the case personally because he had the reputation of being the best with the highest efficiency record in solving cases in department history. He had solved every one of his cases.

As he walked towards Grimes, he informally called out, "Bobby!" getting his attention.

They had been friends since he had gotten out of the academy. The detective was his rookie officer when he was first assigned to the precinct. They had been partners for three years before Kuntz began ascending up the ranks. Kuntz had always thought highly of him. His dedication and efficiency were noticeable, once referring to Grimes as the most intelligent young officers with whom he had ever worked with.

"Was she murdered like Stacy?" Kuntz asked.

"Yes, almost identically," Grimes reported. "We have a man who says he saw someone standing over the body before he—or it—disappeared. Unlike in

Stacy's murder, the description given was not that of a young blond-guy but something completely different."

"Like what?" he responded with his eyebrows raised.

What the man described to the arriving officers was vague at best, like someone who had too much to drink. I'll wait until he sobers up a little and interview him down at the precinct later, after we're finished here. I was told that officers were sent to her home, but I haven't reviewed the report yet. Once we collect the facts, I'm going to begin a detailed investigation. Whoever it was may have possibly committed both murders, but we don't have a motive yet. There's no evidence so far that either woman had been sexually assaulted. Robbery has been ruled out. Apparently, both the purses of Stacy and Kerri were left on the scene with nothing taken. In both cases their IDs were still present, but we have to wait for the autopsy, which I will attend. Once we examine the evidence, we'll have more answers."

Grimes escorted the commissioner to the body explaining all the details. Once they arrived, Grimes drew back the covers to show him what they had. The savagery of the attack and what he saw was disturbing. Kuntz stared at the body in disbelief.

"My God," he gasped. "What kind of animal do we have loose on our streets?"

The two murders almost the same," Grimes replied. "Claw marks across the chest along with two large puncture wounds in the shoulder and around the breast area, and the removal of both their hearts in the same brutal way. The attacks are like that of a large animal. All we found were a few hair samples that we've sent downtown for further analysis to see what turns up."

"This looks like something straight out of someone's demented nightmare," Kuntz replied. "Two young women torn apart like rag dolls, their hearts removed, and not many clues to go by so far. Who or what could've done all this?"

"I don't know," Grimes declared, "but I intend to find out."

"Bobby, I'm counting on you. If no one else can solve this, I know you can."

"When we started our initial investigation on Stacy's case, we spoke with her father along with friends. They had no knowledge of anyone that would've done anything like this; they say she was loved by everyone, but that investigation is still ongoing. Stranger things have happened."

"Yes, I spoke with her father also," Kuntz said. "He was devastated as any father would. Who wouldn't be? I promised him that I was going to do everything in my power to bring his daughter's killer to justice. That's why I handpicked you."

"We're attempting to notify the victim's family as we speak," Grimes replied. "Ms. Barnes was not from here. She's from Louisiana. That's where most of her family is. After school, she decided to stay. She has a roommate we've already contacted. Hopefully, she can give us something to work with, we do have something, although it may be a longshot. Harvey Lancaster, our witness has both mental and alcohol issues, and we believe he had been drinking. We can argue the credibility of his statement due to his state of mind. What you can't argue is the fact that he's a witness. We can argue the validity of it, but he did see something."

Kuntz looked at both detectives and agreed. Kuntz responded, "Whoever or whatever this killer is," we need to find them and find them fast."

"There's one thing I failed to mention, Commissioner," Grimes divulged. "The two women are the same age and size. Although it's still early, my biggest fear is that there may be a pattern.

As a crowd of curious onlookers began to gather outside the yellow tape, Kuntz looked back over at the detectives before walking off and said, "We don't want this thing to become more of a media circus. Keep this animal thing under wraps, understood?" Grimes simply nodded.

The Action News team was the first news outlet to arrive with their lead reporter Terrie Collins. Beautiful and petite, with a light brown complexion, mid-length hair, and a body that would put an athlete to shame, she looked as though she had stepped out of a dream and in front of a camera. When she spoke, her voice had a soft island flavor about it. Articulate and intelligent, she was as confident as she was beautiful.

Her cameraman was a young Jewish kid named Steve Whitman. Cool, calm, and laid back, Whitman was sharp. Straight out of graduate school, he had just completed his first year working with her. His demeanor complemented the style of the savvy and aggressive reporter well.

Her technician, Buddy Long, was short and stout with a lively personality. Always wearing a smile and full of jokes, he was the perfect medium to offset these two extremes.

After they set up across the street, Terrie and Whitman came over to the detective carrying a mic. Terrie asked, "Bobby, what happened here?"

Grimes looked her in her eyes and smiled. They had history—an on-again, off-again relationship that at the moment was somewhere in between, but this was business.

"Is this on the record?"

"No, the mic is off," Terrie said.

"It's too early to know," he responded. "We're still investigating."

"Is this murder related to the one a couple of weeks ago?"

"We don't know yet, but by the way things look, it's a possibility. I can't tell you anything that isn't fact-based, but off the record, it's a very strong possibility."

Glancing across the street, she saw the commissioner standing among a group of officers. She looked up at Grimes and said, "We'll talk later. I think I know where I can get something official." She turned, along with her cameraman, and walked toward the commissioner. As she approached Kuntz from behind, she called his name to get his attention.

"Miss Collins," he greeted.

"Commissioner, we'd like an interview."

After he agreed, she turned and faced the camera to begin.

"This is Action News Team live on the scene in this quiet Bronx neighborhood where another young woman was found brutally murdered. It is a scene that has this local neighborhood shocked, in the wake of the gruesome murder of Stacy Thomas just a few weeks ago, not far from here. This is the second time in less than a month that a young woman was found mutilated and murdered—her heart taken from her body—while police have yet to find any answers."

After finishing her introductory speech, placing the microphone to his mouth, she continued. "We're here with Police Commissioner Kyle Kuntz. With two women found murdered in just a matter of weeks, do you believe that this murder is related to that of Stacy Thomas, or know whether anything has been found that could link these murders?"

Looking into the camera, he stated, "In regard to whether the two cases are related, we do not know at this time. It's too early to make that assessment. Miss Thomas's case is still ongoing. There's not enough information until we complete our investigation. But to answer your question, we have a person of interest, but the identity is still unknown at this time."

Terrie further inquired, "Can the police provide any assurance to the public that our streets are safe?"

"Concerning the safety of our city streets, I can assure you that we are doing everything in our power to ensure the safety and wellbeing of the citizens of the City of New York. We are working around the clock to make certain that the culprit of these heinous crimes be apprehended and brought to justice. In conclusion, I have no further comment while this case is still under investigation. I can assure you that the safety of our city streets is our top priority while keeping its citizens informed."

After his statement, he smiled, stepped from the microphone, and walked away.

"Looking into the camera," she reported. "There you have it, the words of Police Commissioner Kyle Kuntz. This concludes our interview. Terrie Collins, Action News."

"That's a wrap," Steve concluded. "Time to wrap it up."

"Yes, it is," she agreed.

As she and her crew were preparing to leave, there was something that didn't feel right to her. It was an uneasy feeling she couldn't explain, her intuition perhaps. Whatever it was, she felt as though she were being watched. She looked in all directions with a strong inkling to look to up. It was dark, and she didn't see anything.

Satisfied it was probably nothing, she wrote off whatever caused her suspicion as being her imagination. Before climbing into the van to head back, she glanced up at the top of the building one more time before they pulled off.

Grimes also watched her and her crew drive off before turning his attention back to concluding their investigation for the evening. Grimes stood there, his mind on something beyond just the crime scene.

"Hey, Chief," Poles questioned, "how are you and Terrie making out these days? You haven't mentioned her in a while."

Pausing, he answered, "We have our ups and downs. Right now, we're in one of those even moments."

"Yeah, I understand, but I saw a little electricity in her eyes tonight. It seemed to be flowing."

"Yeah, that was tonight, but in truth we both have been busy lately. It's been taking its toll on our relationship. Our work already has caused stress on us, and now this. It's always been tough, but now, we both are working on the same case. You know the strain that will cause—she needing info and me not being able to give it."

"Yeah, tell me about it," Poles replied. "My wife has been on my case about my lack of time spent at home. The long hours can be a killer, and this case couldn't have happened at a worst time. Our ten-year anniversary is coming up, and I've been working like a mule."

Grimes looked over at him and smirked. "You and me both," sharing a laugh. "Tell your wife it's all my fault."

Poles laughed, "You know Monica. She ain't buying that."

"Probably not," Grimes concurred as he laughed.

"Hey, why don't you and Terrie come by the house one evening for dinner? Monica makes the best pasta on the planet. If that doesn't ease tension, nothing will."

Grimes smiled. "I think I'll take you up on that. Always good to see your folks."

"Well, it's settled," Poles proclaimed. "All that's needed is for us to set a date."

"Will do. When I see her, I'll ask her. I'm sure she would love that. All of us need some relax time with everything going on."

The two detectives headed back to the precinct. They had an interview to conduct with their first real witness.

***

Unbeknownst to everyone, above them out of view, there was another set of eyes looking on with interest in the events that had just taken place. Hidden atop an adjacent building sat this silent figure quiet and still. It was Jahir. He was careful to avoid detection by the police chopper hovering above, their lights beaming down on the streets and rooftops still in search of that elusive suspect.

His senses were extraordinary, he could hear and see everything going on below as if he were standing in their midst. Besides everything that was going on, there was something else that had caught his attention, one that kept his eyes glued and fixed—Terrie Collins. There was something about her that took his thoughts back to the past.

On the roof, he had watched as the white news van pulled off until it disappeared amongst the sea of headlights. As he hid in the darkness, something else caught his attention—a familiar face that he had barely noticed.

Standing amongst the crowd was a small, old white-haired lady. She stood out like a ghost. As he focused his eyes on her, she looked up at him and smiled. She was all too familiar to him. Standing up to get a clearer view, the sudden sound of a dumpster being lifted for a late-night pickup distracted him momentarily. When he focused back on her, she was gone as though she were never there. It was like a ghost of his past that disturbed him. He drifted back into the shadows where he once again became completely hidden.

***

Arriving back at the news station, Terrie and her crew gathered their things as they prepared to leave.

Steve looked over at her. "I'm calling it quits for the night. I'm beat," he said.

She smiled. "Yes, get some rest. It's been a long day. I've got a few things I wanna take care of before I head home."

"Did you drive today?" Steve asked.

"No," she replied, "I took the train."

"I can stick around and wait for you if you like, to take you home. Plus, it's getting late. I can rest in my car 'til you're ready."

She grinned; she knew he liked her. She thought it was kind of cute, but her interest lay elsewhere.

"No, you go home. I'll be fine."

"You sure? It's not like I have anything planned, just my bed. My girlfriend just left me," he joked. I can hang around."

"You're so silly," she responded, with both sharing a laugh. "No, I'll be fine. The subway is down the street from both here and my condo."

"You do know there's a maniac on the loose? You might need a protector."

"I have my protector right here," she laughed, pulling a can of mace from her purse. "Trust me, I know how to use it."

"Okay, okay," he snickered, "I get the message. Be safe."

"Goodnight Steve. I appreciate the offer."

"Goodnight," he responded while watching her walk into the building. "That's one beautiful woman," he thought to himself before pulling off.

Walking into her office she sat at her desk. Logging on to her computer she pulled up her notes she had from the previous investigation. She was curious to see the similarities. She had become frustrated with the lack of information along with her sources that were constantly coming up blank. There were no leads or rumors circulating on the street, only fear of the current unknown.

***

Back at the station, Grimes and Poles had begun conducting an interview with their lone witness, Harvey Lancaster. As they sat across from him reviewing the report, Grimes looked over at Lancaster.

"Before we get started, can we get you something? A cup of coffee, some water, anything?" Grimes asked.

"You have anything a little stronger?" he smirked.

"Anything stronger than a cup of black coffee is a no-go," Poles jested. "Besides, I think you've had all you need for one night as it is."

"Don't bet on it," he chuckled, shaking his head. "After what I saw, I'll need a double."

"Let's get down to what happened," Grimes said, interrupting the verbal sparring between the two. "According to your statement, you said you saw someone standing over the body. Suppose you tell me what you saw."

"I was walking down the alley, and I thought I heard something," Lancaster explained. "It was pretty dark. It sounded like someone was dragging something along the ground, then I ain't hear nothing no more. I didn't think much of it, so I kept walking. When I looked down at the ground, I saw a trail of blood. Then when I looked over to the side, that's when I saw it. I thought it was a man. He was big and stocky, wearing a long coat. At its feet, I saw the body. At first, I thought it was a pile of rags or something. Then, I realized what it was.

"What I thought was a man when I focused my eyes looked like something else," he continued. "Its face was half covered with a scarf or something, but I saw its eyes. They were like a cat's. They were yellow with big black pupils. Its face looked like it was covered with fur. He had on a hood and looked like he was wearing a skully under it. He also had dreads coming down from under it. His hands looked like paws with long curled claws at the end of them. I dropped my drink and ran as fast as I could. When I looked back to see if I were being chased, it disappeared into the building. That's the last thing I remembered."

After hearing Lancaster's account, both detectives remained skeptical and silent. To the officers, Lancaster's story was remarkable but more so unbelievable.

"Mr. Lancaster," Poles questioned, "how close were you, and how long did you stand there?"

"About twenty feet, I guess. I didn't stick around. I got outta there."

"How many drinks did you have before entering that alley?" Poles posed another question. "You said it was dark with very little lighting. You sure it wasn't simply a guy with locks?"

"Hey, man, I'm not crazy. I know what I saw. I might have a drinking problem, but if you see something like that, it will sober you up in a hurry. That was my first! I had just gotten out of detox at least twenty minutes before any of this happened."

"That long, huh?" Poles replied.

Grimes glared over at his partner. "Cut it, will you?"

"Sorry, Chief."

Grimes focused back on Lancaster. He thought about asking him a few more questions, but decided that it was enough for the night. What they had heard was more than they could digest in one evening. Due to the circumstances and the source, a lot of it could be disregarded and thrown out of the realm of believability, but Grimes decided to hold onto the possibility, although it would be a distant one.

"Mr. Lancaster, you're free to go," Grimes said. "We may call on you again if we need any further information."

"Okay, will do," he responded. "Hey, can I get a ride down to the shelter? You know it's no longer safe out here, not even for a street savvy homeless vet like me."

"Okay, I'll take care of it," Grimes replied. "I'll see that one of the officers takes you there."

Poles walked over to the door and looked to see who was available. He saw a young newly assigned officer standing in front of a file cabinet. He had just walked in to drop off some files. Poles looked down at his name tag and waved him over.

"Officer Candy!"

"Yes, sir," he replied.

"If you're not too busy, I have an assignment for you."

"No, I'm not too busy, sir. What do you need me to do?"

"Go to the lot and get a car. I need you to see that Mr. Lancaster gets back to the shelter safely, would you?"

"Okay, Sarg."

"Oh, yeah, and rookie," Poles added, "on your way back, stop at the donut shop and bring back a dozen. "And I don't want to see one bite out of any of them, either. Remember, I'm a detective, so I'll see the evidence on your face. I want a whole donut, not half of one, "he snickered.

"Will do, Sarg," Candy laughed escorting Lancaster out to the lot.

Chapter 6:
Enter the Panthiem

Now after midnight Terrie headed home. Frustrated and tired, she couldn't wait to get there and relax. It had been a long, turbulent evening. With most of the staff gone, only the nightly news crews and building security were left to make their rounds.

Before leaving the building, she approached the watchman—a sixty-nine-year-old man with gray hair named Aaron Johnson. He had worked there for about twenty years. "Goodnight, Mr. Johnson," she said.

"Same to you," he replied. "You have a safe night and be careful. These streets have been crazy lately."

"Thank you, Mr. Johnson. I'll be okay, "Besides, the subway is just a few blocks away. I'll be there in no time."

"I'll be praying that you do he said with a smile, watching as she left out the door.

The street was quiet with an occasional passing car. Briskly she walked down the empty street. The day had been long and she was tired. She wasted little time trying to get there. While she hurried along, the same feeling she had experienced earlier came over her—that feeling of being watched. At first, she thought it was her imagination again, but there was an echo of footsteps behind her.

When she turned, she saw a hooded figure with both hands in their pockets matching her step for step. The faster she walked, the more he kept pace. As she reached into her purse, she pulled out her can of mace, making it ready in case she needed it, but the footsteps had ceased. she turned again to see if the person was still there but they were gone, like they had vanished.

Momentarily she relaxed, letting out a sigh of relief. Pausing to look around she made certain everything was clear then put her mace back into her purse. She continued walking while passing a dark alley.

Suddenly someone grabbed her from behind placing their hand over her mouth as she began struggling frantically. Overpowered, she was dragged back into the alley. While being dragged she saw three men waiting, all with their faces covered before everything went blurry.

A blow to her face had dazed her knocking her to the ground. Discombobulated, she laid helpless as the men lifted her off the ground throwing her over a toppled trash can with her facing the ground. One duct-taped her mouth as the others held her down.

Finally, the one following her entered the alley. With her vision blurred, she saw double. She could hear laughter but was helpless as two of the men held her legs apart while another held both of her hands. The one who last entered the alley immediately began unzipping his pants and laughed while she watched helplessly.

"Terrie Collins, that sexy TV reporter," she heard him say. "You are going to really enjoy this."

Preparing for the worst, she wanted to scream but her mouth was taped so tightly that no one could hear her. The man standing behind her pulled out a knife and held it to her throat.

Drawing close he said, "If you fight," he whispered "I will slice your throat, then I'll do you while your body is still warm! Try me."

She felt the roughness of his hands as he grabbed hold of her breast, continuing slowly and reaching down to feel the outer portion of her thighs before slowly moving his hand up her inner thigh. Suddenly, he stopped. There was the sound of yet another set of footsteps walking up behind them.

Immediately, one of her captors was flung over her head at least ten feet in the air like a discarded toy. Terrie rolled over to her side to see her attackers being overpowered single handedly by a huge hooded figure that was tossing the men around like they were nothing. He moved so quickly in the darkness she couldn't get a good look at his face.

Her assailants couldn't lay a hand on him. Her heart was pounding. She didn't know what was going to happen next. They attempted to get away but couldn't. He pummeled them all within moments until he was the only one standing.

After the struggle was over, she saw the silhouette of large man in a hood with his back to her standing in the middle of the alley. Around him lying unconscious were the men that had attacked her, now littering the ground around him. She wasn't sure if they were still alive. Turning slowly, it was Jahir.

In the darkness she couldn't clearly see his face. It was only the light reflecting from his eyes coming from the street light at the alley's entrance. She didn't know what was going to happen next.

He slowly began walking toward her. She didn't know whether he was a friend or someone who had his own agenda, with the thugs simply being in his way. Unsure what was going to happen, she watched him as he approached. Suddenly she heard a sound behind her so she looked back. One of the attackers had keeled over a trash can while unconscious. When she turned back Jahir had vanished without a sound. The only evidence that he had been there was the men he left scattered in his wake. Removing the tape from her mouth she took her phone from her purse. Springing to her feet she hurried out the alley dialing 911. Moments later, officers had arrived. Scratched and bruised, she pointed to the alley, where they found the five men barely alive. She told them a story that seemed unbelievable, but they couldn't dispute the evidence around them along with the word of a top flight reporter to back it up before taking the men into custody.

***

Back at the station, Grimes and Poles were left with the dilemma of deciphering fact from what they perceived as fantasy. Everything they had to assess was based on the account of an alcoholic that said he saw what looked like a cat on two feet, though his blood alcohol levels were off the chart despite claiming he had only the one drink.

Grimes looked over at Poles and said, "We started this case with not much to go on, hoping to tie the two together. The last victim was seen with a young blond man, but no one can confirm the two left together. We have a set of prints no one can explain, an attack that appears to be by a large animal no one has seen with wounds that are obviously real to that effect. This thing Lancaster described cannot be taken seriously as fact, not with his alcohol levels five times the limit. Without tangible proof or other witnesses, his statement is null and void."

"We can call it whatever we like, but he still is a witness who said he saw someone or something standing over the victim," Poles replied.

"Yeah," Grimes replied, "but a witness to what? Something that looked half man, half cat standing over a body in the dark. Now tell me, where do we start searching for this killer, at the pound or at the zoo? Cause I don't know," shaking his head.

"Well boss, that's a start," Poles replied smiling.

There was a momentary silence before both officers chuckled, breaking the somber mood. As they sat, a call came over the air. The dispatcher called for units to respond to an assault with both the victim and assailants still on the scene.

"Still on the scene?" Poles asked, amazed. "It's crazy out there. The streets are jumping tonight."

"Yeah, they are, and so are we."

"Can't argue about that, Chief."

Both sat there going over reports when Officer Candy returned with the box of donuts that Poles asked for. Looking at the two detectives, he laughed and said, "Check the box. They're all there, intact."

Everyone laughed. Poles said, "Take one for your service."

"Thank you, sir, but I don't eat sweets. Interferes with my workout."

Poles laughed and said, "Oh you're one of those."

Candy laughed and then remembered what he had to say. "Hey, did you hear what just happened?"

"Yeah, a call dispatched about a half hour ago about assailants and a victim still on the scene, but no details," Poles replied.

Being new and not knowing the relationship between Grimes and Terrie Collins, Candy replied, "I overheard some officers talking about how that hot news reporter at Action News was assaulted. She was roughed up and dragged into an alley where some men had tried to rape her. But someone showed up and took them out single handedly before disappearing. When units arrived, all they had to do was put on the cuffs and wait for the ambulances to come and pick up the pieces."

Upset Grimes asked, "How badly was she hurt?"

"Don't know," he replied, "but they said she was shaken up pretty good."

"Where did they take her?" Grimes urgently asked.

"Saint Anne's Hospital."

Grabbing his coat Grimes rushed out the door, followed by Poles as he grabbed a donut, rushing by the young officer who was puzzled by their response.

With lights and sirens blazing Grimes was weaving in and out of traffic as fast as he could. Less than twenty minutes later, they arrived in front of the ER of Saint Anne's. Hopping out the car Grimes rushed into the Hospital, with Poles not far behind.

Making their way through the crowded ER, they approached the information desk where the head nurse was standing looking over patient charts. Grimes stepped forward with his partner after they flashed their badges.

"Excuse me. I'm looking for Terrie Collins. She was just brought by ambulance and police escort. Where's she being kept?"

"Around the corner, halfway down the hall," the nurse replied. "You won't miss her. Two police are with her right now."

Grimes nodded; both officers headed toward her room. As they approached, the officers outside recognized both detectives, acknowledging them.

"How is she?" Grimes asked.

"Last we checked, she seemed okay, "She's in there with the doctor."

Grimes stuck his head into her room. He couldn't see her, only the shadowed images of the doctor through the drawn curtain.

Grimes turning to the officers he asked. "How long has the doctor been in there with her?"

"A few minutes," one replied.

Impatiently, Grimes began to pace back and forth before the doctor finally came out. Approaching him, Grimes asked, "How is she, doc?"

"She'll be okay," "She's just a little shaken up. A small bruise on the side of her face along with a few scratches. But she'll be fine."

"Can I go back there and see her?"

"Sure," "We're just holding her for observation. We'll probably release her in another hour or so. I gave her something for pain. She's tough and in good spirits. All she's talked about was wanting to go back to work tomorrow.

After the doctor briefed him on her condition, he left the room. Quietly, walking back to where she was, he peeked around the curtain. She was lying there with her eyes closed. Hearing his footsteps she opened them. Immediately her spirits were lifted while reaching out to him as they hugged.

Finishing with a kiss, Grimes leaned back and asked, "What is this the doctor said? You're talking about wanting to go back to work tomorrow? Baby, you need time to rest and recover. Besides, you now have your own case to deal with. Those guys that attacked you. I'm going to make sure they'll never do anything like this to anyone again."

"Yes, I want all of them behind bars, too," she replied, "and I hope they throw away the key but they're already in custody. It's that monster on the street that killed those women I'm concerned about." Thanks to that big guy that helped me I was fortunate that I got away with a few cuts and bruises It's those other women that I'm concerned about who weren't so lucky. That killer is out there somewhere running free, and will probably kill again."

Grimes's ears perked as Terrie mentioned the man who came to her aid as he glared at the bruises on her face. she continued.

"There's too much going on with that case, she continued. I need to be out there reporting, helping to get the facts out to the public while you try and apprehend this person."

"I understand how you feel sweetheart, but your health is important too and you really need to rest. One thing is for sure—this case isn't going anywhere overnight. Unless there's a breakthrough between tonight and tomorrow, there's nothing new to report. Besides, you're not the only news team at that station. Just give it a week or so."

"There's always new findings and breaking news," she replied. "You know that. Would you want anyone taking over your investigation after the work you put in?"

Grimes hesitated before responding. "No, you're right. I couldn't or wouldn't take off from my duties, short of being incapacitated."

"Well, you just answered your own statement. Neither can I."

"Let's not argue over this. All I want is for you to be okay."

"I know, but I'm going to be okay and up and running soon," She replied, pointing to her face. "A little makeup and no one will notice a thing."

Poles cautiously entered the room. Hearing the two go back and forth over obligations, he didn't want to interrupt. Tapping the wall to get their attention, he slowly stuck his head around the curtains and smiled.

"Hello, I hope I'm not interrupting."

Happy to see him, Terrie smiled, "Hi, Johnny. You're not interrupting a thing. It's always good seeing you."

"I didn't want to get in between nothing so I took my time giving the two of you your space. How you feeling?"

"A little sore, add a headache. Other than that, I'll be fine."

There was another tap on the door followed by a soft voice. "Terrie!" she called.

Both detectives turned curiously to see who it was. After the way the night had gone everyone was on edge.

"Maria," Terrie sang out happy to see her.

Maria and Terrie's were like sisters. They had been friends since their early college days. They even favored one another. They were the same age and the same size; even their birthdays were a few weeks apart. Both were beautiful.

Terrie had called her when they told her she was being released. Knowing that Grimes was working, she called her instead to give her a ride home. After entering the room, Maria spoke to Grimes; Poles she had never met. Walking over to Terrie, she gave her a hug.

"Are you all right?" looking at the side of her face.

"I'm okay," Terrie replied.

Maria's eyes were fixed on the bruises on her friend's face. "Is this where those animals hit you?" Terrie nodded, "I hope they get what's coming to them."

Wanting to know all the details, Grimes focused back on the incident. He asked Terrie if it was all right to ask her the details. "Of course," she replied.

"Tell me everything that happened." Grimes stated. Poles leaned against the wall while Maria sat beside her while they listened.

"First, I was being followed, then someone hit me before I was dragged in an alley. I was still dazed while they held me down. That's when this person came out from nowhere and saved me. A hooded man with tremendous strength fought all of them off of me. It was so effortless."

She continued telling them everything in detail. It was so intense; it took everything in her to hold back all the emotions she felt while reliving those moments. At times, those emotions began getting the best of her as she fought desperately to hold back the tears and anger. She gave a vivid account of everything as it had taken place.

As she explained, Grimes was torn between being her man and being a cop. This was personal but he knew he couldn't act on those feelings. He wanted to break all the rules, punishing those men in ways that were beyond the law, but as a sworn officer those very rules kept him in check.

When she concluded her account of what happened, Grimes's emotional ride that accompanied her story had continued. In order to move forward, he had to suppress those feelings. The men responsible were in custody but a murderer on the loose was not.

He and Poles had a job to do that was beyond these hospital walls. In order to do it, Grimes knew he had to put what happened to Terrie behind him and let justice take its course. He committed to focusing on what was ahead—catching a sociopath. Suddenly, the one that rescued Terrie struck another interest.

Grimes leaned over and hugged her tight as both were caught up in the moment. Terrie closed her eyes, intending to hold back the tears, but couldn't. As they streamed down the side of her face, Grimes attempted to comfort her. It wasn't just Terrie and Grimes that had become emotional;

Maria felt the pain alongside her friend, reaching in her purse for a tissue to stop the tears from flowing.

Poles too was moved by all of this. The whole night had been unbelievably bad and he was trying to find answers for it. As all the emotions began to settle, they attempted to bring some normality back to the moment.

"There's a guy who fit a similar description," Poles told Terrie, saying no more. Remembering the mandate given to them by the commissioner pertaining to the unexplained animal tracks, he didn't share the details as much as he wanted to.

Stepping back, Grimes let the two friends have their time together.

"What time are they going to release you, or was that another one of your stunts, being hard headed?" Maria asked.

"No, not this time. I'm just happy to see everyone. I'm just sorry it had to be like this."

Grimes said, "I could have taken you home."

"I know, but I also know you're on duty so I called Maria. I wasn't going to interfere with you doing your job for a ride home."

Grimes walked over and kissed her. "When you get home, make sure you get some rest. "You really need it. Call me if you need me and I'll be right there. I'll check on you in a few hours."

"Don't worry, sweetie. I'll be fine." She looked over to Poles and said, "Keep an eye on him, will you?

Giving Terrie a wink, Poles said, "I got 'em."

The two detectives left the room. After they left, Terrie's smile slowly faded.

Walking down the hallway, Grimes looked at Poles. "The description Terrie gave sounds an awful lot like what Lancaster described."

"Yeah," Poles replied, "but the difference was that they had opposite results. This has been a very strange night. What do you make of that guy she spoke of, and what if it's the same one our friend Lancaster described?"

"I don't know what to make of all this," Grimes replied, shaking his head. "Another murder, Terrie's attack, the description of a guy, and the events that follow is beyond believable. If I didn't know her, I would've thought that drugs or alcohol were involved, like earlier. I'm trying to formulate all of this in my head. We now have two people we need to find—the blond guy and this mystery person either as a witness or a possible suspect."

"With what Lancaster told us, and now this all in the same night, it all just might be connected. At this point, anything is possible."

"There's already an alert out for one."

After walking out of the hospital, they jumped into their car and headed back to the station. It was a quiet ride with both men silent, each thinking about everything that happened. Once back at the station, each walked separately to their cars that were parked beside each other.

Grimes looked to Poles. "I'm beat. I'm going to go home, get some rest, and call Terrie in the morning. She's been through a lot tonight. Maybe if we sleep on it, we'll have some answers by then."

"Maybe so," Poles replied, "let me get home to my wife and another missed supper. Under these circumstances, she'll understand. It's too late for me to get flowers; everything's closed. Besides, she's probably sound asleep, anyway. Goodnight, Chief. I'm sure Terrie will feel better in the morning."

"I wish she would take a few days off. She can be stubborn when she wants to be. That's one of the reasons we bump heads sometimes."

"Yeah, believe me, I know. Monica's the exact same way when she sets her mind on something."

Shaking his head, Grimes said, "Goodnight, partner. Give your wife my love."

"Will do."

"Oh yeah, by the way, I almost forgot to mention—we need to be down at the morgue early, no later than eight." Grimes replied.

"Why? The autopsy isn't until noon."

"Yeah, I know. I forgot to tell you. I spoke with Tonya Springs, Kerri Barnes's roommate, when you had stepped out the office. She'll be there in the morning to identify the body. I told her if she were up to it, I would interview her when she got there. She agreed to it."

"Thanks a lot, Chief. Looks like that rest you were talking about is going to be very limited."

Grimes chuckled as both hopped in their cars and went home.

****

A little more than an hour had passed since Grimes and Poles had left the hospital. The nurse entered Terrie's room and said, "You're free to go. I hope you feel better."

"Thank you," she replied.

As they left the hospital and got to her car, Maria looked over at Terrie and asked, "Are you sure you're okay?"

Forcing a smile, Terrie nodded. "I'm just a little sore."

The two had been friends for a long time and knew one another like a book. Maria had a feeling that there was more to the story she hadn't heard.

After pulling off Maria looked over at her and asked, "What else is on your mind you're not telling me?"

Looking over at her, Terrie paused while Maria drove waiting on her response. Terrie said, "I had an eerie feeling earlier at the crime. It was like I was being watched but couldn't explain it right before this happened. I looked around but there wasn't anything unusual."

"Wow," Maria responded. "With all the police and spectators around, I'm sure you were being watched" replying sarcastically.

"There were people around but this felt different. It was like a set of eyes were staring down at me from above, not in the crowd. I looked up but didn't see anything."

"With all that going on, you can't help but get the feeling someone may be watching," Maria said, looking at the bruises on her face while remembering the conversation she, Terrie and Bobby had earlier in the hospital. "You know Bobby is right."

Terrie looked over at her trying to ascertain what she meant. "Right about what?"

"Right about staying home and getting some rest. You've been through a lot tonight; this whole thing has been a stressful overload."

With her signature grin Terrie replied, "You both are probably right, but I have a job to do that's beyond me. I don't have time to sit home and feel sorry for myself or have a victim mentality. People need to be made aware of what's going on out here so that they can protect themselves." Shaking her head Maria replied. "Girl, you're something else! That's why I love you. That heart of yours is so big and caring."

Maria pulled up to Terrie's condo in the Bronx. The two embraced before Terrie went inside.

***

Later that night, Jahir returned to the scene after everything had cleared. From the top of an adjacent building he leapt down fifteen stories, landing on his feet without so much of a sound or effort. As he surveyed the area, this time he wanted to make certain there was no one around. All night, he was hearing the buzz from the people below about the mysterious rescuer.

While most had slept comfortably in their beds and others rode out the night in the city that never sleeps, Jahir tried to remained unseen. Since he had arrived in New York, his movements consisted mostly along the uneven rooftops, which allowed him to roam freely. To most, he was but a shadow— a glimpse to those that may have awakened groggy in the middle of the night, dismissing it as merely a dream or a figment of their imagination.

He would maneuver about, carefully avoiding open windows or places that would bring about alarm or suspicion as he had done throughout the centuries. Disguised in bulky clothing to conceal his true identity, this allowed him some freedom. Occasionally he would descend to the streets and alleyways below, moving amongst those too drunk to take notice. His only encounters were with the five men who had felt his wrath, the woman who benefited from his presence, and a homeless man that happened upon him. The untimely arrival of the homeless man had forced him to retreat before he was ready.

For the second time in a month, a young woman had been brutally murdered. Jahir had arrived to the city in time to actively participate in the search. His encounter with the men that attacked Terrie Collins lit a fuse to his wrath, taking him back to when the woman he loved was murdered at the hands of Bultizar. His centuries-long search for the golden wolf had finally brought him to the streets of New York.

When he first arrived, he visited the site of Bultizar's first kill that had happened a few weeks earlier. He attempted to find the direction in which his enemy was beginning his pattern through the images and memories left behind of his previous victim. It was through the pain, fears, and suffering of the werewolf's victims that helped to direct his quest.

Closing his eyes, Jahir stood receiving images of the werewolf through the fading memories of its victim. It was the same image that the previous victim had seen a few weeks earlier, which also allowed him to see the events as they were unfolding. Suddenly Jahir opened his eyes, his face grimaced from the pain of the werewolf's victims, revealing his fangs. He held his chest with paw-like hands that were equipped with six-inch claws. Looking up, he scaled the walls finding his highway along the skyline.

Twenty stories up on the top floor of a vacant apartment complex amongst rows of vacant buildings, Jahir found a dark corner beneath a pile of fallen debris. It was out of the way of any curious passerby that would stumble upon him. A comfort that had been lost to him long ago. Over time, he had simply learned to make the best of it. This was his place of solitude where he reflected on the events of the evening until finally slipping into a restless sleep.

His journey through the ages in search of Bultizar had now brought him within hours, perhaps even moments, away from an encounter with his enemy. For the first time in fifteen hundred years since he and Bultizar were both human, they were in the same place at the same time. This was the closest he had been since that fateful day he was locked in combat with the sadistic overlord. This was before his newfound fate as a monster those many centuries ago.

***

A few miles away, the one responsible for the chaos of the city had slipped away into his place a few hours earlier. Bultizar was a highly respected citizen by day under an assumed identity but his much darker side was unknown to everyone. He found pleasure in his acts on this night—another night in which hunting was good until it was time to choose his next victim, stalking the concrete jungle once more.

Chapter 7:
Truth Be Told

---

8 AM

Grimes and Poles had barely slept. Other than the staff that was working that morning, they were the first to arrive at the morgue. Shortly afterward, Tonya Springs—Kerri Barnes's roommate and closest friend—had arrived to identify her body. One of the on-duty staff members led her down the hallway into the room where Grimes and Poles were waiting.

As the staff member escorted her to one of the refrigerated compartments, he rolled her body out for viewing. Kerri's body had been so badly mutilated that they used a black non-transparent covering instead of clear plastic. As he unzipped it, Tonya braced herself to see her friend lying there.

Laden with tears, Tonya confirmed that it was indeed her friend. She was traumatized to see her mutilated body; it took all her strength just to stand. Gently taking hold of her arm, Grimes escorted her into the hallway to a row of chairs that were lined up. There they attempted to comfort the young woman while she sat there crying.

Finally, Tonya got her emotions under control. Wiping tears away with a tissue she had taken from her purse she sat and stared at the wall in silence, distraught over the loss of her friend.

Both detectives understood what she was experiencing. They had seen it all before. Although Grimes was patient, they had to begin and now was the time.

Looking at the young woman, he said, "I'd like to ask you a few questions, if you're up to it."

Looking back at him she nodded. She pulled all the strength she had inside to share with the two detectives all that she knew.

"When was the last time you saw her?" Grime asked.

With tears trickling down the side of her face, she explained. "Kerri woke up and walked into the kitchen where I was sitting, drinking a cup of coffee. She wasn't going to work that morning. She said she didn't feel up to it. She had been a little apprehensive since her and her boyfriend had broken up a week earlier."

"Did they get into an argument or physical altercation?" Grimes asked.

"Yes. They got into a big argument over at his apartment. She told me he did put his hands on her at least once." Pausing, she looked over at the two detectives and continued. "Kerri told me that she told him she was leaving him. She'd gotten tired of his insecurities and strange habits, and that he was very possessive."

Tonya frowned and added, "I think she was a little frightened of him. I myself didn't really care for him much. For one, because of everything she had told me, and second, what little I've seen from him in such a short time he didn't seem right. She had just met him, then they started dating. They had only been together on a regular basis for a couple of weeks."

"You said you thought she was afraid of him," "Why? "Poles asked.

"Some of the stories Kerri shared were a bit strange. I always thought he was a little creepy."

"What type of stories?" Grimes asked.

Glancing at both officers, she said, "Well, most of them were sexual in nature. Sadistic if you ask me. She said he would sometimes frighten her, handling her roughly. He was a muscular dude, very strong. I'm a woman, and rough can be good sometimes," she explained, "but not excessive, not to the extent she had explained to me. It was a bit much."

Poles, still leaning against the wall, stood up straight and asked, "Like what?"

"She would tell me how he would hold her down so tightly she couldn't move or breathe, sometimes biting her on her breast so hard that he drew blood."

Poles and Grimes looked over at one another momentarily and continued to focus on what Tonya was saying.

"Kerri told me that he would howl like an animal when he climaxed, that she would sometimes have to fight him off of her and that would turn him on even more. I've even heard him howl once. I was sleep and I heard something that sounded like a wild animal, a wolf, a dog, or something. It woke me out of my sleep. Come to find out they were in her room, having sex.

"But she also told me about some things that happened outside the bedroom," she continued. "Once when they were out shopping at a convenience store to grab some snacks he had walked off. Leaving her standing there alone he went down another aisle looking for some chips. A man with his young daughter had approached her asking for directions, telling her that he was from out of town and needed to find a particular address in the neighborhood. She said she told the guy how to get there, which was only a couple of blocks away, but because she was smiling, he accused her of being flirtatious with a random stranger.

"She told me that he hit her so hard she fell to the ground. She wanted to leave him, but he kept apologizing and begging her to stay. Eventually, she gave in, and they continued their relationship, but it wasn't the same after that. Kerri tried to deal with the situation a little longer, but it was too much. She told me he was too possessive."

"What's this guy's name?" Grimes asked.

"Paul Neville," she replied.

"Can you describe him?"

"Yes. Tall, handsome, athletic type, very muscular."

Poles asked, "How tall would you say, giving examples like 5 feet 10, 5 feet 11, 6 feet? Taller or shorter?"

Tonya paused as she thought and then responded with uncertainty. "I don't know." Looking up at Grimes, she said, "About your height. He could have possibly been a little taller or shorter, about 220, 225. I'm not a good judge about stuff like that. He has long blond hair and always wore expensive clothes. He liked flashing his money when he came around. Kerri was always bragging about that—his car, that sort of thing. She always liked bigger guys but his sense of style and fashion is what impressed her the most. Also, he likes to keep his hair in a ponytail. That was his thing."

When she mentioned blond hair and a ponytail, the detectives looked at each other. His description was similar to that of the guy last seen with Stacy Thomas.

"Do you know where he lives?" Grimes asked.

"Yes, in a house not far from here. I dropped Kerri off there once when her car stalled and wouldn't restart. He works for the delivery company DTX-Press. When they first met, he was making deliveries in the complex. They saw one another in passing. He approached her and the two started connecting from that moment. It wasn't the first time they met, though. She remembered when she first saw him, about three years ago. Back then, she thought that he was cute when he delivered her a lease letter, but they didn't talk or interact until recently."

Tonya told them everything she knew—his address and places the two had frequented, one of them being the last place she was seen alive, Tenley's Bar and Grill.

Grimes asked, "Was there anyone else she may have had a problem with? Other friends, anyone that might have clashed with her?"

"No, not that I know of. If she did, she would've told me, but she didn't mention anything else."

"One more question," Grimes said, "then, we'll be finished. Did you and her ever have any serious arguments or disagreements?"

Looking at the two officers, she replied, "No. We always got along. We've never had a single argument or disagreement."

"Okay Ms. Springs, I think that's all I have. Thank you for your cooperation," Grimes replied.

Poles offered to walk her to her car. He had a few unofficial questions pertaining to the case. She accepted.

While Poles went down the hallway with her, Grimes went back in the room where Kerri's body lay. He wanted to get a closer look in examining the body before the autopsy, which was scheduled for noon.

While walking Tonya to her car, Poles asked for more details about Neville's personality. He was looking to find anything about him that the two detectives might have missed during their initial interview.

"He was particular in how he dressed," Tonya revealed, "how he liked expensive clothes. Kerri told me that a lot of things he wore and owned was unaffordable on his salary. Beyond that, I know little else about him. Even Kerri knew very little about his past. And he would get short with her if her questions became too personal, so she let it be."

Once they reached her vehicle, Poles thanked her and said if she thought of anything else, contact them while handing her his card. Closing her door, he watched her pull off before returning to the autopsy room.

Back in the room, Grimes took note of the marks and wounds on Barnes's body. Remembering everything Tonya described of Neville and his relationship with Barnes intensified their interest. Due to the nature of Barnes's and Thomas's murders, he fit the description of the unidentified man.

This raised the possibility of whether he had any connection with Stacy Thomas as well. First, they had to find out when was the last time he had spoken with Barnes and confirm whether he knew Stacy Thomas as well.

This was all speculation, Grimes thought to himself. *There wasn't a shred of evidence linking him to either of the two women the night they were killed. At that moment, there was nothing linking him to Stacy Thomas at all, or whether he even knew her. From the nature of her wounds, it doesn't appear that they were made by a man at all—maybe a trained animal of some kind. That would explain its mysterious disappearance...*

While Grimes played all of these scenarios out in his mind, he continued examining the marks on Barnes's body, comparing the old scars that had already healed with the most recent ones, which were entirely different. The older ones were clearly made by a human being but these current wounds were made by a large animal. Being that this all happened in the heart of the city, he wondered how it was possible without a multitude of witnesses.

How would a large predatory animal roam the streets without a number of people seeing it, especially with nowhere to hide? And what type of animal could it be? Acostas mentioned those strange tracks being from a bipedal animal, but they appeared almost canine. Since neither dogs nor wolves walk on two feet, that made them impossible to explain. Police had also done a thorough search of the area using search dogs and found nothing.

With all of this going on in his head, Grimes continued his examination. He noticed something that could've been easily overlooked—the angle of the blow that entered her chest. After numerous cases he had witnessed, he had developed a keen eye for these types of injuries and how a blow may have been delivered.

Knowing whether an assailant was right- or left-handed, along with the depth and angle in which the injury occurred, was very revealing in these types of cases. After thoroughly evaluating the body, he found that her assailant was neither.

After he completed his assessment, Poles walked back into the room and said, "I asked her a few more questions." He gave Grimes the details.

After listening, Grimes replied, "Whatever or whoever our killer is, he's ambidextrous. The puncture depth was even, no strength variation. And look here," pointing to her breasts. "It looks like the bite marks on her breasts by her boyfriend that Tonya mentioned could be confirmed. But looking closely, it's almost always on the center left side of her breast," he explained, pointing to the spot over her heart.

"Impressive work," Poles said, his eyebrows raised. "Now it's time for coffee and a donut."

"You're not too shabby yourself, partner," Grimes replied. "I think I'll grab a cup of coffee.

As he resealed the victim, Grimes looked over to Poles and said, "Two things—first, we need to go down to Tenley's Bar and Grill. Second, we need to go pay Mr. Neville a visit, today. Let's see what information we can come up with. We need to know if anyone there saw anything, starting with the staff and supervisors. If we're lucky, there may be a couple of regulars that were there during happy hour. Someone should be able to tell us whether she came in with someone who she may have spent time talking with, whether anyone there had warranted suspicion—but most importantly, whether she was seen leaving with anyone. If any of this leads to Neville, I want everything to be in place when we interview him. I wanna see if there are any inconsistencies early in his story."

"Understood," Poles replied. "Now let's get that coffee."

***

Staring across the morning skyline a young real estate baron stood in his office suite forty stories above overlooking one of New York's most prominent business districts. As many of its occupants scurried below, going about their daily activities, he would soon stretch his real estate empire which already expanded from New York to Chicago and most of the Midwest.

His name was Nicholas Wolf—young, ambitious, and extremely wealthy but reclusive. Being the only known living descendant of the Wolvenhunt family, he had inherited a vast real estate empire from his uncle Nicholai Wolvenhunt, whose family roots dated back to an Eastern European lineage.

His uncle was alleged to have suffered from a mental disorder and lived a life of seclusion. He hadn't been seen in public view for decades before his death. His body was found in his home and was later cremated.

Since his uncle's death Wolf Real Estate Corporation was now on the verge of becoming even larger. Like a web, it had spun out in all directions. It was either the majority shareholder or subsequent owner of many smaller companies outright that didn't carry its title—a mighty conglomerate.

As he stood gazing across the city, for a moment he became lost in thought. He was said to be a dreamer, something he kept hidden in his past that never allowed his mind to rest.

"Excuse me, sir," a man's voice rang out to him as Nicholas was in deep thought. "Excuse me, sir."

The voice caught his attention, bringing him and his thoughts back from where they had drifted. With the man's image in the glass windows reflecting back onto himself, Nicholas turned as he heard the sound of footsteps echoing from behind. Reflected in the glass was the image of a young delivery man standing behind him. He was a tall young man with long blond hair pinned back in a long ponytail with the logo of his company on his shirt that read DTX-Press.

With an office full of workers walking around, Wolf casually looked down at the young man's name tag.

"What do you have for me today, Mr. Neville? Or, may I call you Paul?"

It was almost as though he was looking into a mirror, talking to himself. Their likeness was uncanny but they weren't unrelated.

"Either is fine, sir," he said, smiling. "I have a package for you, sir."

Before he could hand it to him, the raspy voice of an older woman rang out from behind him. "Morning," she said, entering the room with a cup of coffee in one hand and a newspaper in the other.

Her name was Margaret Sullivan, Wolf's personal secretary, an older woman with curly gray hair. Her back was slightly hunched. She had been with him since they moved their offices to New York about three years prior. She brought him a newspaper and a cup of coffee every morning. Placing both on his desk, she looked over at the young delivery man.

"I'll take that," she said, signing for the package before placing it on her boss's desk.

"Thank you, Margaret." Wolf replied.

"She then informed him that the Baxter Group and their lawyer would be arriving shortly."

The Baxter Group was once one of the most dominant real estate groups on the East Coast, but its stocks were falling in a downward spiral. Much of the reason was due to Nicholas Wolf. Through shrewd deals and some questionable business maneuvers, he had cut the legs from beneath the company without them ever knowing it. He then positioned himself for a massive buyout—three hundred and fifty million dollars to be exact—to become the majority owner of the flailing company. The buyout only added to his lucrative corporation, thereby increasing his power and already lofty assets.

As both Margaret and Neville turned to walk away, the news was broadcast from his office on the television monitor. While the anchorwoman for Action News spoke, she drew the attention of the employees working in the office. She was reporting the tragic events that had taken place last night before turning the broadcast over to their lead reporter, who was on the scene waiting to give her live report.

Continuing, she said, "Around nine o'clock, the body of another young woman was found in a vacant building of yet another Bronx neighborhood. Her body was mutilated, with her heart violently removed, similar to that of Stacy Thomas weeks earlier. Reporting live on the scene is Terrie Collins with further details."

As the camera switched to the crime scene, she stood in front of the crowd that was gathering. Protesters were standing behind her holding signs in front of the vacant property where Kerri Barnes's body was found. They demanded change and renovations of those properties.

Margaret, Paul Neville, and Nicholas Wolf looked on while Collins gave her opening pitch.

"I'm standing outside of the abandoned apartment complex in the Bronx where twenty-four-year-old Kerri Barnes was found brutally murdered." As she spoke, she gave details of the incident while everyone watched.

"The newspapers have labeled the killer 'the Butcher of the Bronx.' Two people are now dead in separate Bronx neighborhoods, and the community is in shock that something like this has taken place so close to home."

As Terrie continued, she explained, "Only weeks, earlier Stacy Thomas body was also found in an unoccupied apartment complex. She was twenty-four years old. Both were found with their hearts removed in the same violent fashion and both were found in a vacant building—coincidently owned by the Wolf Corporation—leaving many to believe this to be an act of a deranged individual. Some are saying there may be a serial killer stalking our city streets.

"About thirty people are here holding signs in protest," she continued, briefly turning to face them, "signaling their dissatisfaction with the properties—owned by millionaire real estate baron Nicholas Wolf.

As Nicholas Wolf and his secretary looked on, Paul stared quietly with a smirk on his face. Looking over at Nicholas and Margaret he said, "Well, I better go and make my deliveries. I don't wanna get back and find out I've been fired because customers didn't get their packages. Everyone, have a good day," he replied as he briskly walked out of the office.

Without a response, both Margaret and Nicholas continued to watch with their eyes fixed on the big screen.

Looking at her boss, she stated, "I can't believe that you're being accused of being at fault in any way with these two tragedies that took place."

On-screen, Terrie reported, "According to reports, many of its residents say for years this neighborhood has been complaining to the authorities of the rising crime rate. Drugs, assaults, and murders have plagued this affluent neighborhood. Some say it's the lack of attention given to these worn-down buildings by its owners, which could provide affordable housing to those that qualify, is the reason they are a haven for criminal activity. Many of the residents believe that their request to city officials, have fallen on deaf ears.

"Standing beside me is community activist and spokesmen for the AHO—the Affordable Housing Organization—Hakeem Robinson, who's currently running for the open council seat after the tragic death of Morris Rodrigues, who was killed in a boating accident while vacationing in Barbados. Mr. Robinson, you've been fighting against the conditions of such buildings that are owned by Mr. Wolf for the past two years. What are your concerns tonight?" Extending the microphone towards him.

"Looking into the camera Robinson said, "Since he moved his offices to New York three years ago, "We have reached out to Mr. Wolf concerning the unsafe conditions of his buildings along with others. In return, we have gotten no response, whether by email or by phone. Despite our concerted efforts, all of our attempts have been ignored. We've also filed a petition with the City of New York to have this matter addressed, but each time we either received no answers or the paperwork was lost in bureaucratic red tape."

"We have concerns about questionable dealings and campaign pledges from those that would benefit from Mr. Wolf's inaction concerning affordable housing in opposition to those who wish to make a sizable profit," he continued. "They desire to turn the area into a place for high-end establishments and condominiums, which in turn would leave many of its residents either homeless or forced to relocate. Most of these people living here have spent their entire lives in these communities. Many are hardworking people whose only request is an affordable place to live. This is what we are fighting for, but our pleas simply fall on the deaf ears of a millionaire with a callous attitude toward the poor and homeless. I will continue to fight this matter for these people until something is done, even if we have to bring the protest in front of his corporate offices."

Bringing the microphone back in front of her, Terrie turned to the camera. "There you have it, Hakeem Robinson. In reaching out to the Wolf Corporation, all our requests to interview Mr. Wolf have also been denied by his office, and none of our calls have been returned. This is Terrie Collins. Action News."

With the conclusion of the televised report, Wolf stood quietly with a half-smile on his face. He turned off the TV and said, "Interesting." Terrie Collins is a very attractive woman. Maybe I should set up an interview with her," looking over at his secretary. "People need to hear my side of the story."

"Maybe you should, or simply wait to see how all this plays out," she replied. "If you called her, it would appear that you're desperate and that you might be hiding something. Besides, I'm sure they will continue to call us. Grant them the interview when you're ready. Don't let them dictate anything; you do it on your terms."

"You're right," Wolf replied. "I don't know what I'd do without you."

"Yes, Mr. Wolf," Margaret replied, "What would you do without me? Now is there anything else you need, sir?"

He smiled and said, "No, that is all."

Turning to walk away, she paused and looked back. "Oh, and sir, your meeting with the Baxter Group is in ten minutes."

"Okay, thank you, Margaret."

After she walked away, he took a sip of his coffee and began staring at the newspaper headlines, the main one reading: THE BUTCHER OF THE BRONX CLAIMS YET ANOTHER VICTIM. As he sat staring at the headline, he seemed to find pleasure in it. Looking at the clock on his desk, as it was now time he got up and headed to his meeting.

Chapter 8:
The Autopsy, Killer Clues

The city morgue, Kerri's body was taken to the examination room as the pathologist prepared for his examination. Grimes and Poles stood quietly as they watched before he began. Both were anxious, hoping that they would find something that would help link the victims. They already had the strange prints and hair samples, as well as wounds that were nearly identical, but they still needed more.

Dr. Aseem Jindal was the top pathologist in the state. For twenty years, he had served in that capacity, since moving to the United States from a small province in Southeast India. In reviewing the reports, he too was anxious to see what new findings he would discover.

Extending his hand, Dr. Jindal greeted both officers. He had known Grimes for over ten years and had also met Poles previously. Grimes had attended several autopsies Dr. Jindal has performed. This wasn't the first rodeo for either officer in witnessing an autopsy, but for all involved, it was the first of a body this badly mutilated from an attack.

After an exchange of pleasantries, the doctor and the officers gloved and masked up. While the detectives were preparing for the procedure to begin, Grimes pulled a small notepad from his pocket. He didn't want to miss anything he could use while the young woman's wounds were being examined.

Looking over the body, Dr. Jindal first stated the obvious. "The gaping hole in the center of her chest was the coup de grâce that sealed her fate," he said, in his native accent. In closely examining the wound, he was fascinated by what he witnessed.

Looking at the detectives, he added, "Whatever or whoever did this possessed a lot of power." He gestured to both officers to come close to get a closer look as he explained.

Since Grimes had already analyzed her wounds in the pre-autopsy examination, he was familiar with some of Jindal's findings.

The doctor took it a little further as he explained. "See how the rib cage has been caved in? The bone and part of the surrounding tissue have been torn away. This type injury had to be done by someone extremely powerful to cause this type of damage."

"What, like a gorilla?" Poles asked.

"I doubt that even a gorilla possesses that type of strength," the doctor replied while pointing to the evidence. "Also, a gorilla doesn't have claws. Look at the exposed bones. See how the tissues have collapsed inwardly? The marks on her ribcage and breast bones are claw marks. See the angle at which it has penetrated? Whoever did this was powerful enough to plow their hand into her chest upwardly, grasping hold of the heart and tearing apart the inner portion of her ribcage while cracking her sternum. The bones are caved inwardly."

His face cringed. He looked over at the detectives and continued. "The blow was not assisted by gravity." Giving a visual demonstration, he showed how the blow had to have been delivered—in an upward motion, while the victim was still standing upright.

Pausing, Jindal said, "There isn't a human alive who possesses the type of strength capable of doing that type of damage in one fluent motion—to tear through flesh, muscle, and bone to grasp a person's heart, then snatch it from the chest wall. It's an impossible feat, yet the evidence is right in front of us."

Moving forward, he examined the other injuries. He took special notice of what appeared to be a set of puncture wounds deeply submerged into the body.

Using an instrument to measure the depth of the additional tissue damage, he continued to explain his actions. Adjacent to the deep puncture wounds were two claw marks. He followed a trail of damaged tissue, giving intricate details as he moved along. Grimes and Poles paid close attention, listening intensely as Jindal continued narrating the procedure.

This is like watching a real-life horror show, Grimes thought to himself.

With his scalpel, he made detailed and precise incisions to expose the damaged tissue. Grimes moved even closer, looking for anything additional he could use as he recorded everything.

After a more detailed analysis of the wounds, depth of penetration, and superficial and penetrating tissue damage, he began explaining the unusual marks throughout the young woman's body. "They are especially prominent across her breast and neck area. These bite marks are remarkable. I've never come across anything quite like this. See the depth of these wounds? I grew up in a small village on the fringes of the Sundarbans border. As a child, I would sometimes accompany my father into the jungle, or we'd go with a small group of men to fish or to collect timber for the village. Though it was dangerous, being a child there was much I had to learn. My father would always keep his rifle with him because of the tigers that lived there.

"In the Sundarbans, many of them were man eaters. Over the years, several of the villagers would be killed and dragged off into the jungle to be eaten. When their remains were found and brought back into the village, some were half eaten but not like what has happened here. The size of the puncture wounds was enormous compared to those left by a tiger. The claw marks here appear to be directed, more precise. Tigers kill by a bite to the throat, or back of the neck. Its claws are used to hold onto its prey, clamping down the victim's neck or throat while they die. Watching this animal kill from a short distance is something I will always remember.

"In this young woman's case, her attack seems more like some type of ritual. It was as if the victim was tortured before they were killed. Looking at these wounds, I can say there aren't any animals I know of that could have done this. Look at the depth of the bite," he continued as he took a measurement. "See the size of its diameter?"

The detectives leaned in closer.

"It was as if she were attacked by a saber-toothed animal. Had it been a lion or a tiger or even a bear, its depth along with bite force it would have been six and a half, maybe seven inches, taking into account the length of its fangs, which measure about three inches. The pressure of this bite was well over twelve inches, puncturing through tissue and muscle until reaching the posterior portion of her upper body.

"See how the bite extends just past her scapula? When you consider the force and magnitude of the bite, that would be impossible even for extinct animals, the only ones that would've been able to produce a fraction of this type of damage."

Looking over at Poles, who was speechless, Grimes responded, "There's a lot of unknowns here. But two things are for sure—saber toothed animals no longer exist, and these wounds were caused by something, either living or made to look like an animal attack."

Poles concurred. "Maybe a mechanical device or something."

"Maybe," Jindal replied. "But whatever the case may be, it would have to be a very sophisticated device to duplicate the bite of an animal. But anything is possible, looking at her injuries. They were nearly identical to that of Ms. Thomas in almost every way. Gentlemen," he concluded, "it very much appears, though I believe you already have come to the same conclusion, that we have the same killer—whoever or whatever it is."

"Yes," Grimes replied, "but I'm not going to put it out there that there's a possible saber tooth, of all things, roaming loose on the street—a real one with fangs and claws."

Looking to both officers, Jindal asked, "Do you believe it to be possible that someone is wearing a suit or a costume that gives the same effect, like a Bigfoot type of costume made to imitate a bipedal animal?"

"Anything's possible," Grimes replied. "That would explain part of it, and how the footprints are throwing us off."

"Well, if they are doing this in some kind of animal suit with a device, it's sure as hell working," Poles responded.

Jindal looked under her finger nails and took samples. "The strange thing is there doesn't appear to be any traces of skin or blood under her nails. This is very unusual because like I stated, she didn't die instantly by the attack, despite the brutality of it. In a typical homicide case, traces of blood and tissue of the attacker under the nails would indicate evidence of a struggle. We'll have to run more tests to find out."

After the conclusion of the two-hour procedure, the doctor draped the sheet back over the body and had it sent back to storage. "I hope that you find this killer before another innocent life is taken. Good day, gentlemen. I have another body to prepare for in less than an hour."

"Thank you, doctor," Grimes replied quietly as he closed his notepad and looked away in thought.

"Okay doc," Poles replied.

As the doctor walked away, Poles looked over to Grimes. "Unbelievable," he remarked. "Okay Chief, what's our next move?"

Looking back at Poles, he said, "Mr. Neville is up next. After all we've just heard, I'm more confused than I was when this all started."

Chapter 9:
Empty Leads and the Mystery Man

Hours after her interview with Hakeem Robinson at the crime scene, Terrie Collins was back at her desk. She was becoming desperate for new information. After making a few phone calls, she tried to contact her street sources, along with the more reputable ones downtown, yet she came up empty.

Still somewhat shaken, Terrie continued working on her blog concerning the safety in the streets, fueled by her recent encounter, citywide violence, and the events of the past two Bronx killings. The attack against her and the deaths of the young women made her more determined to find answers. Thoughts of her mysterious rescuer still loomed in her mind. *Who is he? Where did he come from? How did he vanish so quickly? And why hasn't he come forward?*

She even wondered whether she had a stalker who happened to be there at that very moment. These were all questions she needed answers to and like the police, her search for missing pieces was also without success.

In her attempt to get to the heart of the story, she realized the only possible lead in the case was vague at best. There were reports of a mysterious young man, well dressed, with blond hair that was last seen talking to the first victim. She believed there may be something even more sinister behind all of this.

Although her main source of information was the lead detective and her lover, she was restricted in what she could report, from fear of potentially compromising potential leads. She also believed that the police were withholding information to prevent public panic while playing down some of the facts, but she didn't know the extent.

There was something else that played on her mind—whether the man that rescued her was connected somehow. So many theories with so few details to go on. Without something concrete, there would be nothing new for her to report. The information she had was no different than what everyone else had.

As she read over her notes, the phone rang. It was Maria.

"Hey girl, how are you feeling?" she asked.

"A little sore still, but nothing I can't handle. What's up?"

"Just calling to check up on my home girl. I watched the broadcast this morning. Had I not known about what happened to you, or seen you in the hospital last night, I would've never been able to tell that you'd been attacked. Doesn't look like you have even a scratch!"

"My makeup artist is a miracle worker. She's excellent. A young college student named Tia Johnson. She's working her way through college. We have a program that allows students to earn credits and a little cash. She did a better job than my professional makeup people. Everyone loved her work. In fact, the whole staff loved her. Some of them have already asked her to come back and do their makeup.

"But Terrie, I know you. You can't fool me. I could see it in your eyes that something was bothering you, but you handled everything well."

"I know, girl. It was horrible. Like I told you in the car, if it wasn't for that big guy, I might not be here. He moved so fast, though. I could have been mistaken about everything. The police are looking to talk to him as a witness but so far, no one has seen anybody that fits his description. The way he tore through those guys like they were nothing! The one thing I do remember about him other than being big and fast were those eyes. It might have been the reflection of light, but they reminded me of a cat. His face was half covered. Looked like he was wearing a mask of some kind but like I said, it was dark."

"So scary, but at least you have a protector," Maria responded.

"I did that night," Terrie replied, "but with what has been going on lately, I wonder."

"Hey, our company is sponsoring a fundraiser to help feed the homeless in about three weeks. I was calling to see if you would go with me. I know you're busy. That's why I wanted to put my bid in early. It will be full of your kinda folks. Celebs from all over trying to give up that pity cash," Maria chuckled as Terrie joined in.

"You know you're wrong for that," Terrie responded, with the two sharing a laugh.

"You know there's got to be a story you can use in the middle of all that pomp and circumstance."

"Stop kidding yourself. You know you're on another one of your manhunts. You just want me there for the ride in case you come up empty. Then, you'll have someone around to keep you company!"

Suddenly changing the subject, Terrie said, "This story really has me swamped. I need to find something that is fact-based out of this, rather than something that is only fit for a tabloid."

"What you need girl, is a break from the action. You need to relax a moment and I guarantee the working parts of the story you're looking for will come to you."

"I hope you're right. I guess I'll try and make it."

"Thank you," Maria responded.

Instantly, a thought came to Terrie and she felt a great sense of urgency. "I don't mean to cut you off. I just thought about it—there's a call I have to make. We'll talk later."

"Okay," Maria responded, hanging up her phone.

Without delay, Terrie logged on to her computer, looked up the number to Wolf's corporate office, and dialed it.

After two rings, "Wolf's office, Margaret Sullivan speaking. How may I help you?"

"Yes, this is Terrie Collins of Action News. I'm calling to set up an interview with Mr. Wolf concerning his thoughts about the recent incidents in and around his vacant properties. Also, regarding the accusations of the

AHO claiming that his company is refusing to address any of the issues pertaining to those properties."

Margaret drew silent then responded. "I am quite sure that he would be willing to set up an interview with you and answer those questions, Ms. Collins."

"Is he available to speak with me directly at this time?"

"Mr. Wolf is quite busy at the moment, but he has given me the autonomy to make that decision on his behalf. I know, however, that he will be quite busy for the next couple of weeks. He will call you back as soon as his schedule clears."

"Okay, thank you," Terrie replied.

"Good day," Margaret responded as she hung up.

For a brief moment, Terrie looked over to the window pleased as a thought came across her mind. *All my previous attempts to get an interview had failed. At least this was some progress.* She grabbed her jacket from the rack and headed out.

***

Earlier that morning, Wolf had increased his real estate assets by a third in less than thirty minutes with his closest competitor, the Baxter Group. With the group on the brink of bankruptcy, Wolf flexed his financial muscle to buy it out, taking control of the majority of its assets. His reputation as a ruthless and shrewd businessman remained intact. He seldom played by the rules, without showing the slightest sign of compassion, leaving many of his competitors financially ruined.

As he began to review some paperwork for a separate business matter, his secretary entered his office.

"Excuse me, Mr. Wolf," Margaret interrupted. "I just took a message from Terrie Collins requesting an interview. I told her your schedule was full and that you would call her in a couple of weeks to set a date."

Wolf looked over at her and asked, "Why so long of a window? They may feel that we're hiding something."

"No, on the contrary," she replied. "It shows that you're confident and that you have more pressing matters than defending yourself against baseless accusations. Besides, we're a busy corporation."

Wolf thought about it, and gave her a nod.

***

Pulling up in front of Tenley's, the two detectives entered the bar. Approaching one of the waiters, they flashed their badges introducing themselves. Grimes asked to speak with the manager. The waiter walked off to get him. Grimes saw the place was half empty but that would soon change. It was just before happy hour.

Coming from the back of the bar, the manager greeted them in good spirits. "Good day, gentlemen. I'm Jon. How may I help you?"

"I'm Detective Grimes, and this is my partner Detective Poles, NYPD homicide. We're here to ask you a few questions concerning a young lady who was murdered last night, Ms. Kerri Barnes." Reaching into his pocket, he pulled out a picture of her and showed it to him. "Her roommate told us she come here to have a few drinks around five during happy hour. Do you or any of your staff remember her coming in?"

"Yes," he replied, "we saw her. She normally comes through from time to time. She sat at the bar in front of the big screen and ordered a Martini. She was alone when she came in. It looked like she had something on her mind. Usually, she's happy and friendly, like she didn't have a care in the world, but not this time. After ordering a drink, the guy she would come in with from time to time showed up and sat next to her."

"Then what?" Poles asked.

"Well, she didn't seem too happy about it. I heard her ask him why he came over and sat by her. The bartender and at least two of the waiters heard her ask him to find another seat and leave her alone."

"What happened next?" Grimes asked.

"He refused," Jon replied. "He didn't want to leave and kept trying to talk to her, but that only made her angry. He began to get upset. He raised his voice, asking her why she didn't want to talk to him, that they could work it out, and that she was acting like a brat. That really upset her. An argument ensued."

"Do you know what they were arguing about?" Grimes asked.

"She said something about him acting crazy like an animal or something."

Probing Grimes asked, "Did it ever become physical?"

"Kinda," he replied. "He had reached out and grabbed her by the arm, but she pulled away before throwing her drink in his face. He got angry and aggressive; it looked like he was going to hit her. At that point, I came over and asked him to leave. He wasn't too happy about that. I watched him walk down the street, throwing expletives as he walked away. She sat there for roughly another forty-five minutes or so, then left. That was the last time we saw her."

"Do you know the exact time she left?" Poles inquired.

"No, I'm afraid not. I wasn't really paying attention at that time."

"Does anyone know his name or anything about him?" Poles asked.

Jon replied, "I think his name is Paul, but I don't know his last name. I heard her call him that the few times they came in together. Before yesterday, they were always laughing and joking among themselves, never anything disturbing."

"Would you describe him for me?" questioned Grimes.

"Yes. Young, athletic build, blond hair. When he came through, he kept it in a 'tail."

"You remember specifically what he had on yesterday?"

After thinking about it for a moment, "He had on blue jeans and a blue blazer with tan loafers, I believe, but I'm not sure."

"Does any of your staff know anything about him?"

"No. We talked about the news broadcast earlier, but no one mentioned anything."

"We'd like to interview the two waiters and the bartender, just to be thorough," Grimes informed. He looked over at Poles. "Do you have anything you'd like to add?"

Poles shook his head no.

Jon called over the bartender first, then the two waiters in turn. After about twenty minutes, all their stories lined up, and both officers were satisfied, thanking each of them for their cooperation. Grimes told them if they needed them, they would contact them.

After the interviews, they had one more stop before heading back to the precinct. It was time to pay Mr. Neville a visit.

***

After finishing his route, Neville arrived at the warehouse, his truck now empty. He had just parked and headed to the office to clock out. The day had gone well. There were no incidents, everything went smoothly.

When he walked in, Grimes and Poles were there talking to his supervisor. They informed him they were there to speak with Neville, they asked him if he would direct them to him.

He agreed then escorted the two officers to him while he was punching out. They approached him, identifying themselves.

"Mr. Neville. I'm detective Grimes, and this is detective Poles. We're investigating last night's death of Kerri Barnes."

"Yes," he replied. "It deeply upset me when I found out about what happened last night. I really cared for her." He looked at both officers as they stood silently and expressionless. "Am I in trouble?"

"No," Grimes replied. "We just wanted to ask you a few questions pertaining to your relationship with Ms. Barnes, where you were, when was the last time you saw her, that sort of thing."

"Sure," he responded. "I want to cooperate in any way I can. She was a sweet, loving person. I don't know who could've done something like this."

Looking over at Neville's supervisor, Grimes asked, "Is there anywhere that we could speak privately with Mr. Neville?"

"Sure, you can use my office," he responded as he pointed to it.

With a window overlooking the timeclock, its door open and only a few feet away, they proceeded to go in and talk. While coworkers curiously looked on, Grimes closed both the door and blinds to the office and began their interview.

"May I call you Paul?"

"Sure," he replied.

"Paul, what was your relationship to Ms. Barnes?"

"We were friends, sometimes lovers. That was before we broke up about a month ago."

"When was the last time you saw her?" Grimes asked.

"Yesterday evening, over at Tenley's."

"You said the two of you had broken up. Her roommate said that she was going down to the bar for happy hour, alone. She also said that the two of you didn't break up on the best of terms, and that Kerri told her that she didn't want to have anything else to do with you."

"Then you showed up at the bar," Poles added. "How did things go after that?"

"We were pretty cordial," Neville responded, "to say the least. Nothing to speak of."

Surprised by the response, Grimes countered his version. "The patrons at the bar said something a little different. They told us that the two of you got into an argument, and that you became aggressive. They also stated that you had to be escorted out of the building not long before she left. She turned up dead a few hours later."

"Pretty coincidental, wouldn't you say?" Poles responded sarcastically.

"Yes, we got into an argument. She was pretty upset that I broke up with her. She didn't accept rejection too well. Things got heated, but I would never put my hands on her or harm her in any way. I don't hit women."

"That's interesting," Grimes said, "because we were told a something a little different."

"That's not the story her roommate gave us or the employees at the bar," Poles added. "The employees at the bar said you grabbed her after an argument. Also, her roommate gave her account of what she knew and what Kerri had told her. She said Kerri told her that she broke up with you, and you became upset and didn't take it very well. Also, that you had violent tendencies when things didn't go your way and that you were very jealous. So, why are you lying?

Responding sharply, "I'm not lying," "It wasn't that dramatic; besides, her roommate doesn't know what she's talking about." I think she was jealous of our relationship. In truth I think she wanted me for herself." And the staff at the restaurant, did they get your actions wrong too? "It wasn't that serious," I never was going to hit her, I was simply trying to calm her and get her to listen." "Calm her huh? That's how you get someone to listen?"

"Regardless," Poles added, "I think everything you just said is a bunch of bull and irrelevant because now a young woman is dead," staring at him suspiciously.   "After you were escorted out of the building where did you go?"

"I rode around a little while, then I went over a friend's house. That was it."

"Your friend, what is their name?"

"Sonja Hart."

After getting her information, Grimes said, "We'd like to speak to her to confirm what you have just told us."

"Not a problem."

"Is there anything else you would like to add?" Grimes asked.

Quickly responding, "All I know is when I left the bar, Kerri was still sitting there. When I got in my car and pulled off, she was alive. That's all I know."

Cynical in his response, Poles said, "You seem really broken up over the death of such a good friend."

"What's that supposed to mean, Detective?"

Poles hunched his shoulders and replied, "Nothing. I'm just saying for someone to care so much about a person, you seem extremely calm."

"We all handle tragedy differently. I keep my feelings inside."

Grimes then intervened. "That's all, Mr. Neville. Thank you for your willingness to talk to us. We'll contact Ms. Hart to corroborate your story."

"Yeah, we'll be in touch, "Poles sharply replied.

Neville looked at Grimes, then to Poles without expression as he left the building.

Thanking the manager for the use of his office, the detectives walked to their car. Poles looked over to Grimes and said, "You believe that crap he was spitting?"

"Not at all. Let's give Ms. Hart a visit and see what she has to say," Grimes replied, looking at the paper with her address and number on it.

The two detectives proceeded to her place to talk to her. When they arrived and knocked on her door, a soft voice spoke out.

Looking through the peephole, she asked, "Who is it?"

Grimes replied, "NYPD Homicide Unit," displaying his badge, stating their names. "We're here to speak to Ms. Sonja Hart."

"This is she."

Removing the chain, she opened the door. Standing in front of them was a small petite young woman. She reminded them of the two women they were currently investigating.

"What is this all about?" she asked.

Grimes replied, "Do you know Paul Neville?"

"Yes, he's a friend of mine. Is anything wrong?"

"It's pertaining to a murder that took place last night, and the whereabouts of Paul Neville at that time. We spoke with him earlier. He told us that he was here with you last night."

"Yes, he was," she replied. "Please come in and have a seat. Would you like something to drink?"

"No, thank you," they replied.

Grimes asked, "How long have you known Mr. Neville?"

"A couple of weeks," she replied.

Poles followed Grimes. "How would you describe his behavior?"

"Very sweet person, and caring. Why do you ask?"

"Does he have any anger issues or has he displayed violent behavior since you've known him?" Grimes asked.

"No, none of that. Why?"

"We're just trying to find out what type of person he is. We're just being thorough.

"Roughly what time did you see him last night?" Poles asked.

"Somewhere between 7:30 and 8 PM. We watched a movie; he stayed the night. Is he in any trouble?"

"No, were just asking questions," Grimes replied.

Poles asked, "Was he upset about anything when he came by?"

"Yes, a little."

"Do you know why?" Grimes queried.

"Yes. He said he stopped by the bar. He had a few things he had to settle, something he had to move on from. He told me he had gotten into an argument and left. He called me about fifteen minutes before he arrived. When he got here, we talked a little; we got comfortable, and he stayed here."

After writing everything down on his notepad, Grimes put it back in his jacket and thanked her for her time.

"I think that's everything we need at this time." "You've been quite helpful."

Both officers got up and headed out. Walking to the car, Grimes said, "Their stories line up. The time they saw each other and the time she left the bar overlapped."

Poles asked, "What's our next move?"

"We continue to hit the streets, door to door if we have to. I want to focus in the area where her body was found. Maybe somebody saw something."

"Yeah, maybe, or maybe nothing at all," Poles said, shaking his head. "Chief, let's grab a bite. All this is making me hungry."

"You treating?" Grimes replied.

"Yeah, I gotcha, but your debt is building. You're gonna end up treating for a month if you keep this up!"

"I got you on the next one," Grimes said. Both laughed and hopped in their car.

Before leaving, Poles asked, "Chief, did you mention to Terrie about coming to the house for dinner?"

Grimes placed his hand on his forehead gritting his teeth. "You know it completely slipped my mind. I was going to ask her the night she was attacked, but with all that going on, I totally forgot. When? "What time?"

Poles thought about it first. "Tomorrow night around 8. How does that sound?"

"Sounds good to me. I'll call her tonight and see what she says."

"Great, sounds good," Poles replied before they pulled off.

***

Sonja slowly closed her door. She had watched the detectives while they sat in their car until they left. The whole episode was disturbing to her and it was written on her face.

The phone rang, breaking her thoughts. When she answered, it was Neville.

"Hey babe, it's me. "I was on my way over. Wanted to see you."

There was a moment of silence before she replied. "Two detectives just came by here asking questions about you and the murder of that young girl last night. Your ex-girlfriend that you happened to stop and see that you claimed you were supposed to be done with before you came over here."

Neville became quiet. He asked, "What did you tell them?"

"I told them the truth, that you were with me last night—which is more truth than you've been telling me. I must be that rebound chick."

"No baby, you're not a rebound. It ain't nothing like that. I just had to straighten a few things out. Get some stuff off my chest so I could move on without having to look back."

Once again, she became silent. "I might be a few things, but dumb ain't one of them."

He sensed Sonja's vibe; he could feel the tension building in her voice. He attempted to plead his case.

"C'mon baby, trust me. It isn't like what you think at all."

"No!" she replied.

"No, it's not," Neville responded.

"Maybe it is, or maybe it isn't. Either way, I don't think it's a good time to see each other tonight. I have a real bad headache, and I wouldn't make for good company."

"Baby, don't be upset, 'cause if you are, then it's for nothing. It was tragic what happened, but our thing was over. What happened to her hurt me to my heart, but there's nothing I can do about it."

"Maybe," Sonja replied, "but I'm not up to having company right now."

She hung up the phone before he could reply. Staring at his phone blankly, he was frozen in place for a moment before he put it back in his pocket and went home.

Chapter 10:

Stalemate, Robinson the Accuser

The following morning at the station while going over her notes, Terrie made a few phone calls while becoming increasingly frustrated. She was still upset about how information had stalled over the murders of Stacy Thomas and Kerri Barnes, and how everything overall had been going so far. She had been at her desk since four thirty that morning, spending hours looking over what she had on both, finding nothing new to report.

I'm getting nowhere, she thought to herself. *My sources are as cold and as dead as the two victims.*

She was trying to ascertain what she could use that was newsworthy. There was the attack on her that continually danced in her mind, and the mysterious rescuer who had come to her aid.

She began to crumple notes and throw them into her wastebasket. Some missed and lined the floor near her desk in disarray. Her phone rang. She answered to hear Grimes's voice.

"Hey, babe."

"Hey," she replied. She could hear the faint noise of Grimes's office in the background.

"You busy?"

"I'm just sitting here going over my notes about the two women we've been following. This has been so frustrating with no witnesses. I was about to call you. I wanted to see if you had found anything new? Anything I could use that the public needed to know."

Grimes listened while thinking about the directive given by the commissioner. Despite their relationship, he knew he couldn't tell her everything. With that in mind, he gave the only answer he could.

"What we have is basically this," he replied. "A boyfriend who Barnes broke up with and wasn't on good terms. But he has an alibi that corroborates his story. Beyond that, we're still waiting for lab results to come back."

"I've never experienced this much frustration covering a story before," she said as she looked up at the clock. "I have to be downtown in a couple of hours to attend a council hearing later today. Hakeem Robinson is scheduled to speak on the housing problem in his ward, and how it relates to Wolf Realty. I'm very curious to hear what he has to say. His thoughts on Nicholas Wolf will be fascinating, to say the least. Their future interests as well as his lack of movement in resolving the renovations process of the buildings will be the focus, especially in light of what's transpired over the past few weeks. "I'm sure it will provide some insight to the public."

"Good," Grimes replied. "But here's the real reason for my call. John and his wife have invited us over to his house for dinner."

"Hmmm, sounds good. When?"

"Tonight, about eight o'clock. How does that sound?"

"Sounds good," she replied. "Honey, I don't mean to cut you off, but I have to finish up here before heading to that hearing."

"Okay, I'll talk to you later, sweetheart," Grimes replied.

After hanging up, her cameraman stuck his head in her office. "We gotta go in about twenty minutes."

Grabbing her notepad and jacket, she left to join her crew.

***

At the precinct, Grimes returned his attention to the issue at hand. He and Poles were in high gear, going over everything they had concerning the two deaths. They pulled every file remotely similar to this case. From their first case leading up to the current one, they had been on the streets, going door to door interviewing family members and friends.

Stacy Thomas's case was more personal to Commissioner Kuntz due to his close ties. Her case had far less material to offer. No real witnesses or leads to confirm. Other than a description of a young blond man that she briefly spoke with, there was nothing substantial. No one had seen her come in or leave with anyone. Outside of him having blond hair and a blue sports jacket, any description of him was limited.

Only animal tracks and the hair samples found at both murders is what directly connected to the two cases. There was the man or whatever Harvey Lancaster had described standing over Barnes's body. His account of what he had seen was questionable, being that he was under the influence.

Whatever physical evidence they found would take several weeks before any lab results would come back and officially confirm anything. Trying to connect the dots would prove a slow and grinding process but Barnes's case was still young.

The two detectives had gone through the list of psychopaths and sociopaths in the system, hoping to get a clue—only to find that most of them were already serving life sentences or dead. The obvious conclusion now was that there was a new player in the game and they had to figure out his next move.

While going over what they had, Captain Hosea Hernandez walked into the office. He was an ex-professional football player who played a couple of years before an injury had stone walled his career. He had a commanding presence at 6 feet 4, two hundred sixty-five pounds. As an officer before moving up the ranks, and one of the best and toughest homicide detectives on the force. He was highly respected among his peers and dead serious about his job.

Entering the room, he looked at both detectives, having high admiration for them both—higher than any under his command.

"Any progress?" he asked, looking at Grimes.

"We're pooling every resource," Grimes replied as he leaned over and handed the captain some reports. "We attended Kerri Barnes' autopsy yesterday morning. The medical examiner confirmed that the teeth marks on the body were the same on both women but still couldn't confirm what it was that attacked them. He said they didn't match the teeth of anything that he knew of living today, and that if he didn't know any better, the bite resembled something like what a saber-toothed cat would deliver—a saber tooth, mind you."

"Yeah, or maybe a saber-toothed wolf," Poles snickered, "That's why the commissioner wants a few of these details kept quiet for now."

"I'm going to take another route—a real life approach," Grimes said. "But whatever it is, it's been very selective in choosing these two women. This killer has been reclusive, waiting weeks before killing again. Also, the bodies weren't eaten—just mauled, and as far as the hearts were concerned, the ribcage appeared to have been caved in by blunt force; the heart was extracted by hand. Beyond the obvious, there was no sign of a sexual assault. No traces of semen or vaginal entry in either case. I've never seen anything like this. No traces of blood, other than that of the victim. You would have thought there would have been some sort of struggle with an attack that violent and head on. The victim would have seemed to at least gotten in a scratch.

"There wasn't any skin or blood found under the fingernails of either woman," Grimes continued. "Both victims were there long enough to do some kind of damage. We have sets of footprints of something that appeared to be a large dog that stood on two feet at both murder scenes. Sample hairs that we have don't match any of the animals we have on record so far. There's no clue where they came from."

"Is our killer a man or an animal?" Captain Hernandez asked. "What kind of sick SOB are we dealing with? And if it is an animal, how could something like that hide in one of the largest and most populated cities in the world, that no one has seen even a trace of?"

"And then there are these long blond hairs that we're still waiting on the lab results for, sir," Grimes added. "And there's the case of witnesses seeing a blond man and another something resembling a cat standing over the latest victim, seen by an alcoholic in a dark alley where the victim was found. Normally, I would dismiss something like that, but by the way everything is going, all doors must remain open, though I myself choose to believe there is a more rational answer. Everything still needs to be investigated.

"All of which is beginning to lead me to believe there may be a man in some kind of customized suit. But that's just my theory. Which brings me to that young man, the boyfriend of Kerri Barnes—who matches that description. But he has an alibi that night. The woman he was with supports his claim when Ms. Barnes was killed, we wouldn't have been able to place him with the victim during the time of the murder. But I'm not quite finished with him yet. Rather than focusing on some mythical creature with saber teeth that I don't believe exists, we need to find the man or woman I believe is responsible. That's where I'm going to start. Out of precaution, we checked with zoo officials to see if they had any escaped animals, lions or tigers or even bears."

"Oh my!" Poles responded, chuckling.

Hernandez looked over at him. "I'm glad you find this funny but until we find the killer, it's far from being a laughing matter."

"Sorry Captain," Poles replied. "I gotta find something to break this tension. If I don't, I'll probably start crying."

Grimes looked over at him and at the captain and hunched his shoulders. Hernandez cracked a smile, then replied, "I guess you're right. Can't let this situation get the best of us."

"We have every ear and snoop on the street," Grimes said. "Every source we've acquired over the last three years, but everything is coming up empty. We've been door to door to every residence within a five-block radius, along with every establishment. We've even randomly questioned every homeless person we came across, searching for something. Taking into account the legitimacy of the one witness who claims to have actually seen something, yet the reports harvested the same results—zero! So, it's back to square one."

"I know the two of you are doing everything in your power," Hernandez replied. This morning, Commissioner called me to see if any progress had been made, especially that of Stacy's. He said the mayor had been on him about the flow of the investigations. I thought I'd come in and see if there had been any progress to relay to him."

"Only what we've told you so far," Grimes replied.

"Twenty-four seven," Poles added.

Hernandez said, "Yeah, I know you two are the closest we have to miracle workers."

"Well Captain, we try," Poles replied. He nodded toward his partner. "Grimes nearly walked across the Hudson River the other day to pull a couple fish out the water with his bare hands to feed the homeless," he joked, easing the tension.

"It appears we're gonna need some type of divine intervention to hurry and solve this case," the captain replied. "Carry on. I'm going to leave you two to do your job, as I have to do mine," he instructed as he walked out the door.

Grimes leaned back in his chair with his hands on the back of his head, closing his eyes trying to focus. All their efforts had failed using their usual sources of information. They were now entering the realm of the unlikely ones.

Less obvious in his approach, Poles was equally as frustrated but had a much lighter attitude about him. "Hey Chief, what do we do now?"

"Keep pressing," Grimes replied.

"Yeah, you're right, Chief," Poles replied. "It's about time to grab something to eat. The wife is a little upset with me about last night. I got home much later than I anticipated. Spoiled the nice little candlelight dinner she set up for us," he said while shaking his head. "She didn't fix my lunch today. Man, these cases are killing me."

Despite his frustration, his lighthearted remarks eased the tension, causing Grimes to laugh.

"How's Terrie handling all this?"

"Handling what?"

"This case as it pertains to your relationship."

"We've barely had time to spend together before, and especially now, since all of this. It's been tough. I guess my main concern was helping her get through that attack she suffered, but all she did was throw herself full throttle into her work. In fact, she was back to work the next day. If you look at her, you would've thought nothing had happened."

"Yeah, she's a tough gal. Now, let's head over to the café across the street. I got a taste for a nice cheeseburger with everything on it and a Pepsi."

"Sounds good. Let's go."

***

It was late afternoon when the council hearings were getting set to begin. The room was filled with cameras, while the politicians, reporters, and concerned voters began piling in to address the current issues, with each reporter having an assigned seat. As Terrie Collins walked toward the committee room, someone called out her name. She turned around to see Hakeem Robinson. She walked over to him; they shook hands.

"I'm glad you could make it," she said. "I hope I have something that you may find of interest, particularly concerning those buildings owned by Nicholas Wolf."

"Well, that's why I'm here—to report the facts to the public concerning what they need to hear," Robinson replied.

"I'll be looking forward to it," she responded with a smile before walking into the committee room.

As she made her way through the conversing crowds on her way to her seat, standing in front of her was an older woman staring at her. Terrie looked back at her; it was like they had already met.

"Excuse me, have we met?" Terrie asked.

"No," she replied, "only if you're able to look through the camera lens and see your television audience," she chuckled. "No, we haven't officially met but we have recently spoke on the telephone."

Confused, Terrie looked at her trying to figure out when. The woman extended her hand as she introduced herself.

"I'm Margaret Sullivan, Nicholas Wolf's secretary. We spoke concerning an interview."

"Oh, I'm sorry," Terrie replied as she extended her hand in response. "I didn't know. Forgive me for appearing rude. Is Mr. Wolf here?"

"No. I normally attend these matters. Mr. Wolf likes to shy away from crowds. I work closely with him. Through me, he gets all his information unfiltered. That way, nothing gets lost in the mix."

"I'll be looking forward to our interview as soon as his schedule frees up."

Margaret said, "I'm going to let you go do your job. I better find a seat before they're all gone. Nice meeting you, Ms. Sullivan."

"No, the pleasure is mine."

"You know, you are even more beautiful in person than on TV."

Terrie grinned. "Thank you."

Both women went in separate directions.

Shortly after the hearings began, each council member along with other officials got up and addressed a smorgasbord of the issues, from education to sanitation along with parks and planning and road maintenance. It was now time for Hakeem Robinson to speak on the housing issues in his ward.

Until now, his concerns had been directed at the Wolf Corporation. The issues included a multitude of vacant buildings that Wolf owned and how he seemed to consistently ignore the concerns of the citizens in renovating them.

As the committee chairperson addressed Robinson, he asked, "With the elections coming up and now that you're running for the open seat following the death of our esteemed colleague and dedicated community servant, what would you like to add to this hearing?"

Robinson took his place at the microphone and began addressing the many issues the community had about the housing situation, crime, and how little was being done to improve the problem. As he spoke, he placed the blame squarely on the shoulders of Nicholas Wolf.

"There is a lack of effort in trying to fix the problem—in trying to restore the community's respectability. Since taking ownership of the properties mentioned, these buildings have been a sanctuary for drug dealings and robberies. Instead of fixing these properties so that people can have an affordable place to live, Mr. Wolf has elected to ignore the pleas of the community.

"Despite making many promises to renovate and restore these buildings so that hard working and respectable people can rebuild the community while raising their families, I believe Mr. Wolf's lack of interest in keeping the promises that were made has led to the direct result of the slaughter of these two innocent women. Had promises been kept, I believe those two women may in fact be alive today."

As he spoke, Margaret carefully listened. Her expression showed her displeasure as to what Robinson was saying. She took a pad from out her purse to write it all down. She appeared even more disturbed as he continued. Also taking interest but with a different demeanor was Terrie Collins as she prepared her notes to ask questions.

"Many violations and codes have been broken or ignored. City officials are not taking action, as though there's some type of hidden agenda below the surface. If actions aren't taken to correct the issue, then I will conduct an investigation. If I win the seat, I will use all my power to investigate and expose any possible corruption. If Mr. Nicholas Wolf has any involvement as I suspect, I promise I'll get to the bottom of it."

After Robinson addressed the council, the room was in an uproar. He sat patiently waiting for it to settle, anticipating questions that would follow. The first to begin the line of questioning was Terrie Collins.

"Mr. Robinson, you stated that city officials have not taken action and that you believe there might be more going on that the public may need to know. You were placing some of the blame for the crimes that have been taking place over the past two years, including the recent murders of the two women in question, on Nicholas Wolf. Please give us more of your thoughts."

Robinson nodded as he responded. "I believe Nicolas Wolf has to share some blame in all of this. Had he taken action as promised, his buildings would not be an issue. Even after the two deaths, he refuses to address our concerns, despite repeated attempts to contact his office.

"As far as questionable activities—I don't know," he continued, "but if elected, I intend to do a thorough investigation. I will increase my efforts to see that something is done about this situation. I promise to use everything at my disposal to get to the bottom of this issue."

After taking a few more questions from the host of reporters present, he got up and left the meeting, leaving the committee with more questions than answers. After he walked out, Terrie scanned the room for Nicolas Wolf's secretary but she was gone. She didn't know his secretary had left the moment Mr. Robinson had finished answering her question. She was not sure what to make of all that Robinson had said, but what it did was ignite some new possibilities and thoughts that there might be more to Wolf than meets the eye.

The meeting had lasted a few hours. It was now time for Terrie to wrap things up. She had a dinner date that evening that she didn't want to miss. It was her time to relax in a cozy setting with her man and some good friends. Like Grimes, both of them needed it, and she wasn't going to let the moment pass.

Finally, she and her crew arrived back at the station where she hurried and gathered her things. All reports and final touches were going to have to wait this time. She took her cameraman up on his previous offer, jumping in his car for a ride home.

***

Grimes and Poles were finishing up a long day of going through files, making phone calls, and following up on dead-end leads. It was now time to close up shop.

Suddenly, Poles's expression changed as he remembered something. "Hey Chief, Monica texted me earlier. She told me she had to cancel dinner tonight. Her aunt had gotten sick and she had to go over there. She had gone to the store and had already picked up everything when she got the call. I hadn't seen her this excited in a while. She loves company. Being around the house all day I guess can get a little boring. Besides, she really likes Terrie, thinks she so cool. I know she's very disappointed over this. I know I am."

"Yeah, Terrie seems to have that effect on people. I seem to be the only one who tends to get under her skin, but I love her. Let me call her and let her know. She was looking forward to coming tonight. I know she's gonna be disappointed."

Grimes made the call from his cell. After updating Terrie on the dinner cancellation, it was evident in her voice 'she was disappointed but understood, expressing her willingness to come whenever another date was planned.

"Well, I'm all done here," Grimes said to Poles. "I'll see you back at work tomorrow."

"Okay, Chief. Sorry for letting you know at the last minute. It simply slipped my mind. I have to make a stop by the flower shop to pick up some roses, for when she comes home later.

Grimes gave him a look shaking his head. "What did you do this time?"

"I didn't do anything. It's just a ritual I do every day before I go home. Helps keep the relationship fresh."

"Man, I never knew you did that," Grimes replied. "Maybe I should start."

"Maybe you should give it a try a couple of times and see what happens. It may do the same for you."

"Maybe I'll start tonight, kinda like a supplement for our dinner date!"

Both laughed. Poles said, "See you later, Chief," as he walked out the room.

"Okay, later partner," Grimes replied as he followed, flipping the light switch while closing the door behind him.

***

As the day slowly gave way to evening, the sun hovered slightly above the city skyline when Jahir began to rise from his loft. He had awakened from another restless sleep. Constantly haunted by the past, visions of unfading memories as though it were yesterday. Finding an isolated ledge beyond plain view, Jahir crouched motionless like a stone griffin waiting until the sun had once again found its place below the horizon. While darkness always provided safety for him to roam freely, he would wait for the golden wolf to reveal himself again.

Beyond the norm of everyday life in the city, everything remained quiet and uneventful. The one they called "The Butcher of the Bronx" had not again emerged, so there were no new cries from the people below. But the cries throughout the centuries called out to him, pleading for him to avenge the many souls that no longer had a voice.

Under the cover of the night, dark alleys and street lights casting shadows provided some cover for him to walk with limited freedom. With his face nearly covered, he walked down the sidewalk, careful to cross the streets only when the crowds became too large, drawing some attention but not enough

106

to matter. He was now in the midst of Bultizar's serenade of death. He had already killed two women. With so many more people living in New York out of fear of this unknown killer, unlike the past where anything unusual didn't warrant as much attention—even in a town as busy as this, where nothing seemed to matter to anyone beyond their own personal space. The world had gotten into a rush since the days when he was last a man.

Jahir needed this, to walk amongst people who made him feel human again, to see what they saw and to hear what they heard, not from above like the castaway he was but in close proximity as if one of them.

Although he was amongst millions, in truth he was indeed alone. As alone as a man stranded on a distant moon. To be human once again was the other piece of the puzzle to be solved with the death of a monster.

Beyond stalking a killer, he had Terrie Collins on his mind. Radiantly beautiful, she had reminded him so much of his beloved. It was the reason that had drawn him to her from the beginning. Her eyes, the fragrance of her smell—all were things he could detect beyond the spectrum of light in the midst of darkness. He could do nothing more than admire her from a distance. Since the night she was attacked he never left her, even following the convoy of emergency vehicles to the hospital, where he remained hidden until she was released and had arrived home safely.

Jahir's ears were keen enough to detect movement within her home from across the street this evening. When he arrived, Jahir knew she was there. Shortly after he arrived, a black BMW pulled in front of her building. It was Grimes, He had gotten a call from Poles, letting him know that their dinner invite was back on. When he had called, she was happy and ready to go. When she came out the house she looked like a star. Grimes got out, giving her a hug and a kiss before opening her car door as they pulled off.

Chapter 11:
Let the Game Begin

Jahir wasn't the only one prowling the streets this night. Bultizar too had chosen to roam. This was nothing new. Throughout the centuries, he had gone decades without a human kill. In the past, pursuing a deer or perhaps a boar was the thrill of the hunt and chase, something that his human quarry was unable to provide. People were usually easy and less of a challenge.

Unlike Jahir, he didn't have restrictions. He remained in human form until the time he would choose his next victim. Considered a ladies' man, he was handsome, and well dressed—drawing his prey until the time he would transform into the beast. Bultizar had held several titles and aliases throughout the centuries, all of which he had stolen from his victims usually a century or two after he had killed them. While hiding his true identity and accumulating wealth, he found pawns he would pay handsomely to serve him until their services were no longer required.

As Bultizar walked down the sidewalks of Manhattan, he noticed someone with less desirable attire than his. As the two crossed paths, they looked at one another briefly in passing. Under the cover of darkness Jahir's face was nearly covered concealing his true appearance. they gave one another a glance as they passed while continuing on their way.

Jahir's curse made him unable to recognize the face of the man he had sworn to kill, passing by him as he would any other stranger. As he walked along, he saw something faintly familiar that caused him to turn his head. On Bultizar's face was a small jagged scar and around his neck was the small, round wooden medallion with the symbol of a wolf.

Although he tried to dismiss it, Jahir couldn't. It weighed heavily in his thoughts with every step he took. Once the two had passed one another, Bultizar took a few more steps and smiled as he looked back. This gave him an even greater thrill. He knew it was Jahir. Knowing that Jahir was there and it was the closest he had ever been to him. He decided to play a game of cat and mouse as he had done before given his inability to sense him as the wolf. Through the centuries he constantly left cold trails and false leads, spreading his kills apart while making Jahir's ability to find him all the more difficult. He always had the upper hand on his vaunted enemy. Time was now running out. Bultizar knew he couldn't play out his scheme by way of time and distance but he could spread things out delaying him enough to fulfill his goal as he quickly left the vicinity.

Jahir abruptly stopped in his tracks, realizing that he might have found who he was looking for.

Quickly, he turned around but Bultizar was gone. Jahir stood there a moment, pondering what had just happened, wondering whether he had missed his opportunity. Immediately, he walked back in the direction that Bultizar was walking. A brisk walk turned into nearly a sprint but across the street, something just as disturbing caught his attention.

Standing in the doorway of a building was a face that had been haunting him since it all began, always appearing in the places where Bultizar had killed. Once again, it was the old sorceress. At that moment a passing emergency vehicle with sirens blasting distracted him. He turned his head a moment before shifting his eyes back to where she was standing, but she was gone.

Jahir began to wonder whether his search throughout the ages had begun to madden him. After their encounter, Jahir took to the rooftops once more. Now on alert, he wondered whether he had lost his opportunity to settle this war between them.

As the crowds began to thin, he descended back down onto the street. He hoped that the opportunity would arise again but everything remained quiet. He didn't want to risk a random gallop that might take him out of position in case the werewolf decided to strike. All he could do now was find the highest and most concealed spot and wait.

***

As the evening progressed, miles away in Central Park joggers were blazing the bike and jogging trails armed with mace or whatever protection they deemed necessary to feel safe. For them, this was a nightly routine. But on this night, there was something else looming in the park.

Unassuming and sitting on a park bench, a predator lay in wait—a wolf in sheep's clothing, the flesh of a man yet something far worse. He had a purpose that was beyond the thrill of the hunt and his love to kill. Although like a game, at times it was much deeper than that. Bultizar had something more in mind than just a random kill. This was personal.

It was clear that the man he encountered was Jahir. Now that he knew his enemy was in New York, he wanted to deliver Jahir a message—one in cold blood. He had always known he was being hunted, and remained several steps ahead of the hunter measured by centuries and decades. He could've faced his enemy long ago—settling this blood feud once and for all—but his purpose outweighed any personal feelings he had. The risk that he might lose was too great, he didn't want anything to interfere with his plans.

Time was getting short. This was the year of the scarlet blood moon, his last chance to claim what he sought, absolute power. The only one who was capable of stopping him had now caught up to him.

In Central Park, Peter Mills was among a group of runners with shared fitness goals. Mills—a 36-year-old avid gun and weapons enthusiast—and a group of business professionals would leave their jobs and meet several times a week for their evening run. They had all met at a local gym a few months back, and preferred the late evening because the park would be less crowded. Although there was a risk in terms of crime, they felt safety in numbers as a group.

Those who knew Mills thought him to be a fanatical narcissist. Strapped with a pistol hidden in pouch and a feeling of cockiness, Mills felt he had all the protection he needed. After he and the group began their run, their pace was brisk and steady passing landmarks that was set along their route. As he ran, he became winded. Not wanting to leave him they slowed for him to catch up but he motioned for them to keep going without him.

As the group passed Bultizar, who was still in human form and sitting on a bench along the path under a light, they barely noticed him. Like the predator he was, he waited for that one straggler who would trail behind the others. As he waited, his wish came to fruition. It was the one who was the most confident.

Mills slowly jogged while turning his headset to his favorite tunes. He paid little attention to Bultizar who was sitting on the bench when he passed by. After a few steps, Bultizar stood up as he watched the lagging jogger fade from sight before stalking him.

Mills stopped, momentary removing his headset trying to adjust them. Behind him, he heard a set of footsteps. He looked back and saw the silhouette of something large, standing on two feet, long tufted ears. Bultizar had changed into the beast. Adjusting his eyes, he thought he was hallucinating. As it got closer, what he saw caused him to freeze before he hurriedly reached into his pouch and drew his gun.

Suddenly, it dashed toward him. Covered with long blond fur and fangs that dropped below its jawline, the creature displayed its weaponry, drooling as if it were savoring its next meal. Mills looked into its pale gray eyes before firing a couple of shots, but it was too late. The werewolf grabbed hold of his gun with it still in his hand, crushing it as he screamed. With its other clawed hand, it sunk its claws into Mills's body like fishhooks drawing him close. Opening his mouth as wide as he could the beast sank his massive fangs into his throat, spurting blood about like a fountain, the bite killed him instantly as he dropped to the ground.

Miles away in the Bronx crouched and waiting atop of its tallest building, Jahir stood to his feet. Bultizar had caught his attention the moment he changed. In that instance Jahir hurried toward Central Park as fast as his limbs could carry him. Knowing that he had little time, Bultizar wanted to leave his mark before his stalker arrived. Quickly he gorged himself on Mills's lifeless body before Jahir or the others could arrive. Jahir moved as fast as he could, galloping across the skyline almost as if he had wings.

Meanwhile the other runners reached their destination point along the path, they had heard the two gunshots from a distance followed by the howl of a wolf. Confused, they all looked around at each other, asking whether they had heard it. They dismissed it as shots that may have come from outside the park, being that they were near the exit. As they waited for Mills to arrive, each was anxious to call it a night.

After ten minutes, they decided to head back on the trail, wondering whether something may have happened. When they arrived at the spot where Mills stopped, they saw a large splatter of blood along the trail. Looking a couple of feet off the trail, they saw the gory sight—Mills's lifeless, mutilated body. They were horrified by the sight of him lying in that condition. Immediately one the women pulled out her cell and called 911 while they began looking around to see if whatever did this was still nearby. A short distance feet away they saw a large figure of what they believed to be a man standing near the edge of the woods,

It was too dark for anyone to get a good look at him, but what stood out was his eyes. They reflected the light of one of the trail lights like a mirror—before he turned and disappeared into the woods.

The blue sweat suit he wore was now shredded and soaked in blood. Lying beside him was his pistol and two empty shell casings.

While they waited for the police to arrive, they were terrified, huddled together not knowing what was going to happen next. Police sirens were heard rapidly approaching in the distance.

After Jahir had disappeared into the woods, the beacon in his head that led him there ceased because Bultizar had reverted back to his human form ending his ability to follow him. For a short while his senses remained silent before signaling him that the wolf was on the move once again.

This time Bultizar was far away in another part of the city as Jahir pursued him, hoping he could catch him still there. With supernatural speed, Jahir covered distances faster than any vehicle on the street could. While he was in the park, he used the treetops like an expressway. Once out of the park, it was time to trade the treetops for rooftops as he left the Park.

When the police arrived, the joggers pointed to where Mills's body was lying. They told police they saw someone standing nearby before they disappeared into the woods. Shortly afterward more officers arrived and began to fan out undertaking a more detailed search of the area.

It wasn't long before the entire park was shut down and filled with police. They had formed a perimeter around the park, covering all access points and beyond. Although they arrived quickly both Bultizar and Jahir were already gone.

While the park was on lockdown, miles away in Brooklyn oblivious to what was taking place across town Harvey Lancaster was sipping on a bottle of wine in an alley. Sitting there nodding off a trash can fell over, causing him to wake up.

Regaining the few scruples he had left, he called out, "Who's there?"

Getting no reply, he sat up and looked around. Other than the occasional car passing by the entrance to the alley, he didn't see anything. Thinking nothing more about it, he took another sip before leaning back against the wall. Closing his eyes and nodding off once again.

Suddenly he awakened, this time by the sound of a dumpster being shoved aside a few feet away. He saw something coming directly toward him. What he saw wasn't a man and before he knew it, it was standing over him.

The last thing he saw were rows of sharp pointed teeth with two dagger-like fangs coming down on him as it seemed to be smiling at him. He screamed, then everything went silent. A few minutes later, three men taking a shortcut through the same alley looked over and saw a pair of legs stretched across the ground behind a dumpster.

On approach, they saw Lancaster's body shredded like a salad covered in a bloody dressing. Quickly, they ran out of the alley in panic, flagging down a passing police car. When they stopped, they told them what they found and lead them to the body.

What they found was yet another mutilated body. Unlike the first two deaths in previous weeks, this was a male—the second claimed this night. With his face bitten off along with much of his torso eaten away, he wasn't recognizable. Only his ID lying a few feet from him allowed them to identify him.

When Jahir arrived, he could do nothing but look down from the roof and wait as police and ambulances were already on the scene. Closing his eyes, he shared the visions of the victim's pain and horror. Also in the visions, he saw something else—the medallion hanging from the neck of the werewolf, their attacker. It was the same medallion he had seen earlier when he encountered the man he didn't recognize as Bultizar.

He also saw the image of the beast appearing to be smiling in the memory of both victims while looking into their eyes just before killing them. He knew that Bultizar was sending him a message through the eyes of these two victims—one that was personally directed toward him before making his kill. It was one of defiance to let Jahir know that he knew he was there, and that there would be nothing that he could do to stop him.

This was a chess match between them, to Bultizar a game in which he had all the advantages.

***

While this game of cat and mouse was played out between the two immortal combatants, a few miles beyond the city limits on Long Island, Grimes and Terrie Collins arrived at the Poles' residence. As they walked to the front door, Poles greeted them there before they could knock. He led them to the dining room while his wife was in the kitchen.

Wearing a blue dress with white trim, Monica, a beautiful well-figured brunette had set the table with candles already lit.

As Poles led their guests to the dining room, they sat as Monica brought out her pasta salad and a bottle of red wine. The couples enjoyed a relaxing candlelight dinner between friends. It was a much-needed break from the stress in each of their lives over the past several weeks. Terrie and Grimes were laughing and enjoying each other's company while Poles and his wife Monica welcomed the soothing interaction.

It was all going smoothly until Grimes's cell phone buzzed. Reluctantly, he answered it. The expression on his face immediately changed the mood with everyone knowing there was something wrong. Grimes looked over to Poles and then Terrie as he listened. Everyone waited in anticipation of what Grimes was about to say. After ending the call, Grimes looked around the table with a solemn stare.

"There have been two more murders tonight. A male jogger in Central Park was killed and mutilated. Another was a homeless man was also found behind a dumpster in a Brooklyn alley in the same condition. Both murders being reported approximately a half hour apart."

"Were their hearts removed, as well?" Poles asked.

"Not according to the report," Grimes informed. "Like the previous murders, blond hair and paw prints were also found. Other joggers said they saw what appeared to be a large silhouette, presumably a man with sparkling eyes, standing not far from the body before disappearing into the woods."

Grimes looked over to Terrie and added, "It sounds a lot like the description of the guy you gave that came to your rescue."

"I didn't get a clear look at his face, but if it were him, why would he kill those people and rescue me? Why would he spare those guys' lives that attacked me?" she replied

"I don't know. I'm going to have to wait for those reports to be sent over to me and see how those findings match up with the ones we already have. All the evidence points to some kind of an animal that is responsible for killing these people but this is the second time a guy fitting the same description was seen at the scene, which now makes this person a prime suspect. Either way, we have to get to the bottom of this madness."

Looking at Terrie, Grimes said, "It's more than a coincidence or a hallucination that this guy has been sighted. He may be behind all this."

Terrie drew silent, while Monica sat quietly listening to their conversation, particularly concerned about her husband's safety.

"Well, that put a damper on what had been a beautiful evening," Poles replied. Looking at Grimes, he added, "We have two days before we're due back to work. That's forty-eight hours to put together a plan on how we're going to approach this."

"Well, I can't wait that long," Terrie declared. "I'm going to see what I can find that's related to all of this."

***

Two days later, the detectives arrived back at their office where they found a new stack of reports waiting concerning these latest murders. Grimes sat down and began going over what new evidence had been uncovered. They still needed the lab reports but that would take a few more weeks.

Grimes began looking at the report of the first victim: Peter Mills, a white male thirty-six. His body found just off the jogging trail. As he read the report, it said that Mills was killed and was carrying a gun. There were no traces of blood found other than his own.

"How could he be that close to his attacker and not hit anything?" Grimes asked.

"The reports state that his wrist was shattered on the same hand that was holding the gun—a sign of an obvious struggle. Whoever did this and the way it was done showed incredible strength. The reports also say that he got off two shots."

"It says they spoke with family members and a couple of his companions. They claim he was a superior shot with both handguns and rifles and was at the range at least three times a week. Those who knew him say he was a firearms fanatic."

"Man, this whole thing is getting weird. No, this whole thing is beyond weird."

Grimes handed the report over to Poles. He looked at the photos before handing them over to him. When he got to the second report he read, "A middle-aged black man—"

When he read the name, Grimes paused. Looking up at Poles, he said, "Looks like the one witness we had won't be around to testify."

"Why's that, Chief?"

Grimes read his name. "Harvey Lancaster."

"Lancaster!" Poles responded.

"Yes, looks like our friend got around."

"Those subways," Poles, replied. "Maybe he was trying to get as far away from the Bronx as he could after what he claimed to have seen."

"Yeah, maybe, but evidently not far enough," Grimes replied, shaking his head.

"Hmmm, subway. That's a thought, Chief. It's possible the killer might have been stalking him that night. Maybe by chance, coincidence, or design, the killer got on the train or maybe used the tunnels."

"Nice thought, but I thought about that, too. If there was an animal involved, then the train would be unlikely, but the tunnels, that could be a possibility. Going with what would be more acceptable, I checked the schedule with the rail system just in case. Between the time the murders had taken place, the tracks were down and under repair.

"Besides, it was quite a distance with road construction and traffic from where the victim in Central Park was found and the second body in Brooklyn. It would be nearly impossible to make that trip through the city with the lights and all the traffic in that span of time without a chopper. As for our two victims, there are no train line between the locations of their deaths."

"You're right about that Chief."

"I'm thinking two things—we may have more than one killer, or maybe a copycat."

"Yeah, but there is one thing that may eliminate the copycat aspect. The same tracks were in both locations. You know we're both pretty sure a man didn't do this but they may have had help. Some kind of predatory animal that has been trained, or maybe a pet or something."

"Logic dictates there has to be a human involved," Grimes replied, "not an animal acting single mindedly, although possible but improbable. Whether it is or not, I believe my own eyes that something attacked and ripped these people apart. In both cases, those same strange prints were found leaving the scene in the same direction, then disappearing each time. I'm going with my instincts on this one."

"We're on the same page, Chief," Poles replied.

"I'm also thinking along the lines of this mysterious rescuer that came to Terrie's aid."

"Yes, Chief. At this point, we can't afford to dismiss anything."

"One thing is for certain— there's now been multiple times someone has seen something that resembles this guy. We played off the first description, thinking it was part of an alcoholic's imagination, but now that he's dead by what looks to be the same killer I would've had a few more questions. But it's too late to ask now."

Poles said, "In the report someone said they saw a glimpse of someone or something that resembles what the old man saw in the alley and what those members of the group saw in Central Park, standing in the woods. Again, they found prints and blond hairs."

Grimes added, "The police had all perimeters covered inside and outside of the park in a very short time. It would have been highly unlikely that anyone could have gotten out of there without being seen. None of this is making any sense, which brings me back to the guy that helped Terrie whose description was also similar.

"It was coincidental that this guy suddenly appeared out of nowhere the night of the murders and saved her. He shows up in the nick of time to rescue her and dismantle four men, good sized men at that, tossing them around effortlessly. It leads me to believe he was probably there hiding somewhere all along. He saw her covering the incident and decided to follow her back to the station and waited for her, then was in the process of following her home when she was attacked. A coincidence."

Grimes paused and said, "That I doubt. Let's head downtown to lock up. We're going to talk to each of those clowns now that they're all finally out of the infirmary."

"Just what I was thinking," Poles replied.

An hour later, the two were downtown conducting their interview with each of Terrie's attackers. One by one, each told their story of what they saw, giving their account of what had happened to them. All of them told the same story, that it all happened so fast they barely saw anything. Each of them said the one that attacked them had his face covered and wore a hood and a skully. Another remembered seeing locks or something coming from under a skull cap but after that, everything else happened too fast.

Each of them told the detectives the same thing—that it was so dark, making it hard to get a clear view of him, that he was so fast and hit them so hard that everything went blank before they could focus on anything.

After their interviews, the investigators headed back to their desks. Although each of their stories had a unique twist to them, they all pretty much added up to being the same. They knew about as much now as they did when they started, which was nothing.

For the next couple of weeks, the story moved along slowly. Known as the city that never sleeps, now it didn't even blink. Everyone in the city, both police and citizens, were on high alert and afraid. Even Terrie was scraping the bottom, trying to find new leads that would help break the story and help the police in finding this elusive killer.

Chapter 12:
A Monster Hunting a Monster

The Bronx, Evening was rapidly falling. It had been a long day in the streets and while many prepared to go home, the servants and workers of the night began their activities. It had been several weeks since the murders in Central Park and Brooklyn, and two since the last victim in the Bronx.

In the middle of rush hour, Tia Johnson was on her way to work, locking her apartment door before heading out. A student by day, she was finding her way through the tough streets. She struggled to make ends meet as she pursued her dream to become a makeup and special effects artist at New York City College. Petite with smooth brown skin, Tia kept her hair short and stylish, enhancing her natural beauty.

The most gifted student in her class, she constantly received high praises from her instructors and dedicated long hours perfecting her craft. Part of her student program included earning extra credit while working at various organizations and businesses which participated by putting aside positions for college students.

She would sometimes think about her aunt who took her in at age twelve, having no other family left. Her aunt did her best in raising her for five years before being stricken with cancer, and transferred to a nursing home, A month before she graduated high school her aunt died. It was then that a young social worker named Danielle Michelle stepped in and helped guide her through those tough times. After graduation, she helped her get a grant to attend New York City College to pursue her childhood dream.

Barely nineteen, Tia was on her own, working nights at Luis', a small café for minimum wage in one of the tougher neighborhoods in the South Bronx depending on tips to get by. She did what she could dividing her time between school and the studio.

This evening, like every evening she walked to work. Each time she passed the same group of thugs who eyed her, saying things in an attempt to get her attention. Some were complimentary with a few comments that were downright disrespectful, making her cringe. Always arriving on time, she clocked in and prepared to start her shift.

***

Rising from his sleep, Jahir awakened, hoping to stop Bultizar's reign of terror.

From Eastern Europe to the Middle East and throughout the civilized world, the stories were the same—a string of unsolved murders, most being young females of a tender age, the same pattern he remembered as when they both were still human. Most believed the deaths were by a madman, while others a wild beast. Only Jahir knew the truth but who could he tell, without the blame falling on him?

To the eye, he was every bit the monster that had been stalking the land throughout the centuries. If any had seen him, he would've been perceived as an ogre or some other ungodly beast. They would never believe he had the heart of an angel.

Now that his enemy was aware of his presence, there was a greater sense of urgency than any time before. Not since the death of his woman had he been more determined. He covered great distances with relative ease gliding amongst stone griffins that decorated the tops and ledges of buildings.

Under his clothes his fur was short and sleek like velvet; its color was so black it gave off a bluish tone. His body was heavily muscular and powerful but agile like that of his namesake. His locks were long as they blew in the wind, flowing from beneath his hood and skully while they streamed down and around his oval shaped ears. Although he was fierce and his appearance sinister, his heart was as pure and gentle as an uncut rose.

Since arriving in New York mostly unseen, Bultizar had already claimed four lives and he wasn't going to stop. Jahir was trying to prevent another. It was frontline news—the ferocity and brutality of these attacks had an entire city in fear. Not since Jack the Ripper of 1888 in London had a city been so terrorized. It was now New York City, the new millennium, where the newspapers tagged him as the "Butcher of the Bronx" which led the media to draw the Ripper comparison. With two more lives claimed in two other boroughs all within the same night he had now broaden his claim on the city.

With a chill in the air, his presence concealed by the cover of night, Jahir moved about unobstructed. Observing the crowds below, he moved silently above them. This was a town littered with the homeless, the part of society most had forgotten. It was also aligned with the rich and famous whose names no one would ever forget. To Jahir, all those people were same.

With his nose in the air, his ears shifted with the wind, acutely deciphering sounds as his senses filtering the noises and smells of the city. He was searching for anything that would direct him toward his equally fierce adversary who had a darker agenda. Despite the noise and pollution, what he sought would ring out like a church bell in a monastery.

Finally, he found a place of his own, crouching down along a corner ledge where he remained motionless—a living, breathing gargoyle that overlooked the masses below. They went scurrying about with cellular phones glued to their ears, unaware of the events that were unfolding around them. On the ledge, he patiently waited for his enemy to reveal himself, setting everything in motion. Tonight, he would descend from the building tops and walk amongst the shadows of men.

He was playing a waiting game, hoping the true monster would reveal himself. Moving along the streets, concealing his face, he helped himself to a pair of shades from a vendor while his attention was placed elsewhere, hiding his yellow eyes.

In and out of dark alleys, Jahir moved stealthily. Although immortal he still hungered, scavenging through garbage cans and dumpsters behind the finest restaurants. To him, it was a smorgasbord of opportunity to fill his ironclad stomach. Over time, he no longer cared. A meal was a meal. Throughout the centuries, he hunted the creatures of the forest like any other predator while the flesh of men had neither been part of his diet nor his desire. To him, sustenance was not his only priority. If anything were to happen, he wanted to already be there to stop it.

Chapter 13:

Fundraiser

As the evening progressed, it was now around 8 PM. Maria pulled in front of Terrie's building in her Silver Camry. After two beeps of the horn, she came out and hopped in the car.

It was the night of Maria's charity event. She had invited her weeks ago. On time as usual, Maria was anxious to get there.

"Hey girl! You ready for a good time tonight?" Maria asked knowing her friend could use some fun.

"Yeah, I guess so," Terrie responded showing little enthusiasm.

"Why'd you say it like that?" Maria asked.

"I don't know. I guess I have a lot on my mind. I can't stay too late. I have a host of meetings tomorrow and a lot of work to catch up on. I was hoping to set up an interview this week with Nicholas Wolf about the issues concerning his buildings, but that's been delayed. His secretary told me he was busy and I had to wait for him to call me back. I have a lot of questions for him."

With a grin, Maria replied, "Nicholas Wolf? That fine, millionaire?"

"Yes, that's the one," Terrie replied.

"Why didn't you say that earlier?"

"Why, what's the importance of that?"

"Because he's going to be the guest speaker tonight."

Surprised, Terrie looked off at the passing traffic somewhat amused.

"You have all evening to have your interview with him," Maria added.

Looking back at her, Terrie replied, "You know you can be a real butt sometimes. That's why I love you!" They both laughed.

Pulling in front of the hotel, Maria handed her keys to the valet.

Looking like bombshell bookends, they walked into the lobby. Terrie was dressed in a thigh-length black leather skirt trimmed in gold with knee high knocker boots. Her hair dark brown was highlighted with streaks of blond, perfectly matching her golden-brown complexion. Maria was almost identical in style, only she was dressed opposite in a white leather skirt trimmed in gold. It complemented fair complexion, as well, with her jet-black hair streaming down just below her shoulders. Both were identical in height and weight and would be a perfect set of book ends.

When they walked into the ballroom, all eyes were on them. While the music played in the background, not far from them was Nicholas Wolf, who had arrived a little earlier. Beside him his secretary, Margaret. Both watched as the two women walked in. Although he admired each for their beauty, Wolf had a special interest in Terrie. While Maria introduced Terrie to some of her coworkers and a few of the people who had helped her organize the event, Wolf walked over to greet them with his secretary, wasting no time to make his presence known.

"Ladies," I'm Nicholas Wolf, but you can call me Nick." He looked over to his right. "And this is my secretary, Margaret Sullivan "he concluded.

She extended her hand to Terrie. As she shook it, Margaret said, "Yes, we've already met."

"Yes, at the council hearings, and we spoke on the phone. It's nice to see you again," Terrie replied. She looked over to Maria and was about to introduce her.

"We've already met," Maria replied.

"Yes, over the phone, while extending us the invitation," Margaret responded.

Surprised by his approach, Maria said, "Mr. Wolf—I mean Nick—I'm Maria Gomez."

As they shook hands, he responded, "Yes, I want to thank you for extending us the invitation to speak at this great event. It's also a pleasure to meet you face to face."

Enamored with his words, she couldn't help but blush. "And of course, you know Terrie Collins."

Wolf took her hand as they shook, but held hers a little longer.

"I'm going to leave the three of you to chat, while I go mingle," Margaret said, turning to walk away. "It was a pleasure seeing you both."

Looking over at Terrie, Wolf said, "Yes, Ms. Collins, I have seen your broadcast. Quite intriguing. I'm looking forward to our upcoming meeting as soon as my schedule clears."

With Wolf standing in her presence, she couldn't let this opportunity to pass without addressing the issue. It wasn't her nature, and she couldn't help herself.

"Mr. Wolf—"

Cutting her off, he said, "Nick, please."

Smiling, she replied, "Nick, regarding the housing problem and contention with the AHO concerning your properties, a lot has been said about the way you're addressing this issue."

Abruptly yet politely, Wolf advised, "Ms. Collins, this is a social event. I only conduct business during my office hours. We will have a scheduled date for your interview as soon as my schedule frees up. In the meantime, let's enjoy the evening."

Looking at both women, Wolf continued, "Let me get the both of you a drink." Shifting his eyes toward Maria, "What are you having?"

"A Martini," she answered.

He looked to Terrie, who tried to hide her disappointment. "I'll have a Rum and Coke."

"I'm scared of you," he said, raising his eyebrows, chuckling before he walked over to the bar.

Maria leaned over toward Terrie and said, "He is so hot!"

"He's not bad on the eyes. I feel like an idiot. I should've waited, but I couldn't stand there and not ask something."

"Aw, don't worry about it. That was nothing. You'll get another chance."

"I know. It's not just that. I have something else on my mind."

Looking over at her after scanning the room, Maria said, "You and Bobby," shaking her head. "If the two of you had a relationship that was in an amusement park, it would be one hellava roller coaster ride."

Unable to help herself, all Terrie could do was laugh. "What can I say? I love him, and we're trying."

"I know you love that man. It'll work itself out, it always does. Look how long the two of you have been together."

"I know. Between our careers taking away our time, the stress of these cases eating at our patience—all of this is taking its toll on us both. Although we did have a nice outing a few weeks ago. That helped a lot. Given the fact that we have a deranged individual out here turning the city into a chapter out of the Dark Ages."

"I know."

At that moment, Wolf returned to the table with their drinks. Looking at them both, he asked, "Am I interrupting?"

"No, not at all," Terrie responded. "Thank you for the drinks."

"No need to thank me. It's my pleasure to serve such beautiful young ladies."

Both smiled as they sat enjoying the music. Wolf had already cut their conversation earlier concerning his properties, but she couldn't help herself and wouldn't let it go. Looking at him, she said, "Your policies on these renovation projects—a lot of people are affected by your actions, or shall I say lack thereof."

Taking a sip, he snickered, replying, "I thought we agreed that we would discuss this during business hours."

"I know, but with you here in front of me, I simply can't act as though it's nothing. With so many people affected in the neighborhoods and community by all of this," As her aggressive nature kicked in, Terrie replied, "For goodness' sake, two people have been killed because of its accessibility to criminals."

Wolf became silent before smiling once again, focusing on his glass of wine while twisting it in his fingertips slightly. Placing his glass back onto the table. "Would you care to dance?" he asked.

Accepting his invitation, Terrie glanced over at Maria. "I'll be back."

Once on the floor, Wolf placed his hand on her waist then took hold of her hand with the other as they slowly danced in rhythm. The two never broke eye contact him finding her intriguing. Ever since her broadcast on the murder of Kerri Barnes, he was fascinated by her.

"Like I said earlier, I don't talk business at social events, but tonight I'll make this one exception—off the record, of course."

It was music to her ears, she wanted to hear what he had to say. Repeating the questions she had asked earlier, wanting his thoughts on the matter, about his plans and his reactions to people believing he shared some blame for the crimes.

He answered her questions with the precision of a surgeon, dancing around some of her questions not giving her anything direct—to her it was utter frustration. In his craftiness, he had a swag about him, his smoothness had softened her aggressive tone, which she found to be different.

After their dance, Terrie said, "We do still have an official interview planned, right?"

"Of course, we do," he said, "Excuse me, I have to go to the restroom." Smiling, he walked off.

Terrie returned to her seat where Maria was waiting, sipping on her drink. "How did it go? Did you get what you wanted?"

"About as much as I expected."

"I guess that was a big 'no' by your expression."

Sitting there, Terrie couldn't believe she couldn't get any real answers, hoping her second interview would fare better.

Noticing her frustration, Maria replied, "You going to be okay?"

"Of course."

"Girl, I need to go to the lady's room. Would you like to join me?"

"No, thanks. I'll sit here a minute."

"Okay," Maria responded, "I'll be back in a few minutes."

Staring at her drink, Terrie took a deep breath and shook her head, frustrated with herself. She looked up and saw Wolf's secretary looking at her. Tipping a glass of champagne toward her from across the room, Terrie tipped her glass back as she continued to sip and think. Margaret got up and walked toward the door, where she saw a young delivery man standing there in a DTX-Press uniform. The two spoke for a moment after he handed her an envelope. She returned to her seat.

Terrie looked across the room to see Maria returning from the restroom. She was on her way back to their table when she spotted the same delivery man still standing by the door to the lobby. She noticed that Maria was surprised when she saw him; it was obvious that the two knew one another. After a brief conversation, he leaned over and kissed her before he left.

When she got back to the table, Terrie asked, "Who's the delivery guy?"

"Who, Paul?" Maria asked while grinning. "A friend," she casually responded.

"A friend, huh? You never mentioned him."

"Yeah, I know. I first met him a couple of years ago. He had delivered my new lease agreement at the time but we never talked. It wasn't until about two weeks ago that I saw him again. He was making deliveries to my building. That's when we actually started talking."

"You know Maria, he and Wolf could almost pass for twins."

"Yeah, they do have a strong resemblance." He's just my little fun bun and really knows how to work it, but that's a topic for another day." As both laughed.

"I was surprised to see him here," Maria continued, "but he said he had to make a delivery."

"Yes, I saw him talking to Wolf's secretary before handing her a letter. I thought it was a little odd and a little late to come to an event to make deliveries. I wonder what that was about."

Maria simply shrugged her shoulders.

Returning from the restroom, Wolf smiled and said, "My first dance was with you," looking at Terrie. "It would be quite rude of me not to extend my hand to the beautiful host as well. Both you ladies look quite lovely tonight."

Terrie smiled and said, "Be my guest. That's why we're here, to enjoy ourselves and support this great event."

Maria got up and joined him on the dance floor. Terrie noticed that the two seemed to click. Their conversation, their rhythm they shared was in tune, especially for Maria, who couldn't take her eyes off him. As the evening progressed, the two went off on their own for a while to find a more personal setting. When Maria returned, she had a look that couldn't be wiped away.

Terrie leaned over and said, "Somebody is having a very good time," a two for one night huh?

Maria leaned over, placing her hand on Terrie's wrist, and laughed. "It ain't bad. I don't have a ring on it."

Moments later, Wolf walked up to the podium and took the mic to deliver his speech. Standing before his peers and the various sponsored charitable organizations, Wolf gave an eloquent thirty minutes speech concerning the need for education while stressing how computers in schools for underprivileged youth was important for the advancement of education. His speech was emotional and moving. He received a warm reception, impressing all that were in attendance, he ended by pledging one million dollars for the program.

When he finished, he looked over at Maria with a look that spoke volumes before verbally acknowledging her for the invitation. Afterwards he received a standing ovation from everyone in the room. He looked over to Margaret, who gave him a nod of approval, Wolf looked over to the table where Terrie and Maria were sitting. They looked at one other as both were impressed by his passion. When he returned to their table, they told him how impressed they were by his words as the evening continued.

Chapter 14:
A Timely Introduction

At Luis, Tia wasn't feeling her usual self. Mother Nature had begun to kick in. She asked her boss to leave early since the evening was running unusually slow for a Friday night. After finishing up a few things, she gathered herself and headed home.

Down the block about four doors away the same group of men she passed earlier were still there rolling dice with their money spread on the ground like a deck of cards. This was the order of the day.

Not wanting to be bothered, she decided to go in the opposite direction. It was a longer route but she didn't care. She wanted to be left alone and go home and get in her bed. Consumed with their game, only one of the guys who was standing off to the side had seen her.

His name was Tony but everyone called him Rock. He was twenty-one and no stranger to the law, with a list of charges on his resume, from theft to drug possession to assault. Since he was thirteen, he stayed in and out of juvenile and adult correctional facilities. He was now ready to graduate with his mind on something that would send him to one of the many penitentiaries that had its doors open and waiting for him. At 6 feet 6 with dark skin and long dreads, he was an intimidating physical specimen who was used to getting his way.

Rock had wanted Tia in his own type of way, although she never showed any interest toward him while ignoring all of his advances. Interest for her ate away at him like a cancer. Every day she passed by, she ignored them as though they weren't there, but he wouldn't let her rejection sway him away that easily. Whenever she walked by, he knew they would say things to her that she didn't particularly want to hear. On this occasion he decided to break away and approach her alone.

Walking down the street, she heard footsteps run up from behind her. When she turned, it was him.

"What do you want?" abruptly she asked.

"Why you gotta say it like that? I just wanna holla at'chu a minute. I see you every night, walkin' down this street with your fine self. I be speakin', and you be acting like you don't be hearin' a brother."

"That's because I'm not interested," she responded, increasing her pace.

"That's whack, baby," he responded, keeping up with her pace. "You ain't gotta be like that. What's your name? You can at least tell me that."

Looking at him while continuing her pace, she said, "I ain't gotta tell you nothing, but if it's gonna get you to leave me alone and back to your game, it's Tia. You satisfied? Now, will you leave me alone?"

When she turned away, he reached out to stop her, grabbing her by her arm, and pulled her toward him.

"Get your hands off of me and leave me alone!" she shouted. "You're hurting my arm!" As she jerked her arm away, she added, "I don't wanna be bothered. Leave me alone!"

Across the street, Jahir had been scavenging behind a carry out, and he noticed them. They didn't know that he was watching them.

Rock wasn't used to taking no for an answer, and he didn't plan on today being the first. He grabbed her again, this time raising his voice.

"Look here!"

Before he could say another word, she reached into her pouch and grabbed her pepper spray, spraying him in his face. While he bent over, his hands covering his eyes, she ran. It wasn't long before he had recovered and began running after her. Unable to outrun him he quickly gained ground. After catching up to her, he grabbed her again.

She attempted to spray him again, but this time he grabbed her by the wrist and knocked it out of her hand. He backhanded her across her face, sending her to the ground. Bending over her, he was about to strike her again but her heard faint footsteps coming from behind him. Holding her arms up to shield her face, she braced herself for another blow, then saw what was behind him. The expression on her face changed as she looked around him, although it wasn't her intent, signaled to Rock that someone was coming.

When he turned, he saw a much larger man standing there in a dark trench coat, a hood draped over his head, his face covered and a pair of dark shades. Jahir stood silently, not flinching a muscle.

"Who are you?" Rock shouted.

Jahir didn't reply.

"If I were you, I'd mind my own business and get outta here," he shouted again.

Still no reply.

Rock reached behind his back for the pistol he kept tucked in his belt. He took a step forward, pulling it from his belt, holding it sideways while pointed it toward Jahir's chest.

"You don't have three seconds to get out of here—you have two. One," he counted, cocking his weapon, "two!"

Rock pulled the trigger as Tia screamed. The bullet hit Jahir flush in his chest.

Not fazed, Jahir took hold of Rock's wrist crushing it. Immediately, he released the gun dropping to his knees grunting in pain. With the other hand, he grabbed him by the throat, lifting him into the air, hurling his two-hundred-and-fifty-pound frame across the alley into a wall. It was a miracle that the impact didn't kill him.

Jahir went over to him, grabbing him by the back of his collar, lifting him up to see if he were still alive. Seeing that he was still breathing, he simply dropped him on the ground. He looked at Tia, and saw that she was okay before deciding to make his exit on foot.

Before he could leave, there were five men blocking his path; it was Rock's crew. They had cut their game short to catch up with him when they saw him follow the girl. Whatever he had in mind, they wanted in.

With his path blocked, Jahir stood silently. As they walked toward him, they saw their man lying motionless on the ground. Seeing one of their own sprawled on the ground unconscious, they wanted blood in return. With bad intentions, each pulled a weapon then rushed Jahir. They were going to return the favor.

Tia had gotten up from the ground and watched as Jahir went to work, tearing through them like a lion amongst sheep. His movements were fast and sleek. None of them could lay a hand on him.

Only by chance was one of them able to hit him on the back of his head with a pipe. It was a blow that would've killed an ordinary man, but it had no effect. He attempted a second blow, but Jahir caught it with his hand without looking.

Swiftly, he turned and backhanded the man, launching him into the air as he landed into an open dumpster several feet away. He quickly finished off the rest. In just a few moments, all of them were lying motionless.

During the scuffle, Jahir's covering had come off his face and head without him realizing. While he was about to make his retreat, he turned to make certain Tia wasn't injured during the brawl. Seeing his face, she gasped in disbelief. At that moment, he knew his covering had come off; he touched his face. Knowing she had seen him, he quickly turned and ran away, but she called out to him.

"No! Don't go!" she shouted.

He hesitated, but he didn't stop.

"Please, don't go," she called out to him again. "Please! I'm not afraid of you."

He was unsure of why he stopped in his tracks, despite every instinct telling him to run away. Standing with his back to her was a silhouette of a man with the face that was a far cry from one. The centuries of loneliness he harbored inside yearned to interact with someone, to make him feel human again.

As he stood over the men that he had just dismantled, he heard her footsteps coming from behind him. When she got close to him, she walked around him so that she could stand face-to-face with him. Fearlessly, Tia looked into his eyes. In them, she saw a tameness within the beast, a gentleness, but she could tell he was a troubled soul.

Seeing he had blended features, the appearance of both man and feline resembling a panther, sleek and black with flowing locks. To her he possessed an unexplained beauty that was fierce in every way imaginable.

"Who are you?" she asked. "Can you speak?"

He hesitated at first. Then, in a low growling voice, almost a whisper, he said, "My name is Jahir—"

Before he could finish, he heard police sirens quickly approaching from a distance. With the commotion that took place in the alley, someone called the police.

Tia looked up at him. "We better go,"

"No, you stay. I must go," Jahir instructed. "You must stay, and tell what these men had attempted to do."

"This? It's too much to explain! I'd rather go. I doubt if they'll be bothering anybody for a while."

Tia and Jahir were looking to go their separate ways, but it was too late to run away. They were trapped between buildings with only one way out. With the police sirens and their lights flashing all around, Jahir looked up toward the rooftops. Surprisingly she looked up at him and said, "Take me with you." grabbing hold of his wrist. With no time to argue he wrapped his arm around her waist and said, "There is but one route."

"Hold on tight, and don't be afraid," I shall not harm you.

With those words, in a single bound he was halfway up the wall of the five-story building with his claws firmly embedded in the bricks. Tia was amazed as she found herself on top of the buildings in the arms of a creature no one would be able to explain. Once on the roof, Jahir flipped the young woman onto his back he said.

"Hold on to me as tightly as you can."

With those words, he began to move gracefully across the skyline. Careful to avoid the police choppers that were rapidly approaching in the distance, he moved as fast as his limbs would allow. From building to building in leaps and bounds, he put distance between himself and the scene they had just left. Satisfied that he had reached a safe distance away from the authorities, Jahir knelt on one knee as she climbed off of his back.

"Wow! That was some ride! What a thrill! I've never done anything remotely like that. Ever."

As they stood there, they could see the length of the city, the lights shining all around as though they were on display for them.

Jahir found a corner off the edge of the roof. He crouched like a cat waiting on a mouse to exit its hole. Not saying a word, he just watched and waited. Finding a place to sit, she looked over at him and thought about how she didn't get an answer earlier because they had to make a hasty exit. She wanted to know who and what he was along with his true purpose.

"Where did you come from? I take it that you won't harm me, cause if that were your intent, you could've done it back in the alley."

He remained silent, debating on whether to answer, wondering if he had already spoken too much, thinking how long it's been since he trusted anyone in his present form before being betrayed. This time, however, he perceived it would be different. He was surprised by the lack of fear the young woman showed, for the mightiest of men quivered at the very sight of him. Jahir made the choice to trust her. Looking down at the streets below, filled with lights that matched the stars above, he began to tell her the story of how he came to be, and the events that had led him on his current path.

Looking into her eyes, he said, "My name is Jahir Amid. I come from a place that no longer exists. A place far across the ocean, in a kingdom that has long been forgotten called Sargonia, during the time you call the Dark Ages."

As she listened, his voice, had a heavy sinister growl. He told her stories of a distant past, things that had been long forgotten. It was a journey through time that only he and one other could tell. He shared with her in detail the curse and how it had come to be. He shared how he still pursued his enemy, seeking desperately to destroy him. As Tia listened, she became enthralled with the story he told.

"I was born fifteen hundred years ago during a time when Roman chariots could still be heard. I was a man once, in love, hoping to start a family of my own before that opportunity was all taken away from me by the hand of a deranged madman. His lust for blood has driven him through the ages, causing nothing but grief and despair in his wake. The one I seek—his name is Nicholai Bultizar, the once ruler of the kingdom I so mentioned. His crimes against its people led to his demise.

"Brutal and unjust, he drained the people of nearly all they had in the name of the title he gave himself. But he also has a much darker side. His lust for blood included torture and murder, abducting young women in the night while committing crimes of unimaginable depth—women with specific characteristics he fancied the most for their height, weight, length of hair, those most pleasant to the eye, much like yourself. He wanted them all for himself at all times.

"He ritualized their murder by claiming their hearts, collecting them in a chest as his prizes. He then buried them beneath the dungeon floors, believing that was where the soul lay and kept them for himself to possess, which also included Kolliana's, who I loved with all my heart."

He told her the story as it was unfolding through his eyes, taking Tia there in her mind as if she were also present. As Jahir spoke, he shared with her everything he had hidden deep within himself for more than fifteen centuries because there was no one else he could trust. As he took her on a journey through time, she envisioned the events as though they were taking place around her. With every word, Tia became more and more intrigued as he told his tale.

Chapter 15:
A Tale of Love and the Encounter

"It was the year 752 AD when it all began. For ten years, the lands of my adopted father had remained unattended until I returned to reclaim them. I had left to live the life of an adventurer. I was both young and unsettled before returning home to find my purpose.

"After the death of my parents, I was taken in and raised by a once fierce and noble warrior named Omon Escar. He had allowed my birth parents to farm and till a small portion of his lands as their own without any payment required from them. The old warrior had grown tired of the wars that constantly raged in the far East and sought a more peaceful existence. Within these lands is where he finally found solace and made his home.

"When the plague came, only the strongest amongst them survived. My parents were among the fatalities. Their dying wish was for their son to be raised by him to whom he gave his word that it would be so. Under his watchful eye, he taught me everything he knew.

"He was a humble man, one that was once of great nobility from distant lands far to the East. He had migrated there long before the warlord Bultizar had masked his takeover after the fall of the Roman Empire. He taught me the true path of a great warrior--the honor and skills that came along with such a title. But most of all, he taught me how to be a man of honor, generous, and compassionate—rare traits during those times. There was also no finer swordsman or fighter in the land. My abilities eventually surpassed that of his.

"After his death, I was now left alone in the world to find my own way, along with my closest friend, Adonis, who also lost his family to the Black Death. Raised by his surviving aunt, they too struggled to survive. Having a more impulsive nature with no one around to temper it, Omon helped him through those troubled times as we grew together as brothers.

"He also taught him everything he had taught me, and like himself, very few could best him in wielding a sword. After the death of Omon and Adonis's aunt, the two us, then in our mid-teens, decided to leave those lands and seek adventure far to the East into Asia to find our places in this vast world. Over time, we both grew tired after years of wars, endless fighting, and death, like the man who had raised and taught me everything I knew. We both had had enough and decided to return home, where we believed it would be as we had left it--peaceful and flourishing.

"I was twenty-five when we returned, Adonis roughly the same. When we returned, everything had changed. The land and its people had been conquered by the barbaric warlord. Under his rule, the people suffered endlessly.

"I returned to the lands of my adopted father, far away from the fortress city of Obi—Bultizar's home—and far away from the prying eyes of the king's watchdogs. After I returned is when I met the one who captured my heart forever.

"Not far from home lived an earnest farmer named Oshimar Omeire and his wife Moria. From dawn to dusk, they worked, barely making their tally of taxes in the form of crop and livestock to the tyrannical warlord each quarter.

"With the aid of their two daughters, Tara, the oldest by one year, and Kolliana the younger, the one who caught my heart. Pleasant to the eyes she was smaller in stature but her proportions were perfect. She was by far the fairest, perhaps in all the kingdom.

"The day we met she shared with me the events that led to our first meeting. After helping their mother with their chores in the house, she told me that she and her sister would go out into the woods daily collecting berries and fruit from the forest, as each also would take turns fetching fresh water from a nearby stream. Each day, Oshimar their father worked his fields behind his oxen's plow and raised livestock in which half were collected each season according to the number of births, which he was required to pay to the king.

"Usually, the portions required were so great that many who worked the fields and raised livestock barely made enough to care for their families. Anyone failing to meet those quotas would be dealt harsh punishments. For some, their farms and their lands were stripped from them, and the former inhabitants denied aid. If anyone dared to help, they too would lose all their possessions and be left to join them, wandering aimlessly until they starved and died.

"For years, Oshimar kept the existence of his daughters a secret in fear of what could become of them because of the fate that many young women in the kingdom faced, if they caught the fancy of the king. He kept his daughters close and out of view the best that he could, and he didn't allow them to venture away from his land. It was the fear that the king's eyes and ears would learn of their existence and bring them to his attention.

"On the morning that we met, I had ventured, deep into the woods to partake in my daily ritual, performing a warrior's dance, of synchronized movements honing my skills. It was there that I came into a chance encounter with the one who would mold my future for years to come.

"Kolliana had gone out into the forest alone without the company of her sister. Carefree and unafraid, she found her surroundings to be a comforting place. Singing and dancing to the tunes that were playing in her mind, she had become lost in her imagination as she wandered deeper than her path normally would take her.

"Hearing my movements as I stepped on twigs and scrubs that echoed through the morning air. She moved closer to get a better view. Hidden behind a patch of tall bushes, she remained unseen watching me wield my sword toward an opponent that wasn't there.

"She was curious by what she saw as I moved about. Moving closer she stumbled before falling to the ground which drew my attention.

"As she rose to her feet, she began to run away. Wanting to meet her, I shouted for her not to run, assuring her that I wasn't going to harm her. For reasons she could not explain, she stopped as she looked back at me while I stood quietly as we both stared at one another. I slowly walked toward her while sheathing my sword, reassuring her that I wouldn't harm her.

"Looking into my eyes, she could have been afraid, not knowing who I was or what my intentions might have been, but she wasn't. It was like a calm fell upon her, finding trust in my words. It was something between us, something we both were feeling—a bond that formed almost instantly the moment we looked into each other's eyes.

"I asked to know her name and where she had come from. She told me and that we were standing on the land where she was raised. She told me the names of her parents and that of her sister.

"After sharing with me everything, she looked at me and asked the same.

"I told her my story and that my home was just beyond the river's edge, the land that bordered her own.

"I told her that the only thing I now sought was peace, which is why I returned to my homeland, finding a far different place than I remembered. She explained in detail how everything had changed, and that it was now full of misery, more than I could ever imagine.

"I told her that I had heard the stories, and that I had returned to re-claim my land.

"She said, *If he learns of your presence, he will demand that you pay a portion of all that you possess.*

"I replied, *When that day comes, I shall be concerned, but for now I will live my life as freely as I always have without conviction. I then asked had she ever left her father's land?*

"Her reply was, *No. My father would not allow it because Bultizar would send those belonging to his most secret circle to abduct young women in the night so that he could have his way. Some had never been seen alive again, so my father kept me and my sister far from the city to protect us.*

"I told her, looking into her eyes, *As long as I am close, I shall protect you.*

"She looked at me and said, *You are just one man against the king and his forces.* She spoke in doubt, but I laughed and reassured her.

"In the months that followed after I had met her parents, the passion we shared blossomed into love. All was at peace as I made the daily journey to see her.

"It was early, Kolliana and her sister were out fetching water when they were interrupted by the sound of horses echoing through the forest. Twenty armed men dressed in armor emerged from the forest and rode up on them.

"Hastily, they approached as horses' hooves shook the ground, startling them both. They were hard men, gruff in their appearance, rowdy in nature, one of them being the lord Nicholai Bultizar himself out on one of his hunting excursions. Finding themselves surrounded by his men she told me they stood quietly as they formed a barricade around them. I listened carefully as she told me her story before my arrival.

"*Well, what do we have here?*" asked one of the king's guards. "*We haven't seen the likes of such beauty anywhere in the kingdom, and two such as you in one place at the same time,*" he said as they laughed.

"Because of the tales that had spread throughout the kingdom, they both were frightened, not knowing what would happen next. They stood quietly at first, too frightened to speak. *"Come now, have you lost the ability to speak or are you deaf and mute?"* he asked.

"Kolliana, being the bolder of the two, stepped forward and said, *That is because this is my home and we never leave it. My father forbids it.*

"Before a reply could be made, a voice from within the twenty spoke out, *Silence!*

"With those words, the men who surrounded them opened a path, allowing Bultizar to come forth. Neither girl had ever seen the king before, but both were afraid of what may become of them.

"As Bultizar approached, he said, *My man is correct. We haven't seen the likes of you before. Had it been so I would've surely remembered. Your beauty surpasses any that I have ever seen to this day.*" While smiling, he asked, *Is she your sister?*

"Kolliana looked back and nodded.

"Then king looked over to Tara and asked, *How old are you?*

"*I'm nineteen.*

"The king paused and replied, *Two so young and lovely, so tender.* Then he looked at Kolliana, finding her the more fascinating of the two. *Who is your father?*

"They both were afraid for their family; neither woman said a word. Bultizar said, *Now, now, not all at once. I will find out, and if I have to take that path, it shall not be a pleasant one.*

"Kolliana then walked up to the king and said, *My father is Oshimar. He is the owner of this land.*

"One of Bultizar's men then shouted, *No woman! Lord Bultizar is the owner of these lands and throughout this kingdom.*

"Looking down at the young female, Bultizar smiled and tilted his head, gesturing that he confirmed that fact. But he had found the young woman to be most desirable, fueling his interest.

"*Ah, I see,*" he replied. Looking to one of his men, he asked, "*Does he pay his taxes?*"

"*Yes, my lord. They all do in this region,* the guard replied.

"Bultizar said to his man, *If you collect, then how is it that none has ever seen two maidens as lovely as these?*

"*They must hide them from us, my lord,* he responded.

"*All we do is collect for the king,* another responded.

"*Oh yes, I see.*

"Once again, Bultizar turned his attention toward the two girls. *Tell your father he must take the two of you to the city one day. There is so much to see.*

"Interrupting the king's thought, in that moment, I arrived. The gallop of hooves as I rapidly approached on top of my stallion. As I emerged from the woods, Bultizar's men unsheathed their swords while forming a circle of protection around their king.

"Bringing my horse to a halt, I looked over at Kolliana and Tara to make sure they were all right. I turned my attention toward the contingency of armed men.

"*Who are you?* I asked.

"One of the guards looked at me and shouted, *Hold your tongue, dog! You are in the presence of the king.*

"Looking at the soldier, I replied, *The king?*

"The guard then replied, *Do you not know who your king is?*

"I told them, *I do not have a king. When I left these lands, they were independent and free. I have just returned after years of absence.*

"The guard responded, *That reason holds no excuse. It is your duty to know to whom you should bow. The punishment for your lacking is death!*

"I quickly drew my sword and said, *If today is the day of my death, then you will also join me to meet my maker.*

"Just as quickly, the others drew their swords, prepared to attack. It was Bultizar who interceded, ordering his men to sheath their swords.

"Looking me in the eye, he said, *I am the king of these lands now and I am feeling merciful today.*

"As he rode his horse towards me, I stood silent, holding my ground. As the king approached, I noticed the round wooden medallion dangling from around his neck with the head of a wolf made of solid gold at its center. I wasn't sure what was going to happen next as he drew closer and grinned.

"*Much has changed since you've returned,* Bultizar said. *You claim that these lands are your home? Then know this—they are a part of my kingdom now, which makes me your king.*

"I remained silent, assessing the situation, weighing the odds. With my hand poised to grab my sword, if need be, I looked Bultizar in his eyes. Everyone was silent as they awaited his response. I had fought many wars and seen kingdoms fall. I knew an unwise answer could mean the death of Kolliana, her sister, as well as, myself. Reluctantly, I nodded, acknowledging him as king.

"Bultizar smiled, looked over at the two women, then back at me and asked, *Are you the protector of these ladies?*

"*Yes, I am. If need be, I'll defend them to the death.*

"He laughed and said, *Such loyalty. I could use one so brave and loyal in my service.*

"*I am not a soldier, just a humble man—a humble man,* repeating my words.

"Bultizar smiled in response. All knew the nature of Bultizar. They knew that behind his words was more than what appeared. Bultizar looked at the scars etched deep into my armor. I remained silent and ready, not knowing if I would live or die this day.

"For one whose beginnings are humble, your armor tells a different tale. Where do you reside, young warrior? Bultizar asked.

"Beyond the river I rest my head, and all the land beyond it, I possess until reaching the great foothills of the mountain.

"Such a broad stretch of land, Bultizar replied.

"I inherited it from the one who raised me.

"And what happened to the man that raised you?

"He died!

"I see, he replied. *So, tell me, how shall you break it up to pay me what is my due?*

"I haven't been here long enough to give it much thought.

"Bultizar led his horse forward a few steps until he was close. He leaned forward, drawing close to my ear and whispered, *You have three days to figure it out. Within that time, I shall send my collectors to stake my claim.*

"I said nothing, I was unsure of what he would do or say next.

"Bultizar simply looked back to his men and said, *I have a hunt to partake in.*

"With a stab of his spurs, he prompted his horse, as well as, his men to press forth as they rode off into the forest. I stood silent while watching them disappear.

"Afterward, I knew trouble was coming. After ensuring they were okay, I told them to get on my horse so I could take them home.

"Shaken from their encounter, Tara remained quiet while Kolliana looked at me and asked, *What did you think of the king's words? Will he will return?*

"I hesitated, seeing that both were still shaken. In an attempt to comfort them, I chose my words carefully. I wanted to reassure them, although I didn't know for certain.

"I told them that no matter what happened, I would be there to protect them.

"Although Kolliana found comfort in my promise, my words did little to ease the fears of her sister. She knew that, alone, my power to protect them would be limited.

"When we arrived at the farm, Oshimar was plowing behind his ox when he looked up to see me with his daughters galloping across the field. It was obvious to him there was something wrong.

"Oshimar stopped what he was doing and stood there beside his ox as we approached. He could see the fear in his daughter's eyes and that I was troubled, no matter how much I tried to conceal it. When we reached him, Tara got off my horse and ran over to him while Kolliana remained.

"As Oshimar held Tara tightly, he looked over to me and Kolliana as she got off the horse and stood beside him.

"*What happened?* Oshimar asked.

"*In the woods,* Tara replied. *Those awful men!* Tears began flowing down her face.

"*It was the king and his soldiers,* Kolliana added.

"As I dismounted my horse, I told him what happened and that the king and I had broken words.

"Hearing this, Oshimar became concerned.

"The secret he had desperately tried to hide was now in the open. All the years he spent protecting them from discovery were gone. Now, both of his daughters were in the same danger that had plagued the rest of the kingdom.

"After his daughters departed into the house, I looked him in the eye and told him that Bultizar may return.

"I knew thoughts of the sisters laid heavily on Bultizar's mind, especially that of my love.

"Her boldness, along with her innocence, fascinated him. I knew he had to have her.

"Before mounting my horse, she ran out from her home calling my name. When she arrived, she jumped into my arms and kissed me, telling me that she loved me. The family knew the bond we shared, a fact that her father accepted. Oshimar knew I would give my life to defend her.

Chapter 16:
End of a Dream

"For months, all had been quiet since the last string of deaths. Far from Obi's walls, Kolliana and I had become nearly inseparable. There had not been another encounter with the king, only that of the tax collectors who returned to my land, where I reluctantly complied for the sake of peace.

"I would go to their farm daily, hunting deer and boar to help feed the family as if they were my own. From time to time, Kolliana and I would take long rides in the forest, walking along the ponds and streams, admiring their beauty as I admired the beauty that resided within her. In return, she showed the love she had for me. We were oblivious as to what was going on throughout the kingdom. It was as though we were a world away where no danger existed.

"I had become set on starting a life with the woman I had fallen in love with. My desire was to start a family of my own. I laid my heart before her and asked for her hand in marriage.

"Before I could complete my thoughts, she jumped into my arms and kissed me with such passion that I could not find the words to explain. It was time for me to ask her father for her hand in marriage. It was late and I wanted the occasion to be a special one, so I waited until early the next morning, I donned my best wardrobe, shined my armor, and put on my most valiant cape. I rode to a place not far from them and picked the finest flowers I could find in the field. There wasn't a time in my life that I had been happier.

"When I arrived at her farm, I expected to find her father working his fields, their mother wringing the laundry. As I approached, I saw that the door to the farmhouse had been kicked in.

"Drawing my sword, I rushed in calling out to them without response only to find what I feared the most—death. Blood was splattered everywhere, her father lying in a pool of his own blood, face down with a pitchfork beside him. He had been killed with a sword. Kolliana's mother was lying beside him. Her throat cut, her eyes and mouth still open—the terror still etched on her face. I found Tara had shared her parent's fate—but she had been stripped naked, and raped before her death.

"It was like a nightmare where nothing seemed real. I moved swiftly, calling out Kolliana's name trying to find her, but she wasn't there. It was like time stood still around me.

"I searched and searched but there still were no signs of her. Whoever has done this had taken her. I knew in my heart she would have never abandoned them and would have gladly died by their side.

Deep into the story and unable to look away, Tia was saddened by the tragedy Jahir shared. She felt sorry for the man inside the beast who told it. Her eyes watered as she listened, feeling his pain as he continued.

"I followed the tracks that were left behind. I counted six on horseback that led onto the road to Obi. I followed the trail for miles before it went cold as the horses went off the road scattering in all directions. I stopped and dismounted my horse, stooping low to get closer examine their tracks. I saw that five of the horses had gone off the trail with one missing.

"I first studied the depth of the hooves I sought. I knew the one baring the heavier load was the horse I was looking for, because those that went off the paved trail were of equal depth. I knew then that the one I pursued was still on the paved road and that was the path I was taking.

"I rode as fast as my horse would take me, full knowing, the king had for her. His secret fetish for blood and young women caused me to fear the worst. All I wanted to do was find her and avenge the death of her family and everyone responsible—even at the cost of my own life.

"Riding toward the city, I came across the one who had sorely been missed—Adonis, my friend and companion on many adventures. I was relieved to see him but had no time to indulge a reunion, with finding Kolliana my only purpose.

"Face-to-face, we extended our arms in a brotherly embrace. Looking into my eyes, Adonis knew instantly that I was troubled. We had fought and saw many of our comrades die.

"He asked what was troubling me.

"I told him, *The woman I love was taken sometime during the night. My beliefs are with the king. It was he who was responsible.* I shared with him I was running out of time to find her with the hope that she may still be alive.

"Adonis said to me that we had ridden together and fought many battles side by side and that he shall not pick this moment to abandon me at a time when I needed his help.

"I told him that I did not want him to endanger his life against a foe who commands a kingdom and an army, although I knew that it would be impossible to do it alone.

"Adonis said to me that I needed not to ask for his help, that I was his friend, and that he would ride with me to the end if necessary. He told me he had much to share with me that may be useful to my cause.

"He began to explain. *There are many who would follow you throughout the kingdom. They, too, have lost loved ones secretly to the king, abducted in the night by his henchmen.* He had heard many of these stories, of how they had ceased for a time but had begun again.

"He had seen the misery and suffering firsthand in this kingdom, and heard the grumblings of the people. They were ready to rise up against the king's rule. All they needed was someone to lead them. He said if I gave them hope, they would follow me. If we could get them to fight, then we will have numbers on our side.

"None of that was my concern at that moment, all that mattered to me was finding Kolliana, no matter where it led me.

"After I had spoken, Adonis drew silent, then exclaimed, *Let us ride, together!*

"Without delay we rode to the palace gates. Unable to gain entry, we stood in front of the castle where I demanded to have an audience before the so-called king. For nearly an hour we waited until eventually the gates slowly opened.

"We were greeted by twelve heavily armed guards. Their commander rode up to me and said, *King Bultizar shall speak to you now.*

"We were escorted to the king's chamber. Once we arrived, we walked into the throne room flanked by six guards on each side. Sitting atop his seat made of gold covered with the finest linen, furs, and stones in the region, Bultizar sat. He had purchased the items from lands afar with the possessions he had stolen from the people of Sargonia. With these callous acts, he showed contempt he had for everyone under his rule. The once prosperous region had crumbled into ruins. He had brought with him only his most loyal, which numbered around four thousand followers, while many others were living in poverty and facing starvation.

"At that moment my only concern was to find my woman. I knew the king held the answer. Standing before him, I spoke with an unbridled tongue full of anger, unfazed by whatever the outcome would be.

"*I followed the path of the butcher, which led to these gates!*" I shouted brashly.

"*The woman I seek is missing; her family murdered. You remember the woman. Her name is Kolliana.*"

"Angered by my words and actions, I wasn't sure of his response, placing my had on my sword as did Adonis we waited, as he began to speak. *You stand before me after making accusations both here and outside my palace gates as though I was responsible. You demand an audience without a formal request or petition at a time in which you desire, and without permission? For such acts I should have your head on a pole on display for all to see, you insolent wretch! Why would I remember one woman? There are many under my rule, both young and old, some fair, others painful to gaze upon.*"

"After listening to his threats, I spoke while my temper inside began to boil. *A few months ago, you and your men came upon her and surrounded her on the southern borders of the kingdom, not long before I happened upon you. It was there when you and I spoke.*

"Bultizar paused, gesturing that he had now remembered the incident. *Ah!* he said. *Yes, I remember now, you and the woman you speak of. As I recall, there was a sister also present, I believe. What a tragedy, I shall not suffer such an act in my kingdom,* he proclaimed.

"Knowing that the truth was far from his lips, I kept my composure and reluctantly said, *Lord Bultizar, then it shall not trouble you if I assist in the search by starting here in the palace, since all tracks led here. I believe the murderer is hiding someplace within these walls.*

"As I spoke, Adonis once again slowly placed his hand on the handle of his sword, knowing the king's reputation of ruthlessness and impatience. He was unsure of how the king would react to my words, believing our time was running short, and fate was now upon us.

"Immediately, Bultizar rose from his throne, with his guards quickly drawing their swords as they moved toward me.

"The commander of the guards looked at the king and said, *My lord*, as he awaited Bultizar's response.

"The king smiled. He looked at me and said, *You spoke to me once in a manner that—had I chosen to—would've had you thrown in chains. Now, you have spoken to me again in a manner that could have your head on a platter. Because you're upset for your loss and your hunt for your missing loved one, I extend to you one last mercy. But this is the last time I shall pardon your insolence. For the next time, it shall be your head I shall remove. I am not without mercy to the people who serve me. I shall see to it that she is found and those responsible punished.*

"Stepping down, he walked toward me, and now face-to-face, he declared that the next time I stood before him without being summoned would be my last. He told me to leave before he changed his mind. Looking over to his guards, Bultizar commanded them to escort us to our horses, and if we returned making such claims, demands, or threats, to kill us where we stood.

"While we walked away, Bultizar looked over to his captain, giving him a subtle nod. Knowing in silence what he was to do on behalf of the king.

"Once we arrived to our horses, I looked over at Adonis and declared, *That lying sack of manure.*

"*What is our next recourse?*

"I told him, *At nightfall, we shall return,* and that I knew she was there, somewhere. *I could feel it and I shall not give up, not as long as there was breath in my body.*

"*You know if we're caught what will happen to us?* Adonis questioned me.

"I replied, *I know, that's why I must go alone.*

"Adonis laughed, looked at me, and confirmed, *We are one my friend, and I shall not let you do this alone.*

"We then mounted our horses and rode out of the city. My plan was to return at nightfall, but first we searched for a place to wait, away from watchful eyes. Word about the death of yet another young girl had reached our ears before we could accomplish our task.

"I now feared the worst, not knowing who it was. My thoughts were only of Kolliana in the hope that it wasn't her. Another body of a young woman had been found mutilated and discarded along an infrequently used path in the woods. Someone else had been searching for their loved one who had been missing just a few days prior and that young woman was roughly the same build as Kolliana.

"Now there was news of yet another woman found in a shallow ditch just hours after Adonis and I had met with the king, not far off the road we had traveled. In hearing this, I hurried to find out if it was as I had feared. When we arrived, the woman had just been placed on a cart and covered. Before she was taken away, I ran over to the body and removed the coverings.

"My fears were realized, it was Kolliana. As with the others that had been found, she was beaten, her heart had been cut from her chest.

"I fell to my knees and yelled out with all the breath that was in me. Finally, after regaining my composure, I stood and began looking over her body and saw that her wrists and ankles bore the marks of shackles. Symbols that were engraved on them marked all prisoners who wore them, as enemies of the king.

"Then a man came forth named Kabar who was traveling with a small group. He was a more recent victim of the king's policies. Everything they possessed had been taken from them. They were fortunate to be alive, yet forced to leave the only home they had known.

"Seeing that I was stricken with grief and knowing what had happened there, he said to me, *We all know it was the king's hand that had taken her life —she along with all the others found murdered since he came to power, with each of them sharing the same fate.*

"As he spoke to us, he said, *A young woman whose name was kept secret to protect her from the hands of the king's henchmen had told of the story how she herself was abducted and beaten. She was to be his next victim before being helped by one of the king's guards who had grown tired of his murderous acts. He was later found hung in a field, stripped of all clothing and armor. His eyes were gouged out, his tongue ripped from his mouth, his body picked by the beaks of vultures.*

"Knowing what had transpired there, and in seeing the grief in my eyes, he trusted me. *Her name is Amara. I know where you can find her, he said to me. Then made me swear that I would never reveal it, for fear that she will share the same fate as the guard who was responsible for setting her free.*

"I gave the man my word. Before I sought her out, I then took Kolliana's body back to the land of her father. There, I buried her alongside them.

"Afterwards, I went in search of Amara for answers. I needed to know everything about the king. As far as Kabar was concerned, despite his efforts, his daughter was never found. The people knew who it was that was responsible and had grown weary of the obstinate king. As instructed, we sought out Amara where she had been hiding. She had found refuge, far from the lands of this misbegotten king.

"At first, she feared we were sent by Bultizar to kill her. She quickly learned that we had a much different purpose—to bring justice to all those who Bultizar had murdered, including Kolliana.

"As Amara told us of her tales of horror, tears began streaming down the sides of her face. She told us that the guard had also overheard the name Kolliana--how he had met her and her sister in the woods and that Bultizar had to have her. We stood before her and listened in detail to every word she spoke until she began to weep uncontrollably, no longer able to bear the memories of that night. Consumed with grief and anger after hearing her words, all I wanted was vengeance.

"I am going to take my sword and return the favor to Bultizar, ending his worthless life! I exclaimed.

"Adonis stopped me and wouldn't let me pass. He knew that I was blinded by rage. I even threatened him if he stood in my way, but his persistence and reasoning prevailed. His words took hold before calmness took control, which allowed me to listen to reason. He placed his hand on my shoulder and said,

"A direct attempt on the king's life would be suicide and futile at best. And that I would never get close enough. He reminded me of the words he had previously spoken to me. That the people were ready to rise up against him. They'd grown weary of his injustice, his cruelty, but most of all, the murders of their loved ones. Although no one dared to speak it, all knew he was the one responsible. He looked me in the eye and emphasized, *The time has come to lead them.* This was something I had the natural ability to do; all they needed was a reason to trust me. And with the death of my woman, that was what linked me to them, directly fueling their cause.

"From that day, I scoured the countryside, looking to find those that were willing to rid themselves of this madman. I was careful to avoid those who were blinded by the king's promises of prosperity, concerned that they would be his eyes and ears. As word spread, more and more were willing to take arms against the king. They were willing to die rather than to have another of their loved ones abducted and murdered. Soon, we began training farmers, turning them into fighters.

"As the months began to build, our fighting force had grown to nearly twice that of Bultizar's. With more and more villagers refusing to pay their portions to the king, Bultizar dispatched contingencies of soldiers to crush what he perceived to be the beginning of a rebellion, only to have them defeated and driven back. Ours were now an army strong enough to challenge Bultizar's forces. With ten thousand strong—we were now prepared to face them. Then we marched on Obi, killing everyone responsible for carrying out his injustice in return for stolen lands and power.

"When word reached Bultizar of the uprising, he was angered. Overconfident, he didn't take the uprising seriously. He believed that they were no more than an army of farmers, and unskilled, posing little challenge.

He stayed within his city fortress, sending instead his most loyal and ruthless commander, Boris the Beheader to lead his army. There he waited, believing it was going to be a glorious victory, crushing the rebel uprising. He gathered his forces that numbered around six thousand, but underestimated our numbers and skill--unaware of our discipline and fight training. Most of Bultizar's men had grown fat and lazy. They had become an army of drunkards due to the spoils they had robbed of the Sargonian people throughout the years, unchallenged.

"Boris also believed he would be facing a small, ill-trained force. The Beheader quickly learned of his error in judgment when his army was utterly defeated while he barely escaped the onslaught to give Bultizar warning. Knowing there would be consequences for his actions, Bultizar along with Boris and about sixty of his loyal survivors fled into the eastern forest.

"I was determined to make him pay for his crimes while avenging the death of my beloved. Throughout the edges of the civilized world into the deepest depths of the wilderness, we pursued him.

"In his travels, Bultizar came across an old man deep within the forest. He told him of a book that ignited his interest, as well as, his lust for power. The old man told him that the book had the power to restore him back to the throne and to make him invincible. In leading him to the place it was kept, Bultizar betrayed him and left him for dead. When we found the old man, he was barely alive. With his dying breath, he shared with us that he had told Bultizar and where to find him. He told us of an abandoned fortress that was ruled by a powerful sorceress they called Mother. She along with her followers had long since vanished but not before legend told that she had placed a curse upon the castle fortress. It was also believed that it was built with the labor of demons, and that whoever entered its walls would suffer death and misfortune."

As Tia sat and listened, it was as if she were in a trance as he told her everything in detail that happened in that castle on that day.

"I have been hunting him ever since."

Chapter 17:
Myth as Fact

Astounded by Jahir's account, Tia replied, "A panthiem and a werewolf." She stared at him in his eyes. "I've heard of vampires and werewolves and all kind of creepy creatures. Until now, I thought these were only fictional stories out of a book. This is all new to me. I've never heard of a panthiem in any story I've ever been told."

"There are a great many things that you have no knowledge of," Jahir responded. "Events that have been lost in time. In your eyes, we both appear as monsters, but there is a difference between us beyond our shape and form. Once the sun sets below the horizon, he can transform at will and act upon those dark desires. Nothing on this earth can stop him except me. Not silver bullets nor anything that is of myth or legend attached to killing a werewolf is true in stopping him. Not any weapon that is made by men can kill him."

Jahir removed his right glove, revealing his paw-like hand. He stretched his fingers wide apart while looking down at them, revealing them to her. Slowly he unsheathed his claws. They were long and curved, six inches in length. Tia's eyes were opened wide as she was amazed at what she witnessed.

"Only when my claws thrust deeply into his chest, removing his blackened heart, can this game come to its true end. The only way this curse can be lifted from the both of us is if I take his heart while he is in the form of the living werewolf. Only then can I once again take my human form and live out my life as a mortal. The horror and the fears of the werewolf's countless victims I see and feel. Through their memories, I feel their pain as claws and teeth rip through their flesh. I am forever linked to each of them throughout the ages, both past and present. He is the reason I am here. Not only must I end this madness and free myself to stop him before he kills again, but there is much more at stake."

"Why can't you find him while he is a man?" she asked. "Can't you smell him or something like animals do, then wait for him to change? Or are you restricted by daylight?"

"No, I'm not restricted by daylight. Only by my appearance do I seek the comfort of the darkness to hide my true self—a lesson I learned through the ages, unless I wish to be hunted like a savage beast because of it. If he stood before me face to face, I would not know who he was. This is part of the curse in which I'm burdened. I can only sense him when his blood boils before the change, which will lead me to him. I cannot not track him until he's fully turned. He is responsible not only for those you speak of but countless other souls. All of this to satisfy his lust and to see the fear of his victim before he robs them of life.

"In human form, I cannot see anything but distorted images in my memories of him, even from the days of our past. If I crossed paths with him, he would be unrecognizable to me by sight or by smell. Over the centuries, he has gathered great wealth. This allows him to move about with relative ease from place to place, from continent to continent, leaving me to track him by whatever means available. And I must follow the pattern of his kills as I have done throughout the centuries, which helps to delay our encounter. Only when breath has left his body will I see him in his human form, and his dark soul finds his deserving place before the judgment of God."

As she listened, a delayed thought came across her mind. With talks of hearts being savagely removed from its victim's chest, coupled with all the recent murders, Tia began to back slowly as fear crept up on her. She began thinking that she might very well be face to face with the real killer.

With a bit of uncertainty, she said, "Werewolves! Until today I thought were a myth, a horror story made to strike fear in the listener, but I got you here standing in front of me, telling me the story. At this point, how could I doubt anything? Hearts being ripped from people's chests, recent killings like the stories you've just told me." After pausing a moment, Tia added, "Even so, I am familiar with something pertaining to those stories. Like I just stated, I've never heard of your kind, this is all new for me. With you standing here in front of me, how can I argue with that, though? The question I have is, how do I know you're not capable of doing the same thing?"

With everything in her, Tia tried to hide the fear that was building inside. Doing her best, she tried to conceal it. Boldly she spoke out.

"How do I know that you're not the one actually responsible or just playing some kind of sick game with me? You could be telling me a bedtime story like Hansel and Gretel, fattening my mind up before you kill me."

Jahir became silent, tilting his head slightly from side to side trying to comprehend what she was trying to say. Looking in her eyes, he moved toward her then leaned forward. With their eyes locked, he remained silent for a moment.

Tia didn't know what to expect. She was too scared to move a muscle. It had seemed like time had stood still. She didn't know whether she was going to get the answer that she had feared. Regardless of the uncertainty, she held her ground and waited for his response.

Breaking his silence, Jahir said, "Child, there is no need to fear me. I smell it coming from your pores. I do not kill or murder the innocent, and I have no such desire to harm you. I shall tell you the nature of the curse that the witch laid upon me, if you are willing to listen.

"Before I was changed into this beastly form, the curse of the Panthiem had never before reached my ears. When the witch spoke it, that was the first I had ever heard that name. I had no knowledge of what was going to become of me. Whether I'm the first or the last, I do not know. I have known no other like myself giving me reason to believe that I am the only one. Once I had awakened from my sleep, I found myself in a cold dark place, entombed behind a hidden wall. I freed myself with strength I didn't know I possessed. I went up a winding stairwell from the depths of the castle's cellar, finding the sunlit floors above.

"The castle had been burned and in ruins for a long time. Looking around through the scorched bricks, broken archways, and rubble, I searched for a clue, trying to make sense of what had happened to me. Seeing my reflection in the pieces of a broken mirror scattered about on the ground, it frightened me. I realized I had been transformed into this monster that now stands before you. I didn't know what I was or what was going to become of me. All I could remember was that while I slept, the dreams of hundreds of souls haunted me. Images of people in my mind crying out to me as they were being torn to shreds.

"Seeing these images in my head, no matter how badly I wanted to come to their aid, I was powerless to do anything to help them. Images of the golden wolf flashed through my mind as he tore through their flesh. I heard their cries ringing out in my head, then the face of the one that cursed me. All the while, her words rang out in my mind over and over again as if she had just spoken them. Looking around, I tried to make sense of it all, finding myself standing in the place I last remembered. This was where the book last rested, but it was gone. The walls had crumbled, its foundation weakened from the fire along with time itself.

"The longer I am in this form, the compassion in my heart grows stronger. I believe if my nature was opposite, both you and your attackers would be dead. What puzzles me is why would one so evil place such a veil around me? Why would she spare me, giving me the opportunity to free myself and simply not kill me and end it? It is as though there's some hidden purpose for me, one that I have yet to know its meaning. I've traveled this journey for centuries unable to share this with anyone because of the fear my presence would bring. Therefore, no one knows I truly exist, but there is something about you that I trust. I haven't the words to explain—just a feeling.

"Through the ages, I see the old witch mingled amongst the crowd or in open spaces. Like a ghost, always near where the victims once lay. Always staring, sometimes smiling but when I blink, it is as though she was never there."

Tia said, "Whatever she's done to you, maybe it's causing you to hallucinate."

"Perhaps! But it is happening more frequently, with each time being the same. Perhaps madness is beginning to take hold of me. I believe all of this is connected to that book. Something I have no true knowledge of or its power—only the words of a dying old man that spoke of its potential. Beyond that, I know nothing and because of it, I am cursed along with my enemy. If he had not sought it, then I would've killed him long ago and would have long since been in the grave."

Returning to the ledge, Jahir resumed his crouched position, looking down at the street below. Tia overcame her fear, putting everything back into perspective. She walked over and sat down beside him.

Looking across at the city lights, she said, "The view is so beautiful from up here. I never realized all the people moving about this time of night until now."

Jahir responded, "Yes, it is beautiful, and so is life. Often, I think of what life could have been for me had it not been for this madman. Nevertheless, whatever my fate would've been, I'll never know. What I do know is this—Bultizar is somewhere out there, stalking his next victim."

Pausing a moment, Jahir looked at his young friend and said, "For fifteen hundred years I've pursued him, first as a man, and later when I had awakened from my sleep as the creature you now see before you. Unless I find and stop him, the killing will continue." Looking away and then back at Tia, he said, "Like in the beginning, when Bultizar lived a life as a mortal man, he would murder randomly. As time went on, he formed patterns in which he chose his special victims with their beating hearts as his prize. When he became a werewolf, he started out the same as he did when he was just a man, killing randomly, seeking the hearts of the ones that moved him the most. These were women that were similar to yourself—youthful, pleasant to the eyes and of similar size. Those are the ones whose hearts he desires.

"I am running out of time to find him. The witch spoke of two moon risings, both scarlet, and on either night if I don't stop him, he could claim his prize. The first rising was in 1888, when the monster arrived in England. It was during that time he nearly obtained what he sought. He appeared in London's East End. The press at the time called him Jack the Ripper."

Staring in disbelief, she replied, "Jack the Ripper? He was a man."

"That's what the authorities wanted the people to believe," Jahir replied. "It would've caused panic had the authorities revealed the truth—*werewolves really existed*. There, he chose prostitutes. Each of them was of the measure he desired. Like now, he also held a city in fear, and through that fear, he had hoped to fulfill his desire. Parading as a gentleman of distinction, he used some discretion to prevent being recognized.

"As he sought the company of women of lower esteem, he believed their loss would be of no concern. This would allow him to choose freely without anyone to care about, or even mourn, their deaths. He went on carrying out these fiendish acts unabated. One by one, he killed and butchered these women, claiming their hearts. He had claimed the lives of five women, then he needed but one more to fulfill his desire. He had nearly claimed his sixth and final victim on that night of the scarlet moon.

"At the stroke of midnight, he was poised to claim his final victim and obtained the invincibility he sought. Fortunately, he was interrupted before he could strike, causing him to flee. Unlike the old myths and legends about werewolves, his bite and kills do not create other werewolves. Silver bullets, garlic, or any other trinket will not stop him. Only my claws thrust deep into his chest," pausing slowly he revealed them while continuing to speak, "claiming his heart while he is still in that form, can he be killed.

"If I fail to stop him before such time, he would then be able to create armies in his likeness that would be impossible to stop. During the time of the Ripper, it was only by chance was he interrupted before he could make that final kill at the appointed hour, robbing him of the power he so desperately sought. Had he succeeded, today would be a much different world.

"He has left a trail of tears and sorrow for me to follow. The pain and images of all those tormented souls delayed my senses as they constantly danced through my mind. I am cursed to relive them one after the other until such time that they would eventually lead me to that particular place and time, three decades later. By that time, I would have been powerless against him. But now that opportunity has come once again and I'm now here. I must find him."

Tia looked over towards Jahir and asked, "How were you able to track him here all the way across the ocean? How were you able to get here? The very sight of you would have caused people to panic."

Jahir looked back towards her and replied, "There is nowhere on this earth I cannot follow or find him. I stowed away on a cargo ship. There I remained hidden until I reached these distant lands." Jahir then changed his focus, looking directly at Tia. "Why do you walk alone in a city filled with all sorts of hidden dangers? Your family, those who are supposed to watch over you—where are they?"

"My mother gave me up to live with my aunt when I was five. The streets were more important to her than raising a young daughter. She did drugs and alcohol while she tricked to support those habits, which were her driving force. Cocaine, her drug of choice before PCP took her over the edge, landed her in a mental institution, somewhere upstate."

Jahir looked over to her and asked, "And your father?"

She became silent, looking down and around, then replied, "I never had a father. If I did, he never came around. For all I know, he could have been anybody. My aunt did the best she could, but she died about three years ago, just before I finished high school. I've been on my own ever since. She was the only family I had left. I was sixteen; there was nobody else except a social worker who cared enough to help me through the tough times after my aunt's death. She helped me enroll in college. If it weren't for her during those tough times, I don't know where I'd be."

"Where is she now?"

Tia smiled and revealed, "She got a better job offer and moved to Atlanta. She told me that I could move there and finish school. There's a world of opportunity in Atlanta for what I like to do. The field is wide open there for me, but I told her no. I wanted to finish here on my own first."

"What is it that you want to do?"

"I'm a makeup artist, but I want to do much more. Special effects for the movies, stuff like that. My aunt had always told me I had big time talent. My instructors also have told me I was very talented. It's a dream I have."

Jahir listened as she conveyed her thoughts. Although he had been a patron through time, not everything was clear to him as he looked on in silence, somewhat confused as it pertained to movies.

Watching him she asked, "You do know what the movies are?"

Jahir replied, "I am familiar, but I have never attended one. Only the images on the television screens that I pass during the night through open blinds and windows."

Tia looked at him and smiled as she reached into her purse and pulled out a picture. It was a before and after picture of a man she had transformed into a monster for a play. Handing it over to him, he stared at it. She explained to him all that it entailed. Fascinated by everything she explained, he became interested in what she did.

"Could you change my face to make me look human again?" he asked.

She looked over at him and gently touched his face. Instinctively, his reflexes caused him to jump back a little while moving his head back slightly.

"Don't be such a wimp," Tia said, giggling. "I'm not going to hurt you."

As she reached out to him again, gently she turned his face to one side examining him, then slowly back to the other side.

"Noooo problem," she replied playfully. "I gotcha."

Jahir smiled. A smile was something he hadn't done for centuries, something that he believed he was no longer capable of pulling out of his almost forgotten former self.

"When do you want me to do it?"

"Soon," he replied. He paused and added, "Like myself, you are also alone in this world, having to find your way, but there is a difference. You have a world of opportunity and a future that can shape your path. I, on the other hand, have only but one recourse—to find Bultizar and end this madness. Afterward, I must resort to an uncertain fate in a world in which I am out of place."

After a brief silence they both looked over the city skyline, Jahir adding, "The streets should have quieted, I shall return you to your home before the hour becomes late."

He leaned over in a crouched position before her. Tia hopped on his back and held on tightly directing him as they moved silently before descending onto the streets below.

Jahir looked at Tia as she hopped off and said, "You're home now and safe."

While he spoke, she could tell that something was wrong.

"What's the matter?" she asked.

He stood silent. He looked around, nose in the air while closing his eyes, as if trying to get his bearings.

Looking over at her, abruptly he said, "I must go." He turned to face the direction from which the two of them had just come. Without answering her question, he simply leaped halfway up the side of the apartment building Then scaling the wall like a cat climbing up a tree, disappearing onto the roof, out of view.

She stood for a moment wondering what had happened before finally, entering her apartment.

Chapter 18:

Big Bad Wolf?

After several hours of speeches and entertainment, the fundraiser was finally coming to an end. Margaret walked over to her boss whispering in his ear. After their discussion, Margaret looked at the two ladies and spoke before leaving. Afterward, Wolf turned his attention towards them, addressing Maria first.

"Thank you for the invite to speak, and for a lovely evening," he said, looking at Terrie. "This has been quite an evening. We'll have that official interview soon. Unfortunately, I have other business to attend and must go," he stated as he walked away.

Terrie looked over to Maria. "It was a nice evening."

Maria smiled. "I have absolutely no complaints," she replied.

"Well, I do have a few things I have to take care of. I need to go, too."

"Okay," she replied as they walked over to the coat closet, retrieving their jackets.

Standing in front of the hotel lobby, Wolf waited for the valet to bring his car around. That evening, he had decided to forego being chauffeured in his pearl white Bentley leaving it home. Instead, he chose to drive himself in his red Ferrari.

Driving around to the entrance, the young valet hopped out of his car. He was excited to have had the opportunity to get behind the wheel of such a vehicle, even if it was around a parking lot.

"Nice ride, Mr. Wolf," he said before handing him his keys.

"If you play your cards right, one day you might own one yourself. Stay focused on the choices you make moving forward."

"I sure will, Mr. Wolf. Thanks for the advice."

"Anytime," Wolf responded.

As he was about to get into his car, Terrie and Maria were exiting the lobby. Maria spotted him and walked over and said, "Nice car. I thought a man of your stature would prefer to be chauffeured."

Wolf smiled. "Every now and then, I love the freedom to go it alone--helps me relate to the less fortunate."

Terrie smiled and said, "Not everyone can feel normal behind the wheel of a Ferrari."

Wolf chuckled, then replied, "Goodnight, ladies!" before pulling off.

The valet arrived with Maria's Camry, handing her the keys.

"Well, it's no Ferrari," she said, as both laughed before getting in and taking off.

While driving, Maria was all bubbly. Looking over at her friend, she said, "Speaking of Wolf, that's the first time I've seen him in person. I never dreamed he was that fine, girl."

"Just like you like them," Terrie responded as both laughed. "He's okay," Terrie added.

"Okay? Stop faking! Girlllll," Maria replied, "you know that man is fine. And his pockets are deeper than the ocean."

"What about the delivery guy?"

Maria looked back at her grinning. "He's nice, something to do. But Nicholas Wolf, on the other hand--that's a long-term investment. That's the hand I wanna play," she said as she displayed her ring finger still absent a ring.

"Well, he may call you sooner or later—that is, if he calls."

"Don't have to," Maria responded, showing Terrie a card, given to her with his name and number on it. "I intend to find out myself sooner than later, if we have that connection."

Terrie looked at Maria, shaking her head and remarked, "Girl, you're so crazy!"

Everything got quiet. With her eyes fixed on the road, Maria glanced at Terrie periodically as she drove along. "I'm sorry things didn't go well with your interview."

"That's okay," Terrie responded, shrugging her shoulders while watching the scenery go by. "It was a little awkward but once his schedule frees up, we'll have our official one."

"You seem to be drifting. What's going on in that head of yours?"

"Nothing really, just thinking about a few things."

"Bobby Grimes. You and that detective," Maria said shaking her head. "You two love birds must be going through another one of your phases. Come to think of it, except for the hospital, I haven't heard you talk about him as much lately."

"Yeah, I know. I think it's our jobs. Before I was attacked, we hadn't spent much time together over these past weeks. That incident brought us a little closer, but there's still a lot of stress. These recent murders haven't helped. They've really gotten him on edge, not to mention having to deal with what happened to me. Plus, the frustration I'm dealing with in trying to pull leads on what's been going on."

Maria pulled in front of Terrie's condo, as the two exchanged hugs. Terrie smiled and said, "Let me go in and unwind a little." After pausing, she added, "I forgot to tell you that I just got a puppy from the shelter."

"A puppy?" Maria responded.

"Yeah, I was doing a short story about pet owners who could no longer keep their pets on my blog. I went over to the shelter to conduct my interview. That's when I saw him. He was the cutest thing! I had to have him."

Maria shook her head and smiled. "You're something else."

"He helps me to relax."

"Yes, you really do need to. What's its name?"

"Max," Terrie replied. "You're right, I really need to, but not now. Too much to do first.

Maria smiled. "Cute name. Well, I'll call you tomorrow, and at least try to relax anyway."

As Maria pulled off, Terrie unlocked the door and walked in to put her things on the table. Then she went over to the cage and picked up her new puppy. As she sat on her recliner with him on her lap, there was a knock on the door.

Probably Maria, she thought as she got up to open the door.

"Gurl, what did I leave in—"

Terrie stopped mid-sentence, surprised to see Grimes standing there.

"—your car," she concluded.

Standing there leaning against the door frame with his head resting on his forearm, was Grimes.

"Bobby? This is a surprise,"

"Hello, baby, I was in the neighborhood. Thought I'd stop by to check on you, make sure you're okay." Looking at the puppy, he added, "Looks like somebody has already beat me to the punch."

They both were happy to see each other.

"With all this stuff going on--these murders, your safety—I've been frustrated and on edge. I've let this stuff get the best of me, and between us. I wanna make it up to you."

Terrie looked down, stepped back from the door, and spoke. "You don't have to stand out there. You can come in."

Closing the door behind him, he said, "Sweetheart, we need to make up, starting tonight. I realize it has been mostly me."

Putting the little dog on the floor, giving him an inviting look she replied, "That sounds good."

Grimes walked slowly over to her and kissed her. Leaning back, looking her into the eyes, he shared, "I can't get you off my mind. I love you, baby."

"I love you, too."

They both resumed their kiss with more passion than they had in a long time. Terrie held him loosely as they both hurriedly began to undress. Backing through her condo with both leaving a trail of clothing on the floor she led him onto her bed. Pulling him down on top of her.

After what had been an evening filled with speeches and promises that were part of the deal associated with high octane socialites with endless pockets, it was now Terrie's time to relax. The frustration and stress that had begun to build was about to be released like an uncapped volcano the moment they embraced. Now engulfed in their own little world, it was their moment.

***

Oblivious to the world, beyond her condo walls that night stood a predator on the prowl. Like a lone wolf free from his pack, Bultizar was again ready to hunt. His blood begun to boil, giving off a signal that he was on the move. Roaming amongst the masses, he viewed them all as sheep, feeling a desire that would prompt his next move.

It had all been a game to him since he arose from his long sleep. The city had much to offer with buildings towering above him like concrete mountains.

He had attended the fundraiser while keeping his true identity concealed. He admired the young reporter and her friend the moment they entered the room. There was something about the two ladies that raised his blood levels, awakening an instinct from his past that flowed through his veins while he waited for the right moment to act. The excitement of it all drove his desire to be alone and on the prowl. But this night neither woman was his target.

It was a Friday night under the lights. He was on the move, his eyes were electric gazing everywhere filled with the anticipation of people looking to have a good time—some in groups, others alone or one on one in their private little cove. There were those that were lonely, seeking whatever attention they could find that would soothe their lonely hearts. They were the ones whose desires Bultizar was seeking. Slowly driving down the busy street, under the moonlight shining overhead, he pulled into a lot and handed his keys to one of the attendants.

Bultizar, now on foot moving amongst his potential prey, looking for the victim that suited his lust. The knowledge that his enemy was somewhere out there stalking him also thrilled him that much more. It was all bizarre—a monster hunting a monster, the difference being that Bultizar took pleasure in what and who he was. In his heart, he hoped this game would never end.

He had the looks that women would literally die for, which was one of his traps. Dressed in the finest clothes with a diamond on his finger that sparked like the brightest star, Wolf was a living billboard advertising that he had something to offer to a young gullible female seeking benefits. Stalking the New York nightlife, he frequented clubs, bars, and hangouts the nightlife offered.

As he walked casually along the busy strip, the people driven by the thrill of the night were the prey. With the eyes of a wolf piercing the darkness, he searched, hoping to make eye contact with one of the beauties he would choose.

Finally, he walked into a crowded bar called Tahoes' to investigate a little closer. The crowd was nice and was slowly beginning to fill. He stood in a corner, patiently assessing its patrons until someone caught his eye. Sitting at the bar with her legs crossed in a red dress with matching stilettos was a young, beautiful woman of Asian descent. With long black hair, sipping on a drink Bultizar had caught her eye from across the room. It was mutual as both exchanged stares.

Seductively, she winked at him. The evening was still young, and she was looking for someone that would offer to buy her another drink.

Making his way to her, the two never lost eye contact. Taking a seat next to her, he looked over at her and asked, "What's the lady drinking?"

"White Russian," she replied.

From the top of her head to her shoes, he looked at her as though he wanted to devour her. She enjoyed every minute of it and would have let him. She didn't know that it wasn't in a manner that she had in mind.

Signaling the bartender he ordered her drink. Then said, "I'll have the same," He turned to her and asked, "Why is such a beautiful woman out alone tonight, dressed to kill, and in red? Don't you believe in fairy tales?" He laughed.

Also laughing, in response she said, "I'm not Little Red Riding Hood, and I'm not afraid of the Big Bad Wolf. Why should I be? My prince has just arrived to protect me."

"That's what I do," he replied, "I'm Nick. What's your name?"

"Sandra," she replied. "I'm into fashion, so when I put on a dress, I like to make a statement."

The bartender arrived with their drinks. They both took a sip and began to engage in conversation that opened up more with each drink Sandra consumed. She was a twenty-four-year-old and a receptionist at Glow Enterprises, one of the top fashion magazines in the city. Lonely and frustrated, she had been involved in a few failed relationships with guys who made promises coated with lies that they had no intention in keeping. She was tired of being depressed and decided tonight was the night to put the past behind her. She was looking for something new, a desire she openly expressed. Before taking another sip, Bultizar offering a toast lifted his glass in the air.

"To something different," he said.

Sandra smiled and raised her glass, then took a sip.

"It feels a little confined in here. Would you like to take a stroll in the fresh air under the night lights?"

"Sure," she replied. "I'd love that my handsome prince." They both laughed.

Bultizar signaled to the bartender regarding their tab. After paying, he offered his arm for her to take hold of. As they walked, she drew closer to him as they made their way through the crowd and exited the bar.

As they strolled down the populated street exchanging thoughts, it was almost midnight. Many that were around them had a similar look in their eyes. Some were much like her, out looking for love. Others just out and about, looking to have a good time.

The night felt special to her. Although they had just met, he made her feel safe and secure. The two continued to stroll casually down the strip, mingling amongst the crowd. People entered back and forth from packed nightclubs.

More than thirty blocks away, Jahir's senses were aroused. Unlike in the past which were vague and distant, this was different. They were stronger but not strong enough to be certain until Bultizar began to change. Jahir felt a sense of anxiety coupled with an urgency that started him on his hunt. If he moved too quickly, he may overshoot his position, which would be critical with time being the essence in the event that Bultizar transformed into the golden wolf. All he knew was that the beast was still in his human form and he was out there, on the move.

He had to wait for the change to know exactly where to find him. He could only hope to reach Bultizar in time to prevent him from killing again, knowing that the odds were against him in preventing it from happening. Nonetheless, he had to try as he leaped across buildings and streets, closing the gap between them. He moved in the direction his instincts were leading him.

While back on the ground, Sandra's mind was so fixed on her escort she hardly realized that the crowd had begun to thin. It was late and Sandra wasn't sure where she was, but they were exactly where Bultizar wanted them to be.

Taking the liberty, he wrapped his arm around Sandra's shoulder as they walked in a synchronized rhythm, Bultizar pulling her closer to him. Comforted by his presence, she looked him in his eyes, and then reached around his waist, solidifying their bond. They must have walked for over an hour. Bultizar stopped for a moment and turned to face her.

Looking into his eyes, Sandra felt there was something different about him, something she couldn't place a finger on, but she brushed it off. While they were walking, she occasionally looked over at him. She saw something she didn't see earlier when they were sitting at the bar. It was a gold chain around his neck. She was so focused on his face and his gray eyes that she simply didn't notice.

"What's that around your neck?" she asked.

Reaching over she gently held it, lifting it up toward her, he replied, "My family symbol."

"It's beautiful," she said, staring at it. "I've never seen anything like this. A wolf. That's your family symbol?"

"Yes," he replied, "but not any wolf. A golden one."

"It's so unique, made of wood and trimmed in gold. It must be worth a lot of money," she replied.

Bultizar smiled and said, "It's priceless."

He then took hold of her waist, gently pulling her close to him. Staring up into his eyes, she noticed something she hadn't before.

"I thought you had pretty eyes, but I didn't realize just how pretty they were. The moonlight reflecting off of them makes them appear lunar, like something I saw on the Discovery Channel. They're pretty, but wild."

Bultizar smiled. "The better to see you with, my dear," he joked, using an old cliché. "Must be the wolf in me," he added, howling up at the moon.

The howl startled her. She became nervous and backed away from him.

"That's not at all funny, especially with the stuff that has been happening over the past several weeks, all those murders."

Bultizar looked at her and said, "I'm sorry, I didn't mean to frighten you. I was only playing, but I do apologize. That was poor judgment on my part. Do you forgive me?"

Pausing for a moment, her tension eased. Bultizar stepped forward and kissed her, gently at first and then aggressively.

Loving every moment, she had wanted to do that with him all night. Bultizar then reached down, cuffing her bottom firmly with both hands. She looked back to where he was holding her and then back at him enjoying the moment.

"You like that huh? No worries I don't mind."

She then reached up, cuffing him by the back of his head, and pulled him back toward her so they could continue their kiss.

When they stopped, she looked around and then at Bultizar. "Wow, where's everybody?"

They were now alone on an empty street surrounded by empty buildings.

"I think we need to be heading back," She said." After all, these streets are not safe."

Agreeing with her, he said, "I know a shortcut but before we go, let me taste your lips again."

"Yes, a little one," she said, stepping backwards. Bultizar then grabbed hold of her once again, drawing her close.

As he held her, she felt his embrace getting tighter to the point of becoming uncomfortable. Opening her eyes, she said, "Stop, you're hurting me. Let me go."

Bultizar smiled asking, "What's wrong? Don't you like being in my arms? Don't I make you feel safe? After all, I am here to protect you."

Now frightened, she struggled to break free from him. He laughed, while his voice began to take on a heavier tone. He had now begun to terrify her.

"Somebody, help me, please!" she cried out then screamed.

A couple passing by in their car heard her from behind the vacant buildings, prompting them to call 911, but they didn't know exactly where as the screams echoed off the surrounding buildings.

At that moment, Jahir moved toward her now several blocks away. With his senses heightened, he had felt Bultizar's presence earlier that evening but wasn't sure where. As he got closer, images began to appear, like blurred images of a video that slowly began to focus. The werewolf was beginning to change as Jahir watched through a terrified woman's eyes. Everything was beginning to unfold. On the street below, Sandra was helpless, unable to break free of Bultizar's grasp no matter how hard she struggled.

While she cried out for help, Bultizar was changing before her eyes as she watched in horror as he once again took form.

With a single swipe of his clawed hands, he raked them across her face, stunning her before digging them deeply over her mouth forming a seal to keep her from screaming. The blood from her wound spurted out and began streaming down her face.

With her cries now muffled, the golden wolf focused on his prey. With her face covered in blood, she looked into the eyes of the beast as he released his grip. She screamed one last time as loud as she could which pleased him. The excitement of the moment gave him a rush; for him, it was a game. Her screams thrilled him before he completed his goal.

With Bultizar fully transformed into the golden wolf, the images were now crystal clear in Jahir's head, guiding him to Bultizar like a beacon in the night. He knew exactly where to find them, but the only question remained was whether or not he could reach her in time. His speed and movements could barely be followed. He was like a blur, a shadow passing in the night.

He jumped across the tops of buildings from ledge to ledge in leaps and bounds without missing a step, ten stories above. He covered distances that no one could fathom, but the question remained—*was he too late?*

Nearly there, this was the moment for which he had waited centuries. This was the opportunity to free himself and save one more life. Jahir felt the teeth of the werewolf as they sank into the woman's body, his claws tearing through her flesh, which pushed him even harder.

He was but moments away when the images of the wolf through the woman's eyes suddenly went blank. He heard the howl of the werewolf as if to mock him before the pain struck him wherever the woman felt his fangs and claws. Although the images were gone, Bultizar's presence was still felt.

Moving as fast as he could, he leapt twenty feet to clear the building's edge, landing lightly on his feet ten stories below. Immediately grasping his chest as though someone had torn his heart from its cradle, he crouched to his knees.

Grimacing in pain, he looked around for his enemy and the woman. What he found was a trail of blood leading into another open doorway of another vacant building. Again, Bultizar was gone--claiming yet another life and transformed back into human form, eluding him once more.

Standing there, he spotted her. Like the others, her heart was taken, and he was unable to stop him. With the flashing lights and sirens of approaching police cars all around him, he had to depart.

The pain from Bultizar's latest victim was still resonating through his body. Quickly, he scaled the building walls, disappearing in the dark. Now hidden, he blamed himself each time he failed to arrive speedily enough to save them. Unlike days of old when everything was a distant memory like an old filtered tape, the images in his head were fresh, clear as crystal, making him truly desperate to find Bultizar.

Jahir attempted to gather his thoughts. The police arrived to cord off everything. It was another gruesome scene--another victim for a family to grieve. They waited for the crime scene investigators who would attempt to put another murder puzzle together with pieces that had yet to fit.

While the police were left to search for answers, and his greatest enemy once again left frustrated, Bultizar was experiencing great satisfaction while fulfilling his desire.

Chapter 19:
A Heart-Filled Place

Like he had always done, Bultizar managed to elude his pursuer while obtaining his prize. Back in human form, he arrived at his destination, moving down into a dark basement corridor that led to a concealed room filled with debris. Clearing it to the side, he uncovered a hidden compartment in the floor and opened it. Inside was a wooden chest. It had six compartments with two of them already filled: the hearts of Stacey Thomas and Kerri Barnes, leaving four that remained empty.

Kneeling over it, he went into his pocket and pulled out the plastic bag with the heart of his latest victim, Sandra Woo. Taking it out of the bag he stared at it, cherishing it, he carefully placed it in one of the open compartments. It was another successful night that drew him closer to his goal.

Staring down at the box he paused, and thought to himself, *Three claimed, Now, three to go*, as he covered it back up.

As he walked away, he stopped, looked back feeling a sense of exuberance. He quietly returned to his place of refuge.

***

Back at Terrie's, the evening couldn't have gone better. After intimacy, they were having a quiet moment. Snuggled tightly against one another, Grimes sat up behind her, slowly running his fingers through her hair. He leaned over and kissed her on her cheek, then on her forehead where the scar from her attack was left as a reminder.

"The night you were attacked," "I keep thinking that I should have been there for you."

"How could you?" "You were at work doing your job, she replied"

"Yeah, I was doing my job, but had I called you like I was supposed to, I would've known you were working late and would've driven the car over to the station and took you home."

"No, it wouldn't have mattered. It was no one's fault."

There was something else on the detective's mind that had been eating away at him—something that he hadn't been able to shake.

He asked, "That guy who came to your rescue, have you been able to remember any other details?"

Pressing back against him, she replied, "It all happened so fast. It was a strange moment when he appeared. I only got a glimpse. All I remember there were bodies flying everywhere. He was so animalistic."

"Yeah, that's what those punks who attacked you said—that they couldn't remember anything either mimicking everything you said.

"I remember his eyes; they reflected the light like our family cat we had when I was a little girl. Every time the porch light shined in his face, the light would reflect off his eyes."

"That was the same thing I read in the police report. The night Mills was killed, the joggers that were with him also said they saw what they believed to be a man, that his eyes had also reflected light from the park lights before disappearing into the woods. Mills got off two shots but we didn't find any traces of blood, only shell casings. At that range, it's hard to fathom how anybody could miss; but evidently, he did. We're still looking but we have no leads on the guy. He could be a valuable witness, but for me our number one suspect."

Terrie exhaled. "That whole evening was strange, but there was something else that was eerie about that night, even before all this had happened. The night of Kerri Barnes's murder while I was about to leave the scene, I felt like I was being watched—from the time I left to the moment I began walking to the subway station."

"Your guardian angel."

"If so, he delivered that night," she replied.

Afterward, everything got quiet. Grimes looked at her before caressing her again.

Reaching over, she turned off the light and the action between them repeated again. The sounds of the night once again commanded the evening. Pleasure and passion were eventually replaced by silence as the night moved on.

At 3:30 AM, Grimes's cell phone vibrated across the nightstand, over and over until finally Terrie opened her eyes. Turning to see it was his phone she shook him.

"Bobby! Bobby, your phone."

Opening his eyes, he reached over, and answered.

"Yeah," he responded, still groggy from his sleep.

"Chief," Poles responded on the other end. "I think you better get over here. We have another one in the Bronx!"

"What?" Grimes replied.

The words woke him like an alarm clock. Gently releasing his embrace, he sat up on the side of the bed while his partner gave him the details.

"I couldn't sleep. This case has been like an anchor on my brain. I needed to get it off my mind so I came in. I decided to take this time and look over a few things. That's when the call came in, and I immediately called you. Another female was killed, and her heart was removed. I'm on the scene now."

Taking a deep breath, Grimes replied, "I'm on my way."

After their conversation, he stared at his cell phone a moment before laying it down.

"What's wrong, honey?" Terrie asked.

Grimes looked over at her and said, "There's been another murder." He paused for a second, "Another young woman with her heart removed."

"What!" Terrie exclaimed. She sat up, then ran her hand through her hair, sharing his concern. "What's happening here?" she asked. "What kind of animal is loose on these streets? Of all the assaults and senseless shootings that go on out here, nothing even begins to compare to this."

Grimes leaned over and kissed her. "I gotta go. John is on the scene waiting for me."

He got up and began getting dressed. Reaching over to open her nightstand, Terrie pulled out a pack of cigarettes and then lit one.

Looking over at her, he said, "I thought you stopped."

"I did," she replied. "With everything going on, I need something to help settle my nerves."

Nearly dressed, he replied, "That's not going to help. All you're doing is killing yourself."

Irritated by his response, she replied, "Bobby, please leave it alone. That's one of your problems—you don't know when to quit. I'm not a child."

"You're right. You're not a child, but when you respond like that, you could've fooled me. I'll call you later," Grimes said as he opened the door to leave.

"Don't bother," she replied. "I'll call you."

He stopped and looked back at her. "You know that's one of your problems. You can't be told anything, even if it's for your own good." He left.

When the door shut, Terrie grunted, hurling the pillow at the door. As she grabbed the ashtray, she quickly put out her cigarette and placed her hand on her forehead as she sat a moment. She stood and walked to the bathroom, staring at herself in the mirror. Beyond their squabble, the news of another murder was disheartening. It was another tragic story to cover with grieving loved ones to interview. Like Grimes, she, too, had a lot vested in these events, trying to gather whatever information she could find that would help.

Max whined and licked her feet. Even he sensed there was something wrong. As she picked him up, she looked at him, kissing him on his whiskers before petting him. When she walked over to put him back into his cage, her phone rang. Answering it, she thought it was Grimes calling to apologize. She glanced at her caller ID and saw that it was her cameraman.

"We have another one," he said.

"I know. Bobby was over and got the call before he rushed out of here. He didn't give any details."

"They're bad just like the last two. Me and Buddy are here at the station picking up the equipment. We'll swing by and pick you up. Can you be ready in, say, twenty minutes?"

"I'll be ready in ten. Just come on."

After hanging up the phone, she started thinking and then made another call to one of her street sources. Known simply as Joe, he liked to keep things simple in case his name came up to the wrong set of ears that could someday cost him more than he could pay. For the latest incident in the Bronx, she knew this was his part of town.

"Hello?" he answered after a couple of rings, in a low voice.

"Yeah, this is me," Terrie replied.

"This sounds like Ms. Collins," he laughed.

"This is serious," she cautioned.

"Isn't it always when you call? Okay. What is it you want?" Before she could answer, he added, "Um, let me see, could it be about this crime scene with all these cops, ambulances, and teams of reporters that you are not a part of?"

"Okay, Joe, cut it. I need any and all the information you can get for me. I'm getting ready while waiting on my crew to come get me."

"And what's in it for me this time?"

"The usual. Fifty bucks."

"You do know this is the twenty-first century, right?" sarcastically replying. "With the way things are going, everyone is at a loss, including the police. My fee is going to double on this one."

Shaking her head, she pondered, "I don't know what's worse—these streets or you shaking me down."

"Now, now, Ms. Collins. Information ain't cheap, especially if you have to put in serious work to get it."

"I'll see you in about forty-five minutes."

Before he could respond, she hung up and then jumped into the shower.

***

After arriving on the scene, Grimes headed to the doorway where the woman's body was found. When he got over there, Poles told him that there weren't any actual witnesses there. He told him that a couple passing by stopped when they heard the screams. They were the ones who called and reported to the police.

They told the officers what they had heard pointing to the alley. When they followed the police in the alley, they told them they remembered her at Tahoes' Bar and Grill." Earlier in the evening, "She was sitting and talking with a guy. Poles explained.

"Tahoes'," Grimes replied. "That's ten blocks away."

"Yeah," Poles responded. "The two were sitting across from her. They described the man as having long blond hair and wearing a blue sports blazer. He was talking to her for a while before leaving the bar together."

"How did they happen to be at this location? Do they live around here or is this strictly a coincidence?"

Poles responded, "They said that they live only a few blocks up the street." After re-reading the couple's statement he looked over to his partner. "We now have our first real lead. A person that now seems to be directly linked to at least one other victim."

"Our street game now has to double," Grimes replied, "I want to interview that couple. I need to find out everything that they saw in detail. We got to catch this monster and in a hurry. We need every contact, every eye we have on the street for this one—including any security surveillance camera footage."

Looking over at Grimes, Poles nodded and replied, "I'm on it." Pausing for a moment, he thought about something. "Hey Chief, you know the thing that baffles me about this whole deal?"

"What?"

"Those strange tracks and the dude that matches the description of the guy who's been hailed as a hero. Where does he play in all of this? We have the tracks of an animal and someone fitting the description of one; it all seems crazy yet the evidence is undeniable. When everything plays out, he may also be tied to all of this. No one has seen this guy on the streets, though. With the features that were described, how could anyone miss seeing him anywhere?

"With so much violence and blood," Poles continued, "I'm shocked there hasn't been more physical evidence left behind of this killer as well, other than a strand or two of hair and a set of paw prints that don't make sense. You would think there was some kind of evidence left under the victim's nails at least. All the evidence points to frontal attacks."

Looking over at his partner, Grimes said, "None of the forensic reports from any of the previous murders have come back yet to reveal anything. Hopefully, the results this evening will render some new clues other than claw and teeth marks from what I can't even begin to know—only the blood of the victims, which so far leads us nowhere. On one hand, it appears she was attacked by some kind of animal, but the last time anyone saw them, they were seen with men.

"Another question is, if they were indeed attacked and mutilated by some sort of animal," he continued, "then why haven't we found any of these men dead alongside them? This is New York City. I know the streets can be rough but these aren't the jungles of South America, Africa, or Asia. There are no lions and tigers running around freely here, other than at the zoo. And . . . they're in cages."

Grimes and his partner were at a loss for words. Their frustration was mapped on their faces.

"Well, partner," Poles replied as he walked away, "let me find the couple who remembers seeing Ms. Woo and see what else I can find out."

Just beyond the alley entrance, Terrie and her news crew had just arrived. While they were preparing their equipment, Terrie looked over toward a small crowd that had begun to gather.

She searched for her eyes and ears she had on the street. Moving forward from behind the crowd was a short, black slender guy about thirty-five years old. It was Joe, her source for a few years.

Finding a more secluded spot, he gave her the signal to join him. Once she came over, he looked around, making sure no one else was around them.

They had previously talked on the phone an hour earlier. She wanted to know had he seen or heard anything since. He told her that there was a couple that saw the victim and a man with her. They had already told the police what they saw.

"Were there any other reporters around?" she asked.

"Nah," he responded. "I was standing behind them and heard everything but so far, that's all I got."

Satisfied, she slipped him two fifty-dollar bills.

He chuckled and said, "It's always a pleasure doing business with you."

With a contemptuous smile, she walked back across the street to her crew. When she saw Grimes standing with his partner, she walked toward them.

Although their words were still fresh, she put it behind her. This wasn't the time or the place to revisit the issue.

Grimes was surprised to see her. Barely an hour ago, he had left her in bed as they exchanged words. He also figured that the station would have sent a different crew. What started off being a beautiful evening was cut short with the call that brought him to yet another nightmare.

"I'm surprised that the station didn't send another team on such short notice."

"My crew was up and already at the station loading up. They called soon as you left and told me they were coming to get me."

Turning her attention to the business at hand, she asked if there were any new viable information that was beyond the obvious. He then gave her what details he could, which was more information than the other news crews had yet to acquire.

She learned that unlike the recent murders in which the two were killed and feasted upon—their first witness, Harvey Lancaster, in Brooklyn, and the jogger in Central Park—Sandra Woo was murdered in the same way as the other two women, which she found to be very disturbing on a personal level.

She had interviewed the female victims' families and had gotten to know them more intimately, thereby gaining their trust. They gave her a detailed window into their lives, giving her the feeling that she was part of the family. And now there was yet another who had died in the same brutal way.

While this was taking place below, above them, Jahir was watching as he sat patiently listening to everything.

He pierced the darkness with the eyes of a cat. His hearing amplified as though he were in the midst of the conversation with hopes of gathering any information that would help guide him close so that when Bultizar transformed he wouldn't be too late to stop him.

Finding Bultizar wasn't the only thing on his mind. Everything about Terrie drew him to her.

Somehow, her involvement was important, something that he sensed. He didn't know why it wasn't clear; he knew, though, he had to stay close. Unable reveal himself to her, he remained aloof. He was the protector she didn't know she had.

Jahir was deeply troubled by this night. He was closer than he had ever been in ending these murders, but at times, he felt as though he was even farther away from ridding himself from his curse.

With the outcome always the same, another soul lost to the fangs of a monster as his frustration grew.

Being so close to his enemy, closer than he had ever been, he knew he could no longer afford to simply wait until nightfall. He had to search for clues both day and night, running the risk of exposure during daylight hours.

Bultizar's prey was now more abundant. He had more choices in the present--the thrill of the hunt with so many to fulfill his morbid appetite. Now hunting in the most intriguing jungle of them all—one made of concrete and steel.

Fully on the prowl and short on time, Jahir could no longer rely solely on his instincts or his usual movements. He must move about on amongst the masses.

Around the clock, he must search for whatever information he could find to help him. More desperate than ever he decided to call on the only one he could trust—his young friend, Tia. He needed her talents and sought her out to help disguise himself so that he could accomplish what he needed to do.

He remembered the pictures she showed him of her work. He needed her to make him appear human which would allow him to go places where he could never go.

Her talents weren't the only things he needed from her. There was information she may have been able to access. Helping him in this way would also put her at risk, which was something he didn't want, but he was running out of options.

Etched in his memories were the words of the scarlet blood moon spoken by the old sorceress. They remained as clear in his head as the day she first spoke to them--that day both he and Bultizar were damned.

Sitting quietly, he watched and listened to everything he deemed important, especially that of Grimes and his partner, knowing they were investigating these murders and if anyone held answers, they would.

***

Turning on the television after arriving to his place, Bultizar was curious as to whether his deeds had been discovered.

To his delight, he was just in time to catch the breaking news as it was being reported. As he stood in front of the TV, he was thrilled beyond measure. It was all amusing to him; this was the mind of a deranged killer, regardless of his form.

The only difference between Bultizar and his beastly form was that as a werewolf, he was nearly unstoppable, and he took pleasure in it. He stood and watched while Terrie was reporting live on the scene. With his eyes glued to the television, she had always fascinated him whenever he saw her face.

"The Butcher of the Bronx has claimed yet another victim," she said, giving her report. His latest victim was a twenty-four-year-old woman named Sandra Woo. She was found brutally murdered, also with her heart removed in the same way as the two women previously found behind a group of vacant buildings.

"The police are looking for a young white male in his late twenties or early thirties with blond hair last seen wearing a ponytail and a blue sports blazer," she continued. "He was also last seen with Woo at Tahoe's Bar and Grill in the Bronx. Police are asking anyone with any information on this individual to contact the police. Police are also looking for possible connections related to the recent attacks in Central Park, and in Brooklyn, where, the lives of two men were also taken.

He is the prime suspect in this case and possibly another. This has been the third female victim whose heart was removed out of the five murders. The two male victims were partially consumed, but their hearts were not taken, bringing into question whether these crimes were committed by the same individual. Each of the women were found in the rear of old vacant buildings coincidently owned by Nicholas Wolf."

Bultizar remained focused on the television as the beautiful reporter gave the details of the women being identical in both age and body type.

"So far," she continued, "city officials and the New York Police Department are baffled by the ferocity of the attacks and motive of the killer or killers. Some believe there may possibly have been some type of religious cult behind these strings of murders, but so far, there has been no evidence to substantiate those claims."

Grabbing the remote, he turned off the television and walked over to the mirror. As he stood there staring at himself his thoughts drifted back in time to past memories. The events that were taking place in the present—the hysteria, the panic, the fear amongst the masses—reminded him of the events that had taken place centuries ago.

Chapter 20:

Gevaudan

1766

It was the year 1766 in the small province of Gevaudan, high in the Margeride Mountains of Central France. Three years prior, Bultizar had arrived there under the assumed name of Auguste Cartier. This was the identity of one of his previous victims over a century earlier—a wanderer whose origins were unknown.

Cartier was one of many faceless persons that he had claimed, building a hidden fortune before fading away again. Dressed in the finest clothing of the time—wearing silk garments and golden tassels—his attire was fitting to that of royalty as it caught the eyes of the local ladies desiring to be in his company. He immediately caught the attention of the town officials. This along with his mannerisms gave him an immediate aura of respect.

Although Cartier was a man of great wealth and education, his origins were a clouded mystery. He was able to read and write at a time when education was at a premium. Understanding the documents of the day gave him an advantage over the common people. His wealth coupled with education bought him power and acceptance, a place of prominence that no one questioned.

Whatever was in his past or wherever it may have led, no one cared. His secret was well hidden as he walked freely amongst the innocent once again. The wealth that he had accumulated over time allowed him to purchase large portions of land. He had become the richest and the most powerful the land owner within this small community,

For the past two years, there had been a wave of killings that had plagued the French countryside. It was believed to be a wolf, or some other wild beast, while some believed it to be much more. Rumors and tales of a werewolf had spread amongst the locals, causing the demand for local authorities to take action.

Being the most powerful landowner in the region, the people began looking to him for help. They grew weary of living in fear, with many losing their loved ones to some creature after the sun set. They pleaded to Cartier, that he would utilize his resources to influence and petition the government for aid.

The attention to the region steadily grew, eventually reaching the ears of a few government officials. Cartier knew it would be only a matter of time before the government sent troops to the region in force. He knew it would obstruct his freedom of the hunt, something he enjoyed. He couldn't help himself. It was all too easy for him. To pluck sheep from this flock without a shepherd to protect them was too irresistible, knowing his time there was nearing an end, and it would be time to move on.

Before he left, he would have something special planned for all those wishing to put an end to their nightmare. Not wanting the government involved, Cartier came forth offering a handsome reward to anyone that could bring the head of the killer back to the township. He set a date, a time, and a place so that everyone involved would begin at the same time. And with such a large reward—a chest full of gold coins and acres of land—whoever claimed it would become wealthy themselves, so no one would bother to be suspicious. The generous reward caught the attention of bounty hunters and trackers in the region, along with anyone who was old enough to carry a musket.

After weeks of petitioning for the hunt, roughly forty men and women showed up with the hope of claiming the reward for themselves. For about a month, they trickled in until finally, the day of the hunt had arrived. As sunset rapidly approached, they gathered in the courtyard. Cartier, who also participated, stood before everyone while his secret remained intact. The whole village came to watch as they prepared for the hunt.

With two of his servants flanked at his side, along with men and women holding torches and muskets. They waited for him to give his speech. Looking over at the crowd, his eyes glistened. He was as eager to begin the search as those who had come to collect the prize, except he had a much darker purpose.

"To all," Cartier declared, "I stand before you to warn that what you seek is more than just a wolf, but a creature of the night with supernatural powers. Bullets of lead will not stop it. Only with those of silver may you be able to kill the creature we seek, for it is not a bear nor a wolf, nor anything of natural birth, but something much more. A werewolf stalks these hills!" he continued, shouting. "Only when the moon is full shall we be able to find and kill it. The one who claims the life of the monster will possess the riches of their dreams."

When he spoke of a werewolf, everyone became quiet, looked at one another, and began talking amongst themselves.

Then a heavy voice in the crowd shouted, "A werewolf!"

He moved forward through the crowd. A mountain of a man standing six feet 9 and over three hundred pounds, having a thick beard and hair as red as fire. His appearance was as rugged as the mountains that surrounded the village. He carried two musket rifles and two handguns, along with three Danish boar hounds that each were nearly the size of a pony—one brindle, one black, and the other a mixture of the two, wearing spiked collars and muzzles made of iron. They were meaner that anything that roamed the woods, whether bear or boar. He along with the others had heard of the bounty, which was more coin than anyone had ever seen.

When he reached the front of the crowd, he proclaimed, "We are all armed with lead, but none of us have any silver. We all have heard these stories and legends of werewolves before. I myself have never believed in such tales. Nonetheless, according to these stories only silver can kill a werewolf."

Another shouted, "What the big man speaks is the truth!"

Then he asked Bultizar, "Why now do you make the claim that what we are hunting is a werewolf, knowing none of us would have silver bullets?"

"Who are you?" Cartier asked. "I have never seen anyone of your stature among these lands."

"I am Philippe Pierre," he replied, "a hunter and tracker from a small village far to the north." His disposition was coarse and gruff, a reflection of the man that had been shaped by the harsh life in the wilderness.

Cartier turned to one of his servants. He nodded for him to go into the stable and bring out a cart that was stored there. When he returned, it was filled with bullets made of silver. There were also daggers and swords laced in silver along with wreaths lined with garlic and wolf's bane to be placed around the necks of anyone partaking in the hunt for added protection. Unbeknownst to anyone, Cartier had spent weeks preparing for that day, taking the time to forge those weapons alone.

"Come get your ammunition and garlic wreaths, for nightfall is upon us, and it is time that we go and hunt the beast," he said.

Pierre being skeptical, he shouted, "A full moon? I have heard of many attacks occurring when there was no such lunar event."

"That is true," Cartier replied, "but it is when the moon is at its fullest when the monster will reveal itself, and that night is now upon us. Tonight, we must track and kill it."

"You say 'we'," Pierre replied.

"Yes, I, too, will partake in the hunt."

"Why do you take such a risk?" Pierre asked. "Isn't that why you put up such a lofty reward, or is it that you really don't want to honor it and save yourself from paying such a sum?"

Looking him in his eyes, Cartier replied, "If I kill the wolf, then the reward will be split evenly amongst you for taking such a risk."

Pierre became silent, pausing a moment. Skeptical of his response, he said, "We will see," as he joined the rest in taking his portion of silver and garlic.

Darkness was nearly upon them. Cartier signaled for the hunt to begin while he kept a watchful eye on Pierre. They began just before the last glimmer of light disappeared behind the trees. A little more than an hour had passed since they had begun. The dense fog rested on the ground around them like a blanket, making it difficult to see even with their own torches. The chill of the evening had turned colder as they slowly disappeared into an overcast darkness.

From the distance his blood boiled, triggering a change. Cartier watched as some began spreading out, setting their own paths. Although some tried to conceal their trepidation by holding both their guns and reefs close to their bodies, the fear was clearly etched on their faces.

Now in the form of the blonde werewolf, he began to pursue the man giant as they moved farther into the wilderness. As the night progressed, the wind began to pick up speed, moving the clouds across the sky while briefly revealing the stars throughout the evening to Cartier's advantage.

It was deathly silent, only the breaking of twigs by Pierre's steps could be heard. Suddenly, breaking the silence was the sound of his hounds barking as there was movement all around followed by a heavy growl. Upon hearing this, he blindly fired his musket twice into the forest. One shot hit one of his dogs, killing it. The other two dogs began to attack the growling beast. It was the werewolf, but they were no match against the beast which slashed one of the dogs nearly in half with the other sharing its fate. For the first time in his life, the big man was afraid. He had reloaded his musket aiming in all directions not knowing which direction the attack would come in the pitch darkness. Everything went silent.

Coming up behind him before he could react, Cartier wounded Pierre with its claws, as he fell to his knees. This was a game he sometimes loved to play with his victims before the final strike. Bleeding heavily from his wound, he grasped it with one hand. Holding his sidearm up with the other ready to fire. Now standing before him with massive fangs on display, the werewolf quickly charged him as Pierre got off a shot hitting the him in the chest. Having no effect, Cartier sank his fangs into Pierre's body as he keeled over.

Cartier was determined that the night would be one filled with screams and terror to keep fear in the hearts of the people, including Pierre, who was still alive on the ground surrounded by his lifeless dogs. With eyes aglow, Cartier moved forward through the darkness to slay all in his path responding to the action. In the distance, he could see hunters losing their nerve—hearing his growl and the screams of the victims he tortured—as they fled back toward the village.

Like sheep, they were being corralled together before the slaughter. Fearful to venture out individually, they were no longer the hunters but the hunted, now relying on each other for protection. Cartier had drastically reduced their numbers. As they stopped to assess their surroundings, they found themselves in the middle of an open field surrounded by rolling hills, with only thick cloud cover above them. The cold, harsh winds left them to huddle close together for warmth. Suddenly, the winds whisked the clouds away, emerging to reveal a moon shining at its fullest.

The golden wolf stood atop the highest point of a hill. His monstrous silhouette the first thing visible, boldly looking down at his pursuers. The light of the moon reflected off his body to reveal his golden appearance. He lifted his head toward the pale moon and gave off a chilling howl that unnerved the hunters below. Some panicked and fled while others fired their muskets filled with the silver bullets he had given them. Reloading as quickly as they could over and over again, they fired into their target, causing the blond beast to fall backward as it lay motionless, eyes and mouth wide open, appearing lifeless. With his tongue hanging from the side of his mouth, they thought him dead.

After a few minutes, they moved in closer arguing over who would claim the bounty. Since Auguste Cartier was nowhere to be found, they considered him to be counted amongst the dead. They surrounded its body as it lay motionless, glassy-eyed, and riddled with silver bullets. As they lowered their guns, some poked it to make certain that the creature was truly dead. Finally, there were cries of joy as they began to celebrate their victory.

Unsheathing a large knife one of the female trackers was about to claim his head. Slowly moving closer, her knife ready, she leaned forward staring into his eyes.

Before she could move or say a word, Cartier focused his vision and grabbed her by the throat ripping it from her. Her blood splattered as Cartier sprang to his feet before letting out another howl. He revealed his fangs once more just before the slaughter. He went through his pursuers with a savagery that was unimaginable, tearing through flesh and bone as quickly as the blowing winds raged through the forest around them.

Those able to reload their weapons fired at the creature, but to no avail. He tore through them all. Body parts were scattered around the open field like discarded waste. Within minutes, he had slaughtered all who remained.

Those who had tried to flee, he swiftly ran them down and slaughtered them along the forest edge. It was a killing frenzy in which he had taken great delight.

Of those that had lost their lives that night, there was one he savored the most. It was Pierre, who he had left alive for last, crippling him so that he couldn't run away. Cartier had intentionally wounded him, choosing him for his more personal desires. He had been the most vocal, as well as, the most arrogant, mocking him before it all began. It was now time for him to pay.

Pierre struggled to get to his feet. Every time he tried, he'd fall back to his knees. Again and again, he attempted to stand but each time it harbored the same results falling back to the ground, until finally trying to crawl to get away. Like a cat toying with a mouse before the kill, Cartier moved a little closer. Pierre grunted while struggling to move forward.

Cartier leaned over him so closely that Pierre could feel the warmth of his breath. Tired of the game, it was time to end it. He walked behind the wounded giant, and in one swipe of his claws, pierced Pierre's spine-- paralyzing him below the chest. He struggled to turn and face the monster. With blood spurting from his wounds, he wanted it to end. Cartier turned him over as he looked up into the face of death as it smiled at him, revealing his teeth but with one final surprise. Cartier briefly revealed to Pierre his human face before returning back to that of the wolf. With his fear now magnified and with all his strength, he turned his body in a futile attempt to crawl away using but his arms.

Positioning himself Cartier opened his mouth as wide as he could. Then sank his teeth to the back of his neck like a pair of hooks, lifting him off the ground like a wolf lifting its cub. With Pierre's lifeless body dangling from his mouth, he carried off his prey to feast on him at his leisure.

Cartier remembered how of the forty that went on the hunt, he was the only one to emerge from the forest with his life. At sunrise, in bloody and shredded garments, he stood before the towns people that were there awaiting their return. Concealing his delight he fabricated his story, describing a large, werewolf—one with long golden long hair and fangs that appeared as daggers. He shared the account of how helpless they all were in trying to stop him, and that garlic, wolf's bane, nor weapons forged from silver were able to stop it.

Everyone there was horrified as he told the story. Listening to what had happened to all those people that night and how horribly they died instilled more fear in their hearts than before. With all believing that a werewolf was responsible, their only question was its identity.

There were mounting questions and suspicions within his story, such as how was it possible that he was the only one to escape the beast. The village physician designated to attend to his wounds, found upon examining, there were none.

"With your clothes tattered and your body covered with blood, how is it possible that you received not a single injury, not even a scratch?" The physician questioned with suspicion.

"It must've come from those around me, the way the creature was slashing about," he replied. "During the frenzy, it must have spattered on me. In the midst of all of his swinging about, its claws must have grazed my garments. It happened so fast; I can hardly remember. I was fortunate to have evaded its blows, with so many around me being killed. In the middle of the chaos, I was fortunate to have escaped."

"I see," the physician replied. "You're very fortunate to have escaped with your life when so many others did not. Who would have imagined that the man who organized this hunt, putting up such a handsome reward from his own wealth, along with supplying the ammunition needed to kill a werewolf, would be the lone survivor in all of this, without even a scratch? Sir, you were truly blessed."

Staring Cartier in the eye, he showed no emotion and became quiet.

Staring the doctor back in his eyes, he replied, "It must have been God's will to have shown me mercy, allowing me to survive through all of this."

Not giving a response, he simply looked at Cartier and said, "Get some rest. You had a long night."

Afterward, he and the others left. Peering through the window as they walked away, Cartier smiled. Knowing that there were those who doubted his story didn't faze him in the least. He also knew it wouldn't be long before the town would share the same thoughts as the doctor, but he didn't care. He knew that he was at the end of the chapter, and he would be moving along the pages of his horror story very soon.

The people of Gevaudan never dreamed that when they welcomed Auguste Cartier into their town with open arms, they had invited a monster into their midst. Throughout the days that followed, his lust for blood drove him, no matter what form he took. The more he killed, the greater the ecstasy. It wasn't long after Cartier had returned that a request was sent to the governor for assistance.

A few weeks later, after troops were dispatched by the governor, they arrived at the village, but Auguste Cartier was nowhere to be found after he had gotten word they had more questions to ask him.

He was never seen or heard from again. He had simply vanished without a trace. With his disappearance, the killings ceased. Not long afterward, the body of a large strange looking wolf was finally killed.

Now satisfied in believing that the killer had been caught and killed, the government closed the case of the Beast of Gevaudan. Although they had the body of the strange-looking beast, many still believed it wasn't a wolf that slaughtered those people that day but an unnatural creature of the night. Although it was never proven, many believed that Auguste Cartier was the real killer, and through the years, his story became a tale of legend in the region.

With Bultizar's thoughts returning to his most recent victim in the Bronx, he walked away from the mirror into which he gazed. He smiled as he departed the room, flipping off the light switch behind him.

Chapter 21:
A Cry for Help

Back at the murder scene, a black van pulled up from the coroner's office. Taking out a stretcher, technicians retrieved what remained of Sandra Woo's body. Terrie Collins and her crew had begun packing up after concluding their interviews. Grimes walked over to the news van. He was obviously troubled, not only about the murder but also about what happened between them.

What started off as a relaxing evening became progressively worse in a hurry. She was still a little annoyed about what had happened and ignored him. He stood behind her calling her name in a low tone. She didn't respond, but continued working. Hesitating for a moment, she slowly looked back toward him.

"Can we talk?"

Terrie looked up at him. "I'm here," she returned sharply.

Remorsefully, he said, "I just wanted to say 'I'm sorry.' I didn't mean to come off at you like that."

With a cold and expressionless stare, held for a moment, she smiled, breaking the ice.

"I guess I can forgive you," she relented.

Relieved, he said, "With everything that has happened to you, I didn't mean to come off so abrasive. I can barely sleep with what's been going. It's like everything is in suspended animation, and I feel helpless to do anything. We don't have any real leads, just a blood trail from our phantom killer. The streets have been silent. No one has any information as to what's been going on. Even the toughest of the tough are scared of what's been happening out here."

Terrie walked up close to him. "I understand. Although our jobs differ, we both are attached to what's been going on. My most reliable sources don't have anything of any substance for me either, and like your people they all have to watch their backs out of fear, which is frustrating. All of us want this matter resolved and this killer found."

Jahir overheard everything.

Remembering his conversation with Tia, she was the one person who might be able to help. If she could create a disguise for him, that would allow him to breach the barriers that currently restricted him because of his current state. This might allow him to go into places during the day and help shed some light on Bultizar's whereabouts as a man.

It may even lead him to the next victim, allowing him to be present the moment of change. With lights above shining all around from the hovering news and police helicopters, Jahir shifted his position to avoid detection.

Below, Terrie and Grimes finished their conversation. They stood momentarily, visually locked on one another as the tension between the two had lifted.

Grimes said, "It would be nice to finish our evening the way it began, lying next to you."

Terrie smiled, "I would love that, but it simply wouldn't be the same. Too much has gone on tonight." Forcing a smile followed by comforting words she said, "Baby, it has nothing to do with you or with us."

"I guess you're right. This thing has blown wide open. And until I can begin to find answers, it will be tough."

Terrie agreed.

Responding Grimes replied, "Once this is over, I promise it will be just you and me."

Hopping into the front seat of the news van, Terrie looked at Grimes, smiling before she and her crew pulled off.

Returning to his partner, Grimes gathered whatever information they could.

"It's been another long night," Poles said. "So many highs and lows, I feel like I just got off a roller coaster."

Looking to Poles, Grimes said, "This was one of those evenings with Terrie that started off great, until this. We smoothed out a few problems, whereas some of them need more work. Now, I'm beat. I think I'm going to head home and get some sleep."

"Yeah, it's been rough on all of us," Poles replied. "Monica called me to apologize for what went on at the house. Now it's time to go home and officially make up with my wife. I guess I'll see you tomorrow, Chief," he said, with a wink.

With an approving look, Grimes got into his car and headed home.

***

After another long night finally at a close, Jahir made his way back to his abandoned loft. So much had occurred. In his mind, he had once again failed. With the sun beginning to rise, its rays seeping through the open window, the events of another deadly evening began to dance across Jahir's mind.

Closing his eyes, he slipped into another unsettled sleep. Jahir's subconscious drifted back in time, to the aftermath surrounding the massacre of the small province in Gevaudan. The memories of the victims killed by Bultizar that night were still fresh in Jahir's head.

It was the year 1802, fifty years after the slaughter when Bultizar had his way as the golden wolf. The trail of death Bultizar left led Jahir to that region of Central France.

There were but a few who remained alive that were able to remember the horrors of those mountains. Many were just babes when it all began when the stories were told to them. Others were old enough to remember the horrors in detail. Unlike Bultizar who could walk amongst the people freely without anyone knowing there was a monster caged inside of him—Jahir could only move about under the cover of night. Finding the place where the wolf had killed, separate images appeared in his head. In his thoughts, he revisited the place where each of Bultizar's victims had suffered, which were becoming unbearable. It was then his friend Tia came to mind and with that thought, remembering their conversation, he believed she might be the only one able to help him.

***

The evening that followed Sandra Woo's death, Tia was preparing to leave her apartment. It was her day off from work and school, a break that she needed. After a contentious week, she was looking to relax her mind. With the latest death all over the news, she thought about everything Jahir had told her. She was still trying to process everything, although it was all very difficult.

After leaving her apartment, she noticed everything around her was different. The thugs were gone after their encounter with Jahir. The street was quiet from all the previous activities. For the first time, everything was quiet as she walked toward the subway.

Passing by an alley, she heard a familiar voice call out her name. Deep and low, but too strong to be a whisper. It was just loud enough to startle her causing her to jump. Looking toward it, she saw a large silhouette leaning against the wall in the dark.

She instantly knew who it was but was still surprised. Placing her hand to her breast, she took a deep breath.

"You scared the heck outta me. What are you doing here on the street? You know it's not safe."

"That is true, but I need your help," Jahir answered.

"My help how?"

"I need you to make me look human. I can no longer simply wait for him to change. I need to be close enough to be there when he does. Usually, I'm too late when I arrive, therefore I must be able to roam freely during the day. To get what information I can't get at night which will allow me to be present to stop him before someone else dies, allowing me to end this."

Looking around to make sure they were alone, Tia stepped into the alley. Looking up at him, she gently reached up to touch his chin. Then she turned his face slowly from side to side, examining his features trying to determine what she had to do.

"Come on back to my place," she said. "I don't have any real plans for the night. I'm going to see what I can do. I'll go in first and open a window so no one will see you come in."

Jahir nodded. As she headed back to her apartment, Jahir took a different route in getting there. When she opened her window, he entered. Quietly, he looked around the room from the ceiling to the carpet. It had been a while since he had been on the inside of an occupied dwelling.

Observing his fascination, Tia said, "It's not much but it's home."

Looking at her, he said, "If you've been where I've been, in the gutters, the plague-ridden towns and villages, this equals a palace of the wealthiest kings."

Tia went into her closet and pulled out a chest filled with makeup and materials to create a mold. Determining the dimensions of his face, she began working her magic, preparing her own ingredients she had developed. It was fast drying and lightweight, the result of the hours spent perfecting her product. As she made her final adjustments, achieving the look she desired, all that was left was to paint and wait for it to dry.

After six hours, Jahir donned the mask. Hesitant at first, he walked to the mirror, not knowing what to expect. As he gazed upon his reflection, he simply stood there for a few minutes amazed. Even Tia was astounded by what she had created.

It had been ages since he had seen himself as human. He saw the image of a young black man, but at that moment he didn't care whether his appearance was an illusion or authentic. All that mattered to him was that he appeared normal.

Looking away from the mirror and back at Tia, Jahir was beyond grateful. He stood there marveling over his appearance, gently touching his face.

His joy was such that he would've shed tears if he could. Instinctively, Tia knew what he needed. She walked over to him and hugged him. Jahir momentarily froze where he stood. He hadn't had physical contact with another human being since he last held Kolliana. Cherishing the moment of human touch, he didn't want it to end, until finally she stepped away.

Looking into Jahir's eyes, she said, "If you need my help in finding this monster, I'll do whatever is necessary."

"I do not wish you to be in harm's way," he responded. "No matter what form he chooses, whether it's a man or werewolf, he will always be a monster and just as dangerous." After a brief pause, he continued. "I don't know how I'll ever repay you for what you have just done for me. I'm just sorry I delayed your plans for this evening."

"There's no reason to thank me," she replied. "That's what friends do for one another. Besides, it's too late to go out now; I'm going to bed. I know that it is something you haven't been in for a very long time."

"That is true," he replied. "It's been a long time since I've slept on anything considered comfortable."

"My couch is a sofa that turns into a bed. If you ever need to, you can sleep here. You don't have to worry about any roaches and the rats. I keep my place clean."

"I thank you for your kind offer, but I have no time to relax. I have to go. Besides, the roaches and rats you spoke of—I am now one of them. They, too, are now my friends," he said in jest. She followed with a laugh.

Turning towards her kitchen, a thought came across her mind. "Would you like something to eat?"

When she turned back, he had left through the window without making a sound. With the curtains blowing in the wind, she stuck her head out the window to see where he had gone, but he had already disappeared.

She closed the window and went to bed.

***

Three weeks had passed since Sandra Woo's death. There was also an urgency that had fully peaked amongst the citizens. Fear had spread across the city like a ripple in water. Police and reporters weren't the only ones frustrated with the situation. Jahir's desperation was at its peak. Although he was no longer confined to stalking city rooftops--thanks to the help of his friend--his ability to descend and blend onto the streets in a near-perfect disguise did not instantly solve the problem. His progress in finding Bultizar still remained at a standstill, proving that waiting for him to make his next move was a game he was losing.

From the timid to the toughest, everyone was apprehensive that someone or something was going to descend upon them and take their lives at any moment. He held the cards while hiding in plain sight. The Butcher of the Bronx was now under the national spotlight.

Chapter 22
A Tragic Tale of Two Cities

Hundreds of miles away in Cleveland, seated in front of a television, was an elderly man. His eyes were glued on his screen, having been following the news story intensely since it all began. Henry Grace, a retired janitor for the Cleveland Public School System, held a more personal interest in what was going on in New York. On his wall surrounding him were old newspaper articles that pertained to a number of unsolved murders, some dating as far back as the 1930s. The captions on the articles had a very familiar ring to them, like THE BUTCHER OF KINGSBURY, ALSO KNOWN AS THE TORSO KILLER. Many were so old that they had turned yellow, some ready to crumble at the slightest touch.

One paper in particular, he had circled a name that held great importance to him—Hattie Grace, his older sister. With his room filled with candles for lighting in her wake, he would often hold his own vigil in her memory. He still grieved over those distant memories and the tragedy of the event decades later.

Everything that was going on in New York was nearly identical to what had taken place during that time. As he sat watching the news, he began to reminisce to the day they found his sister's body. He was a young boy then. She was believed to be the last of twenty victims of the infamous Kingsbury killer in the Cleveland area.

His thoughts flashed back to those haunting memories and the one that was believed to be her killer. A man named Ted Coles had been arrested and charged for those crimes—a claim that was never proven. He remembered the day he last saw his sister alive. She was fancied up and smiling as she awaited her date for the evening to come by and take her out. He remembered hearing the car horn blow and watching from the window as she ran out to the car. He remembered seeing a young man with blond hair and a scar on his face open the door for her as he looked back at the window where he was standing. He remembered the man's face as clearly as though it were yesterday.

That was the last time he saw her alive. It wasn't until days later that the police found her mutilated body with her heart ripped from her chest. They had also found a pair of strange tracks from some type of animal near her body that was never explained. She was thought to be the last of about twenty others he had murdered. When Coles's face appeared in the papers, it wasn't the guy he had remembered.

When he told his father that the man in the papers wasn't the same person he had seen, his father dismissed it. Being that he was so young, everyone assumed he had been mistaken. His father believed that the police had captured his daughter's killer.

Shortly after, a news article with photos was published that featured the power and success of a few local businessmen. Seeing the article still lying on top of a table, Grace still recognized one of the men pictured as being the same man that had come and picked up his sister that day. He was the owner of one of the largest real estate companies in the area, Wolf Realty. Aloof and seldom in public view, Grace noticed that he was always one to shy away from cameras. Any photos or history of him prior to the article published were nonexistent.

After showing his father the man in the picture as being the guy that he had remembered, immediately his father thought about where her body had been found. It was in the rear of an old building at the time reportedly owned by Nicholai Wolvenhunt, the owner of Wolf Realty, which may have connected him to her death. When he went to the police, they dismissed the thought, refusing to move forward in opening a new investigation citing that Wolvenhunt was beyond reproach as one of the pillars of the community. Shortly after his father went to the police, a mysterious fire destroyed the printing office along with the press and template used in printing those photos.

For reasons unknown, there were less than ten copies that were ever printed that went into circulation. The few copies that had circulated had disappeared over time. Grace had the only surviving photo and it too had grown fragile over the years.

Although he didn't understand it at the time, it wasn't until he got older and began to conduct his own investigation, he learned that the city had spent much of its resources and wanted to conclude the case. He learned that Coles had been apprehended hours before she was reported missing. The location where her body was found and where he was apprehended was more than a hundred miles away, which confirmed his alibi and made it almost impossible for him to be responsible within that time frame. They had simply thrown her name in the mix with the rest.

Looking deeper into her death, he found that of the twenty alleged victims, five were females that had the exact same injuries. Each of the five appeared to have been killed by some kind of animal with all of them having their hearts violently removed. They were also found in abandoned properties that were owned by the Wolf Realty, along with unexplained animal footprints. This led to the belief that there were those in the community whose family members were amongst the victims but both police and city officials were being paid by an unidentified source to look the other way.

For years, He had been looking into his sister's death, attempting to find proof to his claims that Nicholai Wolvenhunt was responsible. Years after his sister's death, Henry continued his research. He learned that a few years prior to what happened in Cleveland had also occurred in the Chicago suburbs, with a similar incident leading to the death of a local activist who had constantly criticized Wolf Realty and its practices, since most of the victims' bodies had been found in or near one of its buildings.

The Chicago account was less publicized, with its storylines taking a backseat to the organized crime that was dominating the news at that time. Over the years, He had collected news articles and photos in search of proof that Wolvenhunt was the one responsible for his sister's death, a task that proved to be both difficult and frustrating. Any evidence he had collected only led to dead ends.

Shortly after the Kingsbury murders, Wolvenhunt had become totally reclusive and lived in seclusion from the rest of the world. He would hire people whose appearance was a near replica of his own so they would serve as the face of his company, while he ran things behind the scenes. Other than the news article he had in his possession, no one had seen his face again.

The news of Nicholai Wolvenhunt's passing a few years later ended any hope that his sister's killer would ever be brought to justice. Now in his nineties, it wasn't until the string of murders taking place in New York that once again caught his attention.

***

The day before, a special election was being held in the Bronx to fill the council seat of one of its deceased members, who had died. Although tragic, it wasn't the topic that dominated the news. Instead, people were in an uproar over the butcher of the Bronx. No one felt safe nor believed enough was being done to prevent the murders. The sentiment was that the police were not able to protect them.

Public posturing by local authorities was no longer enough to pacify the community. Protesters began taking to the streets, demanding results and seeking answers. The day before the elections, Hakeem Robinson brought his fight to the doorstep of Nicholas Wolf's corporate office.

Reporting live standing alongside him was Terrie Collins, who was preparing to conduct an on-air interview with the young candidate. Earlier that morning, she had received a phone call from Wolf's secretary, setting up an afternoon appointment later that day—something she had been anxiously waiting for weeks. With cameras rolling, Terrie gave her opening statement.

"Reporting live in front of Nicholas Wolf's corporate office with the latest update on the death of Sandra Woo, receptionist at Glow Enterprises, a Bronx resident. Just last night, Woo's body was found inside yet another of Nicholas Wolf's vacant properties. There has been a total of five victims, three of them have been women that were found murdered and dragged into these buildings. Police say they were led to the scene by witnesses who said they heard screams behind one of the buildings and saw a trail of blood, leading police to the body."

After giving a summary of the events, Terrie turned her attention to Hakeem Robinson, who was the clear frontrunner for the vacant council seat and also served as the spokesman for the Affordable Housing Organization.

Looking at him, Terrie asked, "In the aftermath of this tragic incident and on the eve of the election, what did you hope to accomplish with these protests in front of Wolf's offices?" Placing the microphone to his mouth.

"As I have stated before," Robinson responded, "over the past three years we have reached out to Nicholas Wolf and now everything has come to a head. Over the past three years, we've have worked hard to get the answers but to no avail, despite repeated attempts. During our fight, there have been rumors of corruption among city officials through bribery and payoffs, along with unscrupulous tactics used by Mr. Wolf and his corporation in obtaining many of its properties. Although these are rumors, once in office I promise to use all the resources available to me to get to the bottom of this. I intend to expose all activities and participants if these rumors are proven to be true.

"We are also here to let Mr. Wolf know he is not exempt from blame or responsibility for these and other crimes that have taken place in or around his properties. The conditions created in this environment enable a mechanism for these crimes to take place. In refusing to make these changes, this makes him partially responsible. Renovations of these buildings will help to prevent them from being used as hubs for criminal activities. And now with these horrendous acts of violence and murders plaguing our communities, it is time that he takes responsibility.

"If he truly places value in the community and its people, then he would start by putting his money into helping the people by repairing these places to create homes for people in need. We hope to get his attention and let him know that we are going to bring the fight to him. Those city officials who have chosen to ignore the problems that plague our city will be targeted and exposed as well.

"We have made every effort to meet with Mr. Wolf over our concerns, but he has declined. He has yet to return any of our phone calls or respond to any of our written requests. I promise once this election is final, we will bring the truth to light, exposing everyone involved that has anything to do with criminal activity. We hope by coming here a day ahead of the election in protest would gain his attention and trigger a response.

"I will not leave a single stone unturned and will do all that is in my power to end all corruption as it exists. If we cannot reach him one way, we will another."

After his statement, Terrie turned to the camera and spoke.

"And that concludes our interview, Terrie Collins action news."

After wrapping up her interview, she thought to herself that the day would be a good day. She had started it with Hakeem Robinson, Wolf's chief critic. Later that afternoon, she had an exclusive interview scheduled with Nicholas Wolf. himself. She was very interested in what he had to say in response to everything that Robinson had addressed. This was a reporter's dream—she was going to get the best of both worlds while the storylines were building. This was her opportunity to tap into Wolf's mind, to understand his views and feelings about being somehow attached to a killer who seems to favor his properties to commit these crimes.

While Wolf's offices were under the spotlight, they were not the only place that was targeted by protesters. Hundreds of others led by separate groups were also picketing outside City Hall, demanding that the city officials use more of their resources. Placing more police on the streets was the topic of their demands in order to find this killer.

While the on-air interview was taking place, Wolf, his secretary and staff watched intensely. "How can anyone put blame on you?" a staff member asked. "You're not responsible for the actions of a lunatic." Looking over at him, Margaret agreed then replied, "People look for anyone to blame if they can't find answers." Then looking at her boss, she added, "This Hakeem Robinson seems hell bent on using you as a platform for his own political gain."

Nicholas replied, "It's all politics, always searching for some type of forum, blasting rhetoric just to look like they're doing something. Posturing like he really cares. All of this, though tragic, is at the cost of several innocent women's lives for his political gain. He never mentioned the others that were killed in different parts of the city that are nowhere near anything I own. Mr. Robinson is nothing more than a slight irritation and a side thought in the larger scheme of what direction this corporation is heading in the future."

Wolf looked around at his employees and added, "Well, we all have work to do and deadlines to meet. I suggest we get to it. We have a business to run." Nicholas said to Margaret, "Don't I have an interview with Ms. Collins? "

"Yes, at two o'clock."

"Good. I don't want to miss it. Our last meeting was quite interesting and I'm looking forward to speaking with her again."

Wolf looked over to Margaret glancing toward his office, giving her an indication that he wanted to see her there. Both headed over, closing the door behind them.

Chapter 23:
Deadly Memories

Hours after wrapping things up, Terrie had returned to her office. It was time to return to Wolf's office for their interview to hear his take on everything. Shortly afterwards Terrie and her team arrived at his office where they were greeted by Margaret Sullivan.

"Hello Ms. Collins," Good to see you again, Mr. Wolf is expecting you," she escorted them back into his suite. "Ms. Collins it's a pleasure to see you again. I know our last meeting didn't go as you envisioned, I do apologize, I just don't like conducting business outside my business settings, I hope you understand. "That's ok," I do she replied, May I offer anyone a drink before we start?" After checking with her crew," they passed on his offer.

Margaret asked her boss whether he needed anything.

"No thank you, Margaret," That will be all.

Walking towards the door she looked back at him briefly, exchanging eye contact before closing the door behind her. Wolf turned his attention to the reporter offering her a seat while politely, instructing her to get comfortable.

"I've been looking forward to seeing you again. Our last conversation, I might say, was quite interesting."

"Yes, it was a little awkward, but unfortunately, a few more people have lost their lives since then."

"Yes, quite unfortunate. Maybe now, I can address some of the issues that I've been accused of ignoring. I realize success brings on ridicule, even if you are far removed from any crime."

After her crew confirmed that they were ready to begin, Terrie looked to Wolf informing him that their interview was also being streamed live before asking if he were ready. Giving her permission to start, she wasted little time to get to the heart of the matter.

"Mr. Wolf, there has been much criticism surrounding you in the way that you are handling your properties. There are some accusing you of holding off renovation projects and repairs to properties that are just sitting idle. It has been argued for at least two years that they be renovated and restored, and that in doing so would provide affordable housing for working families needing a place to live. Instead, they've been turned into a hub for criminal activities such as drug distribution and murder. The most recent, we all know, have been the brutal murders of at least three women in various locations you own around the Bronx. What answers do you have for the public?"

Wolf replied, "It is very unfortunate and tragic what has been happening on our streets recently. I too am deeply appalled by what has been going on. But to hold me accountable is absurd. We have a plan in place to restore this community to where the neighborhood should be, but it will take time. There are legal issues I'm not at liberty to discuss at this time that has slowed the progress."

"City council candidate Hakeem Robinson has stated on many occasions that his office had made efforts through the city to get things started, but has been given no answers as to why there's been no progress. He stated that he and his organization have reached out to you on many occasions with no reply. Also, he has stated on record that once elected he would investigate possible irregularities and illegal activities such as bribes and payoffs by your company. What are your thoughts of these allegations?"

"Any investigation that Mr. Robinson wishes to conduct, he is more than welcome to do so. It's just sensationalism by him to get votes. At the election's conclusion, whether he wins or loses there's no evidence to support any of his claims. Furthermore, I believe Mr. Robinson is on a witch hunt, using the deaths of those innocent women as a platform for his political gain. He is using the backs of the poor to stand on while he makes a lot of noise and throws darts at an invisible target.

"Mr. Robinson has not presented a shred of evidence or proof to back up any of his claims that I or my corporation are in any way responsible for those deaths," Wolf continued, "nor is there any proof of any illegal activities going on by me or my company that is keeping any progress from being made. I will say this—I am doing everything in my power to move forward and give to the community all the help that's needed now or in the future."

After asking a few more questions, Terrie realized that not much progress was being made. Concluding her interview, she thanked him for allowing her to speak with him before shutting it down and packing up. In her mind, it was nothing more than a political show. If she didn't know any better, she would've thought that it was Nicholas Wolf who was running for office. He was smooth and clever, sounding less like a businessman and more like a politician than the politicians themselves.

***

In Cleveland, Henry Grace sat watching the live interview to its conclusion on a news app he had acquired. The image of Nicholas Wolf onscreen was exceptionally haunting to the old man. It was as though he had seen a ghost. The sight of him seemed impossible. The man on camera was identical to the man he had remembered when he was a child. He hadn't changed in over eighty years. Watching him was like being in a time capsule, a door to the past that had opened, reliving the events that had taken place in Kingsbury back in the 1930s. Unlike when he was a child and information was limited to radio and newspapers, this was live television and could not be ignored.

Following the case, he knew that everything had reached an impasse. He walked over to his dresser pulling out a drawer. He reached in and took hold of a picture and stared at it. He then carefully began taking the articles off the wall and placed them into a brown envelope. With evidence in his hand, he grabbed his coat and cane, headed out the door to the nearest office supply place with a fax machine.

***

While Terrie conducted her interview, Hakeem Robinson and his staff also watched. In disbelief, they looked around at each another, shaking their heads.

"Can you believe this guy?" Robinson asked, looking at his colleagues. "He's like the president. He believes he's untouchable."

One of the staff responded, "Well, he will see if he has the same confidence once you're in office and is investigated. The election is tomorrow. All we can do is wait for the results."

"Yes, that's all we can do, but until then I have a dinner date tonight with my lovely wife, and that I won't miss for all the elections in the world."

His statement was followed by laughter. After a few hours, Robinson's staff began trickling out the office. Last to leave, Robinson gathered some important papers in anticipation that he was going to be elected. Before leaving, his fax machine began receiving news articles anonymously addressed to him. sent from Cleveland, with pictures and headlines about a serial killer.

At first, he was going to ignore it and wait for the next day but there was an article with a photo that caught his attention. While staring at the picture, his phone rang. He then answered. "AHO, Hakeem Robinson." After answering it, there was silence on the other end.

"Hello, hello!"

There was no reply.

Just before hanging up, the voice of an old man answered, "Mr. Robinson, you are in danger." His voice trembled.

"Who is this?" Robinson asked.

Not wanting to identify himself out of fear, the old man replied, "It's not important who I am but know that Nicholas Wolf isn't who you think he is. He is very dangerous."

"Who is this?" Robinson repeated.

"Listen and listen carefully to what I'm about to tell you. Did you just receive a fax?"

"Yes, moments before this call. Did you send it?"

"Yes, but you must listen to what I'm going to tell you. Your life may depend on it."

As the old man spoke, Robinson remained quiet and listened. He gave him a history of what he had learned and a list of properties in and around the Cleveland area dating back to the Kingsbury murders. He told him of his sister, who was found murdered in the same way as those women in the Bronx, and how the police had found them dismembered or worse. About twenty people in all. They called him the Torso Killer.

"The Torso Killer, yes, I've heard of him," Robinson replied. "But that was a long time ago. Didn't they catch that guy? Besides, even if they didn't, he would've been dead a long time ago."

"They arrested a man named Ted Coles for those crimes," he responded, "but he died without them ever proving it. Most people believed he was the killer except a few of the victim's loved ones. Of his victims, which numbered around twenty-five, they were found in old dilapidated buildings. A few of the women had their hearts removed, which included my own sister."

As he listened, they paralleled the events that were taking place there in New York.

"You recognize the man in the photo?" he asked.

Robinson replied, "It looks exactly like Nicholas Wolf. Are you implying that the man in this photo is Nicholas Wolf? If you are, then that would be impossible, looking at the date of the article—1939. This picture is over seventy-five years old, and judging by this photo, would make him well over a hundred. Wolf is a little over thirty."

"I kept that picture in my drawer for decades. It wasn't until I saw the footage of the man who claimed to be his nephew on the news. I then pulled the picture from my drawer. When I compared it to that of the nephew, it verified my belief. Nicholai Wolvenhunt and the man you know as the nephew, Nicholas Wolf, are one in the same. There is no uncle—there never was. They are identical down to the scar on the side of the face. The building she was found in was owned by a company with another name and an owner no one had ever seen. It was under a group of companies owned by Wolf Realty. Do the math. Wolvenhunt never took another photo since that article was published, always having someone else speak on his behalf."

He then told Robinson that the exact same murders had occurred years earlier in the Chicago area, and that in Chicago there was an activist name

Edward Garfield who, like Robinson, had the same concerns as murders were taking place in the same way, like those in Kingsbury years later and like the ones currently taking place in New York City. Garfield fought against Wolf after finding out he was the real owner of the properties. He began inquiring about payoffs and bribery of local officials that may have been protecting him. When he began to arouse the suspicion of the public concerning his accusations, which threatened to expose the corruption within the local government over housing, he conveniently disappeared.

Garfield was found days later. His body looked like it had been savaged by an animal of some sort. Like in Kingsbury, there were also strange prints that were found which also failed to make the papers beyond the original print, and like the animal analogy it was never emphasized by police.

"The photo I sent you is the only known surviving picture of Nicholai Wolvenhunt that remains from the news article. There may be others but I've never found any. I don't know if any other pictures of him exist in the public."

He explained how the template was destroyed in a fire, and that he believed Wolvenhunt had something to do with it, having had quite a bit of financial influence.

"Why didn't you take this to the police years ago?" Robinson asked.

"Like I said, we tried that once and was spurned by the authorities. They were crooked then and as you have insinuated in your interview, there might be corrupt officials working for him now, possibly even the police."

"What you're saying sounds impossible, unbelievable really."

"You have the picture. You be the judge."

He then hung up the phone.

Afterward, Robinson sat staring at the photo, trying to process everything. Not sure how to take it, he pondered the information in his mind. Filled with doubt he then realized as he looked down at his watch that he was going to be late for his dinner date.

Before leaving, he paused, looking at what the old man had sent him. He then placed everything that was sent in a brown envelope placing it in his desk. The story was incredible and hard to believe, even with the articles. He was in doubt that anyone would believe it.

Chapter 24:

The Robinsons, Unexpected Guests

Hakeem Robinson exited the building locking the door behind him. When he turned, there was a black limousine parked in front with tinted windows and a chauffeur standing beside it. Robinson looked over at both the driver and the limo before the driver said, "Mr. Robinson, Mr. Wolf would like to have a word with you."

"I don't have time," Robinson replied. "I have a date with my wife across town and I don't want to be late. Mr. Wolf has had plenty of time to respond to my requests but hasn't done so."

At that moment, the rear passenger side window rolled down. In the backseat was Wolf.

"Mr. Robinson," Wolf spoke, "this won't take but a moment."

Robinson hesitated at first and then was about to speak before Wolf cut him off. "I'll offer you a ride and pay for your dinner, both yours and your lovely wife, of course."

The chauffeur opened the passenger door for Robinson to get in. "It will only take a moment." Wolf continued.

Robinson stood there momentarily then reluctantly got in. Once he sat down, Robinson impatiently asked, "What do you want? You have to make it quick."

"Yes of course Wolf replied, That's a very nice suit."

"It's off the rack. We all can't afford tailored suits. Now Mr. Wolf, I'm sure you didn't ask me to get in your car to discuss fashions. What do you really want?"

"What do I really want?" Wolf repeated. "What I want is for us to put this negativity behind us and start working together."

He reached into his inside jacket pocket and pulled the envelope. Then he handed it over to him. When Robinson opened it, it was filled with fresh fifty- and hundred-dollar bills.

"What is this?"

"Fifty thousand dollars," Wolf replied. "Just a little something to help make your transition to public office a little easier moving forward. I want to start things off fresh between us."

Robinson looked up from the envelope and over to Wolf and asked, "Are you trying to bribe me?"

Wolf smiled and replied, "Of course not. It's nothing more than a donation. It's a standard thing in politics that helps everything run more smoothly."

"I'm sure, but usually that type of thing is done before or during a campaign, not when it's over. Since I'm no longer campaigning, it sounds like a bribe to me."

"No, bribery is a misleading word. This is a gift."

"Mr. Wolf, to me it's all the same." Changing the subject, Robinson then said, "I received an anonymous phone call not too long ago, giving me a very interesting history about you and your company. I usually don't give much credence to callers that refuse to identify themselves but as they spoke, what they shared was quite interesting,"

Wolf chuckled, "Maybe you found the call interesting because it was something you simply wanted to hear. As far as your claims go—to be frank with you, it all sounds quite ridiculous, trying to link me to those crimes.

As Robinson listened, he handed the envelope back to Wolf. "Call it what you want, put whatever spin on it you like, but to me it's all the same. I'm not for sale. I intend to see this thing through, exposing you and your practices. So, tell me, Mr. Wolf, how many officials have you given one of these brown envelopes to? How many people do you have protecting you so that you don't have to do the right thing? And at what cost? There are hundreds of homeless people needing homes, and you sit up in your loft pretending that they don't exist."

"Hmm," Wolf replied. "Bribery and payoffs are strong words without proof, which makes the person making these allegations liable and open to quite a few lawsuits."

"You handing that envelope over to me proves otherwise," Robinson replied. "Your company has been doing this kind of stuff for decades in different cities, buying properties in the names of smaller companies owned by you. In the Cleveland area, they called him The Butcher of Kingsbury. Officials kept the truth hidden because someone paid them to keep quiet. They even came up with a suspect to cover their tracks. They never proved it was him before he came up dead—mysteriously, might I add. In Chicago, years earlier, the same thing happened, alleged bribes and payoffs to official bodies that were found, including an activist named Edward Garfield who also fought against your company's practices. He too came up dead.

"All the properties were under Crescent Hill Realty before that was owned by the Wolf Realty Corporation," Robinson continued. "In each of the vacant dwellings, like here in the Bronx, only the women were the ones that had their hearts taken. They just didn't give the Chicago murders a name. At first, when I heard this story, I found it hard to believe when it was you that they were implying was responsible, because you weren't even born. After all, you're in your thirties. So, I dismissed it, thinking maybe it had to be a family member with a strong resemblance they were speaking of until I saw an old picture in an article that was sent to me." Pausing a moment, he thought to himself both the impossibilities and danger if his assessment were correct. Determined to get a reaction, he continued. "It was faded, but the image was clear, Mr. Wolf—or shall I call you Mr. Wolvenhunt?"

"You're confusing me with my uncle. Our family resemblance is quite strong. Not to mention, he died years ago."

Wolf then became silent. Looking off through his window at the buildings across the street.

Robinson then said, "You haven't changed in eighty plus years, down to that scar on the side of your face." Robinson then looked over at Wolf, exchanging eye contact and asked, "Who are you, Mr. Wolf? Who are you really? Or better yet, what are you?"

Wolf looked at him and grinned, tucking the envelope back into his pocket. Wolf then called to his driver to open the door, Robinson responded, "Don't bother, I can let myself out."

"I'm sorry we couldn't find a middle ground tonight," Wolf said. "Good luck on the election."

Robinson looked back at Wolf but didn't say a word closing the door before walking away.

With a smirk, Wolf watched him and then said to his driver, "I have an important meeting this evening and I don't want to be late." They then pulled off.

***

Robinson and his wife Jacqueline were enjoying an evening at one of the finest restaurants on Staten Island. Soft music and a candlelight dinner highlighted their evening. This was a pre-victory celebration for him being far ahead in the polls. But looking into her husband's eyes, she saw that they were troubled.

"Baby, What's the matter?" This is supposed to be a special night for us. You seem to be a thousand miles away from here."

He sat there, staring at the stemmed glass in his hand filled with wine. He looked over at his wife and said, "I got a fax today from an unknown sender. In the fax were copies of old news clippings dating back to the thirties concerning an old serial killer. 'The Butcher of Kingsbury' the article read, along with pictures. There was one photo in particular that made my jaw drop. In the picture was a man that looked exactly like Nicholas Wolf standing with a group of businessmen."

"Well, what's so surprising about that?" she asked.

"It was dated 1939," he replied.

Surprised, she repeated, "1939? That was decades ago. It sounds like someone is playing games with you."

"That's what I thought at first, but then I got a phone call right after that. On the other end was an old man who told me he was the one who sent the fax."

217

"Did he say who he was?"

"No, he didn't want to give me his name. It was like he was afraid. At first, I was about to hang up, thinking he was some old lunatic, until he then began telling me a story about events, things that happened in Cleveland and in Chicago, and how he believed Wolf Realty and its owner were involved. I didn't believe any of it at first, but I continued to listen, anyway."

"Eighty plus years ago?" Jacqueline responded. "I don't understand what is there to believe. What does that have to do with now? I don't see how any of that is relevant."

Hakeem began telling her everything the old man had told him, every detail including references to Nicholas Wolf and his uncle as possibly being the same person and everything associated with the crime. After he finished explaining, she wasn't sure how to take it. There was a lot to digest but she remained doubtful.

"There's something else," he added. "I also met with Wolf this evening."

"You met with Nicholas Wolf? You never mentioned that you had a meeting set up with him. I thought he wasn't answering or returning your calls."

"He wasn't. When I was leaving, he was outside waiting in his limo, pressing to speak with me. Initially, I wasn't going to talk to him. I told him I had a date but then I thought the better of it and got in the car. Soon as I sat down, he tried to put me on his payroll. Offered me fifty thousand in cash as a campaign gift to start my political career. I thought about what the caller told me, that I was in danger, that Wolf wasn't who he claims to be."

"I think you should call the police," alarmed Jacqueline replied. "Have you told anybody else this?"

"Yes, Nicholas Wolf. When we were in the car talking, I told him everything. I even questioned his identity. He got quiet; I left."

"Honey, I think you should tell the police what you just told me."

"Tell them what, that he's a killer based on pictures taken in the thirties? Besides, those old murders are public record, a closed case. Me trying to sell to them that he's the real Butcher of Kingsbury and responsible for the murders in Chicago that happened in the twenties and thirties, off the word of an anonymous caller, I would sound absurd. My credibility would be shot."

After thinking about it, he said, "You know, you're right. This is our evening. We can save this discussion for another time."

She picked up her glass as they toasted before kissing. The night was still young. After dinner, they headed home to put a stamp on what turned out to be a very relaxing evening. Leaving the restaurant, they walked down to the basement level of the parking garage.

Strolling along with their arms interlocked, her head on her husband's shoulder, they were in their own world. Approaching the car, the lights in the parking garage began to flicker. Robinson thought he saw movement in the corner of his eye in a dark corner.

When he turned and focused, there was nothing. They both heard something behind them but when they turned nothing. Jacqueline began getting nervous and anxious as Robinson called out, asking if there was anyone there. But there was no reply.

They were but a few spaces away from the car when he unlocked the car door with their remote before hearing another sound. This time, they looked around and saw something in the shadows—a pair of illuminated eyes piercing through the darkness. Both bright and gray, they were reflecting like mirrors from the lights that were still lit in the garage. Slowly, a large blond furry creature emerged.

Both froze in disbelief. Robinson quickly snapped out of it and gave the keys to his wife, telling her to run.

She ran as fast as she could toward their car screaming for help, but no one was around to hear her. In an instant, the blond beast was on top of her husband as he attempted to fight it off vigorously. He tried his best to buy time for his wife to get away but it wasn't enough.

While the werewolf was on the attack, his change had already alerted Jahir that Bultizar had chosen his next victim. Racing across the city, he moved as fast as he could.

Jacqueline made it to the car and frantically tried to start it. She could hear her husband cry out while the growling beast tore at him.

After several attempts, the engine finally turned over and started when the passenger side window crashed in. Reaching across the seat, Bultizar hooked his claws deeply into her shoulder as she screamed. Effortlessly he pulled her across the seat, through the passenger side window.

With her husband already dead, Bultizar attacked her as the car drifted off, hitting several parked cars until eventually smashing into a concrete wall. Just before she died, she saw what the last few victims had seen, death smiling in her face before the end came.

Aware that Jahir was close, to spite him Bultizar gave a howl before returning to human form. Jahir was too late. Bultizar had now added two more to the death toll.

Heading back to their cars a few minutes later a couple happened upon their shredded bodies and called the police. Shortly afterwards, police and security arrived almost simultaneously, preventing Jahir's direct entry, who had arrived not long after. They found the bodies of Hakeem and his wife mutilated, lying in pools of blood.

Crowds began to gather outside the parking garage, curious to know what was going on. The killer still amongst them taking delight in another successful kill. He found this one to be more gratifying--it was personal, and he knew that Jahir was present.

While all the attention was focused on the area cordoned off by police, Bultizar's attention was focused elsewhere. Regardless of his form, Bultizar's senses were still far beyond that of normal human after nightfall. With his eyes penetrating the darkness, he scanned the area until he found who he was looking for. Atop of one of the buildings, Jahir crouched back in a dark corner where he could see and hear everything.

Jahir scanned the crowd, believing the killer was still amongst them. Despite knowing his senses were blocked in finding him, he felt he had to somehow try. During his search, there was one amongst them that was all too familiar to him. Still haunting him was the sorceress Mother, her face in the crowd looking straight at him with pale gray eyes. Like always, when he blinked, she was gone, as was Bultizar as he slipped away unnoticed.

Jahir closed his eyes and began to connect with the last memories of Bultizar's latest victims. For about ten minutes the memories lasted before fading into oblivion. Sensing Bultizar's blood boiling Jahir knew he was on the move again.

***

Sitting at her favorite restaurant in the Bronx, Sonja Hart was enjoying a glass of Cognac. She was in a mellow mood enjoying her moment alone. As she sat there, a familiar face pulled up a seat next to her. It was Paul Neville dressed like he was worth a million dollars.

When he walked in, he immediately caught the attention of the ladies, along with a few jealous fellas who wanted their undivided attention. Sonja felt somewhat apprehensive. Police suspicion fueled her apprehension to turn up further. The discord between them was obvious.

She had mixed feelings about him along with an uneasy vibe. As the evening progressed, whatever tension that existed began to soothe. It wasn't long before their conversation turned to laughter. After sharing a drink, about an hour had passed before they left together.

***

Stepping out from the dark corner Jahir looked in the directions his senses led him. Immediately he headed in that direction as fast as he could, covering great distances with the grace of a cat. With a combination of running on two feet and all fours, he moved as fast as his legs could carry him from Stanton toward the Bronx, across bridges and buildings. His senses were clear. Somewhere ahead of him the werewolf was nearing his full form.

As Jahir got closer, no more than a few blocks away the images of the golden wolf became clear, his teeth and claws were prevalent, followed by fear and pain before the images faded.

Jahir was too late. Another young woman dead, another heart taken. Jahir instantly realized that he had been lured away from Bultizar's real target and prize—the heart of his fourth victim. Jahir, desperate beyond compare, turned once again to the only one he believed could help him—Tia Johnson.

It had been usually busy at Luis' Café for a weeknight. Forty-five minutes after closing time and the volume of customers was still heavy. Tia was beat and was left to close up before heading home. It was later than normal when she arrived. She had to get back up in a few hours, having an exam at school in the morning. With little time to rest, she needed to hurry.

Pulling out her keys to enter her building. Tia heard a voice whisper her name, startling her. Emerging from between the buildings Jahir stepped out into the light, wearing the mask she molded for him.

Tia put her hand to her chest as if she was having a heart attack. "You have to stop doing that. You scared the crap outta me. You have to stop sneaking up on me like that."

"Forgive me. I didn't mean to scare you, but I need your help. Bultizar has killed again--three people on this night. A man and woman in a parking garage on the other side of the city, another not far from here. I arrived too late before he changed back. I know he was there in the crowd of his first two victims across the city tonight, but I couldn't see him and was once again unable to stop him."

There was another woman whose heart he claimed his true target not far from here. He is now close to accomplishing his task. There is something else. The image of the old sorceress once again haunted my mind, smiling up at me with her pale gray eyes before vanishing like a ghost across town. "I saw her not far from here."

"The night of the scarlet moon will soon be upon us and time is running out. My access to acquiring needed information is limited. I need your help. You did work for the reporter Terrie Collins not too long ago and you said she may call you yet again soon. Through her you may begin to find the answers I seek that may lead me to the man so I may be present when he turns into the beast. I can kill him as soon as he changes. You may be able to gain access to find out what she may know.

"When I arrived at the latest murder scene, I saw her and the detective together engaging in a more personal way. Although I can hear them, it's not what I need. Maybe he has shared things with her in private, maybe you can find out something that can help me before it's too late." Tia looked at him and said, tomorrow I'm supposed to be at the studio to do makeup for her and the broadcast crew. If I ask anything directly, it'll draw suspicion. Maybe she might have notes lying around which may be useful." Tia crafted his mask so well; it showed his expressions as though it were part of his face. He thanked her for her help before disappearing into the night.

Chapter 25:
Triple Jeopardy

At 12:30 AM, the phone vibrated across the nightstand. Grimes rolled over and looked at it. The predawn calls had become almost routine over the past couple of months.

"Hello?" hesitantly answering it.

It was one of the on-duty officers familiar with his investigation. He informed him of the murders that had taken place that evening. After hanging up, he placed a call. This time, it was to his partner. Rolling over from the comfort of his wife's arms, Poles answered it.

"Yeah."

Grimes gave him a rundown of what had been relayed to him, Poles sat up on the side of his bed listening, then ended the call telling him he'd meet him at the station.

Rolling over, Monica placed her arms around his waist. "What's the matter, honey?"

Poles simply looked at her.

"Another one," she responded.

He nodded.

"Another woman?"

"Hakeem Robinson and his wife were found murdered in a parking garage on Staten Island. Honey, I got to go," he said as he leaned over to kiss her before getting ready to leave.

Terrie had gotten a call around the same time as Grimes. She grabbed the keys to her Lexus; she hadn't taken the subway since being attacked. When she arrived, her team was there with the van running. She hopped into the van as they headed to the scene of the Robinsons' murder.

Grimes and Poles met up at the precinct, took a cruiser, and headed over to Staten Island. Minutes after the detectives arrived, Terrie and her news crew arrived and began setting up.

The news team began interviewing before beginning the broadcast. Seeing Grimes, Terrie walked towards him. As Grimes examined the bodies of Robinson and his wife in detail, she diverted her questions to others who were present on the scene. Poles went over to their vehicle that was resting against the concrete wall.

"Hey Chief, I think you should see this."

Grimes walked over to him as Poles pointed to the steering wheel that had been dislodged, then to a trail of blood leading across the front seats.

Looking to his partner, Poles said, "Whoever did this reached across the passenger seat, pulling a five foot nine, one-hundred-and-eighty-pound woman out from under the steering wheel, dislodging it in the process, then across the console and out the passenger side window while the car was still moving like a doll being ripped out of its box—all in one motion. You have to be incredibly strong to do something like that. They then killed her over there," he added, pointing to a spot fifty feet from where the car rested.

Shaking his head, Grimes replied, "That explains the wounds on her right shoulder, the broken arm, and femur."

"I found something else," Poles said, walking him over to a puddle between two parked cars. He showed him half of a bloody print that was barely noticeable. "I almost missed it because it was so dark. When I shined my light the first time I didn't see it. It wasn't until I was about to cut it off that I happened to notice it from the corner of my eye. I snapped a picture of it. The crime unit had just left. I don't think they saw it either. I'll send the picture to them when we get back."

"This is becoming harder and harder to keep this information from the public."

"Yeah, I know, Chief, but orders are orders."

"I know, but there's something else that's bothering me." Grimes replied

"What's that, Chief?"

"The way these two died opposed to previous victims. Their deaths appear more personal, like whatever did this was more personally directed, out of rage, though that seems strange to say based on the brutality of all of these attacks. All reports I've heard about him was that he was well- liked and respected, except for the public criticism of Nicholas Wolf."

***

While the Robinson investigation took place, across town, three friends were taking a shortcut through an alley. They had just finished a night of fun and games along with plenty of beer at a local bar.

While walking, they noticed streaks of blood on the ground like someone had been dragged. As they looked over to see where it led, a pair of legs belonging to a woman were stretched in an open doorway of a vacant building. Immediately, one of them pulled out their cell phone and called the police. Fearful of the situation, they ran out to the main street and waited for the police.

***

Back across town, Grimes and Poles were finishing up on Staten Island when the call came in. This time, it was in their own backyard. After responding, the two detectives made their way back to the Bronx.

Almost forty minutes later, the detectives pulled up in front of a large vacant multi-complex apartment building.

In front of it was a sign that read, THE FUTURE VISION OF HOPE, with pictures of condominiums and businesses posted on it. Police had already arrived forty-five minutes earlier to secure the area. Using floodlights, the place was lit up like it was midday.

Poles looked over at the sign. Right below the heading, it read, STARTING AT FIVE HUNDRED THOUSAND DOLLARS.

"That sign has been hanging there for the past few years," Poles said. "Not a nail had been hammered since then." He looked over at Grimes and added, "Guess who owns it?"

"Wolf," Grimes sarcastically replied. "That's real affordable for a community going through hard times. Sounds like to me they're trying to force poor people out and bring in the high-end community."

"Sounds about right Chief," That's a shame.

When the two got out of their car, they were met by Officer Aiyana Cortez. Among the first on the scene, she began giving details of what they had found.

Her description was almost identical to the previous victims who had their heart removed."

When they saw the name Sonja Hart, both detectives looked at each other almost in disbelief.

Seeing their reaction, Cortez asked, "Do you know her?"

"Yes," Grimes replied. "We interviewed her after the death of Kerri Barnes. At the time of Ms. Barnes's death, she was seeing the ex-boyfriend of Barnes—Paul Neville. He was last seen with Barnes before her death. When we interviewed him, Neville said he was with Hart, and she confirmed it."

"We also have the statements of the three people who discovered her body," Cortez replied. "They said they saw her at the bar earlier that evening talking and laughing with a guy before the two of them left."

"Where are the people who discovered her body?" Grimes asked.

"After interviewing them, they went home." She handed Grimes a slip paper with their names and addresses written on it.

Looking it over, he replied, "Okay, I'll contact them in the morning."

Making their way to the rear of the building where the bodies were found, the detectives discovered that crime scene investigator Gabriel Acostas and her team were already there. They were on the earlier crime scene with the two detectives but had left shortly before. "Here we are again, twice in one night." Poles spoke as they approached.

"Yes, unfortunately," she replied shaking her head. "Another young woman, the same as the other three. Her injuries were different from the Robinsons.' Unlike those women, the Robinson slayings were even more brutal in the way their flesh was torn into, especially Ms. Robinson's. The previous three women seemed more ritualized. Again, we found blond hair and a pair of prints that we didn't find earlier."

"We found a half of a print after you left, almost missed it. It was hardly visible," Poles replied as he showed her a picture. "I'll send it to you later," he added.

Acostas looked at the two and said, "Her body was found roughly at 2:45 AM. That's when the call was made." As she kneeled over the body, Acostas added, "She was killed a few hours prior based on dried blood and pooling at the lowest points of her body. So far, we really haven't been able to come up with anything new."

After updating the detectives, she and her team continued with their investigation. Action News had arrived shortly after Grimes and Poles had set up.

Grimes looked over the body to see if there were anything additional he could find—something subtle that might point him in a different direction. He looked closely, detecting another strand of hair. Immediately, he gloved up and placed it in a separate plastic bag using a pair of tweezers. He wasn't going to send this one to the lab. He decided to keep this strand of evidence for himself. He had something else in mind.

Grimes looked over to Poles and said, "Well the Wolf Corp will get a reprieve on this one. The number one advocate for exposing any dirty laundry and business practices has conveniently been eliminated all in the same night—a day before an election that he was projected to win easily,

"Yeah," Poles replied. "What are the chances of that happening?"

"First, we need to find out where she was last seen and who she was last seen with. Places she frequented, and the last time she saw or spoke to Mr. Neville. Also, we need to head over to Mr. Robinson's office and see what we can find out. Who he last spoke with, whether he had enemies other than the one obvious one."

Looking across the street, he and Terrie exchanged eye contact. They could read one another's body language. He walked over to her, giving her whatever information he was allowed to share that she could presently use.

Working her second crime scene of the night, Terrie hadn't been that busy in a long time. Along with hundreds of crimes that had been going on, these murders dominated the headlines. Either way, the answers equaled up to being all the same: zero.

Chapter 26:
Follow the Leads

———

Grimes and Poles hadn't slept, they were putting in double time to find the killer. The body count was growing faster than falling leaves. To date, all physical evidence either led to a dead end or shut door. This was also an election with the projected winner eliminated from the race, along with his wife.

They had spoken to the three friends who said they saw Sonja Hart leave the bar with a young blond man. They had a description of a man last seen with her but they still were no closer in finding what the evidence pointed to—a large animal of some kind that they now believed may have been trained, although evidence hadn't been able to tell what kind of an animal.

The description of the man pointed them in a specific direction, with the first stop on their list being DTX-Press. The two detectives arrived on the lot before the carrier service opened. While each of them sipped on a cup of coffee, they patiently waited.

Shortly before 8 AM, Paul Neville parked his car and headed toward the building before hearing his name called. As he stopped and turned, it was Grimes and Poles in their car. He showed little concern as they got out and approached him.

The detectives knew he and Sonja Hart had a history—how recent a history was what they intended to find out. Watching as they approached, he asked. "Detectives, back again, huh? Is there a problem?"

"Yes," Grimes replied, "we would like to ask you a few more questions."

"Sure, but I'm going to have to clock in. Don't wanna be late."

"This won't take long. When was the last time you saw Sonja Hart?"

"I saw her last night. Why?"

"She was found murdered last night."

Surprised, he repeated the detective's words. "Found murdered? How?"

"Her body was found a few blocks away from a bar behind a vacant complex."

"No!" he replied.

Poles then replied, "Do you watch the news? Her face was all over it."

"No, I don't. I never do."

"Were the two of you at the bar together?" asked Grimes.

"Yes, and we had a few drinks," he said. With a concerning stare.

"After the two of you had drinks, what happened next?" Grimes asked. "Where did you go? Witnesses there said that the two of you left together."

"Yeah, we left. She went her way; I went home and got in the bed. Had to be here at work."

"Is there anybody that can corroborate your story?"

"No, I went home alone."

Remembering how callous he was during their last interview, his answers and attitude didn't set well with Poles. "This is becoming a routine," Poles declared. With a more pointed question, he asked, "How does it feel to have two women that are close to you end up on the news, with both being found dead hours after being last seen with you? What are the chances of that happening?"

"What are you trying to say? Are you accusing me, Detective?" he replied.

Knowing he struck a nerve, Poles was inspired. "I'm not accusing you of anything. I'm just asking a question."

"If you're not accusing me of something, then what are you doing?" Neville asked.

"I'm just curious."

Interrupting their scrimmage, Grimes asked, "Before her death, what was the status of your relationship?"

Redirecting his attention toward Grimes, Neville calmed down and answered.

"We were friends."

"Close friends?" Grimes probed.

"We were okay. She kinda backed off me after Kerri's death. When the two of you questioned her about my whereabouts, it kinda scared her off. We eventually got back into a rhythm but that wasn't how we started off last night. That was the first time I had seen her in almost two weeks. I was hoping we could work things out, and it was beginning to happen, until this." Staring down at his watch, Neville said, "I'm going to be late; I don't want to lose my job. Unless you're going to arrest me, am I free to go?"

"No, we're not, unless you gave us reason," Poles replied.

"We'll be in touch," Grimes followed.

As he turned and walked away, Poles shouted, "You can go on vacation, but you just can't leave town."

Turning as he was walking away, he looked back at Poles without responding, and kept walking.

Grimes looked at Poles and said, "We'll be back. I want to see a copy of his delivery route. Two of the women he met on his route are dead. Let's see if the dots connect to any of the other murders."

"Sounds like a plan, Chief," Poles replied.

Hoping back into their car, Grimes looked over at his partner and said, "Let's head over to Hakeem Robinson's office and see what we can find out, if anything."

After leaving Neville's, they arrived at the Affordable Housing Office. Robinson's former staff and associates were trying to come to grips with the tragic death of their colleague and friend.

The two officers entered the office. After identifying themselves, they spoke to the new director, who was anticipated to replace him once he became elected. Because of his unfortunate and untimely death, the reason for replacing him had changed.

Her name was Martina Estelle. She shared Robinson's compassion for the community. As they began to speak, she looked at both detectives and said, "The office and community are devastated by his loss. He was more than liked; he was loved and highly respected. His compassion for the community was real and couldn't be dismissed. Anything you need, we are willing to help."

"That is greatly appreciated," Grimes replied. "We'd like to interview the staff and have a look around his office, if that's okay."

"Sure," she replied. "Nothing has been touched. We anticipated someone would be here to have a look."

"Did he mention anything out of the ordinary, any problems he may have had with any of the staff or anyone else?"

"No, not at all. We all met yesterday afternoon. He never mentioned anything. He told us he had a date with his wife. A pre-celebration for his anticipated council seat. We had left. He was the last to leave the office. The only issue he had was with Nicholas Wolf and his practices, which was public record. To my knowledge, the two had never spoken but it wasn't because of the lack of trying on our part."

"Do you mind if we have a look around in his office?"

"Sure, please do," Estelle replied, opening his door.

As they looked around, they didn't find anything unusual. Nothing that related to the case.

Grimes turned to Estelle and said, "Before we leave, we would like to interview your staff members individually, if you don't mind."

"Sure," she replied. Both she and her staff agreed.

After a little more than an hour, the detectives were satisfied. They handed her their business cards.

"If there's any additional information, give us a call," Grimes said. She agreed as the detectives left.

Before heading back to the precinct, they went to grab a sandwich from the diner next door. As they sat there, next to them were two men reading the paper. They were regular patrons of the diner. At that moment, they were discussing the murder of Hakeem Robinson. The waiter working the counter overheard their discussion and joined in. They called him Buzz.

Giving his take on the subject, he added, "It's a tragedy what happened to that guy. He was a decent fella. He would come in and get breakfast in the morning. All he talked about was helping people. The homeless issue was his biggest thing. I had just saw him out front, getting in a black limo. The guy he was talking to looked real high dollar."

Overhearing the conversation, Grimes and Poles glanced at each other before Grimes interceded, flashing his badge.

"I'm investigating this case. May I have a moment?"

"Sure," Buzz responded. "Anything I can do to help."

"The limo—can you describe it?"

"Sure. Black, lots of gold trimming. More than I've ever seen on a limo."

"The guy he spoke to—what did he look like?"

"He looked like someone I seen on TV. He had his chauffeur open the door for him. At first, Robinson was hesitant to get in but he did. Then the driver closed the door and got back in the car."

"Did they leave?" Poles asked.

"No," Buzz responded. "They sat there about five or ten minutes. When Robinson got out, he looked irritated. You could see it on his face."

"Did you see where he went after he got out?" Grimes asked.

"Yeah. He got in his car and pulled off, but the limo sat there awhile before leaving."

"Did you happen to look at or remember the tags?" Poles asked.

"Oh yeah, how could I forget? It said 'Wolf' on it in bright gold letters with New York tags."

Handing him his card, Grimes said, "If anything else comes to mind, give me a call."

Buzz stared at the card for a moment. "Will do, lieutenant." he replied.

The officers grabbed their sandwiches and headed back to their car. "We need to pay Mr. Wolf a visit," As they got in Poles agreed, "We're on our way."

Minutes later as they arrived at Wolf's office, everything was quiet. For the first time in weeks, there weren't any protesters carrying anti-Wolf signs. Many were grieving the death of their community leader at the hands of a psychopath the night before. Getting out of their car, the detectives had business to handle on the twentieth floor.

In his suite, Wolf was sitting, doing what he did best, swinging deals. As he watched the latest news updates from the night before, he had been in an unusually giddy mood most of the morning, although no one mentioned it. Everyone knew that the death of Hakeem Robinson, his biggest critic, brightened his day. Although he would never admit it, there was no love lost between the two of them.

When the detectives entered the office, they were greeted at the front desk by Wolf's receptionist.

"May I help you?" she asked.

Grimes and Poles flashed their badges. "We're with the homicide unit," Grimes responded, "and we want to speak with Mr. Wolf."

"Do you have an appointment?"

"No," Grimes responded. "This is official police business."

"Okay, please wait here," she replied before walking away.

While they waited, they stood looking around the office. It's was impressive. Looking over at Poles Grimes said.

"You could fit some people's houses in this place."

"Yeah, starting with mine," Poles replied.

Next to the TV monitor on the center wall, they noticed a portrait of an elderly white-haired gentleman.

"Must be the founder," Grimes said.

"Yeah. One thing's for certain—he won't get any beauty points, especially with that zipper scar on his face," Poles replied.

"I'm surprised the artist was allowed to paint that," Grimes said shaking his head.

Focusing on the picture more, Poles said, "Something about that painting looks awfully familiar, like I've seen that person before. I just can't place a finger on it."

When the receptionist returned, she brought with her his personal secretary.

"Hello, I'm Margaret Sullivan," Mr. Wolf's secretary. I'll take you to him.

While following her, Poles leaned over and whispered in Grimes's ear. "Now I know where I've seen him before. All she needs is a bigger mark on her face," referring to Wolf's secretary.

When they walked into Wolf's office, Margaret introduced them. "This is detective Grimes and Poles. Would you like any refreshments, gentlemen?"

Both officers declined.

"You, sir?" she asked.

"No, thank you," Wolf replied. "That will be all, Margaret."

Looking back at the officers, then her boss curiously, she left the room.

"How can I help you?" Wolf asked.

"We'd like to ask you a few questions about yesterday evening," Grimes replied.

Before Wolf could answer, Poles said, "This is a nice office. You should see what we have to work with back at the precinct. Your bathroom is bigger than our office," he jokingly replied.

Wolf grinned and said, "I'm sure you make the most out of it, Please," extending his hand gesturing them to have a seat.

As soon as they sat, Grimes got straight to the point, "We'd like to ask you a few questions concerning Hakeem Robinson. A witness said that they saw your limo in front of AHO headquarters, and that he was seen getting into your limo. They said the two of you spoke for a few minutes and that he was visibly disturbed as he got out of your car. Everyone we've spoken to associated with AHO has stated there was ongoing tension and discord between the two of you over the housing restoration issue. Would you like to elaborate on these claims?"

"I didn't have any issue with Mr. Robinson," he replied. "Outside of yesterday evening, we've never spoken, directly or indirectly. It was he who constantly criticized me and my company. I've never really had anything to say about the man one way or the other. Outside of my last interview with Ms. Collins, that was the first time I had addressed the issue."

"Yet you came to visit him, right before the election. Why?" Grimes replied.

"I was hoping to find a middle ground in resolving whatever issues he had with me moving forward. I wanted to start things off fresh between us. Sometimes informal, random meetings often render more success than planned ones with an agenda, whether they're straightforward or not."

"In an interview leading up to the election, he threatened to launch an investigation of you and your company's practices. As to the possibility of exposing city officials in the housing and zoning programs concerning numerous code violations, His intentions were clear, "Grimes expressed."

"Something like that could prompt a visit," Poles interjected. "According to the AHO, they repeatedly reached out to you without response. It wasn't until it was pretty clear that he was going to get that seat that you decided to reach out to him, since he was about to be placed in position and would have the resources and power to act on his promises. That is, the allegations he made were true."

"And conveniently he shows up dead the night before the election," Grimes continued. "So, you see, Mr. Wolf, it's the timing of all this that prompts today's visit."

Looking at the detective, Wolf asked, "Are you accusing me, lieutenant?"

"No, I'm not accusing you of anything. I'm simply stating facts. Mr. Wolf, did the two of you ever find a middle ground on this matter?"

"Unfortunately, we didn't," Wolf replied. "Mr. Robinson pretty much had his mind made up, and there was nothing I was going to say that would change that."

During their exchange, Poles looked over at the coat that was hanging on the rack. On it he noticed a strand of blond hair intertwined with a short curly strand. The coat rack was near some framed certificates displayed on the wall.

"Mr. Wolf, do you mind if I look at your honors hanging on your wall?" Poles asked.

"Sure, be my guest," he replied before turning his attention back to Grimes.

While the two were conversating, Poles pretended to be interested making his way to where he really wanted to be. Reaching into his pocket he pulled out a pair of tweezers and a plastic bag while glancing back to see if Wolf was paying attention. Seeing that he was engaged in conversation and focused on his partner, he used the tweezers to place both of the hairs into the bag. After putting it in his pocket he returned to his seat. At that moment, Grimes and Wolf had concluded their conversation.

Wolf looked at the officers and said, "I see where this line of questioning is leading."

Excusing himself from their conversation he turned on the intercom calling his secretary back into his office. Margaret entered and walked over to him.

"Margaret," Would you confirm my whereabouts yesterday evening he asked"

Looking at the officers, she replied," Mr. Wolf and I had been in the office, working from 8 PM that evening until midnight." Her statement made it impossible for Wolf to have been on Staten Island at the time of the Robinson deaths.

"Were you the only two working that night in the office?" Grimes asked.

"Yes," she replied.

Grimes looked at his partner without saying a word then stood up and said, "I think that will be all. If I have anything else, I'll contact you."

"Of course," Wolf replied, "I'll cooperate in any way I can. I hope you catch the culprit of these hideous crimes. I wish you the best of luck. I'll have Margaret see you out."

"That won't be necessary," Grimes replied. "We can find our own way out."

The two officers left while he and his secretary watched.

In the car, Poles reached into his pocket. "I couldn't resist," Poles snickered. Showing Grimes the hair sample he had collected without Wolf's knowledge. "I'm going to send this down to the lab and have it analyzed to see what comes up."

"Good, we need all we can get right now. It's something about that guy that doesn't add up. I just can't put my finger on it yet. Only time will tell."

Chapter 27:
Untouchable

After the returning to the precinct Poles immediately sent the samples he collected to the lab. The day had been fluent. It was time to piece everything together, starting with Neville and his ties to the two women.

He had an alibi the night of Kerri Barnes's death, but it wasn't the same with Sonja Hart. They were together that night. There was no one to cover for him in her death, just his word. His ties to both women placed him number one on the suspect list.

They didn't have enough for a warrant, but they now had a target. They had two women that were murdered in the same way and who were associated with the same guy. From their perspective, what was the likelihood of that?

Still, everything involving him was circumstantial or coincidental; they were trying to find something that could warrant a more direct move on Neville.

Then there was the question of Nicholas Wolf. The one thing Grimes couldn't shake involved the possible legal implications that would provide a motive to silence Robinson which would get him out the way. Wolf's visit with Robinson on the night of his death, coupled with the position he would've been in to act on his promise, made it look suspicious. The fact was that he was in direct conflict with Wolf's interests, but there was nothing directly tying him to his death. There was also a remote possibility that Wolf may have been targeted by someone using his buildings as a convenient source with a hidden agenda, but there was nothing to substantiate that theory either.

His secretary said the two of them were working late that night in the office and couldn't have been on Staten Island. Even with all of that, nothing could explain the evidence of what killed them or who was responsible, if anybody. With no evidence of a tool or weapon, everything pointed to some type of animal being used or even someone in a specially made suit to give that impression, which sounded highly unlikely. So far, the background investigation on all of the victims found that they did not know one another, and that Neville was the only one who had a direct connection to any of them.

For Grimes, there was one thing that remained on his mind—the mystery man who rescued his girlfriend. Who was he and what role did he play in all of it? At least two people saw something but nothing that would confirm whether he was the same guy. It was a hunch that wouldn't go away.

The mystery man made a rescue and then left the assailants unconscious for the police before slipping away. Who he was didn't match the description of the man last seen with any of the females. He did however fit the description of the mysterious figure of what appeared to be a large man who was enormously strong and fast, had locks, and was seen near or around a couple of the victims. No one had been able to give a clear description of him—only that he disappeared without a trace, leaving no other evidence behind.

The detectives wondered whether he was involved in the crimes or just a vigilante who happened to be on the streets at the same time a psychopath was on the loose. All accounts of him were sketchy at best. In either case, he remained a mystery.

After the long hours, it was now time to close up shop.

Turning to his partner Poles said, "I'm calling it a day." Time to stop at the flower shop. Buy some roses, go home, and make love to my wife. Ease some of this stress."

"Yes, sounds like a good idea," Grimes replied. "Me and Terrie are having our issues again. I'm going to have to go home and take a cold shower until we can get it together."

"You'll work it out. You always do."

Grabbing his jacket, Poles gave a nod to his partner and left, leaving Grimes at his desk with his hands behind his head, pondering his next move. Although all DNA came back the same, he still kept hope that would render something new. Now with the inclusion of the most recent samples Poles collected, one being blond and the other gray along with the results of the last set of victims they were both curious to find out what new information it would render. Grabbing his keys Grimes got up and headed home.

The days that followed, the detectives checked their references while going over the evidence. Although circumstances varied, amidst the chaos and the randomness of the attacks, there was a pattern. All the women that were killed—with the exception of Mrs. Robinson—were done in the same exact way. In her case her heart wasn't taken.

Also, all the women were found in a specific section of the city, and that was where Grimes and Poles would focus.

When they arrived to the precinct, the coroner's report sat on Grimes's desk. There was nothing new to go on, which further frustrated the officers—especially Grimes. With their computers on, Grimes leaned back in his chair with both hands behind his head, thinking about their next move, while Poles sat across from him equally frustrated.

Over and over again, they reviewed their notes and checking everything they had. Grimes rocked back in his chair, staring at the map where he had an assortment of colored stick pins marking the places where each of the victims were found.

The ones that were directly in their district he used red pins. He also noticed that they seemed to have a pattern but wasn't quite sure what to make of it. While scenarios danced in his head, an officer dropped off the mail in their inbox.

Noticing a magazine rolled in his back pocket, Grimes asked, "What's that in your pocket?"

As he pulled it out, on the cover was a picture of a werewolf.

"It's a sci-fi magazine talking about mythical beasts," he replied, "a hobby of mine that has fascinated me since I was a kid." He turned around and left.

As Grimes sat, a thought came across his mind. The picture on that magazine had triggered it. Turning his attention from the city map, he began focusing on the State map hanging on the opposite wall and instructed. "John, grab your jacket."

"Grab my jacket?" Poles replied.

"Yeah. We're going for a ride. I have an old friend and classmate I attended college with. She's a professor at Claremont University upstate she teaches forensics. "Claremont University, that's a two-hour drive." he replied.

Yeah, I know. She's also a historian of infamous serial killers of the past. It was her obsession, even back when we were in college."

Walking over to a separate file cabinet, he pulled out a set of keys, opened it, and reached in pulling out a sealed plastic bag.

"What you got there, chief?"

"Another set of hair samples, in case I had to turn to other resources."

"I think she may be able to help us, or at least point us in a direction."

The two officers gathered what they needed and headed on their way.

Chapter 28:

Of Myths and Legends, a Warrior's Tale

After a two-and-a-half-hour drive, they arrived on campus, about twenty miles outside of Albany. It was late afternoon. Professor Roslyn Perry was finishing up a lecture on human anatomy and the basics of forensic science. She was one of the best forensic experts in her field.

Quietly, they entered the auditorium where she was finishing up. No one noticed except the one conducting the class. After she concluded her lecture, she gave her students their next assignment as they began to leave. Making their way through the existing students, they met with the instructor at the center of the auditorium. She was surprised to see her old friend. It had been years since she had seen her old college classmate. Their relationship had been a good one back in their college days. It was a little deeper than anyone knew. When Grimes got close, he leaned over and hugged her, followed by a peck on her cheek. Then he stepped back and introduced his partner.

"Professor Perry, this is John Poles."

"Nice to meet you John," extending her hand.

"Likewise," he replied, shaking her hand.

Grimes got right to the point. "The reason for our visit is because we need your help. Is there anywhere we could sit and talk?"

"Sure, she replied. I knew you didn't ride all this way just to say hello. We can talk in my office. It's just a few doors down the hall."

As they headed there, the two had a brief session of catching up, with Poles trailing closely behind.

After entering the office, Roslyn took a seat behind her desk while the officers pulled up a couple of chairs.

"I know you've heard what's been going on in the city," Grimes began.

"Who hasn't?" she replied.

"Then you may have an idea why I need your help."

"Of course," I've been almost expecting you."

Grimes handed her a large envelope. When she looked inside, there were several pictures of the victims taken at the crime scene. Looking closely at the photos, she became disturbed.

It was all too familiar to her. She had seen wounds like these before while researching serial murders present and past. One of the photos caught her interest.

"Are these animal tracks? Looking up at both officers.

"Yes," Grimes replied. "They were found at every crime scene. Prints were made but no one could find any animal to match them."

"I've never seen anything like this before. They remind me of something I've read but I can't recall where I read it. It will come back to me, but I do have a friend who might be able to help."

As she continued to look through the pictures, she added, "These wounds are almost identical to ones I've researched throughout history, one case specifically comes to mind."

Reaching in her drawer, she pulled out a flash drive, inserted it, and then asked the officers to look at the computer screen. After opening the drive, she began comparing them to the photos that they had given her while explaining in detail.

"These photos were taken during the time of Jack the Ripper," looking at Grimes and then back to the screen. "When you look at both pictures, they're almost identical. I received these photos years ago when I was in London. Either this is a coincidence, a copycat, or your killer is over a hundred and thirty years old. I would say the chances of the latter being a zero. Like myself, your killer may follow historical serial killers with one difference—he's a murderer himself, mimicking them, and then acting upon his desires with precision. The mystery still remains where those tracks came from," she concluded, "but somehow this story has a very familiar overtone."

Reaching into his pocket, Grimes pulled out the hair sample he had put in his pocket just before leaving his office. He handed her the plastic bag.

"If you can," could you see what you can come up with that could help us out? Grimes asked. I took this off a victim's body.

Roslyn smiled and said, "That's why I'm here." She looked closely at them through the plastic bag and then added, "I have a colleague who's a former detective now working at Scotland Yard forensics that might be able to help. He's also a history buff. We both share the same interest. We met during a conference about five years ago in Germany. That's when he told me that they held in storage evidence of the Jack the Ripper case. I remember him once telling me they found samples of unidentified hairs on the bodies— blond hairs, along with a pair of animal tracks."

She paused, looked over at Grimes, and asked, "Do you mind if I send him this sample along with the pictures of those tracks?"

"Sure, no problem," Grimes replied. "Anything you can come up with will be helpful."

"It may take two weeks but if I know him, he may have something more."

"Thanks for your help, Ros. We need to come up with some answers before this monster kills again."

"As soon as I find out anything, I'll contact you," she replied.

After exchanging goodbyes, the officers headed back to the city. Roslyn sat a moment, allowing everything to settle in before picking up the phone. It was 4 PM when she made the call.

In London, it was 9 PM when the phone rang. Still in the office, Colin McRae answered—a former detective and the leading forensic expert in the U.K. He was both surprised and exuberated to hear the familiar voice on the other end. They hadn't spoken to one another in over three years. After a period of catching up, she asked for his help.

"Whatever you need, Ros was his response?"

"I'm sure you know what's been taking place in New York," she replied.

"Yes, it's on all the news outlets."

Roslyn spoke in detail about what she and the detectives had discussed. Colin remained quiet, taking it all in. She emphasized the importance of keeping a lid on everything they were discussing. She told him of the hair sample and tracks found on the scene, which drew his interest. After giving a few more details, Colin became intrigued with what she shared.

"Is it okay that I send pictures along with the hair sample for you to examine?"

"Sure," he replied. "Once I go over everything, I'll get back to you."

After ending the call, Roslyn began conducting her own research to see what she could find.

Later that evening when she returned home, she immediately went to her attic where she kept an old wooden foot locker she kept locked. Inside of it was a set of old books, one of which was an old journal written by the warrior and adventurer Adonis. Within it contained obscure stories of his exploits and an ancient tale. It mentioned a curse that was never seen outside this book.

When Roslyn attended the conference in Germany, during her leisure time, she visited a few small towns and villages. While on tour she came across an old souvenir shop that caught her eye. It was filled with artifacts and obscure books. While she looked around there was one book that caught her attention. It was very old and had a unique look about it.

The owner of the shop said it was written in Latin 1500 years ago by an adventurer who had recorded his exploits. He also said there was a passage in the book with strange symbols of a forgotten language that were too old to be interpreted. The owner was puzzled as to why it was in the text, who would've known how to write it, and what it may have meant. He also told her there was a passage in it about an ancient killer said to be a blond werewolf and a cat creature called a panthiem who was once the warrior's friend when he was human. It was that narrative that prompted her to purchase it.

Taking the book from her attic she began to meticulously review it. She needed to further research the information the detectives shared to expand on it. When first purchased, she thought it was just another collection of myth, but after listening to what Grimes had told her, it was the only story in the book that came to mind, it had a familiar tone, once she found the passages and began reading them in detail.

It appeared to be based on everything that she and McRae had discussed.

On their way back to New York, it was an unusually quiet drive for the two officers, especially for the snappy Poles who seemed to never be at a loss for words. Both were lost in thought over what the next move would be.

Chapter 29:
Heavy Hearts

Sitting at her desk in her office Terrie Collins was writing a blog about the effect of the recent attacks on the city and its citizens. Also on her desk were news articles discussing the latest victims of the Butcher of the Bronx. Every time Nicholas Wolf's properties were repeatedly mentioned, she circled his name. Although there was no proof of his involvement, she too was beginning to think there may be some connection.

As she wrapped up, the producer walked in, nervously excited.

"There's a bank robbery in progress downtown," he said. "A number of people have been shot, and the assailants have barricaded themselves on the scene. Your team is already in the lot waiting and ready to go."

"Thanks," she replied, quickly powering down her laptop she headed out the door.

While she and her crew headed for Downtown Manhattan, Maria was out with Paul Neville. Their relationship had been going on for a couple of weeks but it was Maria's little secret. It wasn't until the night of the fundraiser—the night Sandra Woo died—that Terrie had found out, and that was by chance.

Maria had taken off to have a little fun time as the two were enjoying their day together. As the hours went passed, Maria's phone rang. Looking at the caller ID, it was Terrie.

Maria's answered, "What's up girl."

"Hey", Would you do me a big favor?

"I've been downtown at the police barricade the last couple of hours. Bank robbery in progress. Looks like I won't be leaving anytime soon.

"Of course," Maria replied.

"Would you please go by the studio and get my keys then go by my place, take Max, and feed him? You don't have to do it until later. He's already set up for this afternoon. It's crazy down here and I won't be leaving anytime soon."

"I gotcha girl, but you owe me," she replied. "I'm on a hot date right now that I hope is going to last well into the night," she chuckled looking across the table at him while he listened.

"Who is it, girl?"

"Remember that delivery guy you saw at the fundraiser?"

After thinking about it, she responded, "Oh yeah, your little secret bun you tried to hide from me," she laughed.

"You know it," Maria responded. "Anyhow, I gotcha.

"Thank you, sweetie, and yes, I owe you.

After Maria ended the call, Neville asked, "Was that your girlfriend?"

"Yes, my sister from another mother. She needs me to go by the TV station, get her keys, then go take care of her puppy. But we don't have to go by there until later. Meanwhile, I can think of a couple of things we can do until then," she teased, winking at him.

He looked at her. "I can think of a few things myself," he replied while taking a sip of beer.

Later that evening, Tia was scheduled to do a makeup session for the evening anchors. She hoped that she could find anything in Terrie Collin's possession that would help Jahir.

She knew there would be a very short window of opportunity and Terrie's office was a few doors down from the studio room, next to the ladies' room. While preparing the anchors for the telecast, she knew the evening crew wasn't fully staffed, giving her the opportunity to look around during filming.

While all attention was on the cast and crew, she walked over to the producer. Wasting no time, she asked for directions to the bathroom. She wasn't going to let this opportunity pass. As she walked toward the bathroom, she looked around making sure everything was clear before slipping into her office.

She wasn't sure what she was looking for, or if there were anything there, she could use. All she knew was that she had to try and try it quickly. While searching for whatever papers, notes, or pictures she could find, she saw an article with Wolf's name circled, thinking it might mean something. She folded it and put it in her purse hoping that Terrie would think the cleaning crew had thrown it away by mistake.

When she was about to leave, she heard footsteps in the hallway getting closer. She didn't know whether it was Terrie returning and didn't want to get caught in there without a good reason, but she was too late. Tia's heart dropped as she stood face-to-face with Maria standing in the doorway.

Caught off guard Tia nervously blurted out. "Oh hi!"

Suspicious and slow to reply Maria responded. "Hel-lo," Do you work here? I've never seen you before."

Thinking quickly, Tia responded, "Not really. I do makeup part-time for the studio, part of my college program for extra credit, "I'm Tia Johnson."

"Oh yes", Terrie told me about you. "You did a phenomenal job on her after her incident. She hasn't stopped talking about you since. I'm her friend Maria. Why are you here in her office? She's downtown and won't be back for a while."

"I was looking for the bathroom, and not paying attention. I ended up in here. I must be tripping," she replied, shaking her head.

While Tia walked out of the door down the hallway, still suspicious, Maria watched her then grabbed Terrie's keys out her desk.

As Tia left the building quietly, she wasn't sure whether she had found anything useful. In front of the studio, Neville was sitting in a car waiting for Maria. When she walked by his face looked familiar but she shrugged off the thought.

She also felt uncomfortable by the way he was looking at her. To her, it was almost as if he wanted to hop out of the car and devour her. He winked then howled at her which made her quicken her steps.

After a few blocks, he pulled up next to her, he wasn't alone. Maria was with him on the passenger side. Neville was looking past her with a grin on his face.

"Would you like a ride? We'll drop you off wherever you're going."

Before she could answer, Neville spurted out, "Hello. I'm Paul," as Maria gave him a look.

Feeling uncomfortable, she declined.

"You sure?" Maria replied, "These streets are crazy. "

Forcing a smile, she told them, "I'll be fine. The subway is only a few blocks up the street."

Neville gave her a look which made her uncomfortable, re-affirming her decision as they slowly pulled off.

After catching the subway, she was back in the Bronx. She was going to meet with Jahir before going home hoping she had something that could help. In a back alley not far from her home he was already there waiting. Pulling the article from her purse with Nicholas Wolf's name circled she handed it to him and said,

"I don't know whether it's worth anything, but I hope it helps out." "If anyone had knowledge would know something, it would be her friend, the policeman," Jahir replied.

"Why him?"

"Because the two are close. The way she looks at him is in the same way Kolliana once looked at me. I will visit the police station soon."

"You can't go there and look around, not like this," Tia replied.

"Don't worry. There is more to me than the monster you see. I'm indebted to you. I must go. I'll see you again soon."

Tia watched as he disappeared into the night. Taking her shortcut, she was now headed home. It wasn't a long walk but it took her through a neighborhood littered with vacant buildings with a few that were occupied mixed in.

The night was quiet as she sped up her walk when suddenly, there was a scream. It frightened her but something inside drove her to where she heard it instead of running away. Her conscience wouldn't allow it. She rushed towards the noise.

When she got there, she froze in place. Less than twenty feet away she saw the blond werewolf standing over Maria's body. It wasn't in its full form but was slowly returning to its human appearance. With her heart still beating within its grasp, he grabbed her by the ankle and dragged her lifeless body toward one of the vacant buildings.

At first, Bultizar was unaware of her presence until he caught her scent. She was hiding behind the corner a building. When Bultizar turned, she recognized his face. Terrified, she turned and ran as fast as she could. Bultizar transformed back into his beastly form, pursuing her.

Running for her life, Jahir's senses were already guiding him towards them. The question wasn't whether he would get there in time to save her. Jahir knew Bultizar had already killed and was already heading towards them from above. He had also caught Tia's scent blocks away. On the ground, Bultizar was now within reach.

Bultizar attempted to strike her but miraculously she dodged the blow at the last possible second, causing him to miss as she tripped. Springing to her feet she attempted to flee again but a second blow found its target knocking her unconscious. While she lay there, Bultizar stood over her, revealing his fangs to deliver the killing bite.

Leaping twelve stories down, landing lightly on his feet, Jahir launched himself like a projectile into Bultizar sending him flying backward into a wall twenty feet away. The impact engraved the shape of his body onto the bricks momentarily stunning him.

Regaining his senses, Jahir looked across the courtyard where Maria's body laid. He was too late. He went over and found her still breathing. Seeing her lying there enraged him even more. Bultizar began to creep away. Jahir turned; he was hell-bent on making him pay.

Intercepting Bultizar before he could get away, they were now face-to-face for the first time since they were both human. The two beastly gladiators instantaneously launched their attack. The two embraced like deranged animals tearing into one another, the sounds of their battle were heard for blocks.

Back and forth they went, fueled with rage and unbridled hatred they had harbored for centuries. The golden wolf sank his fangs deep into the panthiem's body, hoping to end it all, while the panthiem tore into the werewolf's body with claws of equal length, seeking to snatch its heart from its cradle.

Each suffered deep wounds but neither found their mark that would end this struggle. At last, Jahir gained the advantage, pinning the Bultizar to the ground. Jahir neutralized his weapons and was poised to deliver the decisive blow.

Before Jahir could end it, Bultizar reverted back to his human form as a police officer arrived, gleaming his light on the two combatants. In his eyes, Jahir was the last beast standing while Bultizar lay there as a helpless victim, his clothes shredded appearing to be at the mercy of a monster.

With no desire to cause him any harm, Jahir had no choice but to flee as the officer froze not wanting to risk shooting the man on the ground, at the same time not sure what he was witnessing. After Jahir moved away, he opened fire as bullets tore into his body before disappearing into a dark corridor between two buildings.

After checking the two victims to see if they were still breathing, the officer cautiously followed Jahir. Shinning his light into the dark space he saw that it led to a dead end but Jahir was gone. Flashing his light all around he then pointed his flashlight upward to what appeared to be scratch marks up the side of the building several stories up.

After calling for backup, more police arrived. They scoured the area for the suspect, before finding another woman's body in the back of one of the dilapidated buildings. This time, they had two living witnesses, both lying and appearing to be unconscious: Tia battered and bruised, and the man having his clothes nearly torn off him, but they didn't find a scratch.

While police were distracted, Bultizar had vanished. Under the circumstances, it seemed impossible but no one saw him get by them, confusing the police. Tia on the other hand remained consciousness. She was immediately taken to the hospital under an armed escort. They hoped she regained consciousness given she was the only witness who could provide them with vital information or locate the other victim.

Grimes and Poles arrived at the hospital shortly after Tia. Approaching them was a familiar face: Officer Daniels.

"Lieutenant," Daniels, addressing Grimes.

"Officer Daniels," Grimes replied.

Daniels looked over at Poles and nodded.

Daniels began his report.

"When I arrived, one of the victims was being attacked by something before it got away. It had a guy pinned to the ground about to strike with those long claws, but when I shined my light on him, its eyes reflected the light before looking down at the man. He hesitated, then looked back at me. At first, I thought it was a large man, but his face looked almost like a cat that was covered with short black fur. It also had locks coming down from under a cap and hood. It showed its fangs and snarled; maybe he had on a mask or something, I don't know; it looked real. I didn't fire at first because I didn't want to risk shooting the guy on the ground.

"When he fled is when I opened fire. I could see the bullets tear into his clothes, but they didn't even faze him. Nothing could've survived that many hits at that range."

"Maybe it wearing body armor or high on PCP or something," Poles suggested.

"Maybe," Daniels replied. "It just took off between those buildings. It was pitch-black back there where I followed it. When I shined my light back there it was a dead end. The way it came in was the only way out. He would've had to get past me. The only other way out is straight up twelve stories with no windows. Even if he did, he couldn't have moved that fast. I was right behind him."

Looking back at Poles, Grimes then asked, "Where's the man he attacked?"

"Gone," Daniels answered. "He was unconscious. During all the commotion when backup arrived, the next thing I knew, he was gone, vanished. This place was crawling with cops, how he got by all of them, I don't know, or why he would want to with what just happened. He was the lucky one. I can only tell you he was a young white male with blond hair. With everything happening so fast, I didn't get a good look at his face. His clothes were nearly shredded off his body."

Daniels continued, "What I don't understand about all of this was with that much damage to his clothing, I didn't see any cuts, bruises, or blood, not even a scratch. That within itself doesn't make since. But the two women didn't fare as well."

Grimes replied, "One thing is for certain—we have to find whatever it is you saw."

"They transported Ms. Johnson to the hospital. She suffered a number of bruises and lacerations to the head. It's a miracle she survived but she still hasn't regained consciousness. We are presuming that she and that guy were together and they happened upon the killer. We believe that's when that thing attacked them. The other victim was already dead. We found her body in the back of one of those buildings, her heart ripped from her chest. We also found several sets of animal tracks leading to both bodies. The tracks had to belong to that thing we saw."

"When you followed it between the buildings, where did its tracks lead?" Grimes asked.

"There weren't any animal prints, only shoe prints come to think of it. It looked like it was wearing shoes. The only one who didn't have on any shoes was the male victim. They must've come off during the attack but we haven't found them." I did see some scratches on the bricks, but it's probably nothing.

Although the detectives found that to be strange, they didn't elaborate on it. They simply allowed Daniels to continued briefing them.

"The victim's name was Maria Gomez," a twenty-four-year-old organizing director at Tech Industries.

"Maria Gomez!" Grimes exclaimed, looking over at Poles. Their faces dropped as her death struck home.

"You know her?" Daniels asked.

Solemnly, Grimes replied, "Yes."

Action News arrived but without Terrie Collins who was still covering the barricade situation. He assumed she didn't know; therefore, he had to tell her.

But first, he needed to go over the crime scene with the hope of finding physical evidence of the thing Daniels reported to have shot, perhaps leaving a clue beyond what they had already gathered. Once again only blond hairs were found. They believed it may have come from the man who was attacked, but to be certain they had to send it to the lab with whatever additional evidence they could find.

As they examined the wounds, the claw and bite patterns appeared to match those applied to the previous victims. This case had now taken a drastic turn. They had multiple witness but Tia was the one who could confirm it all.

Chapter 30:
Bultizar Makes a Hospital Call

After the barricade incident, Terrie finally settled in back at her condo. She had heard that the serial killer had struck again but hadn't heard any of the particulars. She had no idea one of the victims was Maria.

She was beat. Her search for information concerning the Bronx murders without resolve had taken its toll. For the first time in weeks, she didn't want to do anything but be home, spend time with her puppy and rest. She was disappointed when she saw that Maria hadn't been by. Max hadn't been fed and had relieved himself all over the floor. She knew that Maria was hanging out, but it wasn't like her not to show up, text, or call. She then realized she had turned her ringer off. Still, there was no text.

Picking up her phone she tried to reach her but only got her voice mail. Soon after hanging up there was an incoming call, it was Grimes.

When she answered, there was a moment of silence before a hesitant response on the other end.

By the sound of her voice, he could tell she didn't know.

"Hey baby," he replied, his voice was low and descending.

She knew instantly something was wrong. The noises in the background were all too familiar, she knew Grimes was on the scene of an emergency.

"Bobby, what's the matter, another murder?"

"I'm afraid there was, sweetheart," he replied.

"What's wrong? You're scaring me. Where are you?" she asked.

After a brief silence, Grimes replied, "It's Maria."

"What about Maria?" she inquired, with a veil of nervousness in her voice.

"She's dead. Murdered!"

"No," she gasped as everything around her seem to stand still. Tears began to flow uncontrollably. After several minutes, she began to gather herself saying, "I just spoke to her earlier this evening, asking her to stop by the station and get my keys then come here—but she never showed up." The tears flowed again.

In an attempt to comfort her, he said, "I'll be there as soon as I finish up here."

"No!" she abruptly responded. "I'm coming there." She suddenly ended the call.

Grimes looked at Poles and said, "Terrie's coming here. She said Maria was supposed to stop by the TV station before stopping at her place. We need to ask the night crew if she showed up there, and if so, at what time."

"They're still setting up," Poles replied. "I'll go over and ask them."

When he left, Grimes and Daniels went to the area Jahir had fled.

After giving the details, Daniels pointed to marks up on the wall. Grimes stepped back to get a better look. Seeing them engraved in the bricks was baffling. "It appeared to have jumped up there, about thirty feet up," Grimes surmised. "There are no other marks anywhere before those, so, apparently, he scaled the wall like a cat."

"That's impossible."

Grimes looked at him with raised eyebrows, shrugging his shoulder. "You tell me. You shot him. What other explanation, or proof do you have to say otherwise?"

Daniels responded, "Lieutenant, do you expect me to put that in my report?"

Grimes looked at him saying, "That's up to you," and walked away.

Meanwhile, Poles spoke to the news team. They told him both women had been there briefly around the same time. Tia Johnson did the makeup for the evening team, while Maria came by to pick up Terrie's keys. They said they tried calling her several times, but her mailbox was full. Poles asked if she were alone.

One of the crew said that the guard happened to go outside and saw Maria get into a car with a guy before pulling off.

Asking for a description, they told him he was a young guy with blond hair. After Grimes and Daniels finished their conversation, he walked over to Poles who told him what the news team said.

Grimes told him about the marks on the wall and that Daniels said that they believed the blond guy and Tia Johnson were together.

"Yeah," Poles replied." but Maria was seen in her car with someone that fit the description of the victim who disappeared."

"So how is it that he was fighting to protect Ms. Johnson and not Maria?" Grimes asked, looking back at Poles. "We need to talk to Mr. Neville again."

"This whole thing has been a nightmare. What are we hunting monsters or men?" Poles queried.

Grimes looked at Poles and said, "Maybe both. I'm about ready to believe almost anything at this point. Plus, Daniels said he shot it multiple times, but it didn't faze it. Now Maria is dead, while another young woman is fighting for her life, not to mention that may or may not have been in the company of our mystery man who is now somewhere hiding, and we haven't a clue where to start looking for him. Something has to break."

Terrie arrived as the coroner was placing Maria's body in the back of the van. Grimes intercepted her, grabbing hold of her as he tried to calm her. Tears flowed down her face while Grimes attempted to console her.

Grimes wanted to tell her everything that happened. He wanted to share what the officer had seen but he was pressured not to divulge that information and he knew she had no obligation to remain silent especially anything involving the death of her friend. Grimes believed that she wouldn't hesitate for any reason to reveal what police wanted to keep as a secret. Although he knew that withholding information would jeopardize their relationship, it was a risk he had to take.

Still holding her he asked, "To your knowledge, was Maria with anyone?"

"She said she was on a date with her friend, a guy named Paul, I forgot his last name. I first saw him on the night of the fundraiser, the same night

Sandra Woo was killed. I asked her about him after I saw them talking. She said they had only known each other for a couple of weeks. The guy I saw was wearing a DTX-Press uniform."

"A DTX-Press uniform," Poles replied. He then looked at Grimes and added. You said his first name was Paul?"

"Yes," she replied.

"His last name wouldn't be Neville, would it?"

"Yes, that's it," You know him!

The two officers looked at one another. Playing it off they gave her a reason that didn't connect to the case. Seeing that she was highly emotional and broken they didn't want to make things worse. It wasn't until Maria's body had been taken away did Grimes release her. Grimes said, "I think you should go home and get some rest. Let me drive you, John can follow."

"No, I'll be okay," she replied.

"You sure?"

"Yes, I'll be okay."

She hugged him again like she never wanted to let go.

***

Miles away, Jahir found another place to hide far from police and helicopters looking for him. He couldn't hang around like before waiting for the opportunity to descend and link Bultizar's trail.

He had been exposed. He had been seen by the authorities and had to be even more cautious. They had a face to pin on the crime, diverting the trail from the golden wolf.

His heart was heavy due to his friend lying unconscious in a hospital with her life in the balance. He wasn't sure which hospital, but he was going to find and protect her. What troubled him the most was had he not asked for her to help, they wouldn't have met that night and fate may not have placed her in harm's way. His only solace now rested upon images that flashed through his head which did not include her death.

The fact she survived Bultizar's attack was an anomaly, something in which no one had ever done before. Only she could identify him, which placed her life in double jeopardy. Not only was she in danger from the werewolf, but the man himself. He knew that Bultizar would be looking for her and wouldn't stop in any form until he found her.

There was an urgency now more than ever for Jahir to find her first. Also haunting him was that he was so close to ending this game—just a downward thrust from killing his ancient enemy and freeing himself from what seemed to have been an eternity of pain.

He hadn't been this close since the day he faced him at the sorceress fortress. Just like on that fateful day, he was interrupted before he could kill him—the difference being it was the police this time and that Bultizar had seized the moment to convert back into human form, snatching the opportunity from Jahir's grasp once again.

Bultizar had both outwitted and outmaneuvered him, allowing him to escape. Although the night hadn't been in his favor, he wasn't completely in the dark in finding him. Tia gave him a place to start. The information she revealed to him that she had gotten from Terrie's files also led to the detective's office. If he could somehow get there, then he would possibly be able to collect the pieces that would allow him to figure out where the final kill would take place.

With the night of the scarlet blood moon a few weeks away, the whereabouts of his friend lay heavily on his mind. Jahir had to act fast in finding her, knowing that Bultizar would be after her to finish the job. Jahir knew that police would have doubled their security around her to prevent a second assault but there wouldn't be enough to stop the werewolf.

What troubled Jahir the most was that if Bultizar found out Tia was his friend, then he would stop at nothing to kill her. Also, he was too close to what he wanted, making her a liability that he couldn't afford. On the move again, Jahir he had to return to the scene to follow her scent to track her.

***

After his disappearance from the murder scene, Bultizar arrived to where he kept the prize of his victims. As he opened the chest, for a moment he stared at the latest one triumphantly. Feeling gratified, he carefully placed it in one of the last two open chambers leaving one more to fill.

After placing the chest back into its resting place, Bultizar discarded his shredded clothing before taking hold of a large duffel bag he kept close by. The night wasn't completely done. He had one more stop to make.

Reaching in his bag, he pulled out a change of clothes, a black wig along with a pair of gold framed wire glasses. He took out a mirror from the bag to make sure everything was in place.

Satisfied with his disguise, he was now ready to make his move. He was going to pay her a visit before she could open her eyes, and he was prepared to do whatever it took to ensure that she would never open them again.

After what had been a night straight out the pages of a horror story, his latest victim had struck home. It had affected everyone directly involved in the case. The detectives, the lead reporter and Jahir himself were all linked with Tia laying in the hospital in critical condition.

***

Back on the scene, after watching Terrie leave, Grimes turned to Poles and said, "Let's head over to Neville's and see what we can find out being the last person seen with her."

They needed to find pieces to what had been an extraordinary puzzle to be solved. When they arrived, they knocked on his door, but there was no answer.

As much as they wanted to gain entry they couldn't without a warrant. They didn't want to jeopardize the case even if they found something they could use. Grimes said, "We'll get that court order in the morning. Let's go to the hospital to see if Ms. Johnson has opened her eyes yet."

Despite what Daniels saw, in Grimes's mind it wasn't enough. He needed to know everything.

He needed to know exactly what it was that Daniels had seen earlier, and whether it was tied to his girlfriend's rescuer, or the same one who took out the men who attacked Tia Johnson.

He needed to know the connections that Neville had with at least three of the five women that were last seen with him or the type of contact they had with him. He also needed to know why the killer chose to murder only females in a specific way and why only Nicholas Wolf's properties were chosen. Then, there was the million-dollar question that loomed the heaviest in the detective's mind. Why was it that Hakeem Robinson—the biggest advocate for the community along with being Wolf's biggest critic—had been murdered, was it all a coincidence. How did this all tie together, if at all?

Another question was whether the other victims were simply random or done so to throw off the authorities for whatever twisted reason.

All these questions spun in his head like a tornado but it was time to get answers and move forward. He was still waiting to see what Roslyn Perry had for him. He hadn't a clue whether it would be helpful or simply another dead end. All he could do was wait.

At the hospital, Bultizar entered the rear of the building. Aware of the cameras, he angled himself so they couldn't get a clear view. Passing an unattended examination room, he saw that one of the doctors had left his lab coat hanging on a rack with a name tag still attached. Casually grabbing it along with a stethoscope he put it on. As he walked throughout the hospital, he saw that it was crawling with cops. He knew that posing as a physician was his best chance at getting information. Even in human form, his senses were heightened. He could hear staff members talking among themselves.

They were discussing the incident that had occurred earlier—the young patient that was escorted by police. During their conversation, he learned where they were keeping her, which was exactly what he was looking for.

She was in the critical care unit of the east wing on the fourth floor. Catching the elevator to that floor, he reached into his pocket and put on a hospital mask. With a stethoscope around his neck, he blended with the staff members that were walking towards the unit.

Standing in front of the double doors leading into the unit, two officers were posted outside. Without a key card to enter, he pretended he was checking his chart as he waited for someone to enter or leave. He also saw that there was another camera in the hallway facing the double doors. Despite wearing a disguise, he made sure it couldn't get a direct view of his face. He was determined not to take any risks.

While waiting, several staff members walked by him toward the unit. Seizing the opportunity, he followed them before turning down a separate corridor within the unit. While approaching the nurses' station, one of the patient's emergency lights flashed on the panel, turning everyone's attention to the emergency. Seizing the opportunity Bultizar looked at the chart to see exactly where Tia was. As he approached her, his eyes began turning gray, his nails turned into claws, while blond fur slowly sprouted from his hands and wrists.

A full change wasn't necessary but it was just enough to do the job. He was now in her space while looking around to see if it was clear.

leaning forward he whispered, "Such a little one lying here so peacefully. It will be a shame to wake up to a world so cruel. Therefore, I shall allow you to forever sleep."

About to strike he heard a voice behind him calling out to him halting him.

"Doctor," quickly reverting back to normal.

When he turned, both Grimes and Poles, had their badges out.

"How is she?" Grimes asked.

Enraged within, on the outside he remained calm. This was his opportunity and he wasn't certain if another would present itself. Tempted to kill them all, he thought the better of it. He was too close to throw it all away.

He looked at them and said, "There's been no change. All we can do is wait. Excuse me officers, I have to go check on another patient."

Leaving the two officers standing there, puzzling both.

"That was odd. He must've really been in a hurry," Poles said.

Turning their attention to Tia, the resident physician had just entered the unit.

Bultizar walked toward him and the door.

When the two passed one another, the doctor noticed the name tag on Bultizar's lab coat.

He then turned around and asked, "Excuse me, who are you? Your name tag? It belongs to Steven Marcello, a close colleague of mine. Where did you get it? He's off today."

Grimes and Poles heard the exchange, then looked at each other. Bultizar never responded, he just quickened his steps quickly moving towards the unit's exit door. Grimes and Poles approached the resident doctor and quickly identified themselves. He told them that the name tag the man was wearing didn't belong to him, that the doctor to whom it belonged was off and that he had never seen that man before.

Bultizar begun to run down the hallway before exiting down a stairwell. Grimes then got on the radio notifying officers to be on the lookout for a guy impersonating a doctor giving the details. Giving their location, he instructed them to cover all its exits and that they were in pursuit.

Now trapped, there was a window located between floors within the stairwell. With Grimes and Poles coming down behind him and officers coming up. There was only one way to go and Bultizar took it. He leaped through, the glass window as he made his escape. Converging on the location, he was gone. Only evidence of broken glass remained. For the next couple of hours, the police combed the area looking for him but came up empty; Bultizar had disappeared.

Grimes and Poles went down to the security office.

When they arrived, they were met by an aging bald man with gray hair, a bulging stomach and a strong Boston accent. His name was Kevin MacGreg. Flustered by Bultizar's escape, they approached him requesting to see the video footage. Immediately, MacGreg retrieved it, going over it frame by frame, starting with the elevators and the hallway on Tia's floor.

"That's the same guy, but from a different angle," Grimes said, immediately recognizing him. "There's little else we can make out. He never faced the cameras."

"This guy is good," Poles said. "Usually upon entry, you can get some type of facial, but in every angle, he's covered his tracks by not letting the camera get a good view."

They reviewed the footage from around the hospital grounds--absolutely nothing. Bultizar had carefully avoided all the perimeter cameras. For several hours, they reviewed all footage, but they couldn't get a clear view of the suspect in any of it. Frustrated, the officers returned to Tia's bedside.

Bultizar's momentary change, although partial and brief, didn't go unnoticed. It was enough to alert Jahir. He now knew exactly where they were keeping his friend and was going to protect her.

Still unconscious, Grimes felt that for her safety it was best to move her to a more secure section within the hospital, but this time in secret. To make certain that no one else at the hospital knew where she was kept, they handpicked the staff. Only they and the hospital's director knew where she was located. If there were another incident, then he could trace the source of the leak.

Taking further precautions, he directed the officers assigned to protect her to dress like hospital staff to make them less conspicuous while boosting police presence throughout the hospital covering all points of access. He also left specific orders for him to be contacted immediately when she wakes up.

It had been a long night with daylight only a few hours away. The two detectives were beat but needed to be on top of this thing early.

"It's time to call it a night," Grimes said, looking over to Poles, "We'll start fresh, bright and early," We have a lot of ground to cover.

Poles agreed as they left the hospital.

Jahir had arrived on top of one of the buildings across from the hospital. Although he no longer sensed Bultizar, his fears were now realized and she would never be safe. Fortunately, there were no images or sensations that came with a kill. This made him certain that she was still alive but he knew that he would return to finish the job which was something he wouldn't allow. Knowing this Jahir needed to remain close knowing that he would return.

***

After returning to his place, Bultizar was visibly upset. Ramming his fist through a tile wall in his bathroom it was like a sheet of tissue paper. Tia Johnson was a loose end that played on the back of his mind. He knew that they would probably move her to a more secure and secluded place in the hospital. Where exactly, he had no way of knowing, but he did know he had to return before she would awaken.

***

The next morning, Grimes and Poles went down to get a warrant allowing them to search both Neville's home and office. After receiving it, He told

Poles to take a team of officers and head over to Neville's apartment while he took a team to DTX-Press.

Shortly before eight, Grimes arrived at DTX-Press hoping to talk to Neville before he clocked in but he never showed. He hadn't called or spoken to anyone. Armed with a court order, Grimes seized all documents that were associated with Neville. He wanted to check both his routes and his schedule dating back from the time he started working there.

When they got there, he met with Neville's supervisor, presenting him with the warrant to search all files concerning Neville. He was more than willing to cooperate, showing the detective everything he needed to see. As Grimes reviewed everything, what he found was most interesting. His route took him to complexes where at least three of the women he had direct contact with lived.

After checking the addresses of the other two women he had in his notes, he saw that Neville had made deliveries to their complexes as well. While he went over the logs, he found copies of lease receipts that each of the women had signed all on the same day three years ago. While Grimes looked over the information, his supervisor told him he thought that request was very unusual.

"I got a call from a representative from the Wolf Corporation requesting that he be given that specific route three years ago," Brooks said. "I felt that was odd within itself. It was something that had never been asked before from the corporate office which is why I never forgot."

Surprised, Grimes repeated Brooks' statement. "Wolf Corporation! What do they have to do with anything? They're a real estate company."

"Yes," he replied, "but three years ago they bought out this company, becoming the majority stock owner. They're now our parent company."

That's interesting, Grimes replied. Why would they ask for him specifically?"

"Beats me. I asked why he was requested; they never gave an answer. Other than to the ladies, there was nothing special about him or his work ethic. When I asked Neville, he simply shrugged his shoulders, and walked away."

Grimes thanked him for his cooperation, then headed to Neville's apartment to join Poles. While driving, he couldn't rap his mind around why he was specifically chosen.

When Grimes arrived at Neville's, Grimes told him that Neville never showed up or called the job. He relayed everything he had learned and how even the supervisor thought the route request was strange. He told him that the Wolf Corporation was also the parent company of DTX-Press.

After taking it all in, Poles shook his head.

"There must have been something really important that they needed to send someone they felt comfortable with to make those deliveries," Poles replied.

"Yeah, but why?" Grimes pondered. "His supervisor said he thought he was lazy and the only thing that stood out about him was that the ladies loved him. Maybe he charmed one of them in their office."

"Hmm . . . maybe," Poles skeptically responded, "but when asked why they wanted him, he said Neville never questioned the reason. He simply shrugged his shoulders as if he didn't care."

"One thing is for sure—somebody wanted him to have that route, and I'm going to find out why," Grimes concluded.

Poles told Grimes that they searched through everything and found pictures of three of the women that they knew he was involved with, along with boxed documents that, at a glance, appeared non-related to the case.

Not wanting to leave any stone unturned, they confiscated everything. Among the items taken was a blue sports jacket that fit the description a couple of the earlier reports documented witnesses had seen. Along with the jacket, they took a comb with hair on it and a toothbrush. They were looking to find DNA samples that matched anything at any of the crime scenes but there was still no Neville. there wasn't any evidence that he had ever come home that night. All his keys were missing but everything else appeared to be in order.

After about three hours fine combing the apartment, they returned to the precinct. They had a lot to sort out. Things needed to be put in place so they could begin to make sense of this maze of a case that was beginning to sprout in different directions like tree roots.

Chapter 31:
The Package, A History Lesson

At Scotland Yard, Colin McRae sat at his desk reviewing an article in *The London Times* on the latest findings of The Butcher of the Bronx case in New York.

While he sat, his administrative assistant delivered him the package he had been waiting for from Roslyn Perry. They had already discussed its contents; he was anxious to review them. As he read its contents, he was going over it from a historical standpoint. It all had a very familiar sound to it.

As he looked over the pictures and read the reports in detail, he found them to be fascinating. Out of everything she had sent, there were two pieces of evidence that held his greatest interest, the hair sample and the footprints in the pictures.

He took them downstairs to a file room in the basement where old evidence was kept. Walking over to one of the cabinets, he pulled out a large book covered in dust along with documents of similar murders reported—those that pertained to Jack the Ripper in particular.

He brought over other books from the cabinet as he began comparing all the collected evidence. What he saw astounded him. He also retrieved a pair of hair samples they kept in their possession. One was of Jack the Ripper; the other one he had found while conducting personal historical research of old-world serial killers in Turkey bonded to a goblet that dated back to the thirteenth century. It had a unique story attached to it.

According to legend, the goblet was found in the grasp of a woman still clutching it tightly after both she and her daughter were killed by presumably a werewolf. When McRae placed the current sample beside the old one to compare them under a microscope, they appeared to be identical. He needed a DNA test to officially confirm it, but that would take a couple of weeks.

***

In New York, it was still early when the detectives arrived at the precinct. It had already been a long day for them. The only things on their mind were finding Neville and the story Roslyn told them about the golden wolf and the panthiem though barely discussed. It lingered on their minds. Then they needed to know whether the two were somehow connected.

They speculated that it may have been Neville who fought the strange assailant. If so, the question was why did he literally disappear? The samples they collected from Neville's in their mind would confirm whether he was the one on the scene. If not, then that would be a whole different matter for them. There weren't but so many hours in a day, so for the next few hours, they buried their heads into everything they already had.

***

Back at Scotland Yard, McRae was doing the same. What he found seemed impossible, yet everything lined up linking the murders together, both old and new. After studying the evidence, he already had, along with everything Roslyn Perry had given him, he gave her a call.

"Under the microscope, the hairs were a match," he told Roslyn. All he needed was the DNA test to confirm what he had suspected many years ago. In addition to the new samples, the old ones may provide him the proof he needed.

He also told her everything he knew about the Ripper killings, the true story behind them in detail, and much more. Their conversation lasted a few hours. He told her the story of the goblet and that of an old key having the shape of a heart on one end along with strange markings on the other he had gotten from a dealer of ancient artifacts.

"The key has little value," he continued. "I wear it around my neck as a memento. It was snagged on a fisherman's line somewhere in the Black Sea centuries ago. There are symbols on it that can't be interpreted, just like the ones you described in your book."

This new revelation left Roslyn speechless as she listened.

Later that afternoon, Grimes's phone rang. On the other end was Roslyn Perry. He had been impatiently waiting for her call, hoping she had something that would break the stalemate, something tangible that would point them in the right direction. Since they last spoke, he had more to tell but wanted to hear what she had to say.

"Roslyn", We've been waiting to hear from you, "What were you able to find out?"

"Are you alone?" she asked.

"No, my partner is sitting across from me."

Pausing a moment, she replied, "Good! What I'm about to describe, you both need to hear."

Placing the phone on speaker Poles quietly listened, neither knowing what to expect.

"We're ready," Grimes replied. Excited almost to the point of breathlessness, she began.

"In looking at the photos you gave me, I consulted a colleague, Colin McRae. He's a top forensic expert in the U.K. and a former detective. Initially when he and I first looked at them, we were trying to see who they mimicked in past events from Europe, Asia and throughout different time periods. We matched both the brutality and patterns of killers during those times. We thought that your Bronx Butcher may have also been a student of history carrying out these acts in the present day as though he were giving a tribute to those serial killers of the past in a sick sort of way. There was also a story of a blond werewolf, some would call the golden wolf that was linked to these deaths, but that was dismissed, and impossible to prove until now.

"The hair samples you gave me along with the photos of those prints may very well prove to be a game changer. McRae put that sample under a microscope to compare it to two other samples he had in his possession—one that was directly associated with the Jack the Ripper case, the other sample he had found bonded onto a goblet he had in his possession. When he looked closely at the sample from the goblet, he was surprised to find that it never degraded.

"So, here's the backstory about the goblet. During McRae's travels, he visited different countries over the years while collecting ancient artifacts. He bought the goblet at an antique dealer in southeastern Turkey which had several stories surrounding it. The most prominent was that it was found in the grasp of a woman who was also allegedly killed by a werewolf, along with multiple other killings in the area with the same story behind it.

That sample you sent must've triggered something. There was a story surrounding a tomb and tales of mythical creatures but mostly of a werewolf fitting the same description that dated back to the thirteenth centuries. To him, that find only added to the legend. Other than the Ripper case, which had direct historical ties to Scotland Yard, he hadn't given it much thought until I sent him that sample. He ran all the DNA testing that was possible. We're now waiting for the official results to confirm it. Along with the hairs, a set of wolf-like tracks was almost always present. What both he and I found to be most interesting was that the authorities would always suppress that information from the public in fear of the panic it may cause."

Hearing this, both detectives found all this almost hard to believe but remained silent while trying to digest everything.

"That's impossible," Grimes replied. "That would span hundreds of years. The case of Jack the Ripper itself is well over a century ago."

"There's something else he never mentioned to me before," she added, "something he didn't believe until now. He told me the police at the time were also looking for a well-dressed blond man—a high society type who had frequently been seen visiting those areas in London's east end at night seeking the company of prostitutes, The night of the Ripper's last victim, a witness saw a man fitting his description going into a rooming house with a woman and reported it to two officers that were walking the beat.

"There were also two others off duty who happened to be passing through the area. They weren't but a block away. They joined them once they were told what was going on. Once they heard a scream coming from one of the rooms, they rushed into the building before kicking in the door.

Based on their accounts, what they saw was unbelievable. What they described was a werewolf nearly seven feet tall covered in long blond hair. Although she was still alive, she was severely wounded as they fired their weapons. The bullets had no effect. It turned, showing its fangs before leaping through the third-floor window onto the ground, disappearing into the night.

"Other than the police and the woman who died shortly after the attack, there were no other witnesses. Later back at their headquarters, each officer told what they saw and because of their impeccable records, their superiors didn't dispute it. But they feared this information would cause a panic throughout London and the countryside, so they were ordered to swear an oath of secrecy—an oath they took to their graves except one. Thirty years after the Ripper case, one of the officers broke that oath and, on his deathbed, told his grandson what really happened. His grandson then tried to cash in on the information but died shortly afterward. He mysteriously was found dead in his bed, his neck broken, his murder unsolved.

"A werewolf? A blond werewolf?" Grimes repetitively queried. "That's a lot to swallow,"

"Yes, but that's not all," Roslyn continued.

She told them about the book she had and how she had bought it years ago at an old antique shop while in Eastern Europe. It was a story dating back to the Dark Ages that also had paralleled this story.

"The book spoke about a small forgotten kingdom called Sargonia," she continued. "A king named Nicholai Bultizar, who was both a tyrant and a killer of young women. Like the Ripper murders, and the ones that are taking place in New York, the killer took the hearts of select female victims."

She also told them about the young warrior Jahir Amid who led an army of farmers turning them into fierce warriors, many of which had also lost loved ones at the hands of the murderous king. After defeating him, she told how Bultizar and the few surviving followers had fled, fearing the repercussions of their actions.

She told them that in the book, Jahir and the writer had pursued him across Eastern Europe into the forest, where he came across a soothsayer who directed the fallen king to a cursed fortress to retrieve a book that would restore him to power and much more.

She told how Jahir had intercepted him and his forces defeating them," Roslyn continued. "During the battle, Bultizar slipped away to the fortress alone with Jahir in pursuit. Following Bultizar inside, the two faced each before the battle pursued."

She then said, "This is where the story becomes bizarre. She told them in detail about the sorceress and the curse, giving details of everything that was researched.

How the legend states that the gap between them began a hundred years ago, and through the centuries the Panthiem would pursue the golden wolf getting ever closer."

Roslyn began telling the detectives historically documented facts with an underlining undertone that history had chosen not to acknowledge.

"In 1589, in Germany, a rash of animalistic murders was attributed to a madman named Peter Stump, who was plagued with the lycanthropy mental disorder and was executed. Although Stump was tried and convicted of acting like a wolf, some believed it was actually the golden wolf. Since the officials needed a real person—a sacrificial lamb, so to speak—and not a mythical beast, Stump took the fall.

"Over 160 years later—the golden wolf was linked to the Beast of Gevaudan in Central France. But the government hunted down and shot a large wolf just to satisfy the public, although many believed the culprit wasn't a wolf. The townspeople believed it was a wealthy man of prominence, Augustus Cartier, whose origins were unknown and who mysteriously disappeared. Decades later in the wake of these attacks, there was always the shadow of the cat that always appeared decades later in the aftermath."

Referring to the writings in her book, she told them there were other symbols written in the book that were neither translated nor written in Latin. When she had taken it to one of the top anthropologists in the country, he told her that it was an unknown dialect.

After listening, Grimes responded, "There have been reports of a large man or something seen at a couple of the murder scenes fitting that description. There have also been two incidents not related to the murders where a guy fitting this very same description shows up and overwhelms several street thugs on two separate occasions. On one such occasion, they had assaulted my lady friend Terrie Collins, dragging her into an alley.

"The reporter?" she inquired.

"Yes. By her account, he took them out like they were nothing. Then there was another group of men under investigation who suffered the same fate. Fortunately, no one was killed."

Roslyn told them that in the book, the panthiem takes on the nature of its host, and according to the story, this man Jahir had a good heart. There had also been reports by the locals during various points and times throughout history stating that the panthiem had appeared in the same places that the golden wolf had already killed--decades earlier, if you choose to believe everything I've told you."

"You've heard of the most recent murder," Grimes continued.

"Yes."

"Her name was Maria Gomez. She was Terrie's best friend. She was like family."

"Oh, no! Her death must have been devastating to her. To have someone that close to you die and, in this way, —it's very hard to take."

"Yes. This has become more than just a case to me. It's personal. The night that Tia Johnson—Terrie's makeup assistant—was attacked, when the officer arrived, he saw a man on the ground with someone or something on top of him. They said it was by something that looked like that panthiem you just described. Catlike in appearance, with locks, fangs, and extremely long claws.

"He said it turned toward him showed its fangs and snarled, before he opened fire, striking it several times. The officer said the bullets had no effect on it. He said it turned and ran before disappearing in the dark between two buildings. They didn't see any werewolf covered in blond hair. The one thing that none of them could fathom was after such a savage attack, the man who was lying on the ground unconscious had his clothing nearly torn to shreds— not an ounce of blood nowhere, not even a bruise on his skin. The blond hair that was found was presumed to be left by the man who had been attacked by this thing.

"We're still waiting on those lab results. The man that was said to be unconscious vanished during the confusion, we don't know who he is. We still haven't been able to find him. The only other person who survived is still in a coma. Someone pretending to be a doctor tried to kill her that night and would've succeeded had we gotten there a minute later. We chased him but he got away."

"I didn't hear any of this on the news," Roslyn replied.

"No, you didn't. What I'm telling you is confidential, but I'm desperate. Plus, I trust you."

"You don't have to worry, "The conversation ends here with us."

Roslyn continued. "In the story, the werewolf can change at will, and the panthiem always follows in its shadow. The book also spoke of the rising of the scarlet blood moon and what it meant. According to the book, if the golden wolf claims the heart of his sixth and final victim when the scarlet moon rises to its highest height, which would be midnight, at that moment the werewolf must claim his prize to become invincible. Only then will he be able to create an army like himself, unless the panthiem claims his heart first. According to the book, there were two such risings. The first was the night of the Ripper's final victim. McRae's research revealed that he was interrupted before making that strike before midnight, the death blow was dealt too late. There's another but the pages are so faded and illegible."

"You said his sixth victim," Grimes replied. "Whoever the killer is, he's claimed more than six, he's killed nine."

"Yes, but how many were women and how many of them had their hearts taken?"

"I can only go off what the officer saw when he arrived and it wasn't the werewolf. It sounded more like the other guy."

"The man that fought this cat creature and survived without a scratch? How was that possible?" Grimes asked.

"Does that story sound familiar?" Roslyn asked.

Grimes paused and became quiet as he realized the answer.

Roslyn then said, "Ask yourself, why would anyone leave surrounded by so many people who could protect him after an ordeal like that, with a creature that you described to me having just savagely attacked him and was still on the loose? Also, with so many there around him, how did he get by them unnoticed?"

"So, what are you saying?"

"I'm not sure what I'm saying, but if you find that young man you may find those answers you're looking for." Roslyn added, "There's more. After McRae looked over the samples, he did a little more research surrounding the Ripper case. He cross-referenced those murders with the events in New York and also with the death of one of its victims, the political activist Hakeem Robinson. When the Ripper murders were taking place, there also was a community spokesman named John Addison. He was from a working-class family who actively fought for the betterment of the community and campaigned vigorously against the rich, who he considered to be greedy property owners in that section of London. He was trying to make it better for the people who lived in that quarter.

"When those prostitutes were killed, he was their voice, citing that the property owners cared more about money than the safety of the community, and that the property owners provided the mechanism for the killer to operate. Just like Hakeem Robinson and his wife, he was also found brutally murdered in a similar fashion during the time of the Ripper's killing spree with his killer never having been found. Just like in New York, all the women who were killed by the Ripper in London at that time were butchered almost in the exact same way. The only difference was that the women killed in New York weren't prostitutes.

"During that time there were also reports of corruption amongst city officials taking payments not to act upon the activist request to upgrade those old buildings. They were all owned by a reality company called Wolvenhunt—an old company that carried the family's name whose roots went back a couple hundred years out of eastern Europe. It's said that the company had a history of questionable practices and similar but lesser publicized murders. There's been a history of people appearing to have died by some kind of animal in properties owned by that company, too—many of which had simply been lost in time because of the lack of publicity and public outcry. Shortly after the Ripper murders, the company shut down and moved. Where at the time, no one knew.

"Rumors began to surface that they had left Europe and moved to the States under another name. No one knows for sure if it's true, or what name they may have been under. In truth, I don't think anyone cared. "Something to think about, huh?" she concluded.

"That's a lot to absorb," Grimes replied, looking at Poles. "Not sure how to take any of this. It almost sounds like this city is caught in the middle of a war between two mythical creatures."

"Yeah, good versus evil, but the question is: is there really any good in this equation? So far, we've seen only death," Poles stated.

"I know," Roslyn injected. "This is difficult to take in. Who will believe this?"

"The officers on the scene after turning in their reports of seeing this creature were ordered downtown for drug testing," Grimes concluded.

"I'm not even sure how to take this," Roslyn added. "You have always been decisive and exercised good judgment. Just keep an open mind and trust your instincts. If you need me for anything, you know where to find me."

"I know," Grimes confirmed, thanking her for her help before hanging up. Taking a deep breath, placing both hands behind his head, he leaned back and stared at the ceiling trying to take in it all.

Sitting across from him, Poles looked to Grimes and asked, "What's next, Chief? Are we putting an APB out on the wolf man? Are we now chasing myths and monsters? Has it come down to this? What do you really think?"

"I don't know, but if any of this is true, we must find out who the man is first, then we might have our monster. We're running out of options, and according to Roslyn's story, we may be running out of time, as well, to catch this guy. Whether it's true or not, I believe Tia Johnson and our mystery man hold the answer—that is, if one wakes up and the other miraculously shows up."

Taking a deep breath, Grimes added, "According to legend, Roslyn said this Bultizar character was the werewolf that could change whenever he wanted to at night, and this panthiem who cannot have been chasing him over the centuries. Maybe it was this panthiem guy that Daniels saw that night. With two people injured, and Maria lying there dead, we only have him to question as a witness if we choose to take that route in believing that.

Yet more blond hairs were found on the body. Perhaps our missing person is Paul Neville. We won't know that until the lab results come back."

"That's true," Poles replied. "But according to your friend, this panthiem is not the killer but a protector. The only thing we have to go on is an old book that could be wrong. Who really knows?"

"So far, we haven't found any black hairs of that panther guy, which brings us back to the blond hairs and tracks we did find on or around the other bodies, including Maria's."

"Yeah," Poles replied, "the serial killer, the evil dude Bultizar, if the legend is true."

"Yes," Grimes replied, "and according to Ros the hair I found here matches the ones in London." Theorizing what Roslyn conveyed to them, he added, "If what she's saying is true, think about this: What if that panthiem thing that Daniels saw attacking that dude turns out he wasn't a regular dude at all but that werewolf she spoke of? Mind you, if we choose to take this route, that guy Bultizar may have changed from his wolf form back to human just before the police arrived to make it look like the panthiem was attacking a human. In doing so, the blond hairs found wouldn't mean anything, because they would be looking for this panthiem creature. She did say he was able to change at will."

Grimes thought about it and said, "When Daniels pursued this thing between the buildings there were no paw prints, only shoe prints. Yet the only one not wearing shoes was the man on the ground. I find that to be interesting. After all, no shoes were found on the scene at all. Just listen to how all of this sounds."

Poles said, "It sounds ludicrous but look at the facts. On top of what you just said, he was also being attacked by a thing with teeth and large claws. When they checked him, he was lying unconscious without a mark on his body. Everyone else involved received an assortment of visible injuries, just like that French guy in the story of Gevaudan Roslyn told us about."

"Tia Johnson sustained bruises to her head, along with several cuts and lacerations, not to mention Maria and what happened to her. With the place full of cops and bystanders, he woke up in an instant and disappeared amongst all those people. With all those sets of eyes, how could no one have noticed or seen anything? How do you wake from something like that and not be in a state of stupor? Then of course, there are the hair and tracks--the only tangible evidence we have in our possession.

"We also found more blond hair, not black. It could be our mystery guy's. If it matches the samples sent downtown in the previous cases, then it's gonna match that of our killer's. That's why we have to find Mr. Neville, to find out whether he was here.

"Right now, all of this is circumstantial. It will boil down to the lab results and whether the hair we collected at his apartment matches the ones found on Maria's body or those of the killer. Maybe they are both one in the same."

"Yeah," Poles said. "If that's the case, then we'll be able to knock off two birds with one stone, and that mystery man would no longer be a mystery. If not, then that opens up a whole new can of worms, making the werewolf story even more viable."

"Once Neville's samples return from the lab, it will either place him there or exonerate him," Grimes replied. "We need to find out what happened between the time he first saw Maria to the last time he saw her alive."

"Also, according to Ms. Perry, this killer is on the clock," Poles reminded him.

"She gave reference to the rising of a scarlet blood moon and how they would occur over the centuries," Grimes continued. "The first was on September thirtieth with the real killer said to be a werewolf. It was interrupted, preventing him from achieving his goal that night. Now, there are these murders here in New York that resemble the same patterns as the ones that took place in the Whitechapel district of London. The story parallels exactly what's going on here, which brings us to Nicholas Wolf and the Wolf Corporation and how his company like Wolvenhunt back in England seems to have been targeted.

"Also, the fact that both had an activist fighting against the practices of an unscrupulous reality company, just like here with Wolf and Robinson. Both men had accused these companies of dubious practices and corrupt city officials being paid off."

"Yeah," Poles replied, "the most frightful parallel was that both men suffered the same fate."

Grimes then said, "If the killer is following the same pattern, he has one more kill to make, but we have no way of knowing who, when, or where. He's allegedly killed nine but five of the women fits that bill. We have to figure this thing out before it's too late."

The day had been long but an interesting one. The two had been racking their brains trying to piece together the right scenario that would put them on track. Finally, they decided it was time to call it quits for the night.

Looking at his watch, Poles looked over to Grimes and said, "Oh snap! I almost forgot. I gotta get out of here and stop by the bakery and pick up a cake for my twelve-year-old niece. We're having a few family members over for cake and ice cream. I totally forgot. I know this is a last-minute invite, but would you and Terrie like to come by? It might help her feel better, taking her mind away from everything."

"I'd love to, but I don't think she's up to it right now," I'm going by there tonight once I leave here to try to help her get through this. Soon as I finish writing these notes, I'll be heading out myself."

"Okay, later Chief," Poles replied leaving the office.

Chapter 32:
A Deadly Follow-Up

Sitting in her living room with the lights dimmed and her puppy lying near her feet, Terrie reminisced about her best friend. In front of her was a blank television screen. On her phone and in her lap, she held pictures, both old and recent, of them together. They shared a wealth of memories, but just like she was gone.

This was a reality she had to face but found it hard to believe. Everything was fresh, and her heart was still bleeding like an open wound. She didn't want to see or hear the reports. All they would do was add to her pain. She knew that if the case broke, she would get a call. Until then, the best company she could have would be herself.

There was a knock on her door as Max ran to it and began to yap. Picking him up she placed him in his cage. Without inquiring, she opened the door. Standing there was Grimes, the only one who could put a smile on her face. As he walked in, she grabbed him as both embraced. Tears began to stream down her face as they stood holding each other.

Terrie's eyes were red and puffy from constant crying but at that moment, she found comfort in his arms. She led him into the bedroom. She needed him, and he wanted her. They began a path that led them under the sheets. She didn't want to feel anything but him inside of her. She needed to exchange one pain for another that was more pleasurable.

The journey they had taken lasted well into the night until the moment passed, and she was ready to relieve her mind. With her head on his chest, he remained quiet. He knew that sometimes silence is the best answer when hurt is involved. He knew that it was better to let a bleeding heart be the first to express itself.

Lying there, she asked him about Maria and whether there was any new information.

"Bobby," she asked softly, "that guy Maria was with—Paul—were you able to find out anything from him? Did he have anything to do with this?"

Grimes took his hand and gently lifted her chin to give her a kiss. He replied, "No. We haven't been able to locate him but we're doing our best. We have an APB out on him, and a warrant. We searched his place and are still going over everything. No one has seen or heard from him yet. He hasn't been home or at work."

"Nothing new that at least the public should know so they can protect themselves?" she asked. "I don't want anything like this to happen to anybody. When I was reporting on the other victims, I thought I understood their pain, but now I know I really didn't have a clue. I fully understand now."

Grimes thought for a moment before responding. He knew he had to be careful with his words. As much as he wanted to shed some light on this, he knew he couldn't. It was a tricky situation. He was wedged firmly between a rock and a hard place.

If he answered the wrong way, he could break in either direction. He knew if he told her the truth, she would reveal everything. But not saying anything would possibly jeopardize their relationship. With all of this in mind, he answered her question while hoping he was doing the best thing for all parties involved.

"No, darling, everything is pretty much the same. We didn't find out anything new." He hated to withhold information, but technically nothing could be proven yet.

"How could a person do something like this to another human being? I hope you find this monster, and he gets everything he deserves."

"He will. I promise. I'll do everything in my power to bring this animal down."

For a moment, she found his words to be comforting as they both drifted off to sleep.

***

On the roof of the hospital protecting his friend, Jahir provided another dimension of security—one that added supernatural protection. He knew Bultizar would come again to end what he had started. Something he would never allow to happen. In his mind, he was the reason she was there in the first place. It was eating away at his conscience like the monster he was hunting.

Before arriving, he made a visit to Terrie's to see that she was safe. It was a routine he maintained since the night he rescued her. She served as a reminder of his first love, the driving force that had carried him through the centuries.

With that, her safety loomed heavily on his mind, but his real ties lay here at the hospital, on the floor just below him. Although they had moved her, her scent was so strong, he could find her anywhere. He knew she was in a much safer place.

From the hospital wall in the late hours, he would descend down the side of the building, like a spider looking quietly through the window of her room, hoping that she would open her eyes. Afterward, he would return to his perch, watching and waiting.

***

With the authorities now secretly looking for him, Bultizar basked in his triumph over Jahir. Once again, he proved to be too elusive. He had successfully turned the attention off of himself onto his black-furred nemesis. Bultizar knew that the authorities eventually would figure things out, so he threw them a bone, setting up Jahir while clearing his trail. There remained, however, loose ends that could still throw a cog in his wheel.

Sat in his living room sipping on a bottle of wine, Bultizar weighed his options. With Tia in the hospital, he knew he had to strike again. He held the time card with the luxury to punch it in knowing time was getting short and didn't want to take any chances that would delay him.

He wanted to receive his payment of power, something he had long desired even before he became who he was. This game was coming to an end with the question that lingered of who would be next. That was an answer only he would know. In his mind, he was saving the best for last.

He walked into his closet and chose a black suit, then into one of his drawers where he kept an assortment of wigs. Carefully looking over them, he chose one that was more salt and pepper. He had a more distinguished look in mind, one that was different than the one he wore during his last visit to the hospital out of fear that he would be recognized. He then went into another drawer where he pulled out a fake beard and mustache that matched his wig. Now in front of the mirror, he put on a pair of black, thick-framed glasses. With an entirely different look from his last, he was ready to go forth with his plan as he headed out the door.

He was going in the daytime to finish the job where there would be less risk. At night, his anxiety would cause his blood to boil, alerting Jahir increasing the possibility of being interrupted before he could accomplish his goal.

Entering the hospital no one noticed him as he casually walked towards the ER. After his last visit he knew he would need another way to gain access to where they were keeping Tia without drawing further attention. Knowing he had to do something different from the previous night he casually walked down the hallway looking for another way to access the young woman without discovery until he saw his opportunity. If this were a script it couldn't have been written more perfectly. Walking towards him was a man with salt and pepper hair but without the glasses wearing a black suit. As he approached, he saw the name Carlson Martin CEO written on his name tag. Focused on his cell phone he wasn't paying attention to his surroundings. Seizing the opportunity, Bultizar drifted towards him bumping into him causing him to drop his phone. During the exchange Bultizar extracted his name tag off his jacket pretending it was an accident then apologized. Turning as he walked away, Bultizar didn't allow him to get a clear at his face. Briefly glancing back, the man reached down picking up his phone refocusing on what he was previously doing, never noticing that his name tag had been taken. Moments later after pinning on the stolen name tag, Bultizar slipped into the crowded ER casually looking around until he spotted a medical supply closet that was open. With the staff being too busy to notice him, he confiscated a hypodermic needle then after passing a janitorial supply tray he stuck the needle into a bottle of disinfectant, drawing it into the needle until it was filled.

Placing it in his pocket he proceeded to where he believed Tia was being kept. When he arrived, there were neither police nor security; he realized she had been moved. As before, he remained calm on the surface hiding the storm that was brewing inside. Wearing the stolen CEO tag, he stopped at the nurse's station, banking that the title would alleviate any suspicion.

Facing the on-duty nurse, he said, "Good morning. Where has Tia Johnson been taken?"

Glancing down at his tag, seeing that he was a hospital official she responded, "She was moved sometime during the night. No one knows where."

In hearing the response, if it were night, his fury would have been uncontrollable, which may have involuntarily triggered the wolf inside him to explode, killing everyone there. Fortunately, during the day, he was just another man.

Unable to ascertain what he needed from the staff, after walking away he became visibly upset. He took the elevator checking each floor. From the basement, he began a floor-to-floor search until finally reaching the seventh floor, where he found that it was restricted. Not seeing any police in uniforms, he surmised that they were dressed as part of the staff concluding that this was the floor she was being kept. Before approaching the staff, he became reluctant. He thought to himself even with his false credentials the element of surprise had been lost. If caught in his human form he would be vulnerable. Unable to change into the wolf, the authorities would be able to apprehend him which would possibly reveal of his identity. Thinking the better of it he decided it wasn't worth the risk.

Careful not to bring further attention to himself, he turned quietly before getting back on the elevator, pinning his anger inside while punching the ground floor button before exiting the hospital.

While he departed the building to the left, Grimes and Poles had just walked in from the right, with them just missing each other.

When the detectives reached Tia's room, they found that her condition was stable but still hadn't regained consciousness. They hung around for a while before deciding to leave. After getting on the elevator, a thought came to Grimes's mind.

"Let's stop on the fourth floor,"

"Why the fourth floor?" Poles asked.

"I don't believe what happened last night was the end of it," Grimes replied.

Moments later, the two walked into the unit where she was kept the night before. They approached the nurse that was there, reviewing patient charts. Looked up seeing the officers.

"May I help you?" she asked.

"Yes," Grimes replied. "Flashing their badges." Looking down at her tag, Grimes replied, "Hello, Ms. Taylor. I just wanted to ask you a couple of questions."

"You're not here to arrest me, are you?" she jokingly responded

Both officers lightly laughed. Then Grimes replied, "No Ms. Taylor, we're not. We had a patient here last night that we had to move. Are you familiar with that?"

"Yes, I was informed when my shift began," I was also told that there was some trouble last night. Is everything alright?"

"Yes, everything's fine. I am just checking to see if anyone noticed anything strange, anything out of the ordinary today."

"No, not really," she replied, then thought about it and added, "We did have one visitor. One of the hospital directors asked about that patient. I couldn't help him, so he walked off."

The two detectives looked at one another. Grimes asked, "How long ago?"

"About two hours ago," she replied.

"Can you describe him?" Poles inquired.

"Yes. White guy, with salt and pepper hair, a mustache and beard, about your height, wearing a black suit and a pair of black glasses."

Grimes looked over at his partner. "Sounds similar to the guy last night."

"Yeah," Poles replied, "with the difference being without the gray, and the type of glasses.

Grimes turned back to face the nurse. "What was the name on his tag?" he asked.

"Carlson Martin was the name I saw. I didn't recognize him, but when he left, he did seem a little frustrated."

Immediately, Grimes knew his fears were realized: Tia was still in danger. "Thank you. You've been extremely helpful."

Grimes then got on the radio alerting his officers everything he had received from the nurse, his name and description along with what he was wearing.

Poles then turned to Grimes. "I'll check the hospital registry and see if anybody by that name is even affiliated with the hospital,"

"Okay," Grimes nodded.

"This story is becoming more real by the moment," Poles said. "If this guy is really Bultizar, he'll be more determined to end this."

"Yeah, a living witness," Grimes replied. "I'm rapidly becoming a believer in fairy tales."

"Those stories got you spooked I see. I've never seen you like this before."

"If there's truth to any of this," he doesn't want to take the chance of her waking up and identifying him. She could disrupt his plans—that is, if that this story is true. I know it all sounds crazy for me to believe, but we've already lost nine people. If he's the one killing these people, I don't want her to be the tenth victim. Moving her was the best thing. She obviously wasn't too hard to find, unlike our missing person. They are the only two who could shed light on who the killer might be."

"I understand," Poles replied. "If this is any consolation to you and eases your conscience, I'm a believer, too. Sometimes you have to rely on a sense that isn't too common when the evidence surpasses reason."

Grimes agreed, confident that the two were on the same page.

For the next few hours, police and security searched the hospital from top to bottom. The officers had checked all the surveillance cameras again.

They also found the real Carlson Martin who they confirmed was one of the hospital's directors.

He told them that he didn't know that his name tag had been stolen but he did remember a man bumping into him while he was walking down the hall but didn't get a good look at his face because his back was turned.

Satisfied they had covered their bases at the hospital, they refocused on protecting their sleeping witness, but Bultizar was long gone.

Chapter 33:
A Corporate Trail

"When we get back, I want to do some research of my own," Poles said. "I want to pick up where that English fella left off. After everything we've heard so far, it appears that Wolvenhunt and Wolf Realty are the same company. If that's true, I want to see exactly when they showed up in the U.S."

"Yeah," Grimes replied, "I need to follow up on a few things myself."

Once in the office, Poles got on his computer. He tried to follow the path McRae set that might help, tracing Wolvenhunt after it disappeared in Europe. Using a nationwide database, he searched for Wolvenhunt Realty to see if it had picked up again in the U.S. around the turn of the twentieth century.

When he began his search, the trail was cold, all leading to dead ends. It was literally like searching for a needle in a haystack. He decided to take another route based on the information Roslyn Perry had given them. He started searching for unsolved serial murders that mimicked those that were recorded in Europe with a similar flair during that time period. Knowing this process may take a while, he knew he had to stay on it.

Meanwhile, Paul Neville continued to linger on Grimes's mind. While reviewing copies of Neville's invoices, he needed to follow the times and dates to see if there were more connections. He needed to connect the dots concerning Neville's delivery route if there was any hope of linking him to other victims. They knew of his involvement with at least three of the women as they analyzed the route, he had taken. Grimes looked at each one according to the dates and the sequence of when they were murdered.

The request from Wolf's office for Neville specifically to be assigned to that route posed the biggest question as to why. The fact that Wolf Realty was the parent company of DTX-Press was surprisingly unexpected.

He reviewed the case of each victim. Stacy Thomas was first on his list with the dates all lining up. She was the first to be seen with a young blond guy when the first reports came out. The last guy seen with her was wearing a blue sports jacket described like the one confiscated from Neville's apartment.

In an earlier autopsy, a semen sample was collected for DNA analysis, although there were no signs of sexual assault. It was the same with Sandra Woo. The DNA samples found were from the same guy and all pointed to Neville as the prime suspect.

As both officers were working feverishly to put this case together, the phone rang. Grimes answered, hoping it was the call they had been waiting for. On the other end was the coroner's office, giving the grim details of what they had. Neville had been found floating face down in the Hudson River.

His body had evidence of claw marks and puncture wounds. According to the reports, when they pulled his body from the water, they didn't need an autopsy to determine the cause of death. His throat had been torn completely out, and his wounds were all too familiar. After he ended the call, Grimes relayed everything to Poles.

"Now where does that leave us?" Poles asked. Grimes simply threw his hands up in frustration. He could've filled in some of the blanks, if not all of them, especially if it were his hair on the scene.

"We'll just have to make do with what we have and hope it turns in our favor," was Grimes response.

Immediately after receiving the news of Neville's death, they were struck with a double hitter. The lab called with the DNA results. The hairs on the scene matched all previously found hairs, which didn't belong to Paul Neville, so he was officially exonerated.

This posed another set of questions for the detectives: When did Neville and Maria part company? How did she end up dead behind a group of unoccupied buildings while he was found floating in the river miles away with his throat torn out?

It appeared that Neville wasn't the mystery man but Bultizar himself. The death of Neville and the involvement of the Wolf Corporation left more questions than answers. All of this was key if they were going to figure out who Bultizar really was.

Grimes made a call to the lab. With Neville DNA already logged into the system, he ordered them to cross reference them with the semen DNA found in each of the women that was murdered. In Grimes's mind, there now was the possibility that the kid had been set up as bait for these women.

Grimes turned to Poles with his thoughts. "I believe that Neville was made to look like the killer so that he would appear to be the prime suspect. That way, it would steer us away from the real culprit. Then to cover his tracks, he in turn killed Neville, since he didn't need him anymore."

"I'm also thinking that this panthiem thing may have also been set up by that blond werewolf guy Bultizar as well, to take the blame as the animal part of this scenario," Poles surmised. "In truth, we have no way of knowing this panthiem's true nature, other than what the pages in an old book tells us. Mind you, we don't know if any of this is really true."

"I don't know, but what we do know is this—Neville is dead and this isn't a coincidence. I also know that this definitely isn't random."

"Like you said, he may have been baited. But if we follow Neville's trail of deliveries, it may lead us to where we need to go, starting with who really requested him to deliver this route. We know he had a semi-formal relationship with at least three of them, but I believe he was intimate with all of them."

"I believe someone might have known that he had a weakness for a certain type of woman, and when they were all killed, he was last seen with just about all of them. I think the reason he was killed was that he may have been the link that would've led us to the real killer, Bultizar. Neville's DNA would at least confirm that."

At that moment, the lab called again and confirmed that Neville's semen was a match to the samples found in most of the women. As he pulled out copies from the files, Grimes began fine combing Neville's route and deliveries.

Grimes went back three years from the time he first began the route, specifically for that of the victims. He had delivered packages to all five of these women on the same day. The signatures he had received let them know he had contact with each of these women before. Grimes then cross referenced the copies of the company invoices they had received and confirmed each were sent by Wolf Corporation. Then he checked to see whether there were any recent deliveries made, and whether the women were home the day they were made.

With the information he had, all of them were home on the day of delivery. After he cross-referenced them again, he found they were express letters sent from the Wolf Corporation, each stamped urgent.

With circumstances being what they were, Grimes didn't believe it was coincidental that Neville was handpicked to make deliveries to these five women with which he had some involvement, nor did he believe it was coincidental that it was by the same real estate company who had been criticized for not improving the various properties that were used to carry out these crimes.

To further complicate matters, Wolf's biggest critic, Hakeem Robinson, was also murdered just before he could act on his suspicions concerning Wolf real estate and its business practices. And the delivery man had an intimate relationship and was last seen with at least three of the victims, with the possibility that all may have been with him at some point. To Grimes and Poles, all of these were pieces to a puzzle that was beginning to fit together.

Peering down at his watch, Grimes said, "It's quitting time, at least for you. I'm going over to the hospital for a while and hope that Ms. Johnson's condition has changed, or at least I hope it does while I'm there. Then I'm going to stop and get some flowers and pay Terrie a visit. Hopefully, that will help her feel a little better."

"Well Chief," last I checked we were on the same shift."

"Yeah, I know, but I'm going to the hospital to make sure that our witness is safe."

"How's she handling this? I know she's a soldier anytime she can put up with you," Poles laughed.

Grimes chuckled and replied, "She's doing as well as expected, having her ups and downs. She took some time off to help her get through all of this."

"No, Chief! I got this," Poles replied. "Monica is at her sister's house a few days. Her sister just had a baby, which leaves me bored and with nothing to do. Go on over to Terrie's and look after her. I'll head over to the hospital and check on our witness."

"Okay, thanks man. I owe you."

"What else is new? You always owe me."

Grimes chuckled and replied, "Okay, I'm out. See you tomorrow. I wanna check out a few more things before I leave. Later, partner." Grimes then headed out the door.

Poles went back to his computer, determined to find out whether Wolvenhunt had reached the states under a different name or had simply folded after leaving England. After all, it was only rumored that it may have come to the states. In truth, it could have gone anywhere.

Checking an old database, he finally found something. Old public records showed that in 1905 in New Orleans, Wolvenhunt Realty registered its name after it had been rumored to have relocated from the Bahamas. Then two days later, the business name was changed to Wolf Realty. This revelation raised Poles's eyebrows.

Like a lion craving blood, Poles began searching to see whether there were any unusual deaths in the area during that time period. The same year that Wolvenhunt surfaced, three women had been killed and found in an old abandoned rooming house that was never repaired. It was owned by no other than Wolf Realty.

All the women had similar wounds like they had been attacked by an animal, all with their hearts removed from their body with large paw prints found nearby. As with all the victims, the killer was never found. Wolf Realty left the area shortly afterward.

Poles also found that since coming to the states, it had become more profitable for it to expand its brand by buying out smaller companies while allowing them to keep their names as they expanded north to the Midwest like an umbrella to places like the Chicago and Cleveland areas. As he continued to read, he found that for years things remained quiet, then the killing would start up again, always in the same way—by the actions of an animalistic serial killer.

In a Chicago suburb from 1925 to 1927 during the height of Prohibition, gangland murders and crimes were stealing the headlines. Most of those serial style killings drew very little attention in the papers. With the victims consisting mostly of women who were homeless or prostitutes, they were women that society had abandoned or forgotten.

During that time, Poles read that eight women were found mutilated. According to the articles, the attacks on them were reminiscent of the aggressive style of a large predator. They received very little attention, only in short articles consisting of no more than two or three sentences, usually in small print.

In almost all of these cases, the bodies were always found either in or around Wolf properties. Also, in just about every case involved a young, well-dressed man with blond hair was described but never found. The reports would stop altogether as abruptly as they had begun.

As he continued to read, nine years after Chicago's last victim, the Wolf Corporation moved its headquarters to the Cleveland vicinity. Shortly afterward, a wave of serial murders followed on a much grander scale. Twelve to twenty murders were committed in a five-year span.

The newspapers had deemed the killer as the Butcher of Kingsbury, a familiar title. All but five of the victims were either dismembered, disemboweled, or both. Five of the women were found were speculated to have been killed by someone or something else. Their injuries were completely different from the rest. Their wounds were as though they had been attacked by an animal with fangs and claws.

What he found most interesting was that they were all found in old, unoccupied dwellings that were owned by Wolf Realty. Shortly after those murders, it then packed up and moved its headquarters once again, back to Chicago. Wolf Realty, along with further incidents, had become dormant.

With his mind blown, Poles looked at his watch. He hadn't realized that an hour had passed. After packing up, he headed to the hospital to check on Tia Johnson's condition.

Arriving at Terrie's condo Grimes knocked on her door. Terrie's voice was low and solemn as she answered. Missing was her energy but it was understandable. She was still grieving over Maria's death. When opening her door, he handed her a bouquet of flowers.

"Baby, they're so pretty," she replied, leaning forward, closing her eyes, while hugging him. If things were normal, they would've brightened her day, but the burden of her loss was too heavy, the wounds were too deep. Only time would heal her.

Grimes looked and saw that they were red and swollen from endless tears.

"You okay, baby?" he asked, knowing the answer.

"No, I'm not," she replied, her voice on the verge of breaking, but she held it together to continue her thought. "I don't know if I'll ever be alright. I can't believe she's gone. Not like that. I hope you find that guy Neville and get him to talk. I believe he had to something to do with this."

"We found him," Grimes replied. "He's dead."

"Dead?"

"They pulled him out the Hudson River. He was killed in a different location than where we found Maria's body."

"How did he die?" she asked.

"Mutilated," His throat torn out, the same as the others. Unlike the women, his heart wasn't taken. According to the coroner's office, by the marks on his body it was the same killer."

"My Lord," She gasped. "No one should have to feel this pain, especially over something this senseless." Resting her head on his chest, she added, "Have you found anything else?"

"Not yet."

Grimes cringed inside. As much as he wanted to tell her, no matter how crazy it may have sounded, he knew he couldn't. All he could do was play it off. This was the second time she asked, and the first time he was forced to lie. With the evening progressing, his plans were to stay the night with her, and she had no objections.

When Poles arrived at the hospital, he parked directly across the street. He didn't notice the man in a long black coat was standing a few feet away from him who had arrived moments before him. This time, he wasn't wearing a wig—just glasses and a mustache.

Poles's mind was focused on getting upstairs, hoping there was some type of improvement in Tia's status. When Poles got upstairs, he found that there was no change in her condition, pulling out his cell he made a call.

As Grimes's phone rang, he contemplated whether to check it or leave it alone. He and Terrie were having a quiet moment with her head resting on his chest, and he didn't want to spoil the mood. His presence there served to help ease her pain.

After a few more rings, he looked at it and saw that it was his partner. With Poles at the hospital, there was the possibility that their witness had awakened. Thinking there may be a change in Tia's condition, he answered it.

Poles gave him an update on her condition, which hadn't changed, but he had information that might interest him. Poles then proceeded to tell him everything he had found out about the Wolf Corporation. He confirmed that Wolf was originally Wolvenhunt.

He began referencing a trail of similar murders associated with properties that were owned by the corporation. He told him there were similar patterns of serial deaths that took place through the years and how they spread wherever Wolf expanded.

Although there was no evidence that could tie to any of them, he gave the details as Grimes listened quietly. He didn't want to comment, knowing that this would prompt Terrie's attention as he wanted to keep everything confidential.

While he listened, Terrie watched him and his expressions. She had never seen him listen so intently with little or no response. She knew there was something different, but she didn't want to overstep her boundaries.

After the two had finished their conversation, she looked up at him with her head still planted on his chest.

"Is everything all right?" she asked.

He looked back at her then kissed her, replying, "Everything's fine. He was just giving me details on the witness' condition."

Terrie reached over to turn off the lamp on the nightstand as they allowed the mood to continue to flow. While Grimes and his lady were having their moment, Poles found a comfortable seat in the hallway of the hospital ward, giving the assigned officer time to take a break. He reached into his pocket and pulled out a suspense novel while he waited. He had hoped that Tia would wake up while he was there so they would have a definitive direction in which to move.

Jahir remained perched on top of the roof of the hospital. He could do nothing but wait for Bultizar to begin to itch for the taste of blood. Jahir would be there to scratch his claws deep into his chest and relieve him of his itch forever--something that he had failed to do, since the last opportunity proved Bultizar to be cleverer.

Chapter 34:
Reflections of a Killer

While Poles was upstairs indulging in his book, Bultizar stood across the street staring at the hospital, his hair blowing in the brisk autumn breeze. He was close before in obtaining his heart's desire but was interrupted by unforeseen events that foiled his plans. After visiting the hospital earlier, he thought to himself that he would try one more time since his earlier visits ended in failure and he didn't want to make any mistakes.

This time he decided to go natural, only adding a mustache and glasses. For two hours, he contemplated what would be the right moment to go in and finish what he started, but there was an uneasy feeling he had about his surroundings.

Although the detective didn't notice him standing there as he parked and entered, Bultizar recognized him. This was his opportunity to find her, but he sensed something he couldn't put his finger on so he held his ground.

Something wasn't quite right. It all seemed too easy. He had never left anyone alive before. He realized his attack may have drawn Jahir to the site, giving him the opportunity to stop him, allowing him to be already present the moment he started to change. While he stood there contemplating, his mind began to drift to the past.

***

It was 1888 in the Whitechapel district of London. Bultizar had terrorized the city, brutally mutilating five women by removing their hearts, and was on the loose to find the sixth. He had baffled authorities until finally they received several leads, and then narrowing them down to one.

Bultizar had gotten word that they believed it was a gentleman of a higher class, a doctor perhaps who had frequented the bars and brothels over the past few weeks that no one had been able to clearly identify. He was someone with specific knowledge of the human anatomy, judging by some of the wounds.

It was he they were seeking, but like in the past Bultizar had always eluded his hunters at every turn. After months of terrorizing the city, the night had finally arrived to claim his last victim. The moon was particularly bright that evening, giving off a pale reddish glow. It was the first rising of the scarlet blood moon that no one else noticed.

Although many in the city were living in fear, it was especially high in Whitechapel on the east end of London that Bultizar was preying upon. Among muggers, thugs, and thieves, nothing rivaled Bultizar's appetite for sheer and brutal terror. He knew that people who worked the streets at night still had to survive. He watched the ladies of the night walk those streets, frequent bars, and shadow corners, while their overseers also made a profit. Walking amongst them that flocked to those places like sheep seeking their services, he got the same thrill every time as a wolf in disguise with long golden hair and an appetite for murder, soon to devour his final victim.

Bultizar had been watching her for a while. She was a regular at the bar, a most beautiful and talented servicer of men. Despite his severe appetite for other women of the night over the past several weeks, he knew she had little choice in having to survive the only way she knew how—by selling her greatest commodity.

Many had frequented the bar that night but very few showed her any interest. Bultizar made certain to appeal to her on every level that evening as he entered the bar and caught her eye. He took a seat next to her, showing little interest at first. He ordered a round of beer and posed as the debonair gentleman he knew would appeal to a woman like her.

She immediately initiated a conversation that slowly built steam. He could tell that she was on the prowl. She introduced herself as Delightful, but he knew her real name to be Mary Kelly.

Bultizar finally gave her the interest of a potential customer, with her not knowing it was all part of his web, to minimize the attention while hiding his aggression. Bultizar was as cunning as he was appealing, and she would pay the price. As their conversation progressed, he noticed that she was beginning to open up to him in a way that he hadn't expected. Perhaps it was her drink, or his extremely charming nature. Like many women in the past who desired him, her conversation expanded beyond the bedroom.

After finishing his beers, he offered to walk her home. Although he knew her to be a working girl with a show of indifference to her customers, that night she decided to oblige him.

After walking a few streets down, they were in front of 13 Miller's Court, where she invited him in. Across the street was a woman Bultizar briefly noticed who looked familiar to him—perhaps another lady of the night. She was staring at him like she had seen a ghost, but he was consumed with his mission of the moment.

After closing the door behind them, she walked over to him and began kissing him while undressing him. Bultizar stood looking out the window staring at the moon. It was only a few minutes before midnight when his blood started to boil.

She continued to kiss him with her eyes tightly shut. She didn't see the change of his eyes as they reflected off the moon that was shining through her window. While she held him, Bultizar began to change within her grasp, getting bigger in more places than one. She opened her eyes, looked up into his, and immediately jumped back.

Alarmed, she asked "What's happening to you?"

"Nothing is happening. I'm just being myself," he replied, as he laughed.

His face began to change while long blond hair began to sprout from his pores. Claws sprouted from his hands while his fangs began to grow.

She screamed as she attempted to get away but there was nowhere to go. The only way out was around him, but it was impossible for her to get to the door. Immediately silencing her, he swiped her with his claws, repeatedly ripping into her flesh while knocking her into the bed.

He was careful not to kill her before the appointed time, which was only seconds away, as he raised his hand to strike while she lay helplessly on the bed. The moment he had long awaited was finally upon him.

With the second hand of the clock a few ticks away from the moment that would change everything, the door crashed in while the police opened fire, robbing him of the chance to accomplish his destiny. He could've killed them all for unknown reasons he didn't. He leaped through the window and disappeared into the night. With his victim dying, her death would come too late for him to acquire what he had so desperately sought. He knew his chance would come again one day.

***

Bultizar refocused his mind from his past thoughts to concentrate on the present, his second chance that he refused to ruin. Knowing Jahir might be near, he looked around for all vantage points. Realizing there was no better place than up, he looked to the rooftops—the hospital roof in particular.

With his eyes focused in that direction, they began to turn gray like a pair of moons piercing the darkness in search of his adversary. He knew he had to be quick, or risk discovery. Any change, regardless of how slight or brief, would trigger Jahir's instincts and direct him to his location. He quickly reverted back before Jahir could pinpoint him.

The two enemies were connected in more ways than one. While Bultizar had been reflecting back on his past, Jahir saw Bultizar's open jaws and claws while they were tearing through Mary Kelly's flesh. Even the memory of her torment at that moment caused him to slowly react, and although Jahir's reaction was slow, it was enough to alert him that Bultizar was near.

Rising to his feet, he moved to the edge of the roof while scanning the streets below. As he saw only pedestrians walking back and forth, he could no longer sense him. Bultizar had once again outmaneuvered Jahir. The two had briefly exchanged eye contact but to him he was just another face in the crowd.

Bultizar knew that his failed attack on the young woman was what drew Jahir there. He also realized that Jahir's presence at the hospital was in support of the police to preserve the young woman he had intended to kill.

Although Bultizar's hatred for Jahir motivated him to take a more aggressive approach, he decided to abandon his plan. It was too big of a risk, one that he was unwilling to take. He was too close to achieving his prize and refused to let anything stand in his way. Bultizar returned to his place to bide his time.

Chapter 35:
The Hidden Truth

During the upcoming days while the city remained on edge, Jahir was on the move, searching for clues of who the man behind the monster really was with most of his time now spent on the roof of the hospital overseeing his friend waiting for the real monster to reveal himself.

Although Tia's initial recollections of the attack provided a place for Jahir to start, it was difficult for him to put the pieces together with her blurred memory. He needed her awake. She had seen Bultizar face-to-face. She could tell him exactly who he was and perhaps where to find him.

***

A week had passed since Maria's death. Terrie was still trying to cope with her loss. She hadn't been to work. She had to somehow get through this. Although it was hard, she knew she had to do it.

Sitting home only made it worse. Being one of the best in her field, it was time to come to grips with reality and get back to work. The only way she could make a difference and find justice for her friend was to get back out there and do her job. The best way to do it was through her reporting, gathering as much information as possible and telling it to the public. Maybe someone had seen or heard something that they might not have thought was important or was simply overlooked. She felt that with the right information, it may very well prick people's memory for them to come forward.

Terrie arrived at the station determined to make a difference. With the death of her friend fueling her fire, she was more motivated than ever to get in front of the camera.

Walking into the studio, she was welcomed with open arms and a strong show of support. Steve was the first to greet her. Hugging her, expressing his sorrow for her loss. Behind him was Buddy who shared his sympathy, along with the other news crew.

After all the pleasantries, she felt it was time to get down to business. After asking the staff what they remembered or saw, no one remembered anything unusual that night the two were there.

When she asked whether anyone was with Maria, the security guard told her what he had already told Grimes and Poles. He didn't have anything else to add.

Afterward she returned to her desk, trying to catch up. She overheard the staff members talking to a technician that was there on the scene when Maria died.

Not realizing that Terrie was in her office, she heard one say to the other that they overheard officers talk about something that appeared to be half-man, half-cat, and that they fired on it before it got away. Also, they were instructed to withhold that information, not wanting the public to know.

Unable to remain silent she made her presence known interrupting them by asking why they didn't report it. They told her that they didn't have anything to back up the claim. The police weren't talking and without them confirming it, they couldn't report it.

Hearing this, she became upset. Grimes being the investigating officer, he had to know, which meant he lied to her about not having any additional information. This revelation cut deep, playing into her emotions.

Maria was like her sister, and to find out that her man didn't trust her with that information infuriated her. She felt it should have been reported to the public, making everyone aware of what's been going on. She felt everyone should have been told to make that decision for themselves whether to believe it or not.

She contemplated what she would say when she saw Grimes again. She honestly didn't know what would happen.

With the city being wrapped in a cocoon of fear and everyone seemingly held hostage by a cold-blooded killer, most occupants believed it to be a psychopath responsible for the crimes. They didn't know the police had already encountered something that they could not explain.

Despite police reports and testimonies of the officer, many officials still had written it off as a man on PCP wearing body armor and an animal suit. Grimes and Poles believed otherwise. They had more than a reason not to dispel what had been seen as a hoax. They were committed to the notion that they were hunting a beast of supernatural origin, possibly two.

The question that turned in both of their minds was the exact role the alleged panthiem really played in it all. The likelihood that it could have had a role in all of the murders also stayed on their minds. Although the story did come out the pages of a book that many would consider a fairy tale of good versus evil, who was to say the Panthiem wasn't a little of both?

Grimes began to believe that it had been on the scene of every incident they worked and at every kill that was made. He also believed it was he that came to Terrie's rescue, Grimes also thought he could very well have been stalking her as well.

All of these theories were based off an obscure story told to them by way of Roslyn Perry, someone he believed to be a credible source. He also believed that her knowledge validated the evidence they had gathered. Any evidence they would collect moving forward would not be left open for interpretation, regardless of whether it was of natural or supernatural influence. Everything had to be thoroughly investigated.

Of the ten victims found, five women showed the pattern of a serial killer. The murder of Hakeem Robinson and his wife showed a motive based on the timing of his death, with everyone believing he was a shoe-in to win.

With Robinson's statement that once elected, his first course of action would be directed toward Nicholas Wolf and his company's practices, promising a thoroughly investigate if there were any illegal practices involved. that within itself established a possible motive for Wolf to react against him if he had something to hide.

Then there were those that appeared to be killed randomly, they all shared both visual and physical evidence of being killed by the same person, which would link them all together. Both Grimes and Poles believed if they solved just one of these murders, then they would have the killer in all of them.

Hopping in a car they headed to the various real estate companies that had supposedly held leases to each of the murdered women. During their investigation of Paul Neville, they followed his delivery routes directly connecting him to the female victims in the case.

They went back three years from the time he had first made deliveries on his route. In the company logs were signed invoices of registered letters that were delivered to all five of the women on the same day, all of which came from Wolf Realty.

Although none of the women knew one another, Neville was their connection. He had become the prime suspect before he too was found murdered. They still never received a definitive answer as to why he was handpicked for that specific route. Grimes was determined to have that question answered the next time he met with Nicholas Wolf.

Another thing they found strange was why the women signed a lease agreement with Wolf Realty, when each of them were paying rent to five separate complexes owned by different realty groups. They needed to find the reason for Wolf's involvement. In their mind, the first place to begin was with the realty companies to which their rent was being paid.

Their first stop was Summer Hill Apartments, Stacy Thomas's former residence. After walking into the management office, they identified themselves to the building manager. She was a tall, thin woman identifying herself as Carol Bryant. After greeting them, she offered to help in any way she could.

Grimes then got down to business. "Ms. Bryant, Stacy Thomas was one of your tenants."

"Yes, she was," she replied. "Stacy was such a pleasant young woman. We were all saddened to hear about her death. I hope you find this horrible individual responsible, along with those other poor people that lost their lives."

"We're working very hard on it, ma'am," Grimes replied, "but we're hoping that you could possibly shed a little light on the subject of her lease arrangements. In going over the letter, it appeared that she had a lease with Wolf Realty Corporation. It was signed by Nicholas Wolf himself but she paid her rent to your company, Northern Ride, for the past three years. Why would the corporate head of a multi-million-dollar company sign a lease agreement with another company unless there were some sort of ties there? How does that work?"

"That I can't answer, but here's something that I can," She offered. "Wolf Realty Company is our parent company. Although they oversee our business operations, they rarely interfere. By all intentional purposes, we operate independently and retain our own company name with annual meetings to discuss share distributions and other business."

"Is it standard policy that tenants sign their leases with them and pay their money to this company?" Poles asked.

"No, this was rare," she responded. "It's not normal practice. The request came directly from headquarters. I thought it was highly irregular that they would request that from one of our tenants. When I questioned them about it, they told me it was confidential and that the matter would not be discussed. So, I left it alone after that. I had come on board a month or two before Wolf became the majority share owner, and in my four years with the company I've never seen it done before or since."

Looking at both officers, she added, "You can try to find out why, you may have better luck."

After thanking her and departing, they visited the other complexes of each of the women, with the stories being the same—different real estate companies with one hidden owner buyout being the Wolf Realty. With each of the companies inquiring about each of the leases all the answers were the same. This raised more questions that needed answers. Everything now pointed to the Wolf Corporation, Nicholas Wolf in particular.

They had no evidence that would tie him to any of the murders, whether circumstantial or direct. They would have to bring it out of him and that would be a tall order. They wanted to wait before they confronted him. Although they had a confirmed hair sample from the lab, they needed to have something a little more solid that clearly tied him to the murders moving forward if they wanted to put the clamps on him. They didn't want to make any mistakes.

While heading back to the precinct, Grimes picked up his cell to call Terrie. With her returning to work, he figured that she was beginning to reclaim some sense of normality in her life. In thinking that he could help with the healing process, he decided that a nice dinner and quiet evening out would help to ease her thoughts. A little change of pace would probably do wonders for the both of them. They had a favorite spot located on Broadway, a second-floor restaurant they visited on special occasions.

She was sitting in her recliner stroking Max when her phone rang, consumed with her thoughts. Cuddling her puppy helped to ease them. Looking at the caller ID she saw that it was Grimes, she let it ring.

She didn't want to talk. She was upset after overhearing her co-workers talk about a police cover-up of what the officers saw and how they kept it silent.

She didn't care whether he was under orders or not, to her the two of them were beyond that. In her mind, it was the police's obligation to warn the public regardless of what the rumors were, especially if the crimes were real. She was a reporter, and felt it was not only her job but her obligation, along with the police's responsibility to warn the people so they could protect themselves.

When she didn't pick up, he left a message that he wanted to take her out that evening. After listening to her voicemail his gesture couldn't have taken her any farther away from her mood.

After about fifteen minutes, he called again but this time she answered.

"Yes?" answering sharply.

There was a brief pause. To him, her response was an unusually ridged. He picked up on it immediately.

"Baby, what's wrong? I called and left a message."

She hesitated before answering.

"Bobby, you lied to me."

"Lied to you?" he responded. Thinking about it, he wasn't quite sure what she meant but he knew he was about to find out rather quickly.

"When I asked you about any new developments, you said that there weren't any. I overheard two people at work talking about a police cover-up, how they confronted the killer and shot at it."

"It wasn't reported because the police withheld that information. We can't report speculations. We're not a tabloid. That would've been considered bad reporting without proof or witnesses making the story non-credible."

I trusted you and you broke that trust by not saying anything."

"Would it help if I told you there is a departmental gag order in this case? If the story leaked, I could lose my job."

"It was my friend lying in that dump of a building, dead. You and I were supposed to be above that."

"We are," but I also know you. You feel you have an obligation to report the truth. Had I asked you to remain quiet and restrain from releasing that information, it would've been very hard for you to do. With Maria's death, keeping quiet would've literally torn you apart. I didn't want you to have to go through that. Reporting is your life and you've always exercised good judgment, but I believed that Maria's death would have taken you beyond your limits. "I'm so sorry for not telling you, sweetheart," he continued. "I was just doing what I thought was best for the both of us."

Terrie then became quiet. She was feeling too emotional to continue their conversation. Abruptly ending the conversation, she responded, "Bobby, I have to go. I don't want to talk right now. I'll call you later."

As Grimes tried to respond, she hung up.

In the aftermath of their conversation, he stared at his phone then put it back in his pocket. He looked over at his partner shaking his head.

Poles then said, "Yeah, I could hear her through the phone. She sounded pretty upset."

"Looks like I have to cancel that thought of hanging out tonight, maybe for a while," Grimes replied solemnly.

"There's a lot on her plate right now, Chief. You might have to give her some time. She'll eventually come around."

Chapter 36:
Connecting the Dots

Once back in the office, Grimes's conversation with Terrie only added to the burden that had already been weighing on his mind. He knew he couldn't afford to be distracted so he buried their conversation and how he felt. Putting everything together in his head, he came up with a contingency of scenarios.

Clearing his desk, he stretched a map of the city across it. With his main focus on the Bronx and a marker in his hand, he looked at Poles.

"We both know these murders were never random or coincidental," although they appear to be. They were drawn out like a road map. Look at where the first victim, Stacy Thomas, was killed. It was according to where she lived. When you disregard where the bodies were found and focus on where they lived, that alone would make all of this appear to be random. But I believe they were killed in those locations so that it would conceal what this murderer was really up to. Stacy was the first to be killed, having her heart removed. The second victim was Kerri Barnes," Grimes analyzed as he drew a line to show a pattern.

"Like Stacy," he continued, "she was murdered the same way. Then there were two other murders two days later. The jogger in Central Park in Manhattan and then the other, our old former witness Harvey Lancaster, who was found dead in Brooklyn around thirty minutes later on the same night. Although they also appeared random, not showing a pattern, neither of them had a residency in proximity to anyone. I believe they were killed with the specific purpose to appear that way to distract us from what was really going on."

"Yes," Poles replied, "but in that short amount of time, unless the killer was being transported by a chopper that no one had seen, that distance would be impossible to cover in that time span. Then with traffic lights on top of that, having the time to do that amount of damage to each victim would be impossible."

"Under normal circumstances, I would believe that there was more than one killer," Grimes replied. "With the information Roslyn and her friend in London provided us, we can shoot down that theory. With the blond hairs we found on the victims matching those in London, not to mention that thing Roslyn described as a panthiem, along with what Daniels fired on, I would say it's a safe bet we can throw out multiple killers or a copycat one.

"Another interesting point is though all of them were mutilated none of the men had their hearts removed, whereas all the women killed did except for Mrs. Robinson.

As he stopped and glanced up at his partner, Grimes continued drawing a line on the map that connected to the fifth victim, Sandra Woo, who was the third woman to have hers taken. Poles remained quiet, while following his partner's lead.

"This to me is the most interesting piece," Grimes said, "the murder of Hakeem Robinson and his wife in Staten Island. Robinson was a shoe-in for the vacant council seat a day before the elections. He gets a surprise visit that evening from Nicholas Wolf to make peace only a couple of hours before he and his wife turn up dead. The same guy that had crucified him for his housing policies every chance he got in the papers, threatening to investigate him for illegal activities, which included bribery and payoffs to housing officials. Coincidence? I don't think so. I don't believe he and his wife were killed at random but out of vengeance. Their deaths really raised my suspicion toward Wolf."

With that, he connected the line from Sandra Woo to Sonja Hart.

"This young lady was the alibi for our prime target, Paul Neville," Grimes said. "The night Kerri Barnes was killed with her also at the time being the last one seen with Neville, it was Sonja Hart's statement that exonerated him."

He continued to connect the line, finally leading to Terrie's friend, "Which brings me to Maria," pausing once again.

The weight of her death was the heaviest to Grimes. She was like family. She had been out all day with Neville and was even last seen with him not long before her death and his disappearance.

Grimes then said, "Normally this would be a pretty much an open and shut case with all the arrows directed toward Neville. We know by both witnesses and DNA testing that he had been intimate with all five of the women and last seen with most. Based on what Kerri Barnes's roommate had expressed after our interview with her, Neville was sexually abusive towards Kerri, something that could be seen as lewd and deviant behavior.

He had almost fit the profile, but we now know there are at least two reasons that shut that theory down.

"One—he showed up dead, killed in the same way as the others. Two—his hairs came up a negative match in the lab analysis. But those same matching hairs of the killer were found clung to his body, which brings us to the question as to why his body wasn't found on the scene with Maria's. He was killed someplace else and then dumped in the river.

"In light of what we now have, the arrow now shifts in the direction of Nicholas Wolf, or someone associated with his company. Why was Neville handpicked to make these deliveries? They could've used anyone for that."

Poles then replied, "When you look at him, he strongly resembles Nicholas Wolf. Plus, the word was out that Neville was a ladies' man, attracted to young women of a certain stature. They were his type. Also, looking at his salary, he would've had to be pressing multiple jobs to afford the location and style of his apartment. The type of car he drove and the value of the clothes he had hanging in his closet, Neville couldn't afford a tenth of that stuff on his salary. No one that we interviewed knew him or had any knowledge of him working anywhere else."

"Yeah," Grimes replied. "He looked like the perfect candidate for a setup if you wanted someone away from your trail. You finance a guy to make him feel important. Money gives you more control, more power, more confidence."

"Yeah", but, "before we go making those claims, Poles interjected, directing them at someone with all of what we mentioned, we need proof to go along with that theory. We still have that elephant in the room to prove—death by werewolf. Proving that one exists will be like climbing Mount Everest in a diaper—impossible, unless we catch him in the act."

Grimes agreed and they then continued to focus on the map. The connecting lines formed a five-pointed star.

"The distance from each of their residences were exactly three miles apart!"

"Roslyn spoke about a sixth victim," Poles remembered. "That's what we now gotta figure. How does it correlate to this pattern? Clearly it is a five-pointed star on the map, soon to become a sixth victim if we don't stop him. With the pages in Roslyn's book being faded, we don't know when that scarlet blood moon is supposed to rise."

As Poles continued to think, the solution came to him. He looked over at Grimes and asked, "How could I? We have missed it. It was in our face all along. All we had to do was the math. Look at the dates of when these women were killed, starting with Stacy Thomas." After looking over at the calendar on the wall, he then said, "They were all murdered exactly three weeks apart, every one of them. The others were in no particular order but these women were. It's been almost two weeks since Maria died, which places the day of the next kill in the third week."

Poles paused as they both looked at one another. Poles then said, "It will fall on the week of Halloween, but the questions are who the next target will be and where it will happen."

Grimes agreed, without having a clue as to who or where it will be, there's no way to find and protect them—which leaves us with the cat-man, or panthiem. According to that book, he's looking for the killer too, but that doesn't make him any less dangerous to us. He may be driven to kill this werewolf but who's to say humans are not on his menu? These are all questions we don't know the answer to. We have now come full circle, with everything pointing in Mr. Wolf's direction, and that's exactly where we're heading right now," Grimes concluded.

Forty minutes later the two officers had once again found themselves in Wolf's office. When they walked in, it wasn't necessary for them to show their badges. Everyone knew who they were. With Wolf's secretary out of the office, the receptionist led them to the back. They had neither called nor made an appointment in advance. They wanted this visit to be unexpected. They didn't want a pre-scripted statement—only the truth and real answers.

This time, they had questions that needed to be answered. For Poles, it was the picture on the wall he couldn't dismiss, lingering constantly on his mind. The questions that Grimes had for Wolf would be more directed and to the point.

After taking them to her boss, she returned to the front desk. The welcome wasn't as cozy as it was before. This time, it was all business. Grimes was equally as coarse, He wanted answers.

A lot of what Wolf was practicing simply didn't add up. It all seemed scripted. When the officers entered, Wolf immediately offering them a seat and nothing else.

"No thanks, I've been sitting all day. I need to stretch my legs a little. I can never stop admiring your office, by the way." Poles complimented.

"Yes," Wolf replied, "I have an excellent decorator, but I'm pretty sure you're not down here to discuss office space, now are you detective?"

"No, we're not," Grimes replied. "We're here because we have questions concerning Stacy Thomas, Kerri Barnes, Sandra Woo, Sonja Hart, and Maria Gomez and your association with these women."

"I'm afraid I don't know what you mean detective. I never met any of them except Ms. Gomez, and our encounter was brief. I was asked by her organization to speak at their fundraiser, after that I never saw her or spoke with her again," Wolf replied.

While Grimes and Wolf engaged in conversation, Poles casually wandered off to look at pictures and certificates on the wall while searching for anything that may have been lying about that they could use. He was still listening in on his partner's conversation. He didn't have to forewarn his partner. They had been working together too long and knew the other's play like it was their own.

"I'm familiar with their names and faces from the news reports," Wolf continued, "not to mention being held responsible by the late Mr. Robinson simply because they died in or around a few properties I own. It was very sad to hear about their deaths, very tragic."

Sarcastically, Grimes intoned, "Yes, I'm sure."

Sensing his sarcasm, Wolf asked, "Do I hear a hint of skepticism in your voice, Lieutenant?"

"Not at all," Grimes contradicted. "You said you didn't know any of these women. But during my investigation, I found copies of signed receipts that DTX-Press had on file. A company that you also happen to own. The receipts were payments of rent to various realty companies but had a lease agreement with you directly under Wolf Realty—each lease that they all signed three years ago. We checked with Kengrove, Northern Ride, and the rest of these companies as to why, and asked whether that was standard policy.

"They told us it was not and that you were their parent company. Also, that your office specifically requested their leases to be sent there. They also said that when they inquired about it, the office told them it was deemed confidential."

"Detective, I have a multi-million-dollar business, I have hundreds of employees. That's why I hire people to run this organization. If I knew of anyone requesting those leases without my knowledge, we would have given you their names before we fired them."

"That would be appreciated because this case is still under investigation," Grimes stated.

"I'm guessing that whoever did this was probably an employee that no longer works here," Wolf offered. "After all, we do have a high turnover rate in that office, but I'll look into it."

Their conversation was intense. Periodically, Poles looked over to see if he was being noticed.

Grimes said, "Mr. Wolf, the problem is you signed off on it."

"I put my signature on hundreds of documents every day," he countered. "I don't always pay attention to them. Like I said, that's why I hire people to make sure everything is in order, and the company is protected from liability of any kind. Like all companies in this business, tenants come and go for all sorts of reasons. We are no different than anyone else."

"Yes, you are different, Mr. Wolf."

"How is that, Lieutenant?"

"Most companies don't have tenants that have been killed by the same killer in the same manner spread amongst their property locations, especially if they happen to be picked out for no apparent reason. Most companies don't have the problem of their lease agreements being sent to a corporate office that doesn't normally handle leases and then the corporate head signs them, and then coordinates to have those same leases hand delivered by a specifically requested carrier—who also ends up dead by what appears once again to be by the same killer, and in the same manner. Which brings me to my next question: Why was Neville requested for that specific route?"

"You know Lieutenant, I really can't answer that," Wolf replied, still seated, poised, and cool. "I don't know Neville personally. It's probably by the same employee who had those letters sent to the office. It would make sense."

"So, what you're saying is that you don't know anything about any of this?" Grimes asked Wolf directly.

"I can't say that I do," he replied. "Like I said, I will look into it, I assure you."

Still skeptical, Grimes asked, "Where were you the nights that the other murders took place?" He provided the dates of each one.

Wolf chuckled and then said, "Detective, this case has been going on for months. Surely you don't expect me to remember off the top of my head."

"You can try," Grimes snapped in response, with his patience was growing short.

"Lieutenant, I've enjoyed our talk, but unless you're here to arrest me, this interview is over."

There was an extended exchange of eye contact before Grimes responded, "For now."

Wolf said, "If you need anything or think you have something, feel free to give me a call. I don't mean to be rude but I have important business to attend to. I'm sure you know your way out."

Grimes stood up to join Poles saying, "I'm sure we'll talk again."

As they walked away, Poles looked back at Wolf and added, "You can bet on it."

While they departed, Grimes was extremely disappointed. He knew he really didn't have anything that would directly tie him to any of the murders. He tried baiting him but he didn't bite. His interview had gone nowhere. He knew Wolf was lying from start to finish but there was nothing he could do about it.

They were armed with only a theory and a story from a book of myths that no one had ever remotely heard of, so using that as the basis of their evidence would be nothing short of madness.

If they presented any of it in court, it would lead to both officers being charged with incompetency rather than convicting a killer, no matter how it tied Wolf to any of it. With nothing to stand on this case now in a stalemate, Grimes also had a personal life to fix. He wasn't sure of their next move, and all they had was a belief and a story no one would believe. except the cops that shot at the other guy. Once they got back to the precinct, they went over everything,

After they wrapped up their work for the day, Grimes was going to put werewolves and panthiems behind him and try to patch things up with his woman.

Grimes headed over to Terrie's while Poles went back inside to follow up on a few things. He wasn't quite finished for the night. He had a few things gnawing away at him and wanted to check them out.

A short time later as Grimes arrived at Terrie's condo, he knocked on her door. Peering through the peephole holding Max, she watched him knock. After a few taps on the door knocker, Grimes called her name. Seeing the shadow under the door and the darkened peephole, he knew she was there.

Calling her name again, he pleaded, "Please open the door."

"Bobby, please!" she cried. "Go away. I don't want to see you right now. Go home and leave me alone."

"Baby, we need to talk."

"I'm not in the mood to talk," she replied. "Will you please leave me alone right now?"

"Baby, we need to talk!" he implored. "I'm sorry. I know I was told to keep a lid on it, but I should've trusted you and told you the truth about everything. I was wrong."

Terrie took a deep breath before putting Max in his kennel. Reluctantly she opened her door, taking a step back, then walk away. When he entered, he walked behind her, reaching out gently placing his hand on her shoulder, slowing her while closing the door behind him. He then stepped behind her, now with both hands on her shoulders he drew close and began to explain everything that was going on.

He reminded her how he thought she would've felt obligated to her friend after her death and might have felt compelled to tell the public.

She then replied, "Yes, I feel obligated that my friend receives justice, along with all the others, but I would've never jeopardized your career by breaking your trust in doing so. I was hurt because you thought that I would."

The longer the two of them talked, the more the ice wall she had built between them began to melt. Grimes shared the whole story that Roslyn and McRae shared with them. After hearing the story, she realized that what he told her sounded more like an article fit for a tabloid and would have been irresponsible to report without facts to back it up.

As the tension began to subside, Grimes looked her in her eyes then leaned forward and kissed her, instantly tearing down any remaining wall between them completely. This was once again their time to find comfort and relieve some stress, making their way to her bed.

For Grimes, it had been a long and stressful day. His meeting with Wolf didn't relinquish anything that could be used in court. They were back at square one with none of their evidence able to hold up. He was convinced that everything they had was a loss and there was nothing they had that would change anything.

With that in mind, he decided to take a gamble by doing something he rarely had done, if ever. He turned off his phone. He was going to take this time to heal what had been a stressful time in their relationship. He didn't want any interruptions. As he tuned everything else out and enjoyed the moment with Terrie, they slipped into a place only the two of them could share.

Chapter 37:
Roslyn's Call

While Grimes and Terrie were trying to fix things, Poles was back at his desk searching for something that may have been missed. He was looking for something more solid and concrete than what they already had. The play they made on Wolf amounted to much of nothing. Both he and Grimes now believed that if there was a Bultizar, Wolf may very well be it.

With no real evidence to tie him to any of the murders, Wolf was both arrogant and confident. With only a theory based off an old book, it didn't matter what they believed—only what they could prove, and they had none of that. It seemed that Wolf had played with them until he became tired of the game. Then he ended it by sending both officers on their way with nothing to show but their frustrations.

Poles looked around at all the files and reports that were stacked on his desk, appearing as mini mountains. For weeks, he and Grimes had meticulously gone over everything in detail several times over, but Poles couldn't shake the feeling that they had missed something.

A couple of weeks had passed since Hakeem Robinson's death. Martina Estelle had been named the new director of the Affordable Housing Office in Robinson's place. Earlier that morning, Estelle had gone into Robinson's office. As she sat at the desk to review his files, she opened one of the drawers and saw the brown envelope Robinson had placed there before he left. After opening it, she began going over its contents and immediately knew it may be something the police would want to see.

Taking it back to her desk, she remembered the card Grimes had given her, then called for her carrier to take it to the precinct. When he arrived, they placed it on his desk. As more files and papers were brought in, the envelope found its way to the bottom of the stack.

Before he sat down, Poles saw a white envelope labeled "surveillance cameras" and another sealed envelope on Grimes's desk labelled, "lab results." He opened the white envelope first, finding it disappointing because the street camera footage from the Sandra Woo incident was unclear. He surmised the footage they had from the hospital wouldn't take a rocket scientist to figure out if the suspect, based off his actions, had something to do with all of it. He knew the other envelope contained the DNA reports for which they had been waiting.

After grabbing it, He saw a brown envelope more prominent than the others protruding from under the stack of reports on Grimes's desk. Pulling it from the bottom of the stack, Poles saw that it was from Hakeem Robinson addressed to Grimes with attention written in bold wording, and a return address to the Affordable Housing Organization.

Poles believed it had to be pertaining to the case, but first he wanted to see the DNA report. Upon opening it, he saw that it matched the others, with the gray hair being synthetic. Turning his attention back to the brown envelope, he spilled its contents onto the desk. In it were old news clippings and photographs with headlines that all looked nearly identical to the victims in the Bronx Butcher cases.

Poles checked the dates; he saw that they were from the mid-1930s. It was a case he had just recently researched online but the pictures he had seen weren't anything remotely close to the graphics that were in the photos.

In it was something that really caught his attention—an old photo of local businessmen with one of the men circled with a black marker. Poles wasn't quite believing what his eyes were telling him. It was a picture of Nicholas Wolf.

Looking at the date on the photo, he saw that it was taken over eighty years ago. Focusing on the details he checked to see whether it had been altered or interfaced, but the age and the condition of the paper ruled out that possibility.

Normally lighthearted and easygoing, he was now serious and focused. Page by page, he went over each of the pictures. The story that Roslyn Perry had told them was resonating in his head—the story of the chest filled with victims' hearts that Bultizar kept as his prize ate away at him like a cancer. If there was any truth to that story, finding that in Wolf's possession would give them what they needed, which was proof that he indeed was the Butcher of the Bronx and much more.

He remembered the passage of the story that Roslyn shared, that Bultizar kept the chest in a vault deep within the bowels of his castle. There were no castles in New York to speak of but there were luxurious apartment buildings that towered over Central Park like castle fortresses, and Wolf lived in the one he owned. If he was indeed Bultizar, it would likely be there that he would hide it somewhere in the basement if he followed the same pattern.

In light of the information he had just received, if he were going to act on his belief, then the time to do it was now. He couldn't afford to wait. This was the opportunity that he and Grimes had hoped for and all they needed now was to find the chest.

With the blond hairs that Poles picked from Wolf's coat during their first interview, He now possessed the proof they needed to tie Wolf to all the victims but also to that impossibility of being a real living, breathing werewolf.

Picking up his cell, he attempted to call Grimes. He wanted the two of them to get the answers together. In case one missed something, the other would be there to pick up the missing pieces. Grimes's phone continued to ring until the answering service picked up.

After several attempts, on his final one he left a message detailing everything he had found. This was too important to wait. He felt he needed to act on it now. First, he needed to go back to Wolf and have another face to face. He wanted to look him in his eyes and see the expression on his face when he showed him the evidence and how he was going to respond when he was presented with what he believed to be the final pieces to the puzzle.

He knew his reaction would confirm what he had would connect him to not only the women in all of the murders but to Robinson as well. Unable to reach his partner, he decided to do it alone.

When he was about to leave, the phone rang. On the other end was Roslyn Perry. She had the DNA results back from London. Like Poles, she too had been trying to reach Grimes with no luck.

Roslyn called his desk phone instead, Poles answered.

"Detective Poles."

"John", this is Roslyn Perry. I was trying to reach Bobby. I have the test results."

"Been trying to reach him myself, with no luck," Poles replied. "A lot has happened in the past few hours. What were they?"

"McRae called me back to confirm his findings. He tested the samples more than five times and the results were the same, a perfect match confirming that what we have is not a copycat serial killer but a killer that has been around for centuries. In other words, he is a serial killer through time."

Poles became silent for a few seconds then replied, "Incredible. This goes along with new information that literally just fell in my lap, coinciding with what you just told me. I don't want to wait. I'll need to move quickly. I'll just have to catch up with Bobby later."

"If all of this is true, this guy is too dangerous to go after alone, "she replied.

"I'm not going to try to take him in just yet," he replied. "Even with what we have, it still wouldn't be quite enough to stick unless I can get him to react. Knowing he's a monster isn't quite the same as proving that he's one. I need to find that chest. I'm gonna confront him, see how he reacts. If he is this guy Bultizar, then that chest is somewhere close. I have an idea where it might be. We spoke with him earlier, but in light of this new information I've just received, I'm going back to his office this evening and have another conversation."

"It may be too dangerous, maybe you should wait until you talk to Bobby."

"I don't wanna risk waiting. Anything could happen. Maybe if he knew we had something it might disrupt him, throw him off a little, and cause him to make a mistake."

Listening to the determination in his voice, Roslyn feared for his safety. From everything she read, Bultizar was extremely dangerous. She also knew that Poles was determined and there would be little she could say to deter him.

"Please be careful," she pleaded hoping for the best as their conversation ended.

Poles left the precinct and headed for Wolf's office. He called his partner a few more times, without luck. Nothing was going to slow this surprise visit as he arrived in front of Wolf's corporate office while heading up to his suite. He and Grimes had left there only a few hours earlier, and the last thing he was expecting was to see either of them tonight.

As he walked into the suite, the receptionist asked whether they had forgotten anything from earlier. "No," he replied, "but I would like to speak to your boss."

"One moment," I'll let him know you're here."

Not wanting to wait, He walked around her, and said, "Don't bother. I know where his office is."

When he entered, Wolf was surprised to see him. After their earlier meeting, he was one of the last people he expected to see.

"Detective Poles, did you forget something?" Looking past him, he said, "I don't see your lieutenant."

"He's a little tied up at the moment. And no, I didn't forget anything, but I do have a few things I would like a little clarification on."

"Sure," Wolf replied, "but I thought we covered everything. Was there something we missed?"

"Actually, I have something a little different," Poles told him.

"Have a seat."

"I prefer to stand," Poles replied, then handed him the brown envelope that he and Grimes had received.

"What is this?"

"Take a look. Maybe you can tell me," Poles responded.

Opening the envelope, Wolf looked through the photos and news clippings. He looked up at Poles and said, "These photos are pretty graphic, but what do they have to do with me?"

"I thought maybe you would recognize the handiwork. They're almost identical to those women found in your buildings."

With little expression, Wolf calmly replied, "What's your point? Why would I recognize anything pertaining to any murder where none of it is pertaining to me? Especially one dating back to 1939?" Poles then replied, "I beg to differ, sir. Those same murders took place in buildings under Crescent Hill Realty that was controlled by Wolf Realty."

Wolf looked closely at the date of the articles as well as the dates on the back of the photos. and said, "Sergeant, these photos were taken over eighty years ago. You explain to me how I would know anything about this. This business was owned and operated by my uncle when he was a young man and there is nothing on record that this company is involved in any of this. Your claims are outrageous, irresponsible, and most of all ridiculous. I suggest that if you continue this, then you, your partner, as well as the NYPD will be getting a call from my attorney for harassment and false accusations."

Poles then reached into his pocket and handed him the old photo of him. Wolf stared at it for a moment. Poles could see there was a subtle change in his demeanor, enough to know it had struck a nerve.

"What is this?"

"You tell me," Poles replied. "Doesn't this picture look familiar?" Handing it back to Poles, he said, "It bears a resemblance, but it very well may be shopped. Whether it is or not, that doesn't prove a thing. One can pull up unrelated pictures all day long and find people in the past that look exactly like someone walking the streets today. I think if you attempt to use any of this in court, you will look ridiculous after my lawyers are through with it and you, not to mention the legal ramifications that will follow pertaining to your accusations. Now if that is all, I would suggest that unless you have real proof the very next time you show up, you will be hearing from my lawyers."

Poles then said, "There is one more thing I would like to say."

At that moment, Margaret walked into the office holding documents that needed a signature. She looked over at Poles and greeted. "Hello, Detective. You're back again for another visit, I see."

"He was about to leave," Wolf interjected. He directed to Poles, "You were about to tell me something?"

"Yes, but in private," he responded.

Margaret said to her boss, "I'm leaving now. I just needed a signature."

"No, Margaret, you don't have to leave. Anything the detective has to say he can say in your presence."

"Very well," Poles decided. Looking him directly in the eyes, he said, "Have you ever heard the story of the golden wolf and the panthiem?"

"No, I don't believe I have," Wolf stated.

Poles repeated the story as it was told to him, verbatim.

After listening, Wolf inquired, "That story sounds, entertaining, even amusing, but what does any of that have to do with what's going on today?"

Poles looked him in his eyes and offered, "Probably nothing, but everything that's been going on today reminds me of that story. I believe the night my fellow officer arrived and saw what he believed at first to be a man in an animal suit dressed like a cat was this panthiem, but the man on the ground was really Bultizar. I think he changed back to human in the presence of the police, thereby setting up this panthiem to make it look like he was the killer."

"Well, I hope you and your partner aren't basing your case on a child's fable that no one has ever heard of," Wolf recommended. "Let me get something straight. You're trying to implicate me as a suspect with no other evidence but this?" As he shook his head, Wolf declared, "Not only will I have your badge, but I will also file a civil suit if you come to me again with this ludicrous tale."

"I haven't accused you of anything. All I've done is ask you a few questions and told you a story." Poles then added, "I've never asked you what was in the basement of your castle."

"I wouldn't have been able to tell you because I don't own one." Wolf replied,

Poles smirked then said, "Maybe not, but the building you own towering over Central Park sure looks like a castle, your own castle."

Margaret stood quietly next to her boss; Poles looked up at the old photo on the wall.

"Now I know who that picture reminds me of," Glancing over at Margaret deciding to keep his thoughts to himself without saying another word. He looked Wolf in his eyes then asked, "What are you doing on Halloween?"

"Nothing at all, Detective. Why would you ask?"

"The department is having a Halloween party; I was inviting you to come out," he issued, looking Wolf in his eyes.

"I'd love to, Detective, but I don't think I'll be able to make it. Besides, I wouldn't know what to dress up as."

Poles chuckled, "Maybe a werewolf, a blond one."

With that, Poles walked out of the office. He had seen in his eyes what he wanted to see. Wolf was trying hard to hide his true feelings. To the savvy detective, it was obvious to him that he had struck a nerve. Poles took a gamble revealing his hand; he saw the discomfort and irritation in Wolf that he needed to see, but he knew he had to act fast. He had to find that chest. Without it, he wouldn't be able to prove anything.

As Poles walked away, Wolf looked over at Margaret and didn't say a word.

She smiled and said, "Well, I have something I need to take care of, some unfinished work," as she turned and walked away.

Wolf sat there quietly, staring at the picture of his uncle hanging on the wall.

***

It was dusk when Poles first arrived at Wolf's office, and now the sun had slipped beyond the horizon. Accomplishing what he had hoped to accomplish, he was convinced that Wolf was indeed Bultizar. He would now have to find that chest filled with the evidence but first he decided to take the envelope back to the office where it would be safe in case something went wrong. When he got back to the office, he placed the envelope on the top of his desk before heading to Wolf's apartment building overlooking Central Park. When he arrived, he entered the building and down the stairwell to the basement.

There were a few apartments on that level along with the boiler room and a few storage closets. The building was enormous. It wasn't an easy task. If there was a chest, then he could've hidden it anywhere. It was like looking for a needle in a haystack, but Poles wasn't deterred. He didn't have enough to get a warrant. Even if he could, that would take a few hours and he had already tipped his hand to Wolf.

He checked the boiler and laundry rooms, including each storage area. After an hour or so, he was about to call it a night until he decided to look behind a few stacks of paneling and debris that was stacked at the end of the hallway against the wall.

Curious, Poles walked over to it and moved some of it to see there was a door behind it with a padlock. Moving it aside, he had to figure out how he was going to open it without a key or metal cutter. Looking around on the floor, he found some metal wire amongst an assortment of debris.

Having a few years on the job, he picked up a few skills on the streets. Poles worked the wire into the keyhole until finally he had picked the lock. Once he opened the door, he saw that it led down a dark flight of stairs.

Using the light on hid phone he started down the stairwell as it led to another door. When he opened it, he flashed his light around. It too was filled with light debris and pieces of old drywall, boxes, and wood scattered around.

Finally, he found the light switch and flipped it but it didn't work. Shining his light around initially, he didn't see anything that would draw his interest until he saw some blood on the floor in the far corner.

As he got closer, there was a cut in the concrete floor with a groove allowing him to get his fingers under it. After lifting it, he cast it aside, grabbing his light, shining down in it. At the bottom, he saw what he had hoped to find—an old wooden chest.

Reaching down to take hold of it, Poles pulled it up, placing it in front of him. It also had a lock in which he easily picked. Opening it, he was hit with the stench of decay. It was filled with the hearts of its victims with one empty chamber. The smell was nearly unbearable. After pulling a handkerchief from his pocket to cover his nose and mouth, he heard the door close behind him.

Grabbing his light, he shined it toward the door but didn't see anything. He then shined it around and saw a shadow of someone standing in the corner.

Shining his light directly at it, Poles immediately drew his gun and said, "So you're Bultizar. I'm placing you under arrest for the murders of—"

Before he could finish, he couldn't believe what he was seeing before his eyes. The person standing in front of him grew almost instantly from a human to a werewolf as blond hair sprouted from his pores. The face began elongating like the muzzle of a wolf while a pair of elongated fangs began protruding from his gums. His fingernails were replaced by sharp curved claws. Everything happened simultaneously while his body grew in height and mass.

Poles began firing his pistol consecutively. Before he could finish his clip, the werewolf had covered the distance between them in a blink of an eye. With the bullets having no effect, Bultizar reached out with one hand, grabbing Poles by the throat and lifting him like he was a doll.

As he held him upward, they were now face to face, looking Poles in the eyes while the detective struggled to breathe and break free. With his claws buried deep into both sides of his neck, he snatched out his throat tossing his body to the side while he lay helplessly gurgling in his own blood.

Bultizar stood over Poles as he gloated. He was caught up in the moment when he realized he had drawn the attention of another. Bultizar's change had alerted his hunter as he raced toward their location.

Knowing that he needed to work quickly, Bultizar took hold of Poles's body, along with the wooden chest, and carried both away from the building. Dumping his body about a block away, he changed back into his human form. With the chest in his possession, he disappeared moments before Jahir arrived.

Knowing Bultizar was gone. From the top of the building, Jahir looked down at Poles's below.

Jahir knew he didn't die there. His visions showed him in a much darker place, one that was absent of light where his enemy's face was shrouded in darkness. Only his pain could be felt and he would return to the place of his death later.

He knew this victim. The question in his mind was why. He was one of the policemen that was in charge whenever Bultizar killed. Jahir then surmised that the detectives may have been close to finding his identity and posed a threat. If Bultizar killed him, then the other policeman might also be in danger.

There wasn't much time before the day of the rising. Only Tia could tell him who Bultizar was, and only then could Jahir be there to stop him before he committed his final act. He decided to head back to the hospital, hoping she would open her eyes again. He galloped away into the night to check on Tia.

Not long after disposing of Poles's body, Bultizar arrived at a new location. It was another one of his buildings, one that no one would expect. He entered from the rear. It also had a basement—smaller, but it was perfect. Unlike his last hiding place, he placed his prized possession within a small panel of the wall where he knew it would be safe.

He was gloating with satisfaction. Another one of his nemeses was no longer a threat to his plans. He was feeling more than invincible knowing it wouldn't be long before he claimed his heart's desire. With that thought in mind, he could rest easier. Only the anticipation raised his anxiety. All that was needed was patience and then this world would forever be his. Reaching over to the switch, he turned off the light and rested his eyes. As a businessman, he had a long day ahead of him.

***

Back at the hospital, Jahir descended along the side of the building as he looked in on his friend while she was still sleeping. He was her guardian angel in the form of a beast, and she was his sleeping beauty. Looking at her saddened him deeply. He was constantly haunted by feelings of guilt, and he vowed to rectify all of it once he faced the golden wolf again.

Chapter 38:
Beyond Personal

The following morning, Grimes remembered to turn on his phone. The night had gone well as the two lovers made amends. Terrie was making breakfast while Grimes was still in bed.

With his pants lying on a chair beside the bed, he reached into his pocket, grabbed his phone, and turned it back on. That's when the text messages began to come in one after another. Nearly all of them were from Poles, both texts and voicemail.

As Grimes read each of his text and listened to his messages; they were all about Poles going back to Wolf's office to have another conversation pertaining to new evidence he had acquired. Poles didn't go into detail, other than it was too important for him to wait.

Immediately, he called Poles but he didn't get an answer. When he called his home phone, his wife answered. She was crying uncontrollably. Crying out that John was dead, that they murdered him.

Confused by what she was saying, Grimes attempted to calm her. He needed to find out what had happened, but she dropped the phone. She was crying in the background.

Another text message pinged. It was from Captain Hernandez, telling him that it was urgent and to call him ASAP.

Without delay, Grimes called. Hernandez answered.

"Captain, what is going on? I just called Poles's home. Monica was crying, screaming he was dead."

Hernandez began to tell him what had happened. At that moment, Terrie approached with his breakfast on a tray. She could hear the captain's voice on the other end; she saw the expression on Grimes's face as his countenance had dropped. While they were speaking, Grimes sat, then turned toward the side of the bed and leaned forward, placing his hands on his forehead.

Before the conversation ended, Grimes said, "I'm on my way."

Obviously distraught, he glared at the wall with a blank stare. Terrie could see the hurt in his eyes.

"What's wrong, baby?"

He looked over at her and stated, "John was killed last night."

"No!" she exclaimed as she set the tray down on the bed while sitting close beside him. "What happened?"

"They found his body on the side of a building. His throat had been ripped out. They believe he was killed someplace else and dumped there. Had I not turned off my phone, I would've been there, and he'd probably still be alive today."

With the death of Maria fresh, and now Poles, there was a connection with her, too. She knew his pain all too well; this was another addition. Keeping her composure, she had to remain strong. In an attempt to comfort him, she added her thoughts. "You can't blame yourself. You didn't know. How could you?" She hugged him. Being that the killer was so close to home the fear for his safety heightened one hundred-fold frightening her even more. She turned and asked, "Does Monica know?"

"Yes. When I called the house she answered, crying hysterically, and barely able to talk, dropping the phone. That's when I called Captain." He looked at her saying, "I'm sorry, baby. I gotta go."

He showered, got dressed, gave her a kiss and left.

While Grimes headed to the morgue to see his partner's body, Terrie called the TV station to see what else she could find out. But with the death of her friend and Poles, it was too much for her to deal with directly. She needed a little more time. Everyone had their limits, and as tough of a reporter she had been, she had reached hers. Emotionally, she had barely recovered from the last incident. She wasn't quite ready for another so close behind and possibly committed by the same killer.

For Grimes, the loss of his partner was devastating. He was torn inside. They were more than just partners; they were like brothers, and he felt responsible by not being available when he needed him.

When he arrived at the morgue, it was a scene all too familiar to him. He and his partner had been in the place numerous times, but this time, it was his partner and friend lying there, a victim of whom he believed was the same killer they were trying to stop.

There was only one name that came to mind: Nicholas Wolf. There wasn't a doubt that he was responsible. For the second time, someone had been killed who had direct issues with him, his partner, like himself, being one of them.

He waited by the storage unit, standing there with his thoughts while they opened the drawer and unzipped the bag. As he stood over his friend's body, it was like he was in a state of suspended animation. To him, this didn't seem real.

There was a hole in his throat. He couldn't help feeling that it was all his fault. Had he not gotten caught up in his own world by turning off his phone, he believed his partner would still be alive. Filled with both anger and remorse, Grimes had to pull himself together and refocus on what his next move would be.

Poles's body had been mauled like the others, apparently by the same killer, but there was one difference. His wounds were not to the same extent as the others. His death appeared to be swift and clean as if time weren't a luxury.

He was convinced more than ever that Wolf wasn't who people thought he was, and he was even more determined to go after him, no matter what it took. He examined his wounds to find what clues he needed. He had to backtrack his partner's steps--from the time they went their separate ways. The place to start was back in their office.

While leaving, Monica was coming down the hall to view her husband's body. She needed to see firsthand what had happened to him. Because of the condition of his body, Grimes intercepted her. He felt it might be too much for her to handle, but she was too determined not to let anyone stand in her way.

After getting by him, Grimes went back in the room with her. Monica stood there silently, not moving a muscle. The shock of seeing him caused her body to shut down; she collapsed to the floor.

Grimes and the staff came to her aid, calling for an ambulance as she lay on the floor for a minute or so before coming to.

Assisting her into a chair, she started crying. Grimes leaned over and held her.

"How could this happen to him?" she cried over and over again.

Grimes wished he had the answers to tell her, but there was nothing he could say that would soothe her pain. Finally, she got herself together--but barely. The fears she had earlier for her husband's safety had been realized. Seeing that she was in no condition to drive, Grimes wanted to take her back to her home but he had unfinished business to take care of, so he called for a unit to take her.

Three people connected to him were now slain by this killer. Like a terminator, he wasn't going to stop until this thing was captured or dead. Grimes headed back to his office believing if there were anything to be found, he would find it there. It was the last place Poles had been before heading back onto the streets.

When he got back in his office, he went over to Poles's desk and looked to see if there was something that he hadn't seen. Poles had left a note detailing all new-found information and that Roslyn Perry had called, giving him the details of what they learned, along with the results she got back from London, as well as, how everything matched along with the brown envelope. On his desk, he saw the DNA reports from the lab downtown verifying everything.

Before heading over to Wolf's Manhattan apartment building, Poles had come back to the office and dropped it off. Looking over the photos and articles dating back to the 1930s, he began painting the same picture that his partner had painted. Seeing those pictures, he knew exactly why he went back to see Wolf and why he didn't want to wait before acting on it.

He then noticed a footnote on a small sticky pad. Poles had written, *Bultizar kept his chest of hearts in the bowels of a dungeon chamber* with a question mark beside it.

Grimes looked at it as he attempted to figure out what it had meant, and then a light switched on in his head. He had come to the same conclusion. If Wolf was Bultizar, then his castle would be his home, and his residence was as grand as any castle fortress that towered over the park.

He was going to trace his partner's footsteps, believing that not only would he find what he was looking for but also the place that his partner may have also been killed. This time, he was going to do it unannounced, obtaining the evidence before nailing this murderer to the wall. It didn't matter whether he was in the form of a man or that of the beast, Grimes was going to make him pay either way.

Wasting no time, he headed to Wolf's building in hopes of finding the chest, if it was still there. Once he found it on his property, he had all the evidence he needed to bring Wolf down.

When he arrived, he went into the rear entrance and headed down the basement stairwell. After reaching the basement he walked slowly down the long, half-lit corridor, he saw what appeared to be small droplets of blood on the hallway floor—a drop here and there that was barely noticeable. The loosely scattered droplets led in a single direction, straight to the door that Poles had found. This time, it was uncovered.

Grimes from his pocket he pulled out a light, then he headed forward down the dark, narrow stairwell into the same room. After entering, he shined his light around the room until he saw a large splatter of dried blood and empty shell casings next to the small, carved out opening on the floor. To him this was where his partner was killed.

Shining his light down in it the carved opening in the floor he saw that it was empty. Like his partner in the darkness, he too sensed that he wasn't alone.

While moving the light around, it cast shadows, which made the room seem alive. As he scanned, something caught his eye. He slowly backtracked the light before stopping at a corner where two crates were stacked.

When he shined it upward, there appeared to be the same figure the police had described attacking a man the night Maria was killed. Crouching like a cat ready to pounce, the light reflected off its eyes as he snarled.

Grimes went for his gun, but Jahir already airborne, brushed him to the side like a gnat while Grimes fell into debris, dropping his gun. Momentarily stunned with only his flashlight still in his hand, Grimes reached over and grabbed his gun again. He sprang to his feet, but Jahir had already gone.

Quickly, he found his way back up to the basement hallway. Immediately, he called for backup and then rushed out the rear of the building, swinging his body around with his gun, pointing it in whichever direction he shined his flashlight.

As he looked around, he spotted him across the courtyard scaling the building nearly to the top of one that was twenty stories tall. Once he got on top of the roof, Jahir turned to look back before he disappeared into the night.

Grimes stood momentarily contemplating what had just happened, but was convinced it wasn't the killer, and chose not to pursue him. Turning his attention back to Wolf, Grimes wanted blood— Wolf's blood. As much as he wanted to go after him, he still had nothing but old photos and a hunch. He didn't have grounds for a warrant. All he had was a gut feeling that would have been invalidated in any court, but he was determined to move forward no matter what.

In the days that followed his partner's death, Grimes prepared to bury his friend. Both Monica and Terrie shared the same pain. After burying her husband, Monica moved back to Connecticut with her family.

Now desperate, Grimes had run out of options and turned to Captain Hernandez. This seemed to be a daunting task, but he was going to give it a shot.

With everything he and Poles had collected, he went into his office and hoped for the best. When he came in, he sat down and told the captain everything they had been working on, presenting him with the facts they had acquired, which included surveillance tapes of an unidentified man in two separate disguises who came into the hospital two consecutive days looking for Tia Johnson—although with the footage they had, they still couldn't identify him, but they could tell it was the same person in both videos—all the way down to the information they received from Scotland Yard, as well as, from one of the most respected forensic science expert in the states, Roslyn Perry.

Grimes knew that even with the death of Poles after visiting Wolf, he had nothing that the public would remotely believe. Looking Hernandez in the eye, Grimes described what he had seen, that it brushed him to the side as if he were nothing, causing him to drop his gun. He told him that it could have easily killed him but elected not to, instead escaping without harming him.

After listening, Hernandez became quiet. Although the story appeared to be far-fetched, he still had the reports of Officer Daniels who claimed to have seen and shot what appeared to be the same creature. As the captain took it all in, Grimes was surprised he believed him, but it all boiled down to the things that could be proven.

Grimes said, "We can get a warrant based on probable cause."

"On what grounds?" Hernandez asked.

"According to the building managers of five separate companies that were owned by Wolf," Grimes explained, "his office had specifically requested that leases be delivered to the five murdered women he claimed he had no special knowledge of, yet all of which were signed by him. Each of them had stated that it was unusual practice for the parent company to make such a request.

"Also, the delivery carrier of Wolf's company--personally assigned by his request--had an intimate relationship with all five of the murdered women before he himself turned up dead. All of the women had some ties to him and his company one way or another.

"Also, we've got surveillance tapes of an unidentified man in two separate disguises who came into the hospital for two days looking for Tia Johnson. Although the footage is not absolutely clear, we can see that it's the same person in both videos. Poles and I saw him in her room, thinking at first that he was the doctor, but instead, was found moments later to be an imposter trying to reach Ms. Johnson, before escaping."

"What are we gonna tell the court, that he turned into a werewolf—a blond one, at that—and killed all those people? Accusing Wolf of being a werewolf would be lunacy. The court will throw it out while you and I will be fired for incompetence. The only thing you got is that young woman's testimony who's fighting for her life in that hospital, if she wakes up. Even then, there's no guarantee that she'll remember anything. Besides, Wolf's lawyers will tear her testimony apart with the input from their medical experts. They will say that she was delusional, and that it was the result of a blow to her head."

"If she does wake up and identifies Wolf as the killer in transformation, the courts will have no choice but to listen, regardless of how far-fetched it is. All we can do is wait for her to open her eyes and hope for the best," Grimes offered. Hernandez sat quietly, then reluctantly agreed, saying that if she opened her eyes and gave a testimony, we would give it a shot. Now his obsession, Grimes played back in his mind everything that had happened. From the death of Maria to the man he admired like a brother.

It was October thirtieth. If Roslyn Perry and McRae were right, then he didn't have but a few hours to stop him before the clock struck midnight. With that on his mind, there was something else equally disturbing. Like his fellow officer, he had also seen the panthiem firsthand.

The fact that he was face-to-face with it and lived, confirmed what he and his partner already believed: that the story was true. There was a werewolf stalking the streets of New York, and this panthiem was stalking him.

He was also sure that Nicholas Wolf was responsible for his partner's death—that he was indeed the golden wolf, and Poles had come so close to proving it. That's why he was killed.

The story relayed that the panthiem was stalking the werewolf, but other than proving the two were real, who was to say he didn't have a hand in any of the killings? Outside of a few strands of hair, no one had ever reported seeing the werewolf. It was the panthiem that was reportedly seen attacking a man the night Maria died. It was the same catlike figure who fit the description of the men who were found scattered on the ground in the back of an alley. Was he that gentle soul the story described, or was he just as cold of a killer as Bultizar who just had a bone to pick with him?

Grimes thought about how easily he could've killed him, but he still couldn't totally rule out the likelihood of him being a killer. With everything circling inside his head, Grimes looked over the map again step-by-step.

The locations of all the bodies found were both sequential and random. Looking at the latest results Poles had sent to the lab, the samples found on Wolf's coat matched the ones on the scene, according to the report. He could now request a search warrant but there wasn't enough time. The gray hair was found to be synthetic, but there wasn't much else to go on.

As he looked at the clock, Grimes figured he would try the hospital one more time. Maybe this time luck would be in his favor. Tia Johnson may, by some miracle, open her eyes and give them what they needed, identifying the killer of Maria, which would cause all the dominoes to fall. He left to go to the hospital to check on her progress, hoping for a miracle. Hopefully, she would open her eyes in time to help him.

Grimes wasn't the only one headed to Tia Johnson's room. Jahir was also on his way.

Chapter 39:
Hoping for Answers and a Sleeping Witness

It had been three weeks that Tia had been unconscious. Outside her room, two officers were posted dressed in hospital scrubs assigned to both monitor and protect her.

Patiently, they hoped and waited for her to wake up and give her account.

As they hoped, Tia slowly opened her eyes. Her mouth was dry, her vision was blurred. She looked around to see there was an IV attached to her while wearing an oxygen mask. For about twenty minutes, she struggled to gather her senses then she heard a tap on the window. Looking at it, she tried to focus her vision

Staring at her from the outside was Jahir. He had descended down the wall like a spider with his claws embedded within. He placed a finger over his mouth, gesturing for her to stay quiet.

He then pointed to the door. She slowly looked toward it and could hear people talking. Although she was weak, she had enough strength to sit up on her own. Carefully, she removed her oxygen mask and IV, and quietly walked over to the window.

Jahir pointed to the lock, motioning for her to unlock it. After unlocking it, he quietly slipped through the window. She hugged him like she never wanted to let go. If he hadn't arrived when he did, she would have become another of Bultizar's victims.

She had witnessed the beast turn into a man and knew exactly who he was. She remembered running when he turned, and how it caught and struck her, knocking her into the wall. She remembered Jahir having arrived before she faded from consciousness. Though unconscious inside, she somehow believed Jahir would be there watching over her.

Was this fate or a miracle that Tia had awakened this night? It was a question only the good Lord could answer. This was the night of the scarlet blood moon, at midnight, it would be Halloween, a day well-fitted for the occasion. They were running out of time, and Jahir's only chance depended on what Tia could tell him.

Still weak, she began to lose her balance as Jahir caught hold of her, preventing her from falling and placing her back onto the bed. She whispered in his ear, telling him everything she had seen. She told him who it was and where to find him.

There wasn't much time. There were only a couple of hours before midnight, when the moon would be at its peak. She didn't know who the last victim would be, but she knew the best place to find Bultizar. Jahir's fate, along with the rest of the world, depended on whether he could find him in time.

After hearing everything he needed to know, he whispered in her ear, "Ex toto corde meo et ego semper gratus."

Not understanding a word, she simply looked.

Knowing this, he smiled and said, "It is Latin, my native tongue. It simply means, 'From my heart I shall always be grateful.'"

Jahir slipped out the window as quietly as he had entered, seconds before the nurse came in to check her status. When she arrived, she saw both the IV and the oxygen mask had been removed. Tia's eyes were open.

Reconnecting it, she notified the physician on duty. Seeing that she had finally awakened, one of the officers made the call to Grimes. When his cell rang, he had just pulled up to the hospital. He jumped out his car and rushed inside. He hurried to her floor and down the hall. When he arrived at her room, he was briefed by one of the officers on her condition. He told him that she had begun fading in and out of consciousness. When he entered, the doctor was already there. He informed Grimes that she was very weak and needed to rest, that everything surrounding her may be too much for her at that moment.

Time was of the essence, and Grimes knew he didn't have a moment to waste. He knew he might not get another chance. After convincing the doctor it wouldn't take but a moment, and that he would be as brief as possible, the doctor reluctantly agreed.

Grimes approached her, her eyes were closed, he called her name softly.

"Ms. Johnson? Ms. Johnson," he repeated, with no response. As he called her name again, there still was no response.

The doctor stepped in and said, "I'm going to have to ask you to try another time, Lieutenant. She's very weak."

Reluctantly, Grimes stepped back and was about to leave when she opened her eyes momentarily.

Grimes stepped forward before leaning over and said, "I know you're weak right now, and if these were normal circumstances, I'd wait, but if I don't get the answers now, someone might die tonight, and I'm out of time."

She whispered a word before she faded out of consciousness again. The last word she said before going under again was the name "Wolf."

After hearing what she had said, he turned to the officers and instructed them to head downtown to obtain an arrest warrant for Nicholas Wolf, surrounding the murders of Sergeant John Poles, Hakeem Robinson, and everyone else attached to the case.

"Where are you going?" one of the officers asked.

"I'm headed over to pay Mr. Wolf a visit personally."

Using his cell phone, he made a call to have a squad car meet him at Wolf's office. The blond hair sample was consistent with the others they already had in their possession.

Getting in the car, his cell phone rang. On the other end was the forensics lab with Gabrielle Acostas. After answering, she told him about the lab results she had sent to their office. Grimes told her that his partner had received them.

She proceeded to tell him that she had additional information pertaining to the synthetic hair sample she didn't send.

"The gray sample matched an earlier one they found at the scene of Stacy Thomas's murder—but it wasn't found on or in direct proximity to her body. Since no other samples were found on any of the other cases, we listed it as miscellaneous and disregarded it. It wasn't until John brought those last two samples that my attention returned to that singular gray strand that we had put to the side. When I did a detailed scan of it, comparing it to the one we found at the scene of Stacy Thomas's murder, I found that both were synthetic and a match. If we can find the owner, then I think we can start getting some answers."

Grimes informed her, "I think I know where to start."

After hanging up, thinking to himself that since those hairs were found in his office, Wolf's arrogance proved that he knew something. One way or the other, he had to find out.

It wasn't long before Grimes had pulled up in front of Wolf's office. Already waiting there was the squad car with two officers he requested. Entering the building, they walked up to the security desk towards the guard on duty.

"May I help you?"

"Yes, police business," Grimes proclaimed. "We're going up to Nicholas Wolf's office. Have you seen him this evening?"

"Yes," the guard answered, "He left earlier and then came back about an hour ago--he and his secretary, Ms. Sullivan. He never came back down, only Ms. Sullivan did. That was only moments before you arrived."

"Is there another exit to the building?"

"Not without setting off the fire alarm. Everyone enters and leaves the building here through the main entrance after six o'clock, including the loading docks."

"Thank you," Grimes and the two officers went up to Wolf's suite.

After getting off the elevator, the officers headed toward his office. When they walked in, everything was quiet—too quiet. To Grimes, something wasn't right. In light of what had happened, he instructed the two officers to split up and check the other rooms while he checked Wolf's office.

When he entered, Wolf was sitting at his desk facing the window with his back toward the door. He called his name, as he drew his gun, but Wolf didn't respond. He didn't say a word, neither did he move a muscle. Slowly, Grimes circled to face him, not knowing what to expect, then stopped, lowering his gun.

Sitting with his eyes open, he was dead. His throat had been ripped open. The front of his body was soaked in blood as it pooled on the floor in front him.

Immediately, Grimes raised his gun and swung around ready to fire. Calling to the other officers, they rushed in the room with their guns drawn. Seeing Wolf, one of the officers said, "Holy crap! What happened? The other rooms were clear."

"Check the floors. I'll call for backup," Grimes instructed.

In light of what he knew, he ordered them not to split up and to stay together at all times while they searched. They thought that was strange, but they didn't question him, as they followed his orders.

Grimes stood puzzled. Midnight was less than an hour away; he was running out of time. He still didn't have a clue where to begin.

He was sure Wolf was his killer. Everything pointed to him, but now that he was dead, Grimes was fresh out of suspects. He was prepared to stake his career on the man in the chair in front of him. He was sure that Bultizar had assumed the alias of Nicholas Wolf. He couldn't have been so wrong.

Grimes now believed there was something Wolf knew that cost him his life, but what? Or, to be more accurate, who? Everything they had built within their case led to this office, but Wolf himself was too cool and confident when answering questions that directly pointed to him. He never flinched in the face of questioning.

For Grimes, the answer had to lie somewhere in this office. The hairs Poles found directly linked everything there. The last one known to have seen him alive was his secretary. It was in that instance a light bulb turned on in his head as he began to think. It was all coming together now and racing through his mind.

Bultizar must have assumed the name of Nicholas Wolf some time ago, but the man sitting in the chair in front of him obviously wasn't him. He didn't know who he was or where he came from, but it didn't matter now.

He surmised that the real Nicholas Wolf found this guy on the street somewhere. He was probably a homeless addict, a man that was desperate, down on his luck, and hopeless, without any family—someone who was ready to do anything that would allow him to just simply matter.

Since the man Wolf found had a strong resemblance to himself in terms of height, weight, and age, Bultizar chose him. He offered him the deal of a lifetime--to assume his mantle and identity, giving him prestige, as well as, unlimited buying power as long as he played by the rules that he set. He cleaned him up and used him as the face of his company, even providing surgery to perfect his appearance for the transition in playing out this role. He was now the face of a multi-million-dollar corporation with all the perks that went along with it.

Then there was Paul Neville. Grimes believed he served a different purpose in all of this. He was the bait to draw the women. With his looks and swagger, along with the flashy items Bultizar provided, it made everything easier. It helped to attract the women he desired for his ritual. But to pull off his plans, he needed more than one body; he needed two. He needed a fall guy in case something went wrong. In order to lure the women in and trick them, he had to find someone who could make them feel safe and comfortable.

He believed Neville was the one that was set up from the start. He would take the women to public places or meet them there and then take them where Bultizar would be waiting. On rare occasions, Bultizar would pull a solo act and hunt on his own, depending on his mood.

During their investigation of Neville, they found there weren't many people that were close to him or that really knew him, which made him the perfect candidate. There were a few people on the street that knew him, loose associates more or less, that said he was heavily indebted to loan sharks and drug dealers who were simply tired of him for past transgressions and were ready to cash in with the price of Neville's life, whether he paid them or not.

Grimes believed that Bultizar promised to make Neville's problems disappear, making good among his debtors permanently. Then he provided him with money, clothes, and a car that he would have never been able to afford on his salary. Grimes also believed that Bultizar revealed his secret to both men as a form of insurance, letting them know the severe consequences if they ever revealed his true identity to anyone. With the police beginning to turn their attention toward Wolf, Bultizar was too close in obtaining his prize and didn't want anything getting in his way. So, he decided to tie up loose ends by cutting ties with them permanently.

In order to make all this work, Grimes theorized that Bultizar needed to assume an identity that would allow him unlimited freedom and access to stay close to the daily affairs of the company. While he stood there thinking, he looked up at the picture on the wall of his office. It was the old man.

At last, Grimes understood exactly what his partner meant when they first visited Wolf's office and Poles said that the picture looked familiar. Margaret Sullivan was the old man in the picture. She had the same small scar on her face as the old man in the picture. Posing as his own secretary, he made up the identity of Margaret Sullivan. He was the old gray-haired woman.

Using body prosthetics and makeup to alter his real identity, it made him indistinguishable from that of a real female in appearance. It not only allowed him to attend all of the board meetings, it also allowed him to sign off on all the documents while his puppet remained visual to impersonate him. If by chance his impersonator were ever accused of being involved, he could supply the perfect alibi for himself while he implemented his desired plan—which he had done time and time again.

And then there was still the issue of the panthiem. He was the only one anyone had seen attack someone. When Grimes faced him knowing that he himself would have easily been another statistic in that isolated room, he chose to flee rather than to kill him. Grimes dismissed him as being involved in any of the deaths.

Everything now pointed to Margaret Sullivan being Bultizar. The hour was rapidly approaching and Grimes didn't have a clue about who was next or where it would happen. Immediately, he began looking around for clues, starting with papers he saw stacked on the corner of Wolf's desk. While going through them, he saw the names of the women that were found dead in his buildings. All of the names were circled with a red marker.

When he got to the bottom of the list, there was one name and an address that made his heart drop—Terrie Collins. As he quickly thought back on the diagram that he had drawn on the map, there had been a pattern the women had been killed in, but it didn't hit him at the time that Terrie's building was situated in the center of the five-pointed star. Terrie was the final piece of the puzzle, the heart of the five-pointed star. It was there in his face all along in plain sight, and he didn't see it. As he pulled out his cell, he called her, praying that she would hurry and answer.

At her condo, Terrie was soaking in a bath of bubbles trying to relax when her phone rang. While she reached for it, the phone slipped out of her hand and fell into the water. Upset by the phone fumble, she looked to see who had called but the number was wiped clear. She got out of the tub, frustrated with herself, and placed the phone on the counter.

Terrie wasn't picking up his calls for some reason, Grimes continued to called consecutively with no answer. The situation had drastically changed. He knew her life was in danger. He then called for a cruiser to go to her condo, letting them know he was on the way. After hanging up, out of the corner of his eye, Grimes caught movement outside of the window.

Jahir peered through the glass, clinging to the wall with his claws dug in like hooks. Grimes drew his gun prepared to fire. With his powerful limbs, Jahir pushed off the wall, landing on another building across the street.

As Grimes rushed out, he saw the two officers with whom he had arrived. He ordered them to wait there for backup. When they asked where he was going, all he said was he didn't have time. He was desperate. When he reached the outside, it was like the heavens had opened as the rain began. He looked up to see the moon which was hidden behind the heavy cover of clouds. Grimes jumped in his car and floored it. His tires burned tracks through the wet asphalt; his lights and sirens fired under the blinding downpour.

Chapter 40:
The Reckoning

When Jahir was outside of Wolf's office on the wall, he heard Grimes call for officers to go to Terrie's place. Although the feelings were faint, he sensed Bultizar's anxiety, and it was heading in the direction of her home.

It all made sense. Terrie reminded Jahir of his lost love, and it was that same attraction driving Bultizar to murder her. With this as his motivation, Jahir had never moved with such fervor before, despite the heavy rain. He hadn't felt such desperation since his pursuit of Bultizar began.

In front of her building under a steady downpour, a male and female officer had just pulled up in a cruiser per Grimes's orders. They sat a moment, preparing to go up and check on her. The rains were so heavy, it was difficult to see.

As they prepared to get out, there was a tap on the passenger side where the female officer was sitting. It was Margarete Sullivan shouting, "Officer, officer."

Concerned, she opened the door.

"What's the matter, ma'am? Is everything all right?"

With water dripping down her face, Margaret simply smiled.

The two officers looked confused as to the urgency of her need. As they looked into her eyes, they were as gray and full as the moon hidden above them. As she smiled, her fangs became visible. Startled by what they were seeing, they reached for their guns but Bultizar beat them to the draw.

Forcing himself into the cruiser, he killed them both before they could get off a single shot.

After getting out of the tub, Terrie put on her gown and relaxed on her couch.

With the rain pouring down against the window, she heard a sound outside her window. She got up and walked over to see what it was. Looking out, she didn't see anything other than a police car parked across the street. She sat back down not giving it another thought.

A few minutes later, there was a knock on her door. In his cage, Max began barking and growling excessively which was unusual.

"Shush, Max. What's the matter with you?"

Thinking it might be Grimes, she sprung up from her couch and didn't bother to check the peephole.

When she opened the door, she said, "Baby, I didn't expect to see you so soon—"

Her voice faded before finishing her statement. She was surprised to see it was Margaret Sullivan standing there, her clothes soaked.

"Ms. Sullivan," she murmured, surprised to see her at her door, "what are you doing here at this hour? It's pretty late. And how did you get my address? It's not listed."

"I'm sorry for showing up like this," Margaret lied. "Wolf Realty just took over the mortgage financing of this building, and you're on file with us. If it weren't important, I wouldn't have shown up like this, but I really need to talk to you."

To Terrie, the tone in her voice and the nervous movements showed that she was frightened.

Pausing to regain her composure, she said, "It's about my boss. He's not who he claims to be."

Although hesitant at first, Terrie invited her inside. Max continued to bark frantically. When Margaret walked in, he growled like a crazed animal. Margaret stopped and gave him a piercing stare. Immediately, he cowered and retreated to the corner of his cage and began to whine.

Terrie looked up at Margaret and said, "I don't know what's gotten into him. Let me take your coat. You're soaked."

Taking it off, she handed it to her, thanking her as she placed it on the rack by the door. Terrie focused back on the conversation they were having.

"Now, what do you mean about your boss?" she asked.

"My boss. I don't think he's human."

"Not human! What are you talking about?"

"I think he killed all those people, including your friend and that detective."

At that instance, Terrie's countenance instantly changed becoming visibly disturbed. "Then why did you come here and not the police?"

Margaret started to cry, saying, "I wanted to, but I was afraid they wouldn't believe me."

"Why wouldn't they?" Terrie pushed.

Margaret began telling her everything: that two detectives investigating the case had come by to see him, then one came back alone and was killed later that night.

"Wolf didn't like the questions he was asking. He went into a rage after he left. He sent everyone home and told me to stay--that he had something to take care of. That I was going to be his witness for the evening that he never left.

"When I questioned him about why and what he was going to do, he looked me in my eyes and said he was going to kill someone. When I refused to be his alibi, he told me that he would kill me like all the others. When I asked what others, that's when he told me everything.

"That frightened me. I thought he was a crazy person. At first, I was going to tell the police, but then it happened. At that moment, he started to change before my eyes. His eyes turned gray; his face began to grow, along with claws from his hands, and then he stopped. He didn't fully transform, but it was enough to show me he was telling the truth and that he had control of it. I was horrified. It was then I knew he would do it. He told me he knew what I was thinking and that no one would believe a story like that. After that, I had no choice. He was right; the police would never believe me.

"The reason I came to you is because you're a reporter everyone knows. You've been covering these stories from the beginning, and your word and reputation are credible. The police will believe you more than me and would take your story seriously."

Placing her hand over her mouth after hearing this, Terrie had a memory flash. Reflecting on both deaths, the hurt and devastation she felt after Maria and Poles were killed, came rushing back. She didn't believe her after what Grimes had already told her.

"That's not true," Terrie declared. "I know the detective. Lieutenant Grimes is also my friend. I'll call him."

When she went to get her phone off the counter, she remembered it had fallen into the tub earlier while taking her bath.

Looking over at Margaret, she said, "My phone is dead." Remembering there was a car across the street, she inquired, "When you arrived, did you see the police car across from my building?"

"Yes," she replied, "but nobody's in it. When I got there, it was parked and locked."

The digital clock in the kitchen read eleven fifty. Terrie was flustered after hearing Margaret's story. She needed a bottle of water. She offered her some.

"Yes, please," Margaret affirmed.

When Terrie handed her the water, she saw blood on Margaret's arm. It looked like it had soaked through her clothes.

Concerned, Terrie asked, "Are you alright? Did you just cut yourself?"

"Oh, that's nothing. I cut myself on my car door before I came in."

"I have a first aid kit in my bathroom. I also have some peroxide and bandages. Come, and let me take a look at it. I was going to school for nursing before I decided to change to journalism."

When she got up, she headed to the bathroom. Margaret went to the front door, locked the top bolt, then followed her. Max began barking at her again.

When she heard him go crazy, Terrie shouted, "I don't know what's gotten into him. He's never acted like that before."

***

While Terrie was tending to her guest, like a man on fire, Grimes was blazing through the streets weaving in and out of traffic. Despite repeated attempts, he was unable to reach Terrie by phone. He didn't know her phone wasn't working, but he did know that time was not on his side.

When he called dispatch, they informed him that a car had already been sent and was on the scene waiting, but they hadn't responded after several attempts to reach them. Not hearing from the officers worried him even more, pushing him harder to reach her in time.

Farther ahead, streaking across the rooftops under the steady downpour of rain, Jahir was moving as fast as his limbs could carry him. Since he first came to Terrie's aid, for once, he didn't need for Bultizar to change to know where he would be.

Looking up at the sky, he raced against a moon he couldn't see or catch. Without a watch and under thick cloud cover, his instincts told him the moon was nearing its height, and it was just minutes away from midnight.

***

Terrie was in the bathroom with her back to the door. After going into her first aid kit to get what she needed, she turned to find Margaret standing behind her.

"Let me see your wound," Terrie asked.

"Sure," she complied.

At that instant, she grabbed Terrie by the throat, lifting her into the air with one hand while she struggled.

With her feet dangling and kicking, Margaret's grip was so tight that Terrie was unable to speak and was barely able to breathe. With the same grip, she then rammed her against the wall, then slung her against the other wall before she loosened her grip and smiled.

After catching her breath, she struggled to her feet. When she cried out for help, she was quickly knocked to the floor and rendered unconscious. Bultizar, still dressed as Margaret, grabbed her by the arm and dragged her across the condo.

As Terrie began to come to her senses, he picked her up and threw her onto her bed while she frantically attempted to fight back, but he was too powerful. Pinning her down on the bed with one hand, none of her efforts fazed him. He struck her with the back of his hand, knocking her out again. He then tore off strips of her sheets and began tying her arms and legs to the bedpost.

Slowly, she began to regain consciousness as she found herself unable to move. Her attempted struggle to break free was futile. Bultizar was now standing in front of her at the foot of the bed.

"Who are you?" she shouted.

He smiled and then began to pull off his mask and wig, casting it off to the side. He tore off the prosthetic bodysuit of a woman to reveal his true self.

Looking up at him, she lay there unable to break free. She couldn't believe this was happening to her. Who she had thought was a woman, she found to be something else.

Margaret was a man, but not any man. She looked to be Nicholas Wolf. This confused her. Was this Wolf or an imposter? Or the other way around? They looked identical in every way.

Her mind was racing trying to figure it out, "Who are you?" she shouted again, "You look like Wolf."

He laughed, then replied, "I am who I appear to be."

"Why are you doing this? Why are you dressed like that? If you're Wolf, then who's the other person?"

He simply stated, "A useful pawn that once served a purpose but was no longer needed. Therefore, I discarded him like everything else that had outlived its usefulness."

Intertwined in both anger and fear, she lashed out at him. "It was you who killed Maria, John, and all those people! You're the monster responsible!" she screamed.

He laughed. "Such harsh words. They should've felt honored giving their life for a future god. Such a disappointment."

"I don't know who you are or what you are," she snapped, "but you're not a god!"

Smiling once more, he informed her, "After your supreme sacrifice, you will make that possible on this special night. When the moon reaches its highest height at midnight, only minutes from now, it will be your sacrifice—your pumping heart in my hand—that will give me the power to begin a new order in my likeness, thousands upon thousands just like me. I will claim your heart, giving me the power to rule over all others."

As he looked out the window. The rain had just ceased. The cloud cover began to break up because of the brisk winds, creating an opening for the moonlight to shine through.

He asked her, "Don't you see its beauty, the fullness of the moon? Such a reddish glow. Have you ever seen anything like it in your lifetime? Not even the rains can hold her back."

"You sadistic monster!" she yelled, struggling even harder to break free.

"My name is Nicholai Bultizar Wolvenhunt, the ruler of a kingdom before I was betrayed by my people in favor of a false hope. I chose you the moment I first laid eyes on you, while you were broadcasting the deaths of my prey. I've walked a thousand lifetimes on this earth, and now, the time has come where I claim what is rightfully mine."

"You're crazy!"

"Am I?"

With those words, he began his transformation into what he truly was. Horrified by what she was witnessing, she screamed for help. He tore another strip from the sheet, using it to cover her mouth.

"Ah yes, much better," he taunted.

She continued to struggle in a desperate attempt to break free, not believing what was happening before her. His head began to take the shape of a wolf's showing his massive fangs. He put on mass and height instantly with long blond fur overlaying his outward appearance.

***

While Bultizar was taking on his true form, both Jahir and Grimes rushed desperately to get to her before it was too late. One took to the streets below; the other scaled the highway across tops of buildings. Each one faced obstacles of their own, both having separate missions, but each with the same goal.

The ground was slick and wet as Grimes weaved in and out traffic, sliding across the road trying to avoid another vehicle before slamming into a parked car, delaying him for a moment. Those were moments he knew he couldn't afford to lose. High above him, Jahir's movements were smooth and precise. Neither wet bricks nor slated roofs posed an obstacle for the panthiem, who was also racing against the clock.

***

It was a minute before midnight; the moon now a scarlet red. The golden wolf was now in full array, appearing that nothing would be able to stop him from making his final kill. Showing his teeth and growling like a rabid animal, he let out a howl that awakened the neighborhood as he prepared to claim his last heart.

Bultizar stepped forward as he was about to take it from her chest. At that instance, Jahir crashed through the window with the wind and rain blowing at his back, spreading glass and debris all around as he tumbled across the floor and sprang back to his feet.

Jahir lunged toward him through the air displaying both his fangs and claws, while Bultizar's hand was in a downward motion toward Terrie's chest knocking him backward before the clock struck midnight. Jahir had disrupted his moment, ending the hope to claim the prize he had sought for over a millennium.

Bultizar had misjudged his enemy, confident that Jahir would not arrive in time.

Angered by what just happened, Bultizar howled so strongly that it shook the entire building.

This was personal from the beginning, and now, it was coming to an end on the final battleground between the golden wolf and the panthiem.

The two were now locked in a deadly embrace. The ferocity of the battle was intense, beyond one's darkest imagination as the two combatant attacks were both brutal and relentless. From wall to wall, the two behemoths engaged each other, dishing out equal damage.

During the back-and-forth death match, Bultizar saw an opportunity and seized it, sinking his six-inch fangs deep into Jahir's shoulder. It caused him to roar in pain. Bultizar's goal was to rip the throat out of his black-furred nemesis, barely missed his mark.

Finally breaking free of the wolf's jaws with slashing claws, Jahir tore into the werewolf's abdomen, splattering blood and fur across the floor and walls. They locked onto one another once again, bouncing off the walls like a ping pong match, sending neighbors into the hallway wondering what was taking place.

Both were doing damage to one another. One bit harder while the other cut deeper with long curved claws. The sounds resonated like two wild beasts locked in battle. Without either delivering a strike that would kill the other, their bodies mended back into place.

As the battle persisted, the werewolf gained the advantage, pinning Jahir to the ground as he tried again to sink his fangs deep into his throat –ending this struggle forever.

From the bottom, Jahir held the werewolf by the sides of his neck preventing him from leaning forward and making that final bite. As his head inched closer and closer, he was but a few inches from ending the contest. With everything that was in him, Jahir slowly began to push Bultizar's head backward, farther and farther from his throat until he was nearly straight. Bultizar took his hand, knocking Jahir's away to break free then opened his mouth wide, in his attempt to end it.

At that moment, there was an opening. Although brief, Jahir took it. Freeing a hand with all of his might, he thrust his claws under Bultizar's rib cage, grasping hold of his beating heart, and tore it out from under it.

For the briefest of moments, the two looked into each other's eyes as they were but inches apart. While Jahir watched, Bultizar's eyes dilated as life left his mortal enemy forever. Bultizar keeled over onto the floor while Jahir pushed him off to the side.

Wounded and bleeding, Jahir crawled over to the base of the window he had crashed through and sat down next to it, exhausted. His head was bowed toward the floor.

At that moment, Grimes pulled behind the squad car that was parked across the street. When he got out, he looked into the vehicle and saw blood everywhere. The two officers were slumped over, dead.

During the struggle, Terrie had worked herself free. With the neighbors alarmed, curious as to what had happened, Grimes made his way through the crowded hallway. The door was locked; he kicked it open.

With his gun drawn, he looked over at Jahir and was prepared to fire when Terrie took hold of his hands and gently guided them to the floor. Looking Grimes in his eyes, she gestured for him to look to the opposite side of the room. He was astonished at what he was seeing. Bultizar was dead as he slowly changed back into his human form.

"Nicholas Wolf," he said. "His real name was Nicholai Bultizar Wolvenhunt."

"I know. He told me before he was about to kill me."

Grimes reported, "I found his impostor dead in his office. The man we thought was Nick Wolf was no more than a front, allowing the real Nicholas Wolf to dress as his secretary, giving him the freedom to kill when he pleased while providing him with the perfect alibi for himself. After tonight, he didn't need him anymore, so he killed him."

Looking over at Jahir slumped forward with his head down, they thought he was also dead. She began to cry while Grimes held her tight.

Looking up at him, she recalled, "He saved me twice. That monster was about to kill me when he burst through the window and stopped him. I still don't know who or what he was or why he came to help me."

Grimes lifted her chin while staring into her eyes. "He was your guardian angel." He left it at that.

While they spoke, they had momentarily taken their attention off Jahir. When they turned back toward him, only broken glass and debris from the window remained while the curtains were blowing in the wind. Jahir was gone.

Grimes rushed over to the window and looked all around the street. It was almost empty. In the background, the sound of sirens could be heard in the distance as they approached. Across the street from them was a little old lady with white hair wearing a long black coat. Beside her was what appeared to be a man and a woman both wearing hoodies. The shadows cast from their hoods partially obstructed their faces.

Grimes shouted to them, asking them if they had seen anyone jump from the window. The two figures stood quietly, not moving a muscle, not saying a word. The old woman standing next to them simply looked up and smiled.

As they stood, the one appearing to be male whispered in the old woman's ear, saying, "Mother, you allowed them to live to play out this game. Now that it's over, what purpose did it serve?"

The old woman looked to him, smiled, and pronounced, "It is not over, for this is just the beginning. The answer to that question shall soon be answered, and the purpose of it all shall also be revealed."

With the neighbors gathered in the hallway, some tried to peep through the door to see what happened. Grimes looked back momentarily while Terrie closed the door. He turned his attention back to the old woman and the two figures, wanting to ask them another question, but like Jahir they, too, were gone.

It was a strange conclusion to what had been a bizarre night, but he still wasn't quite finished. There still remained the question of the missing evidence, the chest filled with the hearts of his victims. With Bultizar dead and knowing he had taken it, Grimes thought to himself the most likely place—the basement of Terrie's building.

Looking at her, he observed, "I think I know where to find what I'm looking for."

When the police arrived, he asked them if they had seen an old lady standing with a man and a woman outside. They told them they hadn't seen anyone until they got to their floor. Grimes told them to take care of Terrie, that he had to check out something.

Wasting no time, he rushed down the stairs into the basement. He turned on the switch and looked around. The storage area was clear, but there was one locked door, which he kicked in. When he entered, in the corner was a small paneled door on the wall with a padded lock.

There was a steel bar leaning against the wall. Grimes used it to pry the latch open. There he saw what he had hoped to find—the chest that was missing at Wolf's apartment complex. When he opened it, all the evidence he needed was there.

Chapter 41:
A Closure with Honors
An epilogue

Six months later, the city had returned to business as usual. Everyone involved had already begun to rebuild their lives.

Terrie was back on the streets and reporting on city corruption. She also included some of her personal experiences with the Butcher in her blog online. After the Butcher case gained national attention, she turned it into a best-selling novel entitled, *The Butcher of the Bronx: The Monster Among Us.*

After solving the highest-profile case in the state's history, Commissioner Kuntz gave Lieutenant Grimes the highest honor, promoting him to Captain, and appointing him to the head of the NYPD Homicide Division. He also promoted his predecessor Hernandez to become its Director and Chief.

The public never fully learned what *really* happened. They simply pinned the murders to the wealthy psychopath, Nicholas Wolf. Nowhere was completely safe, but at least there was some sense of normality to the hustle and bustle of city life. Like all the cases regarding the killer in the past, authorities concealed the truth to prevent widespread panic.

After her release from the hospital, Tia Johnson fully recovered from her injuries since that fateful day her life nearly ended. After the death of the most notorious serial killer to ever stalk the streets of New York, she could sleep peacefully, along with the rest of the city.

Before heading to work, she remembered she hadn't checked her mailbox in a long time. She was expecting a very important letter, hoping it would contain the message she wanted to hear. It had finally arrived. After opening it, her facial expression told it all. It was an acceptance letter to the university she had applied for in Atlanta.

When contacting the university, Tia learned that Danielle Michelle had once again come to her aid. She had been both her mentor and friend since her aunt passed away when she was in high school. She had sent a letter of recommendation, pulled strings in high places, and with Danielle's uncle on the board, ensured her acceptance.

Despite all of her joy, however, she felt a burden of sorrow. The thought of Jahir was heavy on her mind. She hadn't seen or heard from her friend since that night he came to the hospital. She owed him everything. He also was her guardian, protector, and closest friend. Her very life was indebted to him. Although she was happy, she also was sad, but knew that life had to go on. Her future seemed brighter these days, but she wished he was around for her to share it.

While walking to work with people passing by, she noticed a tall young man leaning against the wall, reading a magazine. He had dark brown skin, a short-groomed beard, and flowing locks. While reading, he never once looked up. There was something very familiar about him; however, she couldn't place it as she kept walking.

Reaching the diner, she clocked in to start her shift. She went to the back to put on her apron then grabbed her pad to take orders. Sitting in the corner, she saw it was the same man she had passed on her way to work. She walked over to him; he looked up.

She smiled and asked, "Are you following me?"

He smiled and replied, "No, I'm not following you. Seeing how beautiful you are, that probably wouldn't have been a bad idea, though. But then, I would've been deemed a stalker, and I wouldn't have wanted that."

"No, you wouldn't," Tia laughed. "Now, what can I get you?"

He paused a moment, looking her in the eyes. "I'll have a cup of coffee. Black, please," he said.

"Coming up!" she responded jubilantly.

As she turned to make his coffee, she thought there was something about him she couldn't quite put her finger on. A few minutes later, she returned with the coffee. She grinned at him and continued with her other customers.

On the wall was a small television screen with the news broadcast. Onscreen, Terrie Collins reported on corrupt city officials.

Jahir's eyes focused on her face. The memories of what had happened were now behind him, and he was finally at peace.

"Enough of that already," a voice spoke out to the TV. It was the diner's owner. "Is there any good news in the world?" he asked while changing the channel from the news to the Knicks basketball game. There were no objections by anyone there.

Jahir finished his coffee. He called for Tia to let her know he was ready for the bill. He paid her and gave her a tip.

"Thank you," she replied. "I hope you enjoyed your coffee. Is there anything else I can get you?"

"No, everything was great," Jahir replied.

When she turned and walked away, he said, "Ex toto corde meo et ego semper gratus!"

Immediately, she stopped. Her eyes opened wide. At that moment, she knew. When she turned around, he was gone. Rushing out the door, she looked both ways; however, he was nowhere to be found.

She went over to the table where he had been sitting and saw that he had left a note. It read, THANK YOU FOR EVERYTHING, JAHIR AMID.

As she stared at it, her expression told it all. From that moment, she knew that everything was going to be all right.

About the Author

Donald R Simpson (D. R. Simpson), born in Washington, DC is a retired DC firefighter and EMS officer.

He graduated from HD Woodson HS in Northeast Washington DC. After being recruited, he attended Rochester Community College in Rochester, Minnesota, and Montgomery Community College, in Rockville, Maryland, Majoring in Advertising & Design, as well as, Creative Writing. Known mostly as an illustrator, he has also been writing for more than thirty years, following his passion for fantasy and fiction now as a full-time fiction writer drawing from the pages of his imagination. He's also written a number of stories ranging from fantasy, horror, suspense and action dramas. He hand-crafts figurines of his characters to bring his stories to life.

In 2018, he published his first novel, a fantasy adventure series, *Another Worlds Kronicles Nomadic Warriors: The Age of Giants Book I.*

Between Fang & Claw: The Butcher of the Bronx is his second published novel and the first in a new fantasy horror series.